MW00583539

Wild Lands

USA TODAY BESTSELLING AUTHOR
STACEY MARIE BROWN

Layout by Judi Fennell at www.formatting4U.com
Cover by: Jay Aheer (www.simplydefinedart.com
Edited by Hollie (www.hollietheeditor.com)
Edited by Mo Siren's Call Author Services (mo@thescarletsiren.com)
Jordan Rosenfeld at Write Livelihood, Developmental Editor (http://jordanrosenfeld.net)

ALSO BY STACEY MARIE BROWN

Contemporary Romance

How the Heart Breaks

Buried Alive

Smug Bastard

The Unlucky Ones

Blinded Love Series
Shattered Love (#1)
Broken Love (#2)
Twisted Love (#3)

Royal Watch Series
Royal Watch (#1)
Royal Command (#2)

Paranormal Romance

A Winterland Tale
Descending into Madness (#1)
Ascending from Madness (#2)
Beauty in Her Madness (#3)
Beast in His Madness (#4)

Darkness Series
Darkness of Light (#1)
Fire in the Darkness (#2)
Beast in the Darkness (An Elighan Dragen Novelette)
Dwellers of Darkness (#3)
Blood Beyond Darkness (#4)
West (#5)

Collector Series
City in Embers (#1)
The Barrier Between (#2)
Across the Divide (#3)
From Burning Ashes (#4)

Lightness Saga
The Crown of Light (#1)
Lightness Falling (#2)
The Fall of the King (#3)
Rise from the Embers (#4)

Savage Lands Series
Savage Lands (#1)
Wild Lands (#2)
Dead Lands (#3)
Bad Lands (#4)
Blood Lands (#5)
Shadow Lands (#6)

Devil In The Deep Blue Sea
Silver Tongue Devil (#1)

For those who curse my name and call me evil…
This book won't change your mind.

Chapter 1

Sweat trailed down my face, my arms shaking as I lowered myself an inch from the floor. Puffing air through my teeth, I locked my jaw and kept my focus straight beneath me, zeroing in on the grainy cement floor.

Gray.

That's all there was. Floor, ceiling, walls. The uniform they put me back in. Even the blanket and pillow on my cot.

Gray.

I think the pillow used to be white, but time and use had discolored it.

Funny. Germs, dirt, and secondhand items used to bother me when I was the girl who went to glamorous parties and fought because she was good at it, not because her life depended on it. Before prison, I used to be a lot of things, and sometimes I couldn't decipher if I'd changed for the better or not. Another thing lost in the in-between.

Gray.

A mix of two things that weren't even considered colors, which seemed perfect for my current state. Suspended between darkness and light, between life and death. I hovered in nothing.

Waiting.

"One hundred." I marked my last pushup before dropping and rolling onto my back with fatigue. My gaze traveled over the small windowless cell, my new home deep under Lord Killian's castle. The scents of dirt, decay, and grain still lingered in the walls. I could tell it had been converted from a food storage cupboard to a cell quickly, like he hadn't been prepared for a prisoner until moments before my arrival. Inside the ten-by-ten room were only a cot, portable toilet, and sink, which had been crudely bolted to the wall.

All gray.

I was starting to wonder if the void of color was its own torture, expanding the days into years, cruelly killing me by dullness and boredom. The days in the House of Death were hell, but at least I had been busy. Here minutes blended into hours. I only filled my time by exercising, aiming to regain the muscle mass I lost in Halálház. But boxing shadows and doing pushups only filled so many hours.

Able to keep time by counting the food trays delivered to my chamber, I estimated I had been here roughly two weeks since that night.

Since *him*.

My chest filled like a balloon, causing me to sit up against the cot with a huff. Razor-sharp emotions of hurt, anger, and embarrassment churned in my body. How had I fallen for his act? I couldn't believe I'd let his half-fae ass twist me into a pretzel and make me believe he actually gave a shit about me. That there had been something between us—something visceral, sliding and rolling against my skin, grazing my soul.

Even now, I swore I felt him skittering around me, tapping at the edges of my unconsciousness. In the moment between sleep and waking, I would hear my name, a tug on my soul, his presence coiling around me like a viper. Then it would be gone.

"Fuck him," I muttered and pulled my legs into my chest, my nails digging into my palms. Half of my fury was aimed at myself. *I* was the one imagining him trying to reach me, that through space, time, and against all logic, he was here, trying to comfort me in some way.

How pathetic was that?

The man completely betrayed me, cut me so deep it was hard to breathe, and I still thought I could feel him like some fucking ghost. Like the myth he was. Warwick Farkas, *The Wolf*, the legend. The ultimate betraying asshole.

Working out helped me forget my moment of weakness. I put a wall up around myself, fighting against my deeply disturbed psyche that called to him instead of Caden.

Caden.

Sucking in, I dropped my head to my knees. The image of my best friend tore another hole in my heart. I had been so close. To home. To him.

Click.

Locks scraped across the metal door, a shrill sound through the cubicle like the wail of a newborn. I lifted my head slowly. I had grown numb to guards coming and going without a word or threat. Day in and day out, they dropped off a tray, took the old one, and did not respond to any of my questions.

Standing up, clothed in just a sports bra and loose pants that hung off my hips, I grabbed my shirt off the end of the bed. I focused on the door swinging open as a guard stepped into the room, his gaze finding me. It was almost insignificant, but his notice dropped to my toned stomach and barely covered chest before darting away.

A ruthless smile curved my lips as I sat back on my cot coyly, my eyes rolling over the pretty fae guard as he scanned the space.

"I cleaned my room, Daddy. Can I go play now?" I taunted, leaning back on my hands, my voice full of underlying meaning.

His cheeks turned red under his pale skin, his teeth clamping together. He looked all of eighteen, but with fae, appearance was deceiving. He could have been hundreds of years old, but this guard seemed especially young and naïve, too easily flustered when I teased him. I had to find my fun where I could.

He stepped out of the room, clearing the doorway, springing taut in a soldier's stance, his chin tilting high.

"All clear, sir."

Then I heard the soles of shoes hitting the stone floor. Alarm sprang electricity up the back of my neck. A figure stepped around the guard and into my space, forcing me to suck in my breath.

Killian. The leader of the fae in Hungary. Power and magic emanated from him, my skin sizzling, my spine crunching against the wall, and my body freezing.

I hadn't seen him since that night, as if the king had forgotten all about the lowly subject locked far below in this makeshift dungeon. I thought he would parade me around, taunting Istvan with his prize. He hadn't.

"Ms. *Kovacs*." His smooth honey voice poured over me, slipping effortlessly down my torso to my thighs. I clenched my legs. His voice was the opposite of Warwick's rough, deep timbre—as if you crawled through gravel, rubbing against every erogenous spot. Killian's voice glided silkily over your skin, skating against you.

Fae had the power to glamour and seduce humans, reeling us in like fish on a hook with their incredible looks, magic, and pure sexual magnetism.

He took a step closer to me, sliding his hands into his trouser pockets, demonstrating he had not one inkling of worry of me attacking him. Even with just one guard, I was no threat to him.

The fae ruler wasn't in his position for nothing. The stories and rumors about him were almost as legendary as Warwick. Killian was ruthless and cruel, but where Warwick relied on brute physical strength, Killian was strategic.

Even within the walls of Human Defense Forces, he was considered extraordinarily handsome. Exquisite. If you could call a man that. Beautiful and sexy, he pulsed with power, confidence, and entitlement. His violet eyes popped against his dark brown hair. Wearing a dark suit, his scruff and hair were perfectly trimmed. He looked to be only in his early thirties, but I knew he was far, far older. Tall and built, oozing charisma, he reminded me of men I saw in Western glamour magazines I used to smuggle into my room as a young girl.

His attention locked on me, the magic he held vibrated off the walls, digging into my soul. Shifting on the tiny cot, the metal squeaked as I adjusted my weight as I moved.

"I apologize for not coming down to see you sooner." His charming tone made me think of a pinata, harmless on the outside but stuffed with implication. "You have made quite a mess for me to clean up." He strolled slowly around, his power pushing against me, trying to intimidate me.

"Halálház is in complete ruins, and the new one must be built in a secret location at night. Half of the convicts have escaped, and because of you, I had to give up one of my most prized assets." He tipped an eyebrow at me, but I stayed silent. He watched me for a full minute before he spoke again.

"Little did I know some no-name thief in my prison would be the ward of General Markos. A fragile human who still had the capacity to survive through it all, including the Games, and captured the most feared and brutal killer's interest enough to get out safely."

"Wasn't he doing it for you?" My lip lifted.

Killian's mouth curled with a tight complacency. "It took a little *persuading* to get him to do the right thing." Killian stepped closer. He pulled one hand out of his pocket, rubbing his chin. "What is it about you? You are not fae; you should hold no sway over us, no power to fight our glamour. However, you have *resisted* it when no others have. How?" He tilted his head, his gaze pinning me to the wall.

Resisted it? What was he talking about?

"You are a conundrum, Ms. Kovacs. A wave crashing into everything. Twisting, breaking, and flipping everything upside down the moment you enter." He smirked, his fingers tapping his full bottom lip. "I have known Warwick for a long time. Ruthless. Cutthroat. Cruel. But with you…" He shook his head. "You even have my sentinels here completely bewitched."

My gaze dropped to the blond guard behind him. He still stood at attention, but his eyes darted to me, his cheeks blooming with a deeper shade of crimson.

Killian folded his arms over his chest. Even in his fancy suit, I could tell the man was muscular.

"What should I do with you, Ms. Kovacs?"

"Is this a multiple choice or fill in?" I countered. "Because I vote you set me free."

"I could always kill you." The sentiment rolled over me like butter, hiding the danger in the velvetiness.

"But you won't."

His eyebrows curved up. "And why is that?"

"Because you need me for something. Bargaining. Leverage. I don't know, but you didn't scour the Savage Lands for me, lose your greatest asset, and keep me here for weeks just to kill me."

A slight smirk tugged on his full lips, his eyes running down me. "You are nothing like I thought you'd be." His violet eyes locked on mine, holding me like I was caught in a web. My heart sped up under his scrutiny. "You're right. I would not kill you right away, but you're wrong for the reasons why I want you. I don't care about your pathetic humans. The ones whose arrogance let them think they have a hold here when all it would take is a word from me to end them."

"You don't want to use me for bartering with Istvan?" I swallowed.

"Barter?" Killian's head tipped back with laughter, the sound plunging tingles of warmth through me, hitching my chest. Fury at my body's response to him showed on my face. I tugged my legs tighter into my frame.

"What would I possibly need to barter for, Ms. Kovacs? I am quite curious what you think I'd need from your kind." He tipped his head to the side. I pinched my lips together, not answering. "You humans always believe you are far more important than you are. Your lives, your needs, are above all else: earth, animals, nature's resources, even people of your own species." He smiled. The flare of something feral underneath his pristine image radiated off him, his eyes flashing. He leaned into my face, and I could barely breathe. "But it's a lie, Ms. Kovacs. You can all walk around in your delusions, telling your offspring the same falsehoods. But your species is at the bottom of the totem pole. And in a blink…" He snapped his fingers against my cheeks. His breath brushed down my throat, hitching my own breath. "You can be taken out."

Air ripped raggedly through my airways, his words settling in around me. This whole time I thought I would be a carrot to be dangled, a prize to be used against the Human Defense Force's general. It was something Istvan always warned Caden and me about—that our enemy would use us.

"So, what do you want with me then?" Dread sparked with adrenaline tore through my nerves.

"Wrong question." His voice slipped down my neck, spearing my skin with shivers. "It's what am I already doing with you, Ms. Kovacs." His fingers slipped over my ear, tucking a strand of hair, sparking goosebumps down my flesh. "You are turning out to be far more interesting than I could ever have imagined." His proximity pinned my spine to the wall, my lungs hitching as fear rushed into me. His eyes drifted over my face. "I can't figure out why you are different from the others. Why have you not succumbed? How are you able to resist it when no others have?"

"What others? Succumbed to what?"

A sneer curved his mouth, his violet eyes glistening. He stepped away from me, his hand digging into the pocket of his jacket, pulling out a tiny pill, holding it up.

My gaze dropped to the object, my throat clogging at the sight of the neon blue pill between his fingers. I recognized it instantly, the color so unique. It was the same kind I had stolen from the train the night I got captured.

"As soon as I discovered who you were, I had your items sent here from the night you were apprehended. I was curious. Why would the ward of General Markos be on the train robbing from her own kind?"

I locked on the strange pill, my throat bobbing.

"Tell me what these are."

My eyes darted up to his, my jaw locking down.

"Why were you after these?"

Nothing.

"You think it's wise to defy me?" Anger bloomed in a blink, his eyes igniting in fury, enveloping me. "Speak!"

Silence.

"I order you to talk, Ms. Kovacs." His lids narrowed, his focus sharpening. A swirl of energy crackled around me, tugging at my tongue and jaw, but broke like waves against the rocks the moment the magic touched my skin.

His nose flared; a nerve in his jaw twitched.

"Answer me. Now!" I could feel the power of the order. The demand hissed in my ear, but I only locked my teeth together, pushing against the sensation. "I said speak!" His hand caught around my throat, slamming me back against the wall, ripping air from my lungs. His form seemed to expand, magic emanating from him. "Last chance."

"I don't know," I croaked out.

"You expect me to believe that?" His face was an inch away from mine, his thumb pressing into my throat enough to make my heart jump and stutter. "I found your bag full of these pills. Tell me why you were taking them. What do you know about them?"

"I don't know anything," I spat. "I swear."

"I have very little patience today." His cheek twitched, his thumb sliding up and down my neck as if he were taunting me.

"I told you I don't know what they are."

"Do. Not. Lie. To. Me." He clamped down harder. My nose flared. My chest puffed up and down, searching for air, my spine protesting as he continued to push it against the wall.

"I'm not." Holding up my chin, I stared at him, oxygen wheezing through my nose.

His unsettling focus stayed on me for another full minute before a smirk hinted on his lips. "Fine. You want to play it that way. You will find soon, Ms. Kovacs, this isn't Leopold. You push... I don't push back. I obliterate."

"I survived and escaped your impregnable prison, *Killian*. You want to torture or kill me? Bring it," I snarled back.

"Don't *ever* call me by my first name," he growled, his hands clenching, his shoulders lifting. Names held power to the fae. Intimacy. "You call me King."

"There's only one king in this world. His name is Lars," I spit through my teeth, my head swimming for the lack of air.

"He's not king here. I am."

"Just because you call yourself king doesn't make it true." Saliva dribbled down my chin as I struggled to get out each syllable.

His fingers squeezed tighter, stealing all my air. I clawed at his hold, which did not budge his fingers, as blackness dotted around my eyes.

"Watch yourself, Ms. Kovacs. I am known for having an extremely short temper when it comes to disobedience." His breath curled around my ear, sparking energy through my skin before he ripped his hand away, stepping back.

Air rushed back into my lungs with a gasping cough, my hand flying to my throat as I gulped in oxygen.

7

Stacey Marie Brown

"You want to know what I want with you? What I am already using you for?" Killian snapped back into his cool, composed demeanor, turning around and heading out the door. "Then you will see firsthand." He flicked his head to the guard. "Cuff her. Ms. Kovacs is going on a little field trip."

8

Two guards escorted me from my chamber in handcuffs, their grasp on my arms and neck secure, preventing me from trying to make a break for it. I wouldn't have bothered. Not right now. I had to be smart, learn this place. Find its weaknesses.

I took in everything we passed. They took me farther down a stone corridor through two heavy security doors with code locks, hauling me into an elevator that needed Killian's magic to activate it. Instead of going up, we went down. The deeper we descended into the earth, the more my stomach twisted. It was a tomb underground, reminding me all too much of Halálház, distancing me from my chance at freedom.

The elevator dinged, and the doors opened. Killian twisted his head to peer back at me, but I looked away from his chiseled cheeks and jaw. "You think you are ready for what's ahead, Ms. Kovacs?"

Sniffing, I lifted my chin, facing him with no emotion.

"Humans. You think yourselves so tough." Shaking his head, he strolled out.

"I've survived so far," I muttered as the guards shoved me forward into a newly built area. It was a stark contrast to the old stone castle I had been housed in. This area was cold, sleek, and modern and looked very new, the smell of paint still emitting off the white walls.

"You *have*." A strange threat twirled around the two words. Killian's violet gaze drew over my frame slowly. Curiously. "Like a cockroach. But it's why you fascinate me so much." He swiveled back around, his shoes tapping over the tile floor, going through two more security doors, which also had guards.

What the fuck does he have down here? And why does he want me to see it?

We stepped into a small chamber with a large window allowing you to observe what was in the attached room. I blinked, my eyes and mind trying to take in everything I saw. Before me was a large room filled with science equipment, fae machines, microscopes, things I couldn't even describe, and a handful of figures dressed in white coats.

A lab.

"What is this?" Bile burned the back of my throat as my nerves jumped around, a sickness souring my stomach. "What are you doing?"

"What your kind has made me do." He came up next to me at the window. His rich smell of crisp-forest-after-a-rain-with-a-splash-of-sweet was powerful in the sterile room, soothing the panic wanting to explode from me. "What *you* made me do, Ms. Kovacs."

My head jerked to him. "Me? What are you—"

"My lord?" A woman's voice cut me off, drawing my attention to the door near him. A technician stepped into the room, blasting the small space with electricity, igniting my skin, pulsing my core. *Holy fuck.* She tugged down her mask, displaying her ethereal face and eyes. They were the color of amber sap freshly weeping from a tree. Her magic felt like a brush of wind across my face. I saw traces of red hair from underneath her cap.

She was tall, thin, and moved like a leaf in the wind. Everything about her was graceful, strong, and sexual, licking the air with desire and need.

"Willow." Killian turned to her, his head dipping at her in greeting.

"We have the latest results in." She stepped closer, holding out a file to him, her eyes moving down my figure then moving to Killian hungrily, causing a slight moan to catch in my throat. Biting down on my lip, I swallowed it back, but I felt her magic move down my limbs, caressing my thighs.

The young guard behind me groaned under his breath into my ear, pushing into my back. I could feel his excitement, his need. The other guard gripped me harder, his hand sliding around my hip.

My body responded instantly, feeling the spark of her energy kiss my skin, even though my brain told me it was wrong. Gritting my teeth, I tried to push it away, but whatever she was, she inundated the small space with her lust. I longed to step back into the warm bodies behind me, to feel them against me, but I froze in place, ignoring the need.

"Thank you." He took the folder, opening it, his attention on the documents inside, seemingly immune to her power. "What about Subject Eighteen?"

"Final stages. No different from all the others before. Well, except Subject One." Her words were matter of fact, but they seemed to purr from her, her intensity pricking at the back of my neck.

"Interesting." Killian's attention drifted from the papers to me, the force of his gaze hitching my breath.

Lust.

Hunger.

Raw need.

He blinked, snapping his head back toward the window, his expression blank again. "Thank you, Willow. You can go."

"Yes, my lord." She bowed her head, her tongue sliding over her bottom lip as she turned and sauntered back into the lab room, peeling back the heaviness of the room.

"Fuck," I hissed. "What the hell is she?" Air gushed from my lungs. The guards behind me sighing in relief drew Killian's notice.

"A tree fairy. Nature's scientist. They are incredible at mixing and testing potions. Finding cures and medicines." His eyes rolled over me again, going back to searching me like a bug pinned to a board. He flicked his chin at my babysitters. "You are dismissed."

"Sir?" the young guard replied.

"Ms. Kovacs won't do anything foolish. She has nowhere to go or any way to get out from here. She understands how pointless it would be if she tried, doesn't she?" Killian tilted his head at me.

My nose wrinkled as I glared at him, which only made him smile, twisting my gut again. And it wasn't in fear. Anger ballooned in my chest, along with disgust and irritation.

"Uncuff her, Iain. I think I am perfectly capable of handling her." He nodded to the younger one I toyed with earlier. Iain did as he was told, both guards stepping out of the room, but Iain kept watchful eyes on me until the door clicked behind them.

"Someone wants to impress his master." I rubbed my arms, the blood tingling through my fingers as I tried to push off the lingering desire to rub up against the man in front of me.

"Put these on," Killian clipped, tossing a face mask, booties, and coat at me. "Don't want your human germs and diseases contaminating any of the experiments."

"Experiments?" My lungs fluttered as I put on the items. I had no choice but to go forward, my curiosity driving me to find out what he was up to.

"Do not touch anything, Ms. Kovacs." He pushed a button, opening an airlocked door, which hissed controlled air into my face. It held no odor, no hint of life, only cleanliness.

Apparently above wearing anything that might wrinkle his expensive suit, Killian strolled into the lab with authority and righteousness so fast I had to rush to catch up.

Shockingly, not one technician looked up or greeted their lord, acting as if he were an ordinary co-worker moving through. I would have thought his ego would demand they all take time away from what they were doing and bow to him.

Not giving me much time to decipher anything they might be studying, he moved us quickly through, stopping at another door. This one was thick, similar to a walk-in freezer door, with a tiny window at the top to look through. He typed in another code, the lock clanking, the noise making me tense.

"I warn you, Ms. Kovacs. Prepare yourself," he said ominously as he swung the heavy door out.

"For what?" The words barely made it out of my mouth when gut-wrenching screams crashed into my eardrums, and the air went from sterile to putrid, punching my senses.

Bile lunged up my throat as my hand slammed over my covered nose and mouth. I gagged at the stench of rotting flesh, piss, vomit, and feces that drifted through the mask. Wails skated down my spine, my bones trembling. It sent me right back to Halálház, but this felt even worse—if that was possible.

My heart slammed against my ribs, panic fizzing over my body as I followed Killian. We turned a corner, and my feet came to an abrupt stop.

Oh, gods.

My gaze moved over the space, but I could barely take in what was in front of me. A dozen thick-barred cells built into the earth lined one side. Every single one occupied people with different sexes, ages, and nationalities, but I knew in my gut they were all human by their flaws—gray hair, bad teeth, plain looks. Things the fae were exempt from.

Guards were stationed on either end, ladened with every weapon possible, like they were ready to go up against an army.

In prison, I had seen a lot of things that would make most people lose their minds: guts being ripped out of people's bodies, torture, death, people sleeping in their own shit, crying in agony every night. Nothing prepared me for this.

From the first cell to the last one, it was like watching the stages of a horrendous disease strip the life out of every person. The first individual seemed healthy enough, dirty and scared, but plump and present. Looking down the row, they grew thinner, crazed, muttering to themselves, some pacing inside the cage. Around the middle area, the figures no longer moved. They stood there at attention, staring vacantly ahead as if they were waiting for direction. The people in the two cages on the end screamed in agony, clawing at their skin, holding their heads, curling on the floor, crying for death, only skin and bones. The final cage was empty.

"Wha-what is wrong with them?" I croaked, emotion filling my eyes, anger flaring up my neck. "What are you doing to them?"

"Me?" Killian twisted to me, one eyebrow hooking up. "Of course, you'd think this is my doing. The big bad evil fae would relish torturing humans for fun."

"Seems like something you'd enjoy," I spat.

In a blink, he gripped my wrists, slamming my body into the wall, his frame looming over mine, his lips tucked into a snarl. "I have no interest in you humans. Torturing or otherwise. This, *edesem.*" *Sweetheart.* "It is all your kind's doing."

"What?" My head snapped up to him.

He pressed in closer, his frame lining up with mine. "What your beloved master is doing to his own people while killing mine."

"Istvan? What does he have to do with it?"

"Do you want to know what those blue pills do? What you were stealing?" He let go of one of my wrists, his hand sliding down my arm, igniting shivers along my nerves. Tugging down the face mask I wore, he clutched my chin, pinching it between his fingers as he stared at me. "Why are you so different?" he whispered, like he was talking to himself.

I couldn't respond, feeling every part of him press into me, his intense magic overstimulating my senses and tricking my brain.

"Get off me," I hissed through my teeth, countering what my body wanted, stirring up abhorrence.

His gaze went to my mouth, neither of us moving for a moment. Then he shoved me back, his head shaking, his fists rolling into balls.

"Come, Ms. Kovacs. See firsthand what your guardian is smuggling in those crates to other countries." He whipped back around, striding up to the cells, yanking a clipboard from a holder. "Meet Adel. Thirty-five-year-old worker in the Savage Lands. It's her first day taking the pills. How are you feeling, Mrs. Denke?"

She was huddled on a surprisingly nice mattress dripping in clean blankets and pillows, a tray of untouched food and drink next to her. She looked up, shrugging slightly, not saying anything. Sadness was etched on her face.

"You think you're not evil and sick?" I stomped up to him, motioning to the cage. "Kidnapping and testing innocent humans because we're nothing more than livestock to you?"

"Mrs. Denke?" Killian lowered himself down to her level, his voice softer than I would ever have thought. "Were you kidnapped and forced into anything?"

Her expression cracked with pain, but she shook her head. "No."

I huffed, my head shaking. "What else would she say? She's in a cage!"

"The bars are for her protection as well as ours."

"You are a monster."

He exhaled sharply, as though trying to keep calm. "My friend here doesn't seem to believe me, Mrs. Denke. Will you tell her how you came to be here?"

She nodded, wiping her eyes, folding her arms tighter around her legs. "He saved my family from starvation and desolation. I volunteered."

My forehead wrinkled. "You volunteered?"

"My family now has a roof over their heads, food on the table, and my husband has a well-paying job in the palace."

My throat tightened. "You mean they get paid in exchange for this torture?"

"I'm not well anyway." She shrugged. "Knowing they are taken care of makes whatever will happen to me worth it."

My glare shot to Killian as he stood back up. "Everyone is here by their own will."

"Because you preyed on their weakest point. Took advantage of them," I bellowed.

Rage flashed through his eyes, his jaw tightening. "I am a lord, Ms. Kovacs, not some saint from one of your make-believe stories." He stepped back up to me, his force shoving at me. "I am giving them a lot more than your own dear leader does. At least it is their choice, and their family benefits from my gratitude."

"You are vile," I snarled.

"Whatever lets you sleep at night," he scoffed, his breath trickling across my lips, making me realize how close we were. "Let's finish our tour, shall we?" He rotated, motioning to the second cage.

An older, gray-haired man sat on the bed, rocking, his lips moving, muttering to himself, but I couldn't make out his words. "Mr. Laski has been on the pills for two days. Mr. Petrov." He pointed to the next cell, a younger man, but life had not been kind to him. His pants were almost falling off, his skin a yellowish color, and he talked to himself like he was having a full conversation, sometimes bellowing out words. He paced the small cell, scratching and pulling at his hair, not taking notice of us at all. "He's been on for three." Killian continued on.

"But Ms. Kinsky is where things start changing." He paused on the next cage. The girl was no more than twenty, but again you could see her life had not been easy. Her skin was drawn and sun-damaged, scarred along her face and arms. She stood stock-still, her eyes vacant. Her thin frame was not even trembling from weakness. "Day four is the shift."

"The shift?" I stepped up to the bars, peering at her. She took no notice of us, not even a flinch or blink of her lids. I reached out, touching her hand. Nothing. "What's wrong with her?"

"You really have no idea what those pills do?" Killian eyed me.

"No." I shook my head, snapping my fingers in front of her face. No reaction. "How long has she been this way?"

"She stopped pacing twenty-four hours ago and hasn't moved since."

"Twenty-four hours?" My mouth dropped.

"They stay in this state for days. So far, the maximum time has been five days, but she might be the first who surpasses that." Killian flicked his chin down the row to the ones wailing, nothing but skeletons. "Next, this starts to happen… and then…"

I gulped. "Then what?"

"Their brains pretty much melt, and they finally die."

My hand went to my stomach, pressing in.

"They don't eat, drink, or defecate. But when they reach this state?" He gestured back to Ms. Kinsky. "They are incredibly easy to control."

"Control? What do you mean?"

"Ms. Kinsky?" Killian addressed her, though she did not respond. He moved us away from the bars, pointing at me. "Kill her."

As if a monster took her over, she lurched for the bars, making me jump back with a cry. A guttural howl echoed from her, bouncing off the walls as she clawed for me. Her face twisted, her bones cracking while she tried to force herself to fit between the bars, tearing at her flesh.

"Stop!" Killian ordered. She went still, and she stood there like a robot again.

"Oh, my gods." A bitter tang coated my tongue, my heart thumping in my chest.

"It took us a while to realize when they reached this stage, they were waiting for orders." He watched the girl, not looking at me. "They also have triple the strength of a normal human and are slightly harder to kill, as if their senses don't tell them when they're in pain."

My head wagging, I swallowed. "I don't understand. Who would do this?"

"Come on, Ms. Kovacs. *Who* do you think would benefit from an army of people who don't feel pain and will attack anyone they are told to?"

"You're saying Istvan is doing this?" I sputtered, laughing. "We protect humans; this is the opposite of that. This is something you fae would do."

"*We* don't need to." He spun to me, his statement flat and matter of fact. "Plus, why would *I* hurt my own people to achieve something we already have?"

"What do you mean?"

"You haven't guessed what the main components in these pills are?" His violet eyes burrowed into me like he was trying to excavate into my brain and pluck out what was hidden in there. "What is giving these humans this ability?"

I didn't answer, my jaw locked tight. Dread swirled in my stomach because deep down, I was afraid I might already know. And I'd have to face how naïve and blind I had been when it came to Istvan. What he had been doing.

Fury flickered in Killian's eyes. "You look at us like *we* are the monsters when it's been you humans the whole time. Who forced us into hiding for centuries, who slaughtered us by the thousands, who denied our existence. Because in truth, humans have always been jealous and wanted to be us."

Oxygen clogged in my airways. "No." I shook my head, denying what I feared was coming.

"There is only one way to get *fae essence* like this." He snarled, moving closer. "By *harvesting* it from fae and half-breeds."

Sucking in sharply, the cascade of his declaration cracked over me.

"And you know what I found even more interesting?"

"What?" A hoarse whisper came from my throat.

"You."

"Me?" I pointed at myself. "Why me?"

"Because, Ms. Kovacs, every test subject has responded in the same exact way, until succumbing to it. Every. One. Of. Them... *except one*." He slid his hands into his pockets, stepping up to me. "Subject Number One."

"And where is Subject One?"

He smirked. "Standing in front of me."

"Wha-what?" I rasped. A flood of burning ice stabbed through my veins, terror flushing through my body.

"You, Ms. Kovacs, were my first subject. For two weeks, you have been taking the pills, crushed into your meals."

I couldn't move my limbs; my lungs struggled to take in any air. The drug causing these people painful deaths had been in my system for weeks now?

"While nothing happened to you, the other subjects became more fae-like before they started to falter and die. Organs failed. Some faster, some slower, but in the end, all their minds would bend, taking orders before perishing." His shoes hit my covered toes, and he leaned over me, his brows wrinkling, his voice threatening. "But not you. You have become even more guarded to fae glamour."

My brow furrowed.

"Tree fairies are very sexual. Almost equivalent to sirens in carnal energy. If a water or tree fairy targets you, no human can resist. Most fae can't." He picked up a strand of my hair, playing with the end. "I told Willow to focus all her magic on you. My fae guards were about to fuck you on the spot. I was—" He broke off, swallowing. "But you didn't break."

I almost did.

He laid the end of my hair down, his fingers brushing my collarbone.

"You are *not* fae. But no human has survived yet. Around thirty have come after you, Ms. Kovacs, and seventeen of them are dead. But not you. Why is that? What makes you so special?"

"Nothing," I whispered, my head spinning with this truth. "I'm an ordinary human."

"Lie." He inched in closer, his mouth hovering over mine, sliding the same strand of hair behind my ear. "You and I both know you are far more than that." His bright eyes searched mine. For a brief moment, he let down his walls, letting me see a softness in his look, making my throat tighten.

"Then what am I?" I swallowed, terrified, but not for the reasons I should have been.

"I don't know." His voice was low as the screaming and muttering from the cages tapped against the bubble we seemed to be in. "I just know you bewitch and intrigue almost everyone you come into contact with." His fingers slid through my hair. "You can block fae glamour, and, it seems, our *essence*." The last word curled around me with sexual energy, pulsing around my thighs.

My lungs pumped, frozen under the fae lord's attention.

"I am the most powerful fae in this country. I don't like not knowing something," he spoke. His voice held irritation, but his eyes still moved over me with open interest. "Either I figure it out or..." His head tilted as if he was going to kiss me, oxygen sucking through my nose.

"Or?"

"I crush it." He turned around and strode out, the door slamming behind him. He left me gasping for breath, my head spinning, feeling like I had been hit by a wave—crushed, flipped, and flattened. Killian ripped the ground from underneath me, letting me float out to sea.

"Kill. Kill. I must kill them. That's the only way." A voice drew my attention back to a cell. The younger man, Mr. Petrov, muttered over and over, his arms twitching and moving like he'd lost control. "Purify the world. They must die."

"Who? Who must die?" I took a step to the cage.

His head started wagging, his arms flailing. "Die. Kill." He started to rock, not appearing to hear or see me. I stared down the row at each one, my chest heavy with sadness and fear.

I could have been one of them. Why wasn't I? What made me different?

A scream belted from the last occupied cage, the skeleton-like figure who had been wrapped up in a ball let out an anguished wail, spinning me around. Blood gushed from her nose and eyes. Her mouth opened, her bony hand reaching out through the bars to me, her eyes vacant and clouded over. She barely resembled a human, but I still wanted to help her. Fear thudded in my ears, but my feet moved to the cell, where I crouched down next to her.

"I'm here. You are not alone," I said softly. Pushing against my disgust, I took her hand. I couldn't tell if she understood or even knew I was there, but I held her hand, feeling her life drain from her, blood pooling underneath her head. And then she stopped breathing.

"I'm sorry." My throat clotted with emotion, thinking of the pain and fear she must have gone through. It was all my fault. I brought this to Killian's door, and I also felt guilty for surviving when they didn't.

Emotion filled my chest. These were people, ones I met at Kitty's like Rosie, or my maid, Maja's, kids, trying to survive in the Savage Lands, doing what they thought was the best for their families. A surge of heartache and grief cracked against my ribs.

Suddenly the woman sucked in a violent gulp of air, lifting her head. Her emaciated fingers clutched painfully at me, digging into my skin. I jerked back with a shriek. I scrambled away as the woman's head dropped back to the ground, her body still while blood oozed from her mouth and nose.

Dead.

Gasping for air, I slumped into the wall, my body trembling. *What the fuck?* I knew near death your muscles and nerves could pulse out one last surge, but it didn't make it any less frightening to experience.

"Ms. Kovacs?" At the sound of a male voice, I looked to the left. Iain, the young guard, stood there. "Time to return to your cell." He held up a pair of cuffs.

I nodded, shakily standing up, numbly watching him restrain me and walk us back to my cell.

Just because the pills had not affected me yet didn't mean they wouldn't. I could have been down here, taking the place of the woman, muttering to myself, waiting for my brain to become liquid.

I had to get out of here. My gaze drifted to the Iain, his eyes trained ahead, but I saw his cheeks blush under my scrutiny.

He liked me.

And I was going to use that to get free.

"Damn it, get your finger out of her nose." A voice hummed through my dreams, walking the line of semiconsciousness. The familiar tenor dredged up the only happiness and safety I had felt at Halálház, making me cling to the dream.

Chirp.

"No, I don't think she secretly likes it."

Chirp.

"That's a lie! I do not."

Chirp.

"You promised to *never* speak of that incident again. I did not enjoy it there either," the voice hissed, sounding very real, rousing me from sleep. My lashes blinked away something gummy as I skimmed up to consciousness. My blurry eyes opened on two faces only a breath away from me, and I realized one had a long finger up my nose.

"What the hell?" I mumbled, jolting back, my head ramming into the stone wall as my brain tried to take in the bright colors exploding against the dull gray.

"Ah, little Fishy is awake."

Chirp.

"You're the one who woke her up. Don't blame me."

My mind scrambled to make sense of what I saw. Was I still dreaming? Was I still in Halálház and everything after had been a nightmare?

No... my gaze drifted around. I was still in the palace's cell where I had been living for weeks. The cot and lumpy pillow were the same, but the figures in front of me did not fit in this new terrain.

"Opie?" I gaped at the familiar figure holding a broom. The brownie with his heart-shaped face, large nose, slightly pointed ears, brown eyes, brown hair, and beard stood before me. On his back, a tiny, large-eared creature flipped me off.

Bitzy.

"Hey, Fishy." He grinned, brushing back the gold tassel on his head.

"Opie..." I repeated, my brain not wrapping around what my eyes were telling me.

Chirp.

"No. I'm sure she's not brain dead."

Chirp.

"Hey. I am *quite* rememberable, thank you very much." He huffed, putting his hands on his hips, glaring back at the imp. His outfit almost blinded me. His bottom half was wrapped in bright teal handkerchief-like booty shorts. His top half was red and yellow buttons strung together with pink laces, like a bra, and a gold curtain tassel for a hat. His beard was braided with purple ribbon.

"Oh. My. Gods." I sat up, my head shaking in happy puzzlement. "Wha-what are you doing here?"

"What are *you* doing here?" He folded his arms, quirking up a bushy eyebrow. Bitzy rocked her head in an accusatory expression. "You escaped Halálház, without a goodbye, let me add."

Chirp. A finger flew up, telling me off in multiple ways. "To end up here?"

"Wasn't my choice." I frowned briefly, thinking about Warwick's deceit, but seeing Opie and even Bitzy again had me bubbling with glee, unable to hold on to my anger. "But seriously, what are you doing here?"

"Master Finn is beholden to Lord Killian." He swung his head, pushing the tassel to the other side. "And since the prison is in temporary shutdown, we've moved here. Which is a million times better. He has much nicer stuff. At first, we were in his upper chambers, but..." He fixed the knot of his shorts. "Once *again*, I drew the short straw, cleaning the prisoners' cells down here."

My lids narrowed. "Just curious. How many times do you draw the short straw?"

"*Every time!* Crazy, huh?" He tossed up his arms dramatically. "Master Finn says I have awful luck for a brownie."

Chirp.

Opie's smile fell, but he didn't respond to Bitzy, brushing his broom back and forth on my gray blanket. It had nothing to do with luck and everything to do with Opie not following the norms of brownie behavior. This was their way of ostracizing him. But I couldn't be more thankful he was here.

"That's okay. At least I can get away with not having to *really* clean." Opie continued to sweep absently at the blanket, forcing a smile back on his mouth. "I mean, upstairs everything has to be perfect, but down here?" He motioned around with a shrug. "Minus the shit, vomit, piss, blood, or brain matter, it's the easiest job ever."

"Brain matter?" My eyes widened. Was he cleaning the cages down in the lab?

Chirp.

"Bitzy thinks you're an idiot." Opie skipped over my question.

I pinched my nose, still trying to accept they were here. They were real. "Shocker."

"Do you enjoy being in a cell so much you had to find another?" Opie sighed. "I mean, I've heard a lot of women are into being chained up, especially by Lord Killian, but this seems a bit excessive."

"Gross." I gritted my teeth, a flush of chagrin heating my neck. "That man is arrogant, heartless, and—" My mind rolled back to the night before, the feel of his body pressed into me, his power vibrating down my bones. The intensity of his gaze as his finger grazed my neck.

"Hot?" Opie pipped in.

Lowering my lids, I glared at him.

Chirp.

"What?" Opie peered between Bitzy and me. "Like you two weren't thinking it."

"No."

Chirp.

"You are both full of shit." He rolled his eyes.

Chirp.

"Please, how many times have you wanted to put your finger up his nose or other places?"

Bitzy blinked, her head tipping in thought.

"Double gross." I rubbed my head, sitting back more firmly against the wall, dragging my knees up, yawning. After the traumatic, emotional day before, I pretty much had passed out, my night haunted with cries, blood, and skeletons attacking me. "Any way you can sneak me coffee down here?"

This place could be considered more ruthless than Halálház; at least there, I could get coffee before lashings.

"I'm sorry, do I look like a barista to you?" He motioned down to himself.

"In your outfit, you'd be a good one at Madam Kitty's."

"Kitty?" His eyes bulged, peering around him. "Where? Where?" He crouched down, his arms poised to fight.

Chirp.

"I can so fight."

Chirp.

"I did not scream like a peacock and hide under a pillow."

Chirp.

"Well, the cat was huge! And I swear it was out to get me." Opie circled his arms in some generic karate move. "And don't get all cocky. You hid under the pillow with me. I didn't see you running out and challenging it."

Chirp.

"Okay." I broke off their repartee, holding up my hands at them. "What is going on?"

"You said there was a kitty." He kicked out his leg. "Come on, fuzz bucket. Come face me now!"

A laugh burst from my chest. It was like clearing out the cobwebs in an abandoned house, letting light into my soul. The giggles bubbled from my mouth, making me feel lighter. I couldn't even remember the last time I laughed.

"What?" Opie peered back at me.

"There's no cat." I held a hand to my mouth, the giggles bursting through my fingers.

"No cat?" Opie lowered his arms slowly, still gazing around.

"No." I shook my head, wiping away a drop of moisture that escaped from the corner of my eye. A tear shed in amusement, not pain.

"Then why did you say there was?" Opie huffed.

Chirp.

Finger.

"*Madam* Kitty. She's a person. She runs a brothel in the Savage Lands."

"Savage Lands?" Opie went still, his mouth dropping. "You were there?"

"I was." I tipped my head back to the wall, every detail of my time there still vibrant and loud in my mind. "Only for a few days, but it definitely made an impression. I think you'd fit in well where I stayed."

"What's it like?" Opie stepped closer to me, his eyes glistening with wonder. "I've always wanted to go, but Master Finn says only the depraved and disreputable brownies go there. We should appreciate what we have and not venture out of our world. We already have the best. No point to see anything else."

"The best for who?" I flicked the tassel out of his eyes, hitting Bitzy in the face. She glared and flipped me off. How sad that her gesture felt so comforting to me. "Best is relative, isn't it? What's best for asshole Finn might not be best for you." Damn, if I didn't sound similar to my old Druid friends. I thought about Tad and Kek a lot, hoping they were okay. That they escaped and were safe somewhere. "I was raised with the same ideals... why leave if what I had was what everyone wanted? But the more I've seen, the more I've learned..." I sighed, staring off.

When I was in the Savage Lands, all I kept thinking about was going home, not realizing the little taste of the outside world had seeped into my bones. Changed me.

Could I go back to my walled world and be okay with it?

Keys rattled in the lock, spiking alarm down my spine like a javelin. My gaze darted to the door. Even though it was probably just my breakfast of hot gruel, as it had been every day, my nerves felt thin and raw, as if they had been pulled and worked like taffy.

My eyes flashed back to where Opie and Bitzy had been. Gone. In a second, they'd vanished. I searched the basically empty room to see if I'd see them scurrying away.

Nothing.

The door swung open, drawing me back to the figure strolling in, a sharp inhale pushing me against the wall.

My breakfast was being hand delivered.

"Did you sleep well, Ms. Kovacs?" Killian, looking unfairly beautiful, was dressed in a fitted navy suit, a light blue tie and handkerchief, holding a tray with eggs instead of my usual hot cereal. His impact was like a punch to the lungs, and I looked away. Staring off to the side, I tried to ignore his energy bursting around me.

"Not speaking to me?" He walked up to the edge of the cot, waiting for me to respond. He wasn't quite what I thought he'd be. I expected the same cruelty as I'd received in the House of Death from this man who designed it. Not for him to display a strange politeness to his captives like he did with me or Adel in the cell below. It made me feel unstable and skeptical, waiting for the whip or his fist to bring me down. "I see."

He set the tray down on the end of my cot. The aroma of cheesy eggs, crispy bacon, fruit, buttery toast, and... *coffee*... curled in my nose, making my stomach growl and my mouth water, beckoning me to fall face-first into the plate, moaning in ecstasy.

A breakfast fit for a lord.

My jaw cracked as I turned away again, the smell bringing me to my knees. The last time I had real eggs, bacon, fruit, and imported coffee was back in HDF. Months ago, which felt like years.

"I assure you, there is no poison in it. No crushed pills." He stood over me, folding his arms.

I stared at a tiny hole in the wall.

"I wouldn't bother lying to you now, Ms. Kovacs. You have already proven yourself immune."

I turned to look up at him, my lips pinching.

He smirked as if he could read me.

"Not only were you on them for two solid weeks, but they were in every meal after the first few days passed. Those you saw below took only one pill a day. It didn't seem to matter: weight, sex, or health. They were all affected within the first twenty-four hours." He settled back on his heels. "I wish to test you another way, if I may?"

"If you may?" I sputtered, anger lashing out like venom. "Please, you are not asking my permission, Killian, so drop the act."

In a flash, his face was in mine, his hands flattening me back against the wall.

"I told you. Do not call me by my name," he seethed, his irises bursting with color, his nose flaring. We stared at each other before he cleared his throat. "Don't push me. Unlike your last companion, I do not feel the need to use violence for everything." His mouth brushed my ear, which made my lungs constrict. "But if it is the only way you to obey me, I will." He pushed back, tugging at his cuffs. "Eat your breakfast. A guard will be coming for you in ten minutes." He swiveled around, exiting.

"Oh my…" A voice jerked my head back to the tray of food, half a sausage sticking out of his mouth. Opie stood there, fanning himself. "He's so yummy."

Chirp.

"No, I don't think he'd be into that."

Chirp.

"Bitzy!" Opie's mouth fell open. "He's our master. Don't put those images in my head."

Chirp.

"You're right. I totally already thought about it. He's probably into that stuff behind closed doors."

"Please stop." I rubbed my face. "You're making me queasy."

"Oh, then you won't be eating this then?" he mumbled, his mouth sounding full.

My head snapped to my breakfast, seeing a slice of bacon sticking out of Opie's mouth, while Bitzy's finger stirred the coffee, licking it off and sticking it back in the cup.

Folding myself over my legs with a sigh, I said, "No. All yours."

"Oh, good! I know we had a stack of pancakes twenty minutes ago, but I'm starving." Opie crammed in a piece of toast, butter trailing down his chin.

The lock on my cell clinked, the door swinging open. Peering back at my friends, once again, they vanished as if they'd never been there.

"Let's go," a woman's deep voice barked, jolting me back to the door. I was shocked not seeing the young cute guard, Iain, standing there. The woman wore a signature guard outfit with Killian's symbol on her chest, a sword dangling from her waist. She was over six feet, with a sharp nose and wide shoulders. Her feather-like short hair was various shades of brown and gold. Acute gold-brown eyes narrowed on me with utter disgust. "Move it!"

Fuck. I got to my feet, stepping cautiously toward the door.

"Where's Iain?"

"Did I say you could speak, prisoner?" She shoved me forward, my shoulder ramming into the stone wall across the hallway. "You shut the hell up and do what you're told before I stop being nice."

"Someone spit in your coffee too?" I muttered.

Her large hands grabbed my hair, yanking me back, her expression twisted. "Whatever spell you put on the men won't work with me. That's why they have me watching you. Iain was growing too fond of you."

Dammit. Killian saw the weakness before I could exploit it. "I want nothing more than you dead. So, remember your place, human. Or my knife might accidentally slip across your neck, as you deserve." She thrust me forward, my feet scrambling to keep up.

Shit, what had I done to her?

I stayed quiet the rest of the trip to the lab, but she took every opportunity to shove and push me into walls and doorjambs. My arms were bruised by the time we entered the lab.

"Nyx." Killian's voice cut through the air as he stepped into the room with the window, meeting us. "That's enough."

"I disagree, my lord. I think the prisoner has grown too comfortable and has forgotten her place. What she really is."

"And what is she, Nyx?"

"Lucky! I haven't stabbed a hole through her chest yet," she replied.

A hint of humor flashed over Killian's face, his eyes meeting mine. "I see you made a friend, Ms. Kovacs."

I glared back.

"You are excused, Nyx. I will let you know when she needs to be returned to her cell."

Nyx dipped her head at his order, snarling at me before marching back down the hallway.

"Better be careful. Hawk-shifters become intent on their prey and are hard to sway off their target. And she really wants any reason to kill you."

Hawk-shifter. That didn't sound good for me. "What the hell did I do to her?" I rubbed at my sore arms. "Or is it just because I'm human?"

"The human part is what I want to figure out." He moved right up to me, his solid body evident under his nice suit. "But that's not why she wants to kill you."

"Then why?"

"Because you murdered her partner, Yulia." He lifted an eyebrow. "Put a bullet through her lover's heart and watched her fall into the Danube the night you escaped Halálház."

I blinked and glanced back at the doorway. Holy shit... Yulia. Her girlfriend was the owl-shifter I shot while Warwick and I were fleeing Halálház?

Fuck.

"She watched it happening live, so I think that gives her an exceptionally good reason to want you dead." He twisted around, going for the door. "You will do as I say, or I will let her seek the revenge she craves."

Chapter 4

"That is enough for today." Killian's silky voice caused my lashes to flutter open, and I took in his familiar build strolling up to the bed I was lying on. He clicked off the machines surrounding me with their rhythmic beeps and hums, which had lulled me into dozing. "How are you feeling?"

"Better if I had a cookie." I tried to hold back my grin.

"I'm sure I could find you something sweet." His violet eyes lifted to mine with a playful smile, making my chest clench. I turned my attention back to my hands. *What the hell, Brex? He's the enemy.*

It was getting harder to remember that.

It had been more than a week and a half since he first brought me down here. Every day I returned, but instead of forcing pills down my throat, I went through every type of test imaginable: blood, physical, psychological, x-rays, brain waves, fae woo-woo stuff. And in that time, Killian had been by my side. I stopped questioning it after the third day; his constant presence was the only thing giving me comfort. He only left when business came up, but he returned the moment he could. Because I was doing what he wanted without a fight, his threat to punish me if I didn't drifted away with each passing day. But I was no fool. I understood it could all shift in a blink, and he could easily kill me.

I expected the tests to start bordering on cruelty. But besides a basic physical examination, I got to lie there and eat cookies later. In my book, that was a holiday.

"You look a little pale today." Killian peeled off a monitor attached to my temple. "Might benefit from some fresh air. A walk, maybe. Would you join me?"

My head jerked to him.

"Actually, I have a little surprise for you."

My brow crinkled. His kindness bypassed every one of my defenses. I doubted his intentions and my own judgment of character.

Killian was nothing like I imagined or what I had been told. He didn't have human slaves bringing him trays of food while he tortured, killed, and raped our kind. He was compassionate toward me. Attentive. I found myself laughing and teasing with him the longer we spent together. It disturbed me.

"Can I ask you something?"

"Of course." He gently tugged out the needle in my arm.

"Why are you here?" I watched him do everything himself instead of a lab specialist. He had all week. If he was by my side, then he dismissed the technicians and took care of me himself.

"What do you mean, why am I here?" His brow furrowed, grabbing a cotton swab to pat the drip of blood from the puncture hole. "This is my lab. My palace."

"Exactly. Yours. You have dozens of staff at your will who could be here instead."

He didn't respond, still putting pressure on the wound.

"Don't you have other obligations? *You are* the leader. Shouldn't you be, I don't know, running your side of the country instead of being my nurse?"

"My focus is precisely where it should be." His eyes met mine. "And I enjoy being your nurse."

I sucked in, his gaze heavy on me. "Why?"

He stepped back, tossing the swabs into the wastebasket.

"Come," he ordered, advancing for the door, ignoring my question.

Blowing out my breath, I slid off the bed, following him out. Nyx waited at the elevators for us, her glower darkening the moment she saw me.

"Lord." She dipped her head, pulling out a set of handcuffs. "Should I take the prisoner back to her room… smother her with a pillow?"

He chuckled, shaking his head as he stepped into the lift. "Not tonight. I will be escorting Ms. Kovacs myself. You can take the rest of the night off."

"Sir?" She blinked at him in horror, the handcuffs in her hands. "Shouldn't I at least bind the captive?"

29

"No need." His regard slid to me as I moved into the elevator with him, then back to Nyx. "I think I can handle her."

"My lord…" Nyx shook her head. "Yes, she is a weak, disgusting, vile human. But I'm concerned you are not seeing clearly."

"Are you second-guessing me, lieutenant?"

"No, sir." She bowed her head deeper. "It's my job to keep you safe. To see all threats."

"I hardly think a human is any threat to me." He pushed the button on the elevator. "Good night, Nyx."

Nyx's mouth remained open, her eyes wide as the doors shut, taking us up.

"I think she's really beginning to like me." I peered over at Killian, his regard meeting mine, a smile hinting on his mouth. I had seen more and more of this side of him in the last week.

"I daresay she is," he replied, his stare not wavering, forcing me to look away as tension billowed in the tiny space.

The doors opened, finally breaking Killian's attention from me as he stepped out into a large room. A gasp caught in my lungs as I followed him out, twisting around to take in all the grandeur and the opulence reminding me of home.

He had brought me up to his palace. His home.

The huge gallery was laid with marble flooring and rich red carpet. Excruciating detail was sculpted into the arched ceilings far above our heads. Exquisitely carved statues of fae lined the room, invaluable murals painted on the ceilings and walls. Every space dripped with crystal and pure gold chandeliers, ornate rugs, oversized fireplaces, and excessive riches beyond anyone's imagination.

I recognized it; it was very similar to HDF. Here, the fat cats lapped at the cream, while most others starved and begged in the street for crumbs.

When I was at HDF, I used to stare at this castle from across the river. I knew the building's shell was left intact, but from old pictures, it was clear Killian had the interior updated, removing the human influence of its previous owners.

It was now more modern, clean, but oozed decadence and money. Paintings of fae mythology replaced portraits of human leaders, and Killian's insignia was everywhere: two intertwined, detailed circles with a sword cutting through the middle, the blade and handle encrusted with Celtic symbols and blazing with light. It symbolized the Sword of Nuada, an old-world treasure said to have been destroyed around the time of the Fae War twenty years ago. Though, some still believed it had made it out, hidden somewhere in the world.

The time alone with Killian almost made me forget who he really was. Seeing this was like a punch to the face. He was the fae leader. My enemy.

My soft slipper-type shoes skated over the cool floors. My skin prickled, and my lungs sucked in the fresh air blowing through the open windows, where sheer drapes billowed like sails on the open sea. The early evening set deep purples and blues along the horizon and cast the room in shadows. Warm buttery light spilled from the chandeliers and sconces.

Killian strolled out onto the balcony, glancing over his shoulder at me. Stepping beside him, I took a deep breath, tears prickling at my eyes. The scent of the Danube rolled over me, smelling familiar and comfortable. My breath shuddered as I took in the glowing city across the river. The lights of the Human Defense Force twinkled at me like an old friend, beckoning me over. I bit down on my lip, longing and sorrow stabbing my heart. Home.

I could feel Killian's weighted gaze on me, but I couldn't look at him, lost in the view. The hint of fall kissed the air. It had only been a handful of months since my capture on the bridge below, but standing here next to a Seelie fae, the lord of Hungary, staring at my old home from his castle, alive and unscathed, I realized how much had changed for me. I lived lifetimes in those months, experienced things I never imagined.

The girl who used to sit up on the roof of HDF staring at this palace would not recognize the girl who looked back now.

"You won't let me go, will you?" I asked, my voice unemotional.

Killian glided his hands into his pockets. "Is that really what you want?"

I glanced over at him, perplexed by his question.

"Could you imagine yourself returning to what you were doing before?" He flicked his head toward HDF, the lights from the gardens glinting off his dark hair and reflecting in his stunning eyes. "Training to kill fae, listening to them repeat over and over what monsters we are." He curved toward me. "Could you go back? Back to wanting to kill fae... to kill me?"

"How do you know I don't want to now?" My voice wobbled more than I expected, my throat coiling on itself, trying to ignore how stunning he was.

"Do you?" He stepped up to me, his body only a breath away, his face far too close to mine. "You want me dead, *Brexley*?"

I inhaled abruptly as though he'd shot a bullet straight through my chest. The potency and intimacy of my name on his lips pulsed through my stomach and down between my thighs.

31

"Power of a name," he muttered, leaning farther into me.

Was this what it was like when I said his first name? Then I could understand his anger at the time. Holy shit…

"Normal humans do not feel the intense weight of a name as we do." He tipped his head to the side, studying me. "But there is nothing normal about you, is there?"

I swallowed, trying not to move or breathe.

"I think Nyx may be right about you."

"That I should be smothered by my pillow?" I croaked.

He huffed out a laugh, his head wagging.

"No." His hands came up to my face, sliding over my cheeks, my lungs hitching. He cupped my face, his gaze dropping down to my mouth. "That you are a threat to me. I cannot see clearly when it comes to you. I cannot explain it, but you make me feel alive. You are a force I'm drawn to, and I can't seem to help but want to follow."

Without warning, his lips came down on mine, locking my muscles up in shock. His mouth was warm and inviting, lighting passion through me. Sparking that need for touch, for a moment of pleasure against all the cruel harshness. To not feel alone and scared.

I slowly responded. Opened to him. He hissed, reacting to my voracious reply, his fingers clasping my face harder, his tongue slipping through my lips, curling against mine, deepening the kiss.

This was like when Zander kissed me. A burst of fervor flared up my vertebrae, taking over. I returned his kiss as if my life were on the line, but I wasn't getting what I needed. Our mouths moved hungrily, but still, I needed more. Demanded it.

Then something shifted when he pressed his body into mine. He seemed larger than I recalled, letting me feel everything. His need. His desire. Pulsing and extraordinarily massive. Everything about him encompassed me like he had suddenly grown feet taller. Wider, more muscular, consuming me. His mouth moving against mine was so utterly divine, for once I was satisfied. And fuck… horny as hell. Our kiss raked thick desire into my core, bowing my legs, adding more desperation to my kiss.

"Fuck, Kovacs, after weeks, I can't say I mind being greeted this way." A deep gravelly voice scraped over my skin, slipping between my legs like fingers, hardening my nipples instantly. My lids burst open, jerking me out of corded arms.

"Oh, my gods." I stumbled back, blinking in confusion and fear, gaping at the huge figure standing before me, completely blocking Killian.

Warwick Farkas.

A cocky grin tugged the side of his mouth, his aqua blue eyes glowing like lights in the evening, his intensity slamming into me. Raw. Savage. Brutal.

"Missed you too, Kovacs," he rumbled, his thick eyebrows lifting. Every syllable struck me, slipping and clawing over my skin as if they owned me. *"Looks like you are doing just fine. Though it must not be that good, because you're still thinking about me."*

"No," I snarled, stepping farther away, gripping my head. This wasn't real. He wasn't here. *Wake up, Brexley. Wake up.*

"Don't..." Warwick reached for me, his lips rising in a snarl. *"I finally got in... Don't push me out yet."*

"Get the fuck away."

"You can't trust him..."

"I can't trust *you*." I shook my head, covering my face. *Wake up! Wake the hell up now!*

"Brexley?"

"Get away from me!" I screamed, squeezing my lids tightly.

"Brexley...?" A hand touched me. The voice was soft, soothing the burns I still felt on my skin from Warwick's touch.

I pried my lashes apart, turning my head up into a beautiful face, the eyes the color of lavender. My head snapped around, searching for Warwick, knowing I would find nothing but shadows and whispers, my imagination conjuring him up like a spirit.

My throat dry, I licked my lips, standing straight.

"Are you all right?" Killian asked, hurt etching the corners of his eyes. He peered around, hunting for whatever caused my reaction. "I apologize if—"

"No. It's fine...it wasn't you." I exhaled, touching my forehead. "I'm sorry. I must have lost too much blood today. I'm a little out of it."

We both felt the lie.

"Of course." He cleared his throat, no longer close to me, his hands in his pockets, the connection we had broken and scattered over the balcony like glass.

Fuck you, Farkas. You're not even here, and you still wreck everything.

"Let me escort you back to your room." He quickly switched back to the detached, aloof leader, as though he hadn't been kissing me moments before. Killian held his head high, strolling back inside, leaving me frazzled, confused, and a little disappointed. I didn't want to think it was because I actually liked him. That was not acceptable.

Neither was the way my body reacted to the phantom of Warwick. Was I losing my mind? Why did he feel and look so real? Why was I imagining him here?

Sighing heavily, my eyes flicked back across the water, hearing the slow river lap against the stone walls of my home. So close.

The longer I was outside the walls of Leopold, the more I forgot myself. Soon I would be unable to recall the girl I had been. I needed to get back. Be with my friends—with *Caden*. Then all would make sense again. It had to.

I still felt Warwick around me like a ghost, the sense of him brushing against me, his presence even in my imagination, overwhelming and solid.

Let me in. His words whispered through me again.

I snorted, my head shaking. "Hell no," I muttered. I would do everything in my power to block him.

The only important thing was getting home.

In the distance, I heard the roar of a motorcycle, making me shiver. A chill seeped into my bones, as if a warm blanket had been tugged from my frame, unsettling my stomach.

Wrapping my arms around myself, I turned away and headed back to my cell, ignoring the sense of being off-kilter and floating away without an anchor.

Empty and scared.

It reminded me of the night Warwick left me in the showers after my kills, ripping away the strange comfort he had provided. As if he was the only thing that could secure me or let me drift off into oblivion.

Chapter 5

Killian greeted me right after my breakfast of French toast and fruit. He was distant, his shoulders pinned back, his expression a mask of indifference.

"Come," he ordered, already pushing past Nyx. I stared after him, taken aback by his icy mood.

"When the fae lord commands you to do something," Nyx growled at me, grabbing my arm painfully, "you do it." She yanked me to my feet, roughly thrusting me out into the hallway. "I live for the day I can slice your throat and watch your blood gurgle out as you choke on it." Nyx's mouth hummed by my ear, her threat full of abhorrence.

Kicking the back of my heels, she pitched me forward, my feet trying to catch up with Killian's silhouette down the hall. This was the opposite way we had gone every other morning.

"The lab is the other way." I thumbed back behind me.

"Thank you, I'm aware." Killian kept his head forward, his shoulders rolled back. No trace of the intimacy we shared the night before remained. He clearly was pretending it never happened, and I didn't know if the tightness in my stomach was from lack of sleep or if I felt hurt.

No, it's lack of sleep. It must be.

I had gone to bed thinking about how I had kissed the leader of the fae, but my dreams were filled instead with intense turquoise eyes and a deadly smile hunting me from the dark.

Nyx kept close to me now but left me uncuffed while we made our way down the corridor, entering another lift and heading up several floors. The silence in the closed box felt stifling, but I kept my lips pinned together as we rose. When the elevator finally came to a stop, Killian strolled out, not even looking at me.

"Move," Nyx hissed, shoving me forward into an enormous, decadent corridor that dripped with more gold and crystal, naked fairies and shape-shifters painted onto the arched ceilings in suggestive positions and group situations.

Swallowing nervously, I followed behind him. All the doors we passed were closed to my curious eyes.

Finally, he stopped in front of a door, his expression blank as he reached for the doorknob. The door swung open, flooding morning light across the floor and onto my feet. He nodded for me to enter, and I did.

Glass covered almost one entire wall in front of me, large doors opening up onto a balcony. The sun glistened off the Danube and buildings across the river, which warmed the room like a blanket.

My mouth loosened in awe, taking in the room before me, my eyes flinching at the onslaught of beauty. My world had consisted of gray and metal for so long, I couldn't fully take in the rich colors and soft textures.

The bedroom was larger than the one I had in HDF. The elegant headboard went halfway up the wall, and the massive king-size bed was layered in creamy whites, buttery yellows, and soft blues. All the furniture was modern and simple. Silks, linens, velvets, and cashmere swathed the room, offering a warm invitation that whispered for me to run into its arms.

The girl I'd been a few months ago wouldn't have even hesitated. Wouldn't have thought twice about exuberant luxury. This would have felt normal. Familiar. Now I didn't move.

"Do you not like it?" Killian stepped around me, his hands in his pockets. I was starting to realize he did this when he wanted to come across as composed, but I heard a twinge of doubt in his tone.

I touched nothing, moving robotically to the windows, and looked out. Below, a handful of horses and carriages moved over the Chain Bridge, and sounds of motorcycles and clipping of hooves touched my ears. The street bustled with people living their lives. The dome of the old parliament building stuck up in the distance, twisting at my heart. Everything felt vibrant and active. It was the first time I had seen daylight in weeks, animating all I had not been able to see last night.

"There are other rooms you can pick from. But I thought you'd enjoy the view." Killian moved next to me, swinging my head to him.

"Why?" I spat. "To torture me? To show me how close I am, but I will never be able to reach it?"

His jaw tightened. "That was not my intention."

"What *is* your intention, *Killian*?"

He jolted at his name, his eyes darkening.

"I'm still a prisoner, no matter what bed I sleep in." My eyes kept locked on his face. "At least my cell is more honest."

He breathed through his nose, his focus not leaving me. I couldn't make out any emotion underneath, but I could feel the weight of them, words dropping from his tongue, wanting to lash out at me. The tension between us threaded through the room, strangling out the air.

"Sir, you requested me?" A man's voice broke through the discomfort, the familiar pitch jerking my head to the doorway. It felt as though the room tipped, an internal gasp twitching my limbs.

Chocolate brown eyes shot to mine from across the room, a slight frown wrinkling the space between the horse-shifter's eyes as his look darted between Killian and me before his expression went neutral again.

Zander. The only guard who had been kind to me. Kissed me. Helped me escape. He was the reason Warwick and I got out of Halálház. Why would he help us but work for Killian?

"Yes." Killian cleared his throat, stepping away from me. It wasn't until then I realized how close we had been standing. "Thank you, Zander." He strolled to his guard. "Let's go to my office. There is much to do to prepare the new location."

He didn't say, but I understood, they were talking about the new prison. The original site had been compromised, so he would have to rebuild it somewhere completely unknown.

Zander dipped his head, waiting for Killian to exit first.

Killian made it to the door and stopped, looking back at me.

"We can discuss your accommodations later. But please enjoy the room until I get back. I am suspending your testing for the day." His eyes couldn't quite meet mine. "If you need anything, a guard will be right outside." He rubbed his chin, hesitating before he whipped around, leaving the chamber.

Zander grabbed for the knob, his gaze slamming into mine. It was so slight I almost missed it, but his head dipped, his eyes never breaking from mine, like they were trying to speak to me.

"Miss," he said, as though we had never met.

I watched him close the door, wanting nothing more than to run after him, demand to know why he'd helped Warwick and I escape. Was he someone I could trust or not? If I had any chance of getting out of this place, it just walked out of the room.

"Oh yeah... rub it! Harder!"

Chirp!

The late afternoon rays pushed through my lashes as my body curled on top of the huge bed like a cat. Not able to fight the lethargy after my lunch was served, the warm sun stretching across the soft bed had summoned me to it.

Now my brow furrowed as splashes and squeaks came from the stunning en-suite bathroom, lifting my head up.

"What does this button do?"

Chirp!

"Ooooohhh yeeeahhh," a small voice moaned.

Rubbing my face, I got up and strolled into the bathroom. I clasped a hand to my mouth, holding in laughter as I leaned against the doorjamb, taking in the scene inside the bathtub.

Dressed in what looked like a modified neon pink rubber glove, Opie wore it like a scuba suit, and attached to his knees, ass, and elbows were cut-up pieces of an orange scrubber. The jet spurted out water while he wiggled his butt back and forth, his eyes closed as he ground against the surface.

Bitzy floated on a sponge near him, her head and tiny form covered in the same rubber material.

"Take that, jet tub... You like it? I bet you do, you filthy thing."

A snort broke through my hands, jolting the two tiny figures.

"Holy scrubbing loofah!" Opie grabbed at his chest dramatically. "You about turned this water brown, Fishy."

"And I thought you could never sneak up on a brownie." I smirked at him.

"Well, normally, you can't." He cleared his throat, tugging at his skintight suit. "But I was really immersed in *cleaning*."

"Is that what you call it?"

Chirp.

"I was not!" Opie's eyes widened in shock. "I would never do such a thing. That would be vulgar."

Chirp.

"Can't prove it." He sniffed, turning away, busying himself with scouring the already pristine porcelain.

Chirp.

"You promised to never bring up that incident again either. It was a misunderstanding."

Chirp.

"It was too," he countered. "Master Finn still hasn't let me anywhere near a vacuum cleaner since."

"Oh, gods." I laughed, my face planting in my hand, trying to squash the visuals in my mind.

"Like I said, it was a misunderstanding. I got caught for a moment... in the suction."

Chirp.

"It was not five minutes."

Chirp.

"We're not talking about this." He huffed, turning away, his shoulders sagging.

I hated seeing him so sad, like he was "wrong" because he didn't fit in.

"Well, if you ask me, I think this Master Finn would benefit *greatly* from five minutes with a vacuum."

"That's what I told him." A tiny smile hinted on Opie's face. "He had me scrubbing toilets for ten months afterward."

Strolling over to the tub, I shut off the water, sitting on the side. "How did you know where I was?"

Opie scoffed, facing me again. "Please, you are easy to find. You have a particular smell, Fishy."

"I smell?" I frowned, pinching my top, sniffing it. I knew I didn't smell the best, but I had recently taken a shower before testing and had been given a new gray uniform. I was a lot better than when locked away in Halálház.

"Not bad-smelling or anything. It's hard to explain. It's pleasant. Like the moment at night, right before the sun rises. Clean, fresh with a dash of sweetness." Opie tapped his nose. "We sub-fae have excellent noses."

Chirp!

"And ears." He motioned to the imp. "Obviously."

There was a rap on the bedroom door, and I jumped up. In less than a second, I looked back to my friends. Gone. Only the sponge Bitzy had been lounging on still twirled around the bottom of the tub. Damn, they moved fast.

Frantic knocks tapped at my door again, so I hurried to it, my stomach knotting in strange anxiety. Killian would never knock like that or at all. Neither would Nyx or Iain. I was a prisoner, not a guest.

The moment I reached for the door, I heard my name whispered low. "Brexley, it's me."

Swinging the door open, my chest thudded as Zander's wild gaze landed on mine.

"Zander," I breathed out his name. He shot a glance around him, checking to see if anyone was there before he slipped past me, shutting the door.

"We don't have much time." His movements were jerky and anxious. "I told Iain I'd stand guard until Nyx came on duty." His hands came to my waist, then up to my face, taking me in. "Gods, I was so worried about you. Seeing you this morning... I could barely keep it together." He cupped my cheeks, his touch intimate. "I knew you were here, but I wasn't expecting to see you *here*... with him."

"Zander." I gripped his hands, pulling them away, glancing back at the door, afraid at any moment Killian would walk in. "You need to go! You can't get caught. What are you even doing right here?"

"This has been the only place I've thought about being all day. It was so hard to concentrate, knowing you were so close. I had to make an excuse to even be up in the residential wing." His eyes moved over me. "Gods, it's so good to see you. I'm so glad you are all right." He held my face again. "He didn't do anything to you, right? Taken any liberties?"

"No. Killian has been surprisingly kind."

"I wasn't talking about Killian." Zander frowned. He meant Warwick. "I hated watching you leave with him. It killed me. Though I was glad he helped get you out."

"Why *did* you?" I stepped back, putting space between us. "Why are you here?"

"What do you mean, why I am here?" He scowled.

"I mean, what is going on? Why did you help me escape Halálház? Don't you work for Killian?"

He tilted his head to the side, blinking. "You mean Warwick didn't tell you?"

"Tell me wha—" A door slammed, the snap of footsteps coming up the hallway.

"Dammit." Zander huffed through his nose, sounding like a horse. "We don't have time. I will be back, I promise." He hurriedly kissed my forehead. "Just stay safe and be ready."

"Ready for—"

The door clicked, creaking open as Zander lurched away from me, grabbing the glass door leading to my balcony, opening and slamming it, his voice angry. "Last time I tell you. You are not to leave this room. Next time I find your head peeking out the door, I will chop it off."

"Oh, was our little prisoner being bad?" Nyx stepped into the room, her irises glinting with bloodlust. "Can I punish her? Kill her?"

"I handled it." Zander nodded, stepping around me toward the door.

"What are you even doing here? Where's Iain?" Awareness crinkled Nyx's forehead, her wariness dropping my stomach. "You have no reason to be over in this wing watching the prisoner."

Panic thumped at my heart, but I kept my expression bare of what I felt inside. Nyx was not stupid, and she already thought I "bewitched" every male who got close to me.

"I'm training Iain tonight. Came to find him falling asleep on his feet. I told him to go, and I'd finish the watch. Good thing, because she had almost made it outside, probably to wave down a boat."

Nyx's glower targeted me with a promise of punishment. Of brutality.

I understood Zander had no choice but to toss me under the bus. There would have been no other reason for him to be alone with me inside my room unless I was trying to break out.

"She understands her mistake now." He touched the sword on his belt, as though he had threatened me with it. "She will behave. I can guarantee it." He nodded at Nyx, half out of the door. "Good night."

"And Iain?" She twisted to him.

A moment of confusion fluttered on Zander's face. "What about Iain?"

"Will you tell Lord Killian? He needs to be disciplined for failure to do his job. He could have been the reason she got away. He cannot go unpunished."

Zander's mouth pinched for a moment, his head dipping. "He will be reprimanded severely in training tonight. He won't do it again."

Nyx dipped her head shallowly. Zander's eyes flitted to me one last time before he closed the door.

Nyx watched the door for a beat, a strange look on her face, knotting my stomach. She turned back to me, an evil smile curling her mouth.

"After my lord learns what you tried to do after all he's done for you—finding out what a deceitful, conniving bitch you are—I don't think he'll mind if I teach you a lesson." She yanked the pair of cuffs off her belt, her fingers rolling into fists. "Don't worry, I won't kill you. Yet." Her fist struck me as fast as a viper, flinging my body to the ground, pain bursting behind my eye like a bomb. The sudden attack snatched the oxygen from my lungs. She leaped down, clutching the fabric around my throat, and hauled me back to my feet before slamming me back into a chair.

"That was for Yulia," she spat, cuffing my arms behind me. "But until I spill your blood, she will not be avenged, and I will not rest."

"You think Killian will understand you disobeying him?" I huffed through my nose, my eye already swelling. "That you are taking liberties he has not ordered?"

"He said not to kill you… but nothing about beating you within an inch of your pathetic human life." She grabbed my hair, yanking it back until I heard a pop, strands tearing out of my head. "I have been his faithful guard for over four hundred years. You won't even be a flicker in his memory. And eventually, he will see you are nothing more than a waste of space."

Without hesitation, her hand smashed into my gut, heaving me over with a gasp, a blaze tearing through my organs. A desolate wail shredded from her throat as her knuckles crashed across my cheek, pitching me off the chair to the floor.

"You took her away from me!" Her boot cracked into my ribs, the feeling all too familiar. "You took everything!"

Crack.

My bones protested as her foot dug into my stomach.

"I want your death to be so slow and tortuous you are begging me to end you." She smacked my face, the sound of knuckles against cartilage ringing in the air.

"Nyx!" A voice boomed. Magic burst violently into the room, my body freezing from the onslaught. "Stop!" His power dominated every molecule in the space.

Nyx drew in sharply, halting, her teeth bared, a trickle of saliva leaking down her chin.

"Move away from Ms. Kovacs." Barely disguised anger hummed in his voice. "Now."

She wiped her mouth, stepping back. Killian stood in the doorway, his jaw clenched, his frame rigid.

"Get out." His voice was low.

As if she snapped out of a trance, she peered down at her hands, taking in the blood dripping off her knuckles. "My lord… I'm…"

"I. Said. Get. Out!" he bellowed, and I was surprised to see her jolt back in fear. She swallowed, dipped her head, and turned away, rushing toward the door.

He watched her, his expression stone, but a nerve along his neck convulsed, his jaw rolling. She bowed her head in submission.

"Keys." He vibrated with rage.

Her throat bobbed, placing the cuff keys in his palm. "My lord—"

"I will deal with you later," he seethed. "Leave."

Her thick, tall frame trembled under his power. She dipped her head again before exiting the room.

He closed his eyes briefly as his fingers curled around the keys, his nose flaring. He took another breath before he bent his head over me.

I couldn't move, pain eclipsing my ability to function. The desire to close my eyes seeped in at the edges of my vision.

There was no sentiment as his gaze moved over my body, curled up in a ball, blood pooling from my nose, coughs hacking from my lungs.

He stooped down and unfastened my arms. Without a word, his hands tucked under me, picking me up, and carried me into the bathroom, where he set me down on the rim of the grand bathtub.

He leaned over, turning on the water.

"I'm going to undress you," he said matter-of-factly, his palm resting on my shoulder.

I nodded numbly, my face aching too much to speak.

He stood in front of me, slowly lifting my gray top over my head, using it to wipe the blood from my nose before tossing it in the corner. His gaze snaked down my torso. I barely had any curves left, but the low dip of my sports bra displayed my pert breasts.

He reached out, his fingers grazing over the bruises already forming over my ribs. His soft touch, filled with magic, made me inhale sharply, which sent spikes of pain through my lungs.

Steam swirled around us as he turned on the hot water. He leaned over, his eyes staying on me as he slid off my pants. Pain coursed through my veins, but it was the ache tightening near my thighs that had my breath puffing harder.

I stared at the blood marks I left across his suit, oddly concerned I messed up his expensive clothes. I reached out and touched the silkiness of his yellow tie.

"Brexley," he whispered, his mouth close to mine.

My lashes lifted up to his dark irises, desire heaving off of him in waves.

"You better get into the bath before I do something very foolish. *Again.*"

Swallowing, I looked away from him.

43

He's the enemy, Brex. Don't be an idiot.

I moved to climb into the tub, a moan slipping from my lips, my arms quaking as I lowered myself down into the water. By chaining my arms back, Nyx made sure it hadn't been a fair fight.

"I will have someone bring healing salts and potions." He stood.

"You're leaving?" Did I sound disappointed?

A small smile hinted at his mouth. "I will be back. A matter has come up. I was just stopping in to check on you." He ran his hand across his chin, his brow furrowing. He shook his head, clearing the emotion away. "I will return as soon as I can. I promise." He leaned over like he was about to kiss me, but stopped. His eyes widened for a moment before he pulled back and hastened out of the bathroom, the bedroom door shutting a few seconds later.

Sighing, I slumped deeper into the hot water, willing it to heal and dissolve away the pain. The warmth instantly tugged my lids down, exhaustion and pain slipping me quickly into defenseless sleep, with no barriers against the monsters trying to get in.

Chapter 6

The sensation of calloused hands skating up my legs made me groan, replacing the throbbing pain with pleasure.

A bell tapped the back of my head, but I turned away from it, letting myself drown in the bliss, sinking deeper into pleasure. Into a peace I had never known.

Palms grazed my ribs. Heat pulsed against them like a magical rope wrapping around the cracked pieces, fixing their fractured parts.

As if lips grazed over my nipples through the thin fabric of my shirt, my back arched, demanding more. Another soft moan puffed from my lips.

A growl hummed against my ear, once again tickling at my unconscious. I had a distant awareness of water swishing against my skin, cool air caressing my breasts under the wet cotton.

"Fuck, Kovacs." His gritty voice dragged over my body, yanking me out of the last bit of oblivion. My eyes opened with a start, my spine knocking against the tub as a man crawled over me.

Feral.

Ruthless.

Savage.

His severe energy punched my chest with a gasp. As if I had been asleep for weeks, the hit of adrenaline burst through my veins, everything in me screaming with both life and death. Peace and violence. Lust and abhorrence. Calm and terror.

His long, dark lashes lifted to mine, pinning me in place, his face only inches from mine. The weight of his physique, his skin touching mine, his wet clothes rubbing against my mostly naked figure was so real.

"Getting into fights again, Kovacs?" he rumbled, his thumb passing over my cheek, his lids flinching as if he experienced the pain I should have felt from his touch. But there was only warmth. Fear blocked out everything other than my pounding heart. How was this possible? Was he actually here? Was I dreaming?

"Can't leave you alone for a moment." He smirked, his lids narrowing on me. "Even got Killian wrapped around your finger." His hand trailed between my breasts, over my stomach, gliding over my underwear, tracing over my folds. I inhaled sharply, my hips reacting without thought, seeking the unbelievable pleasure from his simple touch. "I told you. Your life is mine. I own you... and I own this." He rubbed harder, my lids fluttering, my mouth gasping.

"Fuck you. You betrayed me." Anger and desire choked my throat, my voice low and tight. "And I told you. No one owns me."

"Really?" He snorted. "Look around you, Kovacs. You are someone's pet. Soon you will have a shiny collar to match."

I snarled, but my body behaved in opposition to my hate, tilting into his touch.

"Time to stop playing house, Kovacs." He grunted into my ear, pressing his erection into me, his mouth grazing my neck. "Be ready... It's all about to go to hell... in three, two, one..."

Boooooooom!

The explosion ripped through the air, hurling me back to reality with a violent jump. I bolted up as tremors shook the room.

What the hell was that? What was going on? Confusion caused me to tremble as I pitched forward, scrambling out of the tub. I was alone. I had been dreaming. Though inexplicably, I still could feel the imprint of where he had touched me, his lips on the curve of my neck.

"Brexley!" An anxious voice screamed for me, lurching me toward the doorway. Zander's expression was etched with tension, but he came to a stuttering stop, his gaze moving down me.

My eyes lowered, aware I stood before him in only knickers and sports bra, both white, wet, and see-through. But it wasn't that which flooded me with shock and fear. My skin was unmarred.

Not a hint of a bruise or cuts where Nyx had kicked and beat me. It was all completely healed. Gaping, I glided my fingers over my pale skin, feeling no pain.

What the hell…?

Boom!

Another blast rattled the crystal chandeliers, jerking me to the window. Smoke and fire billowed up into the twilight from the river right below the palace gates.

"We have to go!" Zander snapped out of his trance, heading to a cupboard.

"What's going on?"

"Put this on now!" Zander tossed me a pair of pants, a shirt, and slip-on shoes. I hadn't even noticed the closet had been stocked with items for me. "Hurry!"

"Zander?" I grabbed the garments as the bellows of guards filled the corridors. My heart leaped into my throat, my brain still trying to wrap around all that was happening.

"Getting you out of here." He jogged back for the door, putting his ear against it to listen to movement on the other side.

I quickly dressed, his statement sinking in. Leave. Escape. My stomach tightened, a whisper of sorrow trickling into my gut. *No! You want to leave, Brexley. What is wrong with you?*

"Come on! We have to go now." He bounced at the door, waving me forward. Shoving my feet into the shoes, I ran to him.

Cracking open the door, he peered out, every muscle tight and ready to react. He motioned me forward, creeping down the corridor. My pulse echoed in my ears. Distant shouts, bangs, and movement haunted the hallway, scraping my nerves. We could be caught at any time.

Zander led me down the hall toward the lift, but he skirted me to a bookcase, his hands pushing and stabbing at every book on the shelf.

"What are you—" I yipped in surprise as the bookcase shifted, swinging in. Stone steps descended into a pit of blackness.

"Stay close." His hand clutched mine, pulling me in. The moment the door shut behind us, a firebulb flickered on, giving us enough light to see in front of us.

"Killian and his main guards use this tunnel all the time, but it's the only chance we have." Zander moved down the steps. "If they decide to use it…"

"We're screwed," I finished.

"Basically." His warm brown eyes glanced back at me, his fingers threading through mine. We padded down the secret stairs, passing a few doors inserted deeper into the stone wall, heading under the ground.

Zander came to a sudden stop, going rigid, his head tilting to listen as he sniffed the air. Below, a door slammed, and so did my lungs. I swallowed back the rush of fear, feeling my heart rebound off the walls like it was trying to tattle on me.

The thud of footsteps hitting the stone beat in tune with my heart. We were done. Our escape was about to be exposed in seconds.

Zander's head snapped around frantically, his eyes locking on something behind me. He surged for me, his arms wrapping around as he yanked me into a doorway we had recently passed. His hand covered my mouth, his body tucking me tightly to his, trying to make us dissolve into the shadows. He pressed us against the corner, the uneven stone cutting into my vertebrae.

The steps grew closer, our pounding hearts knocking against each other.

A crackle of a voice filled the chamber, the guard's gait slowing.

Oh. Baszd meg… of all guards.

Nyx came into view, half her face swollen and cut as if she had been violently reprimanded. She brought a device to her mouth. "I'm heading to her now, my lord."

"If you hurt her, I will kill you, Nyx. There are no second chances if you disobey me."

"Yes, sir." She clicked off, pausing on the same platform as us, a snarl curling her lip. "*Szuka…*" *Bitch.*

Terror engulfed me. I couldn't breathe or even think. All she had to do was shift her eyes just a little more toward the door, and she would see the lumpy silhouettes in the corner. Discover us.

She rolled her head, letting out her annoyance. Her frame went stiff, her hand reaching for her gun.

Fuck. Fuck. Bile scorched my throat.

A distant boom seeped through the tunnel, and she took off, racing up the steps. Her footsteps ebbed away.

My body sagged into Zander's, relief whimpering in my chest. Zander exhaled, his hands rubbing my arms. "That was close."

I scoffed. "That was beyond close. I thought we were done."

"Come on. We have to go." He squeezed my hand, pulling me back down the steps. My legs wobbled under the stress, but my training kicked in and I stayed upright.

We descended quickly to the bottom, then ran down an underground path, stopping at a heavy door. Zander dug out a set of keys, and potent magic hummed off them, telling me this door was protected with a spell. No one could get in or out unless they had the key to the spell.

He unlocked the door, but instead of opening it, he turned to me, hands gripping my shoulders, his gaze drifting back and forth between mine.

"Once again, I am forced to watch him take you away."

My brow furrowed with confusion, but he gave me no time to ask. Pulling me into him, his mouth slanted over mine, and he gave me a quick kiss, his lips soft.

"Our paths will meet again. I promise you." He cupped one side of my face, his eyes filling with adoration. Then he shook his head, inhaling, and yanked the door open, letting in the commotion outside. "Head that way." He pointed behind me. "Go!"

I jolted between the doorway and Zander.

"Hurry!" The intensity of his voice shifted my legs, and I scrambled out the door. *Act first; ask questions later.* It was instinct. Survival. I peered over my shoulder at him. He gestured, pointing the way. Deep purples and reds painted the sky, reflecting the last bits of light in his brown eyes. They were filled with a sorrow I didn't know how to decipher.

The roar of a motorcycle wrenched my attention away from Zander to the outline in front of me. My feet came to a grinding halt, my heart leaping up my throat as my gaze took in what my brain had yet to fully comprehend.

No.

No way.

"Come on!" His deep gravelly voice vibrated through my body, like his words could physically touch me.

My muscles were frozen, oxygen blocked from my lungs, tilting me off-kilter as if I were hallucinating again. I could think of no other way he would be here. The man who betrayed me. The reason I had been locked up here in the first place.

And he was even sexier than I remembered.

"Goddammit, Kovacs! Hate me later. Just get on the fucking bike," Warwick growled, his aqua eyes burning into me like fire through the dusk, the bike engine revving.

Was this another trap? He had already betrayed me once.

"Stop!" A voice shouted from behind me.

We'd been caught. There was now only one direction I could go.

"*Megallas!*" Halt!

Bullets vaulted by my head, making me duck, lurching out of their direct line. Killian had been kind, but I knew if I was caught trying to escape, it would be a betrayal to him. And as I'd seen, he had no tolerance for that.

"Kovacs! Now!" Warwick yelled. The back wheel squealed as he twisted it around, dust and smoke billowing up off the cobbled street in a hazy mushroom.

Shoving away my doubt, I sprinted forward, jumping on behind him.

"Hold on tight." He punched the accelerator, lurching us forward, forcing me to wrap my arms around his thick muscular torso to stay on. Twisting the motorcycle sharply, he aimed for the only single, winding cobble road exiting the side of the castle. Screaming guards ran after us, my heart leaping into my throat as pops of gunfire pinged off the back of the bike and ground. Night blended the bike into its embrace, making it harder to see.

Zooming around a curve that led around the front of the castle, Warwick hit the accelerator again. To the side, built into part of the old city wall, a metal gate squealed, rolling open. The sound of men and engines crashed against my nerves when we passed until we turned the opposite way down a lane.

Warwick's muscles strained underneath his shirt, his head darting behind at the sound of other motorbikes coming alive behind us. Following his gaze, I spotted six guards on motorcycles and a huge SUV barreling out of the tunnel underneath the castle. Headlights broke through the dusky light, trying to pinpoint us and lock on.

"Don't you have a gun?" I patted his sides, searching for a weapon.

"You think they'd let me close to the palace with a weapon? Killian has never trusted me."

Huh?

"How do you think I even got up here? He thought I was here to see him."

"A matter has come up."

Warwick was that matter?

I was sure there were guardhouses on every road leading up to the castle, probably several layers of them to go through to get to the king himself. I realized Warwick wouldn't have been able to sneak up there. He used the connection to Killian to get close. And now Killian would know he outright betrayed him…

A barrage of bullets came at us.

"Shit." I pressed so tightly to him every breath he took vibrated through me. His hands clamped down on my thigh, ramming it against his hip.

"This is going to get very bumpy. Do not let go for any reason," he ordered over his shoulder. He didn't give me a chance to respond before he hit the gas again, traveling down toward a walking path, my ass almost slipping off the tiny speck of seat I had. I clamped down like an octopus, every muscle locked around his frame. Bullets raced by me, the motorcycle flying down the dirt road, cutting and weaving through the winding park lane, taking us down from the hill the palace sat on.

Gunshots licked us, one almost taking out a tire. Warwick's attention drifted to the perfect position the caravan had above us on the switchback lane.

"Warwick!" I screamed, pointing ahead at a truck up the road, coming for us, headlights bouncing, taking up the entire stone archway of the guard gate. The man behind the wheel noticed us too late.

"Fuck!" Warwick yanked the bike to the side, the tires skidding, his leg stepping out to keep us upright as he stopped us from colliding with the vehicle. He looked ahead, and I followed his gaze. I could almost see his face, feel his smirk, feel the decision clicking into his head.

"No." Fear sucked the air from my lungs. "No. Fuck. No."

"Come on, princess, where's your sense of adventure?" his voice whispered from behind, like a ghost, leaving residue, sticky and warm, though what he was thinking was impossible.

Bang!

A bullet clipped by our heads, ending any other thought than our immediate situation.

Warwick tugged me closer as the bike ground toward our only exit.

"Fuckfuckfuck." I tucked into him, gripping with my muscles so tightly it hurt.

The bike hit the crumbling stone stairs heading down to the river, no longer used by tourists, nature having reclaimed the unused path. My body jolted as the bike struggled over the loose terrain, the weakened steps disintegrating, slipping as we headed down the violent bumps. My teeth crunched together, my brain like scrambled eggs. The thick vines took payment as we passed, cutting through my cotton pants and shirt like they were warm butter, then slicing into my limbs and face.

Closing my eyes, I curled into Warwick's broad, muscular back, trying to ignore the lashes of nature's whip. I concentrated on his heartbeat, his warmth, his rich woodsy smell that trickled down my throat like a swig of the best whiskey I could ever taste, easing my breath, pushing everything away as if it were a dream.

Everything disappeared except him. A sensation of calm claimed me, like I was on another plane. My brain flashed with an image of a screaming baby, coated in afterbirth, the night sky igniting in vibrant colors above the baby, then it switched to a man lying motionless in blood-drenched grass. Warwick... his eyes closed, his form black and burned, his neck at an unnatural angle, the same night sky cracking and glowing over him.

Bang!

Shots cut through my reverie, my lids bolting open, the images dissolving faster than they came, slipping through my fingers like they never happened. With my world back to the present, my head snapped around to see a few guards aiming guns at us from the bottom plaza, their guardhouse close to the dock where people could step into Killian's realm.

We hit the bottom of the stairs, my head pounding from the brutal terrain as more slugs whizzed at us, nicking our legs. They clearly weren't trying to kill us but slow our advancement.

Warwick tensed, a growl vibrating his throat, his head set with determination. He hit the accelerator, driving the bike through the throng of men, forcing them to jump out of the way.

Zigzagging slightly to miss their bullets, we were about to curve around a corner.

Pop!

The back tire hissed, tugging the bike down like we were driving through mud.

"Fuck." Warwick growled, his head twisting down to look at it. He gave the engine more gas. We couldn't stop. Panic pounded in my chest as the bike lagged while air continued to slip from the tire.

"Hold on, Kovacs," he yelled, drawing my attention forward, where locked gates loomed ahead of us.

Groaning under my breath, I strung my arms around him tighter, once again hiding my face in his shirt, his warm skin feeling like the safest place in the world. Revving the motor, he tried to enhance the speed, the motorcycle struggling at the demand, not quite barreling us toward the twenty-foot metal gate.

Please be old and not magically locked.

The front of the bike slammed into the gate, the impact reverberating through the metal and blasting into my bones with an audible crack. My head snapped back and then forward, digging into Warwick's spine, pain zinging up my nerves so forcefully I swore I could feel his body screaming with agony.

The shredding noise of twisting metal sliced into my eardrums as the lock snapped, the chopper forcing the gate to bend on its hinges. Destroying the front of the motorbike, the gate finally gave, coming apart, and with it, a tickle of magic crawled up the back of my neck.

The sight of another set of stairs made me whimper. He grasped the handlebars firmly as we bounced and crunched down the short flight, the back tire blowing out completely as we hit the bottom and exited onto the main roadway.

Horse carriages squealed, horses neighed, motorcycles and a few cars honked and swerved as Warwick skidded the dilapidated bike onto the busy street. The odor of burning tires made me gag.

This side of the river was much more up-to-date on magic-designed automobiles, though far more horses and carriages trotted in the slow lane than autos.

The sight and smell of the Danube kissed my face, my eyes tearing up. The sun slipped completely over the horizon, HDF glowing brightly from across the river, a beacon of hope in the distance. Once again, I was so close I could feel it, but I knew we were far from safe.

A piercing squawk jerked my head up to the sky, and I spotted a hawk heading for us. *Of course.* Not only were hawk-shifters some of the greatest hunters, this one came with a personal vendetta. Nyx. That bitch hated me.

"We have company," I warned, wishing we could go faster. The flapping tire was starting to shred, and the bridge to the Pest side felt farther and farther away. Warwick grumbled under his breath.

Nyx swooped down, sharp claws scraping my scalp.

"You bitch." I swiped at the air with one hand, feeling her feathers slip by me again. Her loud screech was filled with rage. While she dipped and clawed at me, Warwick turned the bike toward the Chain Bridge.

"Fuck." Warwick's tone filled me with dread. I sought what had made him react. When I did, despair filled my stomach, hollowing out my chest.

"No," I whispered. I couldn't bear being this close again and not making it.

In the middle of the bridge, which separated the sides, was a blockade right on the dividing line. Only a few guards stood around an SUV. They scrambled together, pointing their weapons at us. It was enough to stop us.

I could hear the motorcycles of the guards coming behind us, the hawk-shifter circling over us, the blockade in front, and prison coming down around me again. I had been living in a shiny prison, the glitter distracting me from the truth—I was still a captive. Now that I was out of the palace, I tasted my freedom.

"Go." My voice came out cold and determined.

"The chances of us getting past them are less than zero. We have no weapons, a bike barely moving forward, and only two of us."

"I don't care." My knees dug into his thighs. "I won't go back. Better to die free than live a life in a cage."

Squawk!

Nyx dove for us again, swooping across Warwick's face. Her first and last mistake. A hawk might be a hunter, but the legendary wolf was a predator, his attack quick and lethal.

His hand plucked her from the air like a striking snake. Bones crunched and snapped as his large palm crushed her neck, then flung the carcass on the ground.

My mouth hung open. The speed and detachment with which he could kill stirred both awe and fear deep in my bones. I hated her. She had tormented me and beat me, but seeing the corpse of the woman who lost her lover scarcely one bridge down cracked grief into my heart. A poetically sad ending for them both.

"You feel bad for her." Warwick's head snapped back to me, his brows crunching together. "Why?"

"I-I… Wait, how did you know I felt bad?"

He blinked at me, his mouth opening, but before he could answer, gunfire rang out from behind. The guards from the castle gained on us, not caring about innocent pedestrians in the way.

Warwick's lids narrowed to slivers before swiveling back around. "You ready, princess? We might be dying on this bridge as well."

"Yeah." I relaced my arms around his torso, feeling oddly calm. "You and I have already died a dozen times. What's one more?"

He turned his head enough for me to see his profile, his eyes darkening, the intensity like a capsule around me where I could forget death waited for us in the middle of the bridge. We were riding the lethal line between safety and peril.

I should have died when my mother gave birth to me. When I was shot in the back. In Halálház, many times. From the pills Killian had given me.

Death seemed to reject us both, letting us slip by. So, if this was when it finally took its claim, the price for all the leniency…

So be it.

I would die free.

Chapter 7

Burning rubber and gasoline scorched my nostrils as mushrooms of smoke swirled and clotted the air, the motorcycle protesting the advancement, ready to end its journey right here. But as if Warwick commanded its allegiance to him, the bike surged forward, giving its last effort, heading into battle with everything it had left.

Bang. Bang. Bang.

Gunfire pinged off the road and metal of the bike, the front wheel hissing as a bullet tore through it. Chaos filled the night like untuned violins, shredding the air. Guards bellowed from ahead and behind, the squealing of the tire rim sending sparks into the night sky.

I heard the sound of flesh being hit, and Warwick's spine curled forward with a grunt.

"Warwick!" Grabbing for him, I sought the source of his wound on his side and covered it with my hand, trying to limit the oozing blood. A painful piercing dove through my own side in the same spot, as if I could feel a bullet tear through my flesh, forcing a gasp from my lips. I reached down but found nothing there.

Warwick slumped forward, almost falling off the bike.

"No!" My hands clutched him harder to my chest, trying to keep him upright, his body and the bike swaying. Warm blood flooded my palm from the wound.

My panic was so deep it felt as if something came and scooped out my insides, dumping them on the pavement, leaving me cold and empty. The idea of losing him barreled into me like a train. No. Not this close to freedom.

Adrenaline twisted my senses, making every sight, smell, and sound tangible against my skin, but strangely from far away as well, as if nothing could touch me. The feel of Warwick's bulk pressed into mine; his heat wrapped around me like a shield. Once again, he felt as if he had climbed inside me, slipping through my skin like he had the right to consume me, to give me the pain he was feeling. I only plunged deeper, shoving away all logic and following an instinct I didn't even understand.

"You do not get to die. Not today," I muttered over and over. My hands didn't move, but I felt a strange sensation that I was grazing his skin, everywhere, weaving in and out, circling his wound. The agony in my body was so painful and tight I could barely breathe and thought I might pass out. I swayed, almost tipping off the bike, but Warwick's hand wrapped around me. A deep growl vibrated through him, rocking against my chest. His head lifted, his shoulder rolling back. Regripping the bike handles, his muscles tightened.

The guards ran around placing gates to barricade us, wanting to stop us from crossing the invisible line between the sides.

A roar thundered deep from Warwick as he pressed the accelerator to the max. I tucked into him with a gasp. The barrage of bullets and yells strangled my throat with fear. The crippled motorcycle plowed into a makeshift fence they'd put up. The bike squealed and moaned, hitting the barricade, the impact flinging us into the air. My bones crunched as I hit the pavement, rolling, and the asphalt tore my skin. I whimpered as pain volleyed through every nerve.

My body had hit a curb, my head spinning, my stomach filling with nausea. Blinking, I stared up at the early evening stars, twinkling and growing bolder. Beautiful and peaceful, impartial to the battle below.

Kovacs...

I felt more than heard my name glide over and through me, jolting my head.

Pushing myself up, my head spun, my throat thick with bile. Pain sizzled along every inch of me, but I was still mostly numb to the true agony permitting me from moving. When I did so, I took in the massive figure lying several meters from me.

"Warwick," I grunted. Struggling to my feet, I hobbled over to him. It was then I realized there was no longer any gunfire, no guards seizing me. My head snapped to the men only meters away, standing at the painted line on the bridge as if an actual wall blocked us, their guns lowered, their faces full of horror…

Because we did it. We somehow made it past them. We were safe. Unless they were willing to start a war.

Margaret Bridge and the Chain Bridge were the only bridges divided between fae and HDF. The other ones were treated as neutral territory and "gray" areas. Between these bridges, the two sides resided, silently challenging each other. Only the divide of the Danube kept them from shoving each other like bullies on a playground. I felt it would be only time before one took the first swipe. And I didn't want to wait and see if today was going to be that day.

"Warwick?" I wheezed, dropping beside him. His shirt glistened with blood, saturated and dark around the gunshot, though it no longer seemed to be oozing blood. His face was masked in abrasions, cutting into his beard, painting his dark hair auburn. Road burn stamped over his skin like a branding iron. His lids closed, his chest barely rising, as another shot of adrenaline shot through my veins. "Wake up!" I shook him.

Nothing. "Warwick!" I shook harder.

Behind us, a guard spoke into a walkie-talkie. "What do you want us to do, sir?" His voice came from behind me, and it was as if I could feel Killian through the contraption, a link to the man I had just betrayed. Fear thudded at the base of my neck.

One word, and they could forget the fragile treaty they had with Istvan. Not losing me might be worth it.

"Get the fuck up, Warwick!" I gritted through my teeth. In terror, I slapped his face, trying to stir him. A grumble rose from his chest, but his lids stayed pinned together.

"Wake. Up!" I demanded, my palm pulling back to smack him again. His hand darted up, his fingers wrapping around my wrist, stopping me in a blink. His sudden movement hitched my breath with an audible hiss. Aqua eyes opened, blazing up into mine.

Something about the moment whooshed a strange sense of déjà vu through me, capturing the air in my lungs like a vault, setting me back on my heels. But as fast as it came, the image slipped away, not letting me hold on to anything.

"I enjoy it rough, but don't think now is the appropriate time, princess." A smirk twitched his cut lips.

I let out a breathy exhale, closing my eyes briefly in relief, determination set on my brow.

"Come on." I bit down painfully as I rose to my feet, helping him up.

His massive body leaned into mine, swaying while he tried to get his feet under him. Both of us were torn up from the crash, blood dripping onto the cement from our wounds as we took steps away.

Oddly, my right side ached the most, as though I was the one who had been shot.

Warwick should have been unconscious if not dead from the bullet. We both should have been. "Guess death didn't want us today either."

Gripping me, he turned to glance at the busted bike, our escape vehicle lying on the ground, shredded and twisted, leaking its fluids.

"It took one of us as payment," he muttered, then swung us back around. "Let's get out of here."

Both of us hobbled off the bridge as a crowd lined up at the Pest end, watching the drama unfold in front of them, their mouths open in either awe or fear.

The fae sentinels stayed silent behind us, letting us amble away. I felt uneasy that Killian would let the two of us go so easily. He seemed to think humans were below him. Why did he bother with the treaty?

A cool breeze whipped at my knotted, grimy hair. The throng parted, letting us pass. Briefly, I peered back, seeing the palace lights glow from the other side. The place, which held me for weeks, appeared picturesque and powerful on the hill, a silent beauty. Yet I could feel in my bones a change in the delicate line of truce HDF and the fae had been walking for years.

I had upset the balance and tipped the first pin over.

"You are a conundrum, Ms. Kovacs. A wave crashing into everything. Twisting, breaking, and flipping all upside down the moment you enter."

"A single drop of water can be the one that breaks the dam."

Warwick and I trudged our way north, my muscles feeling heavier every moment, as if I were taking on Warwick's hurt and pain as well as my own. Turning the corner, the wall of Leopold stood a couple hundred yards away, the main gate coming into view. My eyes clogged with tears of relief and happiness. I made it home.

Warwick stopped, my attention jerking to him.

"What? We're almost there."

"You are." He peered down at me. "I did my part."

"What?" I could hear commotion stirring at the gate, voices and movement from people alerted to our presence, but it all was background noise when I looked up into Warwick's battered face.

"You are home and safe." He nodded, stepping away.

"But... you're hurt. Let our doctors look at you."

"I'm not welcome here anymore than I was welcome on the fae side." His voice slid over me while his boots took him a few more steps away. "Don't mention me. You've never seen or heard of me."

"What?" I sputtered, feeling a stab of his rejection. "How can I not? You saved me."

"You are pretty capable of saving yourself... if you had *wanted* to." His eyebrow rose as he receded deeper into the shadows.

With the immediate fear and danger gone, the memory of what he did, the deep betrayal... I stepped back, anger bristling my neck. "Don't accuse me of something when all I was trying to do was survive."

"Survive?" He snorted. "You looked to be doing far more than that. And *you* were judging the workers at Kitty's."

"Fuck you," I seethed, feeling the anger I put aside as we escaped bubble up. "You betrayed me! You were the reason I was even there."

His head tipped back, peering down at me, his nose flaring.

"Why did you give me to him to only help me escape?"

His jaw rolled.

"Why?" I shoved at his chest.

"None of your business." He grunted, waving behind me. "I got you back home, princess."

"That's not the point!" Hurt laced around my vocals, fury flushing hotter through my veins. "Tell me why you would do that. You made me think I could trust you."

"Your first mistake," he growled, getting into my face. "Trust only yourself."

"You are a vil—"

"Who's there?" A spotlight came down, cutting off my words, trying to lock on the source. "We will shoot if you don't identify yourself."

"Better tell them who you are." Warwick's feral eyes blazed from the dark. "Be really tragic to get all the way home and be shot by your own people."

"Identify yourself," a man bellowed.

"Tell them," Warwick huffed.

I heard boots hitting the cobbled street, guns cocked, ready to fire.

"But I..." I didn't know exactly what I was going to say, but a sudden panic fluttered in my belly.

"Have the life you wanted, princess. He's waiting for you." He stepped back into the shadows.

My mouth parted. As angry as I was, I felt like he was ripping out a part of my soul, which made no sense. He betrayed me. He was the reason

I'd become Killian's prisoner in the first place, but the thought of never seeing him again thumped my heart. The moment he stepped back into my life woke me up, stirring me to action.

"Why?" Noise around me cut out to a dull hum. "Why did you come back for me?"

His emotionless eyes met mine, his jaw rolling.

Our gazes locked, and the sensation of him curling around me tightened my throat. I wanted to ask him so much more, to understand, but nothing came out, words meaningless as the intensity of his stare filled me with emotions I could not explain or define.

"You are home. Safe. Go to him." Warwick's voice nipped at the back of my neck, whipping my head to see who was behind me, though I knew no one was.

"Wait." My legs stepped toward him as if they had already decided which way they were going to go.

The spotlight locked on me, freezing me in place.

"Brexley?" Disbelief and shock rang behind me from the gate.

"I was never here," Warwick muttered right when my name rang through the night again. The familiarity of my name in a voice I knew so well broke my focus from Warwick.

"Brexley!" The boy I had loved almost all my life dropped his gun, running for me, his beautiful face ignited with utter joy and disbelief.

"Caden!" A surge of love at seeing my best friend again punched through my chest, my feet limping to him. His body collided with mine, a sob tearing from his throat as his arms went around me, pulling me into his chest, engulfing me.

"Oh, gods, Brex." His voice cracked with heavy emotion, his grip on me so tight, his hands rubbing and touching me everywhere as if he wanted to make sure I was real. I didn't care that my bones and wounds throbbed in protest. I could take this pain forever if it meant I had made it back to him.

"I thought you were dead..." He cried into my ear, tucking me in even tighter. "I can't believe you are here. You're real. I dreamed so many times you came back to me."

My throat was too heavy with emotion; all I could do was sob, letting the months of agony, the torture and defensive walls, drop away. My shoulders sagged, my face burying into Caden's chest.

"You're truly here... I can't believe it." He kissed my temple, his body and scent so comfortable and familiar. "I was sure I had lost you forever." Caden hiccupped, his hands kneading and caressing me.

My head lifted. "I'm here."

"I don't understand… H-how are you here? How is this possible? Where have you been?"

My neck twisted over my shoulder to where Warwick had been.

Gone.

But I still felt him, like a predator in the bushes, making my gaze dart around in search of him.

"It doesn't matter. You're home and safe. With me." Caden circled his arm around my shoulders, pulling me toward the gate, kissing my cheek, not caring about how dirty and beat up I was.

I swore I could feel those predatory eyes burn into my back, demanding I turn to look once more.

Forget about him, Brex. He betrayed you. You are home. You are back where you are supposed to be.

The moment I stepped through the gate, the iron bars clanking shut, I pushed against the feel of him, slamming the door on him as well as the last few months of hell.

I wanted to put him behind me.

"Brexley!" Rebeka's elegant figure ran for me, her exquisite dress swishing the floor, heels clicking the marble floors. Her glossy hair and perfect complexion were a juxtaposition against my scarred, bony, dirty carcass.

The opulence of the room also contrasted with the state of me. Not a thing had changed from the last time I stepped through the doors of HDF, but I stared at everything like a stranger. Every day of my life, I had walked through the main hall, growing numb to the decadence and riches. One encrusted jewel in her dress or the gold used to paint the ceiling could feed a family in the Savage Lands for months.

"Oh, my dear girl. Where have you been?" Rebeka's painted lips parted, her head shaking in disbelief as she peered at me. Caden kept me tucked into his side, not ready to let go, even as his mother's arms wrapped around me gently as if I would break and turn into dust on the rug. "I cannot believe you are alive. We were all so heartbroken." She quickly pulled back, a slight frown at my filthy clothes and face. "My gods, what you must have been through."

My mouth seemed to be sewn together. The surreality of being back, of my wish coming true, had not settled the way I imagined. I felt I was acting out a play. "It was…" I swallowed, memories of being beaten, tortured. Killing to survive. "Hell—"

"Well…" Rebeka's hand went to my cheek, cutting me off, her expression back to perfect detachment. "That is no matter anymore. You are home and safe and can put all of it behind you."

A stab of resentment burned between my ribs. It was the aristocratic way. Shove all the icky, uncomfortable things under the table, and pretend our lives were suited for our station. Stay pleasing, perfect, and uncomplicated.

She wouldn't want to hear I had been whipped until my bones broke through my skin, my guts spilling onto the ground. That I had been assaulted by guards and inmates, slept next to my own feces, or that I had been held in the fae lord's palace for the last month. Pretenses and lies held up our walls. She would not tolerate me speaking a word of it out loud. As if it never happened.

"You look awful. Too skinny now. Oh my, look at your skin, hands, and your hair." She sucked in, then shook her head, swishing her hand. "Nothing a mask and deep conditioner won't solve." She touched my knotted, dry strands, tears glistening her eyes. "We must get you into a bath right away." She clicked her fingers at a servant. "Retrieve Maja. Have her get a bath ready."

"Mother…" Caden's hand rubbed my arm. "Give Brexley a moment. She just got back."

We all turned at the sound of noise in the hallway and found Istvan striding into the room. Dressed in his uniform, the medals dancing on his chest, his gaze found mine, his eyes widening as if he'd seen a ghost, his feet coming to a slow stop.

"Brexley?" The man who had raised me for the last six years, never showing an ounce of emotion, gaped at me as though overcome. "I heard, but I did not believe it." He strolled cautiously up to me. "You are back…"

It felt like an odd thing to say, but Istvan wasn't good at showing emotions.

"You are all right?" His scrutiny jumped around my figure, his firm, familiar tone back in place.

"Yes."

He cleared his throat with a nod. He stepped up to me, his brow furrowing as if he didn't know how to respond to my return. Finally, he leaned over, curtly kissing my cheek. "It is so good to have you home and safe. We all feared the worst. This is extraordinary…" He rolled his shoulders, regaining his posture. "Glad to know you're all right."

"Thank you," I muttered, so quietly I barely heard myself.

"It's been months. Caden said he saw you get shot. Where have you been this whole time?"

For some reason, my mouth wouldn't move.

"Father..." Caden warned. "She just got home."

"Enemies won't wait for her to take a bath. I need to know if we are under threat. What she knows. Where's she been. I need a full debriefing right now."

"No." Caden pushed out his chest, his arm coming around me tighter.

"No?" Istvan's eyebrow went up.

"She's been through so much. Let her settle in. I'm sure she'd love to have a bath. Something to eat. Relax."

I was in a bath less than an hour ago... in Lord Killian's guest room. Now I was home.

My head was having trouble wrapping around the sharp turn of events.

"Istvan." Rebeka touched his arm, taking his glare off his son. "She's not one of your subordinates. She's family."

"She's one of *my* soldiers," he snapped at his wife. Rebeka pulled her arm away, her mouth pinching. He took a deep breath, looking back at me. "Brexley understands the importance of questioning. She is a soldier first. Duty and honor. The smallest thing could be vital to our fight, isn't that right?"

I dipped my head.

"Please, Istvan. She's like our daughter."

A daughter they had sold for marriage to align two countries and gain more power.

He pinched his nose, inhaling. "You get an hour. I will send the doctor to your room, and after you refresh, please come to my office."

"Yes, sir." I nodded. The words came off my tongue robotically.

"Good girl." A rare smile hinted on Istvan's mouth, his palm squeezing my shoulder. "I knew you would. You always understood the importance of warfare. The tiniest thing could tip it in our favor."

My mouth pinned in forced agreement.

"I will send Dr. Karl to check you out now." He patted my arm again coldly. "So happy you are home." He dipped his head, turning and striding across the room toward his office.

Caden huffed, shaking his head in aggravation, but the moment his eyes came back to me, they lit up with affection and happiness, pulling me into his chest. "Come on. Let's get you cleaned and fed."

Chapter 8

Caden didn't want to leave my side, but Maja shooed him out when Dr. Karl came, saying how improper it was, which was hilarious to me. After everything I had been through, being seen naked seemed so insignificant. In Halálház, I'd showered as people fucked next to me. Shit in a room full of people. I had been stripped, beaten, and stabbed around crowds of people. I saw prostitutes walk around naked, felt them pounding against the bedroom wall I shared with the most feared legend in this country.

I had murdered.

The old doctor checked me from head to toe, taking my blood, getting my vitals, and even though I said I had no sexual encounters, he still demanded a pelvic examination.

Finally, after he left, Maja shoved me into the tub. She massaged shampoo through my hair, talking nonstop about my miraculous return, how her god heard her prayers and brought me back.

Only I knew I was sitting in this tub not because of any god—though I bet he considered himself one—but because of a folk tale. A confounding one. Why had Warwick come back for me? He destroyed any alliance he might have had with Killian. Why had he betrayed me and given me to Killian only to risk everything to get me out?

"Let the conditioner sit for a bit; your hair feels like straw," Maja twittered.

"I need to go see Istvan now."

"Oh, *lófütty!*" *Horse's whistle!* She swished her hand. "He can wait." She fluttered around like a mama bird, fizzing with elation. "I will go get you some tea. Nothing better than a cup of tea to make everything better."

Tea. Sure.

"I have missed you so much, *baratnom*." *My girl.* She clasped her hands over her heart. "You coming back to us is a miracle. It will bring life back here again. To Caden." She brushed a tear from her eyes. "He was not right with you gone. Empty and lost. As if all life had left him." She sniffed, whisking away her sorrow, pinning a smile back on her face. "Oh, right, your tea. I will be back." She bustled out, closing the door behind her.

Her departure left me with a strange fear. As if I was left in an unknown place, not the bathroom I used for the last six years.

The events of the day finally hit me, and I glanced down at my trembling limbs, noticing the deep abrasions, which covered my flesh earlier, were already looking better.

"What the fuck?" I looked over the leg I had fallen heaviest on. It was still covered in bruises and cuts, but all the wounds were closed. Healing. Scars and marks decorated my body, but nothing looked new or fresh like it happened only an hour ago.

Between Nyx and the crash, I should have been in the hospital, unable to move for weeks.

My pulse tapped rapidly in my neck like Morse code, my breath struggling through my nose, my head spinning. I was practical—facts and science. Not that I didn't believe in magic; the air was filled with it. But there still had to be a logical reason. Fae could heal quickly. Humans couldn't.

My hand flattened over my racing heart. I slowly sucked in air, squeezing my lids shut in an attempt to calm myself. The need to feel safe, not drifting away in space, had me tugging my knees into my chest. *Breathe*, I ordered myself. *There is a perfectly good reason for this.*

A derisive scoff pitched my lids back open, where a massive figure leaned against the door.

"Oh, gods." My spine splashed back into the tub, water gushing onto the floor, my lips gasping out a cry.

Once again, the abundance of ruthless power and raw sexuality smacked into me, ripping the air from my lungs.

"We really need to stop meeting like this, Kovacs." Warwick smirked, folding his bulging arms over his naked chest. His body was also covered with injuries, the bullet wound in his side red and angry, but it also looked as if it had been healing for weeks. "Starting to think you enjoy me watching you take a bath."

"How-how are you here…?" My tongue stumbled over itself, faltering as I peered around. I was in my bathroom.

"Me?" One eyebrow drew up, his mouth twisting into a deeper sneer. "This time it's all you, princess."

Did I fall asleep? Was I dreaming him like I had earlier? The pinch of my skin against the porcelain suggested I was awake. You didn't feel pain in dreams. "How did you get in here?" I searched the room, knowing there were no windows. The only way in was the door he leaned against. "Get past the guards?"

He snorted, rubbing his beard. The intensity of his gaze felt like he could see through the bubbles. The sensation of fingers trailing up my inner thigh bolted me out of the water. I grabbed for a towel, my guard up and locked on him.

"Now you get modest? Seems pointless since I've seen everything multiple times." His mouth twitched, staring at the towel I tried to cover myself with. "And we've been through this many times. You're not my type, princess."

"You keep saying that, but here you are, finding me once again naked in the bath."

"For a second time, this is all you."

"Me? How is your being here my fault?"

"You brought me here."

"Huh?"

"I was about to enjoy four curvy women who are about to fuck me into oblivion." He tilted his head. "The last place I want to be is here. Unless you want to watch…"

Suddenly I was no longer in my bathroom, but standing in an all too familiar room. The bedroom we shared at Kitty's. Four naked women squirmed on the bed, curling their fingers to him, touching his chest, kissing his torso. One of them I recognized. The siren, Nerissa, who had called to him the first night we arrived. The women did not look over at me or seem to see me at all, their focus on the beast in front of them, their hands tearing at his dirty and ripped trousers hungrily.

"What the hell?" Terror and shock gripped me. My gaze flipped around wildly. How was I there? How was this possible? I had to be dreaming. Must have fallen asleep in the tub.

"Not a dream, Kovacs. Believe me…" He hissed as Nerissa yanked down his pants, taking him in her hand, cooing and moaning for him.

"Baby, you know I can make your wildest dreams come true," she said to him, licking her lips. With a humming sound, she leaned over, running her tongue along his erection, then took him in her mouth as the others moved around him, touching and kissing him.

Shock, embarrassment, and disgust screamed in my head to turn away, to wake up. But I didn't. I couldn't. Against my will, my nipples hardened, and an ache throbbed between my legs as he bucked against her mouth, his moan spearing me with pure lust. I inhaled violently, his groan wrapping around me, sliding down my hips, licking my pussy.

"You like that, Kovacs? Watching?" He breathed out heavily, his hips bucking, head tipping slightly back, keeping his eyes on me. "Wish it was you?"

Yes. I felt the answer in my body. I swallowed, turning my head to the side, my veins burning with heat.

I was losing my mind. This was not real. *Wake up, Brex.* I shook my head, trying to rouse myself.

I heard him chuckle. "Keep trying, princess."

"I am." Nerissa looked up, replying to what he said to me. "But you're fucking enormous. Gods, Warwick, you are making my pussy so wet, and you know how much that turns me on." Nerissa lowered her mouth back down on him, clearly struggling to take all of him in. Another woman lowered herself to her knees, licking and sucking the area Nerissa couldn't reach. The other two fae circled around him, enjoying the rest of his body.

I rolled my eyes with annoyance, staring at the far wall.

"Anything in what she said not true?" he rumbled, his voice once again was like stroking hands, slipping up underneath the towel. It was true, but it sounded so cheesy, and his ego didn't need any more fluffing.

"I've seen better."

He snorted again.

"Are we not pleasing you? What do you want us to do?" A prostitute I didn't recognize dropped to her knees behind him, grabbing his ass. She flicked her long, forked tongue between his ass cheeks, causing him to grunt, his hips rocking harder, and I almost choked on my saliva. She was a snake-shifter, and I didn't want to think about where she was putting her tongue right now.

"*Baszd meg.*" *Fuck you,* I hissed, turning away, but his energy shoved me, skimming and skating over every inch of my skin. My spine arched, my breath quickening, my skin aching and alive.

"You can leave at any time," he growled at me.

"Never... we begged to be here," one of the girls responded, groaning with need. "Let us pleasure you." I could hear sounds of their eagerness, wanting to satisfy the great Warwick Farkas.

I felt sick. Anger, desire, and another sensation I didn't want to acknowledge coated my tongue.

The feel of him behind me, pressing into me, hitched my breath in fear. I knew he hadn't moved, still standing across the room from me.

"How?" I choked, oxygen barely touching my lungs, making me gasp for more.

"How do you feel me?" His harsh voice was in my ear, freezing me in place. *"I don't fucking know, but tell me how, right now, I have a siren humming and singing around my cock like it's her only mission in life to make me pass out... and all I feel is you, Kovacs, since the moment I met you?"*

Blistering heat pulsed through my core painfully, desire tingling my skin, drying my throat.

He snarled against my neck. *"I thought it was gone. For a month, I had peace. Now you are everywhere. In fucking everything."* Fury trailed down the curve of my neck, inaudibly parting my lips. *"I want nothing except for you to get out of my head."*

"Same, Farkas." I gritted through my teeth as yearning crawled over every inch of me.

"And yet here you are," he taunted.

"Why did you come for me?" The question came out involuntary.

A needy moan came from one of the girls, and I couldn't stop from looking over my shoulder.

His eyes glowed, burning into me as he quickened his pace, grabbing Nerissa's head, pushing her to take him even deeper, her song filling the room, bringing everyone to ecstasy. The other fae with Nerissa sucked and played with his balls, the snake-shifter still behind him, licking him, as the fourth laid on the bed spread open, pleasuring herself for his viewing enjoyment.

I felt his fingers trace through my folds, as his gaze locked on mine.

"Because..." he growled, slipping in a finger deep inside me. I slammed my eyes closed as I moaned.

Loudly.

"Brexley?" The familiar voice jarred my eyes open, blinking in bewilderment, absorbing my location. Marble tile, white walls, and a crystal chandelier hung over my head. Pristine and perfect.

Caden peered around the bathroom door, still wearing his uniform from guard duty, his forehead furrowed, his eyes darting around suspiciously. "Are you okay? I heard you cry out."

I gulped over my dry throat, nodding, expecting to see a semen-covered bed with a man and four naked women in the corner.

It wasn't real. You were dreaming the whole thing.

Sleeping while standing up... Sure.

I bunched the towel tighter around me, my toes curling into the soaking bathmat, water pooling on the floor.

"Brex?"

"Yes." I jerked up to look at him. "Fine."

No, I was not.

His eyes moved over me, a fire sparking in them, his steps bringing him an inch from me.

"Gods, I've missed you," he whispered hoarsely. "Part of me died when I thought I lost you. I haven't been right, Brex. I don't work without you. I lost it."

"I heard."

"You heard?" His head tipped to the side.

Right, they didn't know about Aron. That we had been in the same place. That I had killed him.

Swallowing the lump in my throat, I glanced away. Caden's hand slid over my cheek, curling into my wet hair.

"Brex." He whispered my name, his eyes darting between mine. "You don't even know... that night on the roof has haunted me every night. Tortured me. I was such a fool. I regret my choice. But I have a second chance now." His eyes dropped down to my bottom lip, which made my stomach twist. He tugged my body flat against his, his mouth inching toward mine. I was getting what I always wanted. What I always dreamed of. "I want you." His lips grazed mine before he fully claimed my mouth.

Over a horse-shifter or fae lord... and certainly over a betraying asshole, Caden's kiss should've dissolved them all away, the boy I had loved almost all my life. He finally felt the same way as I had. He wanted me too.

"Stop thinking about me, Kovacs," Warwick's deep voice rumbled in my ear, jerking me back. I searched the empty space behind me, my eyes scanning everywhere.

"Brex?" Caden dropped his grip to my arms.

Fuck, Farkas. He had to ruin everything.

"Brexley?" Caden's tone went up, bringing me back to him. Confusion strained his handsome features. "What's wrong?"

"Nothing." I wagged my head. "I'm sorry."

"Don't be sorry." He wrapped his arms around me. "I know you've been through something very traumatic. I want you to feel safe and loved again." He tucked his chin over my head. "I love you, Brexley. Losing you made me see how stupid I was for pushing you away. I want to be with you."

I blinked, staring at our images in the mirror.

He had finally said the words I dreamed about hearing since I was fourteen. The words I longed for…

The girl who had sat on the roof that night, the one who would have given anything to be with him. Begged for just a kiss.

She was no longer the woman reflected back at me.

Chapter 9

"Can I say I'm against this? She should be resting." Caden huffed in the seat next to me, motioning at me. "Or being force-fed! Look at her, Father. She looks like she's been starved and beaten."

Ninety minutes after stepping through the door, I was examined, pricked, prodded, bathed, conditioned, dipped in lotion, and immersed in any beauty treatment Maja could fit in. Now I found myself sitting in Istvan's office, my body limp and exhausted from the day's events.

"Caden." Istvan strolled behind his desk, annoyance coating his tone. "Didn't *I say* if you were to join us, you were to stay silent? You are technically still on duty. I am being generous to allow you a break from your responsibilities."

Caden huffed again, sitting back in his chair, his hand curling over mine. He couldn't stop touching or looking at me, as if he blinked, I would disappear again.

"Brexley." Istvan sat down in his chair. "I can't begin to say how good it is to have you home safe." He said the words, but everything about him was aloof and distant, back to the man I knew. "We were quite beside ourselves thinking we had lost you."

The door opened behind me, and one of Istvan's assistants rolled in a tea cart: sandwiches cut into tiny triangles, scones with imported jellies and creams, teas from China and England. He rolled the cart near me, bowing, and headed out. A throwaway snack, which cost at least a month's pay, if not more, for someone like Rosie.

"Please." Istvan nodded toward the cart. "I know you must be hungry."

I should have been. I hadn't eaten for a while, but for some reason, my stomach rolled at the sight. Yet I knew if I didn't eat, the food would be tossed away, fed to the pigs and horses. Swallowing the tightness in my throat, I grabbed a sandwich, taking a tiny bite, the soft fluffy bread sticking to the roof of my mouth and back of my throat.

"Bet that tastes like a steak dinner to you." Caden's touch directed my attention to him, his gaze holding pity. Maybe in Halálház it would have, but Killian had been feeding me exceptionally well the last few weeks.

I set the sandwich down, peering back at Istvan.

He watched me, his icy blue eyes trying to peel through my layers, seek every morsel he could against his enemy.

"What happened, Brexley? How did you survive? Where have you been?"

Shifting in my seat, a weight came down on my chest. I couldn't even describe why a barricade popped up in my mind. I gritted my teeth together, selecting the information I would tell him.

You tell him everything. What is wrong with you? The logical part of my brain tried to unknot my tongue. *You are back home with your people. You give them everything you can against the fae.*

"Start from the night on the bridge." Istvan leaned back in his chair, his fingers steepled, waiting for me to tell him the story. "Where were you taken?"

The bread lumped in my gut, feeling like the yeast was expanding around my lungs, forcing out the oxygen.

"Father..." Caden sat up, noticing my response, his hand covering mine.

"She needs to tell us, Caden. She is a soldier first. I would ask the same from you." He leaned forward. "Brexley...?"

I nodded, sucking in. "I was taken to Halálház."

Halálház was more than a place; it was a presence that lingered inside me. It marked me. Changed me. It was my past, present, and future. A nightmare and my reality. Long ago, but so vivid I could taste the sour stench of blood, sweat, and feces.

Both men jolted, frozen with the same violent movement, as if I had laid a bomb on the desk.

"What?" Caden's mouth parted in horror and shock.

"Halálház?" Istvan hissed, pushing up to standing, his eyes locked onto me.

"No one survives that place." Caden still gaped at me, his head shaking. "I don't understand? How did you get out?"

"Where. Is. It?" Istvan leaned over the desk, his voice strained.

The strange urge to clamp my mouth together caused my jaw to ache. Halálház had stolen my humanity, tortured me, made me play a game to the death, forced me to murder a comrade, and I still fought the urge to keep it from them.

What is wrong with you? You are home, back with your family and humans. You should be giving them every morsel you can.

Halálház was gone anyway, being rebuilt in a new location; my information would not help Istvan anymore.

"The Citadel." I clutched my hands together. "It was built into the mountain."

"The Citadel?" Caden bolted up, knocking over his chair. "You mean right across the river from us?" He motioned dramatically in the direction. "It's been right there the whole time."

Istvan watched me, his gaze tearing into me, as though trying to see the full truth of my claim underneath. "There was an explosion up there about a month ago." He was calm, but an almost accusatory tone laced the statement.

"Yes." I nodded. "That was when I escaped."

"A month ago? Where have you been since?"

Caden put his hand on my arm.

"Don't mention me. You've never seen or heard of me." As if Warwick was sitting next to me, I could hear his demand, my throat closing on itself as if he cursed me.

"I-I had to go into hiding." I lifted my chin, staring bolding back at Istvan. "They, of course, were looking for me because of who I was. It took me this long to get back."

Istvan's scrutiny did not relent, his face a mask of stone. Only a slight twitch of his eye suggested he didn't fully buy my story. Lying to someone like Istvan was putting enough truth in the details to make it sound real, but not so much you'd trip yourself up. HDF taught us this in training, in case we were caught by our enemies.

"I'm curious about who bombed it and why." He tapped on the wood. "Who would have the knowledge of its location and also the ability to blow it up?" Every word of his sounded more like an accusation than a question. "Who has the power and money to attack the fae lord?"

I stayed silent, keeping my face blank. Though I didn't know the answer, I knew someone who might.

"Father, you've heard rumblings of a rebel gang in the Savage Lands." Istvan's head shot to his son, his glower telling him to shut up.

"The Sarkis Army? They are nothing more than a bunch of half-breed hooligans. They could not do this." He wagged his head. "This took planning, money, intelligence, and precision. They are just a few dumb ruffians in the Savage Lands. The only rebels who have the power to do something like this would be the Povstat Militia from Prague."

The revolutionary group, Povstat, based in Prague, had grown big enough to become notorious and feared in the Czech Republic, their fame spreading to surrounding countries. Their leader, called Kapitan, spurred them to be more "radical" in their approach. Using violence in the fight against both the human and fae leaders.

"The Povstat?" Caden rubbed his jaw. "But why would they care about Budapest?"

"Who knows why these lowlifes do anything. More power." Istvan snarled, flipping his gaze back on me. "Please, Brexley, tell me everything about Halálház."

Caden grunted low, pacing, ignoring his father. "I can't believe it's been this close the whole time. Directly in front of us. That fucking vile fae lord was rubbing our noses in it. Probably prancing around, gloating about how stupid humans were. I want to kill him, stab him in the heart, and watch him bleed out… while I laugh."

"He hasn't even given you a thought," I snapped, my mouth replying before my brain could warn me to shut up. A suspicious icy silence ballooned in the air. "Or at least I'd figure." My teeth sawed together. "You know fae put themselves far above humans."

Caden scoffed in agreement with me, the stiffness leaking out of the room.

"Halálház is destroyed now. Any human prisoner who was left behind either perished or would have returned home. There is no point in attacking it now." Or ever. Killian wasn't rebuilding it there.

"Did you…" Caden shifted on his feet, his head bowing. "Did you see Aron there? He was captured. I figured that was where they took him."

"Brexley! No! Pleas—" *The splatter of his warm blood across my face, the sickening sound of the spike tearing into his throat.*

I looked to the side, my lungs grappling for air, hearing and seeing his murder with perfect clarity.

"Brex?"

"I did." I nodded, swallowing back a knot of emotion. Enough truth to sell the story. "He didn't make it."

Because of me.

"Fuck!" Caden swiveled around, slamming his fist into a bookshelf. "It should have been me... not him."

"Aron was a less-than-par fighter and soldier. He was reckless, arrogant, and compulsive. His death was inevitable," Istvan replied coldly.

I stared at him. Aron could be a jerk, but to brush his life off so easily, as if it meant nothing?

"You look at us like we are the monsters when it's been you humans the whole time."

"Is that what you think of the people you've tested your pills on?" Once again, I spoke before thinking. "Of the fae you killed to make them?"

Istvan's head twitched back, his nose flaring, but just as fast, confusion wrinkled his brow. "Pills? Tested? What are you speaking of?" The honesty and puzzlement in his eyes and tone crushed my outrage.

What if Killian was tricking me? Playing me for a fool the whole time. Pointing a finger at Istvan while it was him all along. Who benefited more from turning humans into mindless machines to fight against their own? Even if he had to "harvest" a few fae to do it?

No one would suspect it.

It would be the perfect weapon.

Az istenit, Brexley. You are such a gullible fool.

"What are you talking about? What pills?" Caden's voice broke me from my thoughts. "And isn't the more fae dead, the better?"

I shook my head "Nothing. Just rumors inside Halálház."

Istvan kept his gaze on me, but I could not sense his emotions at all.

"What rumors?" he asked coolly.

"Nothing." I shook my head. "Not important."

Istvan's focus did not relent. I knew this trick. He wanted to make me squirm and blurt out whatever I was hiding. But the ploy he used on me as a girl no longer worked on the woman before him now. I held my ground, staring back.

"Where were you hiding for the last month?" He finally broke, shifting his shoulders.

The question weighed on me since I didn't really know how much to tell him.

"Uh... the Savage Lands." Part truth.

"So *close*." Istvan perched down on his chair. "Curiously, only thirty minutes before you miraculously returned to us, there were reports of several explosions coming from across the river near the fae palace, and a chase with a man and woman on the bridge. There are reports they even put up a blockade to try to stop this pair. Happened right before you arrived."

"I don't know. I came from the side where Caden and the rest found me." If they knew it was me, coming from the fae side with a man, there would be too many questions, opening a flood of interrogation, all pointing back to Warwick and Killian.

Something kept me silent about both.

If they knew I had been with the fae lord. Been with the enemy... been his captive, his experiment, and his...

I wagged my head, pushing out the memories of us, the way I actually looked forward to him coming to my cell in the morning to get me, the intimacy of the few days we spent together. Was it all to twist me around? Play his fae tricks on me?

Was there anyone I could trust?

"Good timing then." Istvan tilted his head, his fingers pushing into his desktop.

"Yes, it was." I nodded, rubbing my head.

Istvan opened his mouth to speak as a knock on the door sounded.

"Sir?" Dr. Karl poked his head in. "I have the results back."

"Yes, please come in." Istvan gestured him to advance. Standing back up, he moved around his desk, meeting the doctor.

My attention went to the folder in the doctor's hands, my stomach twisting. They should be normal. Nothing different, but I couldn't fight the fear twinging in my gut, recalling the oddity Killian's people found about me. It wasn't something I could push away because fae and humans were different. I wasn't fae, but...

Would Dr. Karl's results say anything about me? Be abnormal?

Dr. Karl handed Istvan the folder, his brows furrowing.

"It's the oddest thing I've ever seen."

Fuck.

"What?" Istvan opened the file, staring down at the results.

"Ms. Kovacs has extraordinary levels of what is called Immunoglobulin M."

"What does that mean?"

"There are antibodies that protect us from what the body would consider foreign bodies, like a virus, infection, or a disease. Though when they get too high, your organs usually begin to struggle to function. Ms. Kovacs' levels..." Dr. Karl's glower hit me like an accusation. The pause dangling me in the room like a noose. "Are off the charts—so extremely elevated—her organs should have completely shut down. She should be dead." The doctor peered over his half-moon glasses, scrutinizing me. "However, every test shows they are as healthy as can be. It is beyond explanation, sir. Absolutely astonishing. Her body is using these antibodies instead of fighting them."

Every muscle locked in place as all eyes landed on me. Killian's words came back to me.

"For two weeks you have been taking the pills, crushed into your meals. While nothing happened to you, the other subjects would become more fae-like before they started to falter and die. Organs failed. Some faster, some slower, but in the end, all their minds would bend, taking orders before succumbing."

The intensity of their eyes, their confusion, and speculation strangled me like a rope. Humans disliked difference. If there was something unusual about you, something that did not meet the norm, you were treated with suspicion. Mistrusted.

The knot in my throat expanded, not letting a word slip out.

"Maybe the test is wrong." Caden spoke first, easing the tension asphyxiating the room. "Happens all the time. Contamination."

Dr. Karl's shoulders shot back, insulted. "They were not contaminated or done wrong. I tested her blood three times to make sure."

"Do it again," Istvan ordered.

Dr. Karl puffed, his face turning red.

"Then she is to come to my labs downstairs." He turned to me, glaring as if it was my fault. "Even though I know nothing was wrong with the lab tests, if it's to be insisted on, she comes to a sterile environment this time."

"She will be there first thing tomorrow," Istvan replied, his gaze going back over the file. "Other than that, she is fine?"

"Yes." Dr. Karl dipped his head. "No signs of sexual assault. Only slightly dehydrated and malnourished with obvious scarring over her back and stomach. But shockingly, she's in excellent health. Though I had to go back over my records…"

"For what?" Istvan asked.

"Her gunshot wounds. I don't remember ever seeing Brexley for a gunshot in her leg or back."

"Why would you?" Istvan looked to me, then to Caden as if we had hidden some secret from him.

"Well, because the healing around them appears to be at least three years old. Much longer than she has been away."

Istvan's blue eyes met mine again briefly, making me feel more like a specimen than a person.

"Thank you, Doctor." Istvan dismissed him.

He bowed to his general, exiting the room.

Istvan strolled back to his desk, tossing the file down. "Caden said when you were caught you were shot in the back."

"Yes, sir."

"A wound you sustained about five months ago." His lips pinched. "The way Caden described it… it should have been fatal."

Silence.

I understood his meaning. An average person would have died; an extremely lucky person would at least still be recovering.

"Who knows what those fae bastards gave her?" Caden folded his arms. "They probably loved healing humans with their voodoo magic shit so they could tear them apart again."

"Is that what happened there?"

"Yes." Again, not a total lie. *That bitchy healer injected me with something before I went to prison. Though, Halálház didn't put any resources into healing you before they came for you again.*

Istvan looked only at me, but his head eventually dipped in acceptance. "Did you have any contact with the fae lord or any of his top people?"

"No." *The lie slid off my tongue like butter. Why didn't I tell him? Divulge every detail of Killian's palace, every secret I could.* "I only dealt with the fae soldiers at Halálház. None of them seemed high enough to be anything but guards."

"No one knew your true identity?"

"No." *Like Jenga pieces, the lies stacked up.*

"Anyone help you escape?"

"No." I rubbed my forehead.

"Father…" Caden sighed. "Come on. She's exhausted."

"Is there anything else you can tell me, Brexley?" Istvan ignored his son. "Anything at all. You know how important any detail can be."

"No, sir," I replied. "Surviving Halálház was my only focus."

He tilted his head. "It's a miracle you escaped. No one ever has."

"I would have died there. Only the bombing saved my life."

Istvan sighed. "We will pick this up again tomorrow after you see Dr. Karl."

I nodded in agreement.

"Come on." Caden grabbed my arm, tugging me up. "Better go before he changes his mind."

"Brexley?" Istvan's voice stopped us at the door. I turned my head. "I am glad you are back. What you have been through… your father would be so proud of you."

Stab. Twist. "Thank you, sir," I croaked, tears skimming my eyes.

"Same time tomorrow, Brexley."

I dipped my head in response, letting Caden pull me out of the door, away from his father's prying questions and severe gaze.

"I'm sure you want nothing but to crawl into your bed and feel warm and safe again." Caden's arm went around me. "You're home now."

Home.

These walls, which used to be so comforting and familiar, brought me no sense of safety now.

If anything, I could feel them thrumming with warning, telling me life inside would never be the same.

That I no longer belonged here.

Chapter 10

"I don't think she likes that."

My mind hovered at the edge of consciousness, not ready to let go of the protection of dark and warmth.

Chirp.

"I know, I don't get it either, but she gets all frowny."

With an irritated groan, I dug my head into the fluffy pillow. Awareness seeped in. My brows crunched... My pillow in the cell wasn't this fluffy or covered in silk.

Chirp.

"No, I really don't think she'd prefer that either, but I know it gives me a jump-start in the morning."

Slowly, my lids opened to find two brown eyes surrounded by bright colors and a long knobby finger near my nose.

I blinked, wondering where I was, a surge of panic popping my eyes fully open. Then I saw my bedroom, the four-poster bed, my dresser, pictures of my father and me. Like a slap, every memory of the day and night before poured in on me at once. I sat up.

I was home, back at HDF.

Gaping at Opie and Bitzy, knowing Caden had slept next to me all night, my head jerked over my shoulder with fear. The spot next to me was vacant, but the pillow was still indented from his company.

My attention shot back to the tiny figures on my bed in shock. The two things did not go together.

I flinched at Opie's outfit, my eyes not ready for this level of abuse yet.

Wearing a bright fuchsia helmet with scrub bristles Mohawked down the center, his chest was bare while his lower half was skirted in multicolored feathers you'd find from a duster, his feet strapped with blue microfiber dusters. On his back, Bitzy had a smaller scrub brush duct-taped down her head, her large bat ears twisting and twitching, her finger flipping me off.

"I-I don't understand?" I gaped. "This... how... but how..."

"Uh-oh. This one might be broken." Opie patted my hand pityingly. "My name is Opie; this is Bitzy. We are your friends. You always give me things like shiny coins, glittery fabrics, and sparkly jewelry." He spoke slowly, as if I were mentally defective. "Do you understand me? Should I draw pictures?"

"I don't give you things."

"Ohhhh nooo, you must have memory loss... or possibly brain damage. You also give me food... like bacon."

I glowered at him. "I meant what the hell are you doing here?" I motioned around. "How are you here? It's protected so no sub-fae can get in. There are traps and poisons."

Opie twisted his head and peered at Bitzy for a beat before they both erupted in laughter, though Bitzy's was just louder chirps.

"You think traps and poisons would stop sub-fae from coming in?" Opie howled, hitting his knee.

Chirpchirpchirpchirp.

"Shhh." I looked at the door, ready for Maja to come running in.

"Oh, you're hilarious, Fishy." He chuckled, wiping his eyes. "You humans think it's the same as catching a domestic rat. Please, I munch on the cheese while I use your snap traps for leg lifts." He curved to the side, rubbing his butt. "Makes my ass look good."

"So... if sub-fae can so easily get in, why haven't they?"

Chirp. Bitzy rolled her eyes at me, basically telling me I was an idiot.

Crap. I was starting to understand her.

"First of all, we have, but humans never want to think about how little things go missing. They blame it on a maid or forgetfulness. We don't get caught because we can glamour ourselves to look the same as everyday rodents. Plus, we move far faster than the human brain can comprehend. And most of all, why would we want to be here? Humans do not appreciate what we do." He sniffed, brushing his feathers.

"I do."

Blush colored Opie's cheeks.

"But it still doesn't answer why you are here. Why aren't you back at the palace?"

Chirp. Bitzy flipped me off.

"I did not come for her." Opie shot back at Bitzy.

Chirp.

"I did not," he exclaimed. "I just like being around her. She appreciates my outfits."

Chirp.

"Take that back." Opie stomped his foot into the comforter.

Chirp.

"I would never. Master Finn is… To hear such disloyalty to him."

Chirp. She double flipped me off, making Opie gasp dramatically, his hand covering his mouth.

"Bitzy…"

She shrugged, looking bored.

"What?" My eyes danced between them.

Opie glanced around like he was afraid someone would pop out suddenly.

"She said…" He shook his head in shock. "That I choose *you* to be my master instead, that my loyalty is for you now. Crazy, right? Sedition to speak against Master Finn like that. He's my superior."

Chirp.

"Yes, he is!"

Chirp! Chirp! Chirp!

Opie's mouth fell open.

I inhaled and leaned away from her force and pitch. "Fuck, I don't know what she said, but she really meant it."

"I don't think he could reach his own ass and do that." Opie looked down at himself, curving as if he was trying to see if what she said was possible. "I mean, if he could, I don't think he'd be so cantankerous all the time."

My hand came to my face, a chuckle springing out.

My life was so confusing right now. I felt so deeply for these two creatures, who I should have despised and possibly tried to kill by the standards of my own people. Even Bitzy. Yet, they helped me make it through Halálház. My body had been broken there, and they kept my mind together, making me laugh or comforting me, getting me through some horrendous moments. They saved me from myself, became part of me, and I knew in my soul I would protect them with everything I had.

A firm knock sounded at my door, and I knew without even looking they were already gone.

"Come in."

Maja opened the door, hustling in. "*Edesem.*" *My sweet.* "It's time to get up. Lord Markos wants you in his office the moment you are done with Dr. Karl. He is in quite a mood this morning, so please, don't dally." She was already racing for my closet, pulling out an outfit for me.

I had never thought much about how controlled my life had been. Clothes, food, even... men. I hadn't often made my own decisions.

I peered back at the extra pillow. Caden and I had slept next to each other so many times, but last night felt different.

His arms wrapped around me, snuggling me tightly to his chest. He didn't try to push for more than sleeping, assuming I must have been exhausted and traumatized.

I felt the difference in the way his fingers lingered, tucking under my nightshirt, his mouth grazing my neck, the way he rolled into me, letting me feel his clear attraction for me.

I just lay there after he fell asleep, staring straight ahead, restless and empty. I had everything I wished for. I was safe back home with the boy I loved who wanted me in return. So why didn't I feel a flutter of excitement at his touch? It would have only taken a little encouragement from me, and we could have been together. Finally.

I loved him. That wasn't the question, but something felt off with me now. As if I had returned... wrong.

"*Edesem*, get up! Get up!" Maja whirled her arms at me, tossing a nice pair of slacks and blouse on the bed. It was an outfit I had worn a lot when I wasn't training. Rebeka liked when I dressed nicely when I didn't need to be in workout clothes.

I snorted. Hopping off the bed, I went straight for my cargo pants and a tank.

"But you are not training today." Maja reached for the items, but I pulled them out of her grasp. Giving her a look, I walked past her to the toilet, shutting the door.

"Dr. Karl says not to eat or drink before you see him," she yelled through the barrier.

"Okay. Thank you," I replied absently, lost in my reflection. I had been so rushed the night before, I never really looked at myself. The girl looking back even appeared different somehow. To everyone else, she was the same, but I wasn't. I could never be again. I thought returning here would make everything right again. Instead, it only emphasized what was wrong inside me.

Too much had happened. And no one here would ever understand that.

They already wanted to put me back in my box, as if that would make me forget. Forget I killed, forget the fear, the starvation, and the fact the people I cared most about and who I'd developed close relationships with were fae. Forget the nights I spent with a vicious half-breed, the feared legend who gave me comfort after I murdered my friend, making me feel as if I could breathe again.

Stripping down to my knickers, I stared at my naked figure, running my fingers over the various puckered scars. Stabbed, beaten, whipped, and shot. All in the last few months.

"The healing around them appears to be at least three years old."

Fear clotted my throat. Humans didn't heal like that. It was a fact.

Am I not human? A bold voice shot into the back of my head, forcing me to suck in, gripping the counter. Terror wrapped around me, air struggling to move in my lungs. *What am I?*

A deep scoff made my eyes leap up, my gaze seizing on the reflection behind me. Holy shit. Not again.

Warwick leaned casually against the doorjamb, arms crossed. He was fully dressed this time in jeans, shitkickers, and a black T-shirt, which snuggled his chest and arms. His hair was down and loose, framing the intensity of his features.

His aqua eyes burned into me as they moved slowly over me, igniting every nerve to life. A smirk hinted on his mouth when my nipples visibly hardened.

"Now I know you want me to see you naked, Kovacs." His eyebrow lifted, mockery lingering in his tone.

Last night I could write off the bathtub incident as exhaustion. A dream. A moment my brain decided to take a field trip. It was perfectly acceptable after all I had been through.

Standing here now, wide awake, feeling the cool tile under my feet, the counter pressing into my hips, I couldn't brush this off. No way to deny it.

"Am I going crazy?"

He snorted again, lifting off the door. "You already are, princess, but that has nothing to do with this."

"I don't understand…"

"You think I do?" He glowered at me, stepping closer. His aura filled the entire room, consuming me, busting it at the seams, wanting to take up more space. "I have no idea what the fuck is happening. Nor do I want it."

Ouch. Though I didn't either. I didn't want some bizarre link to this man.

"Me neither. I want my life back."

"No, you don't. This is no longer your world, is it?"

My breath hitched, my eyes widening.

"Can you read my thoughts?"

"No…" His lids lowered, shaking his head, moving closer.

"How is this possible? How are you here?"

Suddenly my surroundings shifted, and I found myself standing in the alley in the Savage Lands. The smells of coffee, piss, body odor, and cheap perfume punched up my nose so strongly I had to fight not to gag. I could see the sunshine beaming down through the awnings, warming my bare skin, and heard the people buzz and talk as they moved around us.

"How are we both here in your bathroom right now?" He held out his arms, making some people duck and get out of his way. A girl looked back to see who he was talking to, but her eyes never landed on me.

No one saw me. I was not here… But to Warwick and me, everything was real.

When I turned to peer at him again, we were back in my bathroom, his form stepping so close his clothes brushed my skin. I could feel the heat of him. A groan tried to climb out, but I gritted my teeth, shutting my eyes briefly at the sensation of his breath sliding down the back of my neck.

"Why?" My focus went on him through the mirror again.

"I don't know that either… I just know from the moment you walked into the mess hall that morning in Halálház, you've screwed everything up. Like a fucking succubus… pulling all my attention, demanding it, moving me around you like a planet." He wrapped his fingers around my throat, his bulk pushing into the back of mine, pinning me against the counter, the feel of him through his jeans pressing into me.

For a moment, we were back in the congested lane outside Miss Kitty's, the cool breeze licking my skin and across my nipples. People stared at him, giving him a wide berth. To them, he held nothing but air, their heads shaking at the insane man as he gripped my throat harder, his other hand gliding across my stomach.

"This needs to end," he growled into my ear, lighting every molecule in my body on fire. "I was content… I like death. Feeling nothing."

"I don't want this any more than you do," I breathed, his touch and the wind speckling my skin with bumps.

Even when it seemed we were back in the bathroom, I could feel the cool outside air. It was as if we were in both places at once.

His fingers skated lower, skimming my newly waxed area. I huffed air through my nose, my hips automatically opening to him.

"Back to the clean, good girl… on the outside," he rumbled in my ear, our eyes locking in the mirror. "You can pretend all you want, princess. Play this part until the day you die, but I know better." He yanked me firmer against him, his thumb pushing down on my throat. "You enjoy it dirty and rough."

My nose flared, my lids lowering in a glower, but everything else betrayed me, wetness seeping from me, the frosty air of the outside gliding between my legs as figures moved around us.

A deep noise vibrated from his chest, his lip rising. "I want nothing to do with you, Kovacs. I gave you back. It was supposed to end there. Stop thinking of me and get me the fuck out of your head."

"You first," I snarled. We were back in my bathroom again.

His jaw twitched, his eyes burning as if they were true flames. For someone who liked death and feeling nothing, he felt like life itself. Vigorous. Raw. Fierce. A fire that raged inside me.

His hand inched lower, my back bowing, not caring if this was right or wrong, real or not… I just wanted it. I felt so alive, so vibrant I wanted to crack out of my skin.

"Fuck. Kovacs," he said so low I barely heard him, his fingers slipping between my folds, sinking into me.

I gasped sharply, my head tipping back into his shoulder, my lids shutting as pleasure so intense it burned lashed at my bones like whips. "Oh, gods…"

"*Edesem?*" A tentative voice bolted my head up and my lids apart. I spotted Maja standing in the doorway, her eyes wandering around the room before landing on me.

Alone.

Chagrin burned my face, humiliation at not only being caught but for the person I was imagining touching me. A fae. Even worse, a half-breed.

"It's not—" My hand dropped away.

"I-I'm sorry. I heard you talking… then moaning." A deep rose color flushed her cheeks, realizing what I was doing. "I didn't know. I'm sorry." She backed out quickly, closing the door. There were a few beats, but I heard her prancing outside the door. "It's just… Dr. Karl called up to your room asking where you were."

"I'll be right there." I scoured my face, trying to not only shove back the shame of being caught, but also the fact that I could still feel Warwick's touch. The warmth of the sun still baked into my skin, the cool air and harsh smell of the alley still lingering around me. My imagination was not that good. I was logical, never one to color, write, or play pretend as a child. I grew up participating in strategic games and logic-based scavenger hunts. I didn't get to practice piano as an art, but as a skill to have in my repertoire. All things Istvan thought helped Caden and me be better game pieces for him to use.

I would never come up with something this crazy. So, if it was real…? What did it mean? How was it possible?

"Brexley?" Maja tapped again.

"Yes, yes, I'm coming." I yanked on my pants and tank and washed my face before rushing out, heading for Dr. Karl.

He would be able to tell if I'm human or not, right? The thought made me want to laugh. But after everything I had faced, the laugh became residue on my tongue.

I couldn't be totally normal.

"Brexley!" Heading to Dr. Karl's office, my name shrilled through the air in an excited shriek. "Oh. My. Gods!"

Twisting my head toward the voice, I saw my friend, Hanna, running for me. She wore her training outfit of cargo pants and white tank, her blonde wavy hair up in a ponytail. Her heart-shaped face was makeup-free and bursting with smiles. She was a badass, you had to be in our mostly male world, but visually she and I were night and day.

Her body slammed into mine, almost knocking me on my ass. Her arms wrapped around me, a sob erupting from her chest. She was about my height, trim from combat, but had far more curves than I did. Especially now I'd grown so thin.

"I can't believe you are alive," Hanna croaked, hugging me tighter. "You're here… you're actually here!"

Squeezing her back, I felt my own eyes water up. As the only two girls left in our year, we had naturally grown closer, having each other's backs. It wasn't until now I realized how much I had missed her. I had been so consumed with Caden I didn't appreciate my other friends as much.

"I missed you so much." She struggled to swallow back her sobs.

"Me too." I crushed her to me again before letting go, leaning back and looking at my friend.

"I can't believe this." She sniffed, wiping her eyes. "We all were sure you were dead. We had a funeral for both you and Aron."

My head lowered, and I blinked away the surge of heartache and guilt.

"There are rumors you were in Halálház?" Her blue eyes widened.

I nodded my head in agreement.

"Holy shit," she gasped. "No one has ever made it out of there before. Is it as bad as everyone says?"

I couldn't respond, my brain flashing with guttural screams, the sound of the whip cutting across skin, guts and blood soaking the dirt in the pit, the endless torture in the hole, the sharp smells of urine and blood.

"Hey?" Hanna touched my arm.

I forced a smile on my face. "I'm alive."

"Is it true you saw Aron? He's dead?"

My head snapped to the side, my chest filling with concrete.

"Oh." She bobbed her head, understanding me without my having to say it.

A bell clanged in the distance, letting us know a new hour was upon us.

"Shit, I have to go." She pulled me back into a quick hug. "Let's hang out and catch up. Maybe leave the party early tomorrow."

"Party?"

"Crap! Bakos is going to give me hell. I'll probably be doing pushups for days." She turned to leave. "When are you coming back to class? I so miss you… just isn't the same without you."

"I don't know. Soon?" I replied, but no excitement danced in my stomach at the idea. I used to love training; it was my life. I was always the first one there and the last to leave, working harder than anyone.

"You better. I know you, of all people, wouldn't want to miss what Bakos is teaching us now." Her eyes glinted with excitement. "We are learning the best techniques to cut off a fae's head to make sure those vile monsters are dead. Especially demons; they're the same as cockroaches."

Bile surged up my throat, ice flushing my heart.

"Probably more than ever, you want to destroy and rip apart every fae you see. I'm sure you'll have so many stories to tell. You could probably teach us better than Bakos how to kill them. Am I right?"

The thought of a blue-haired demon filtered into my mind. I saw Kek's intimidating smile as she stood guarding me against the humans threatening my life. A twisted old Druid who instantly took me in. A quiet, tiny fae who stood up for me, taking my whipping to protect me. Zander, Opie, Bitzy… Warwick and even Killian.

The fae had stood with me while my own people turned against me. How could I go back to thinking they were soulless and needed to be destroyed? Before, I hadn't even thought about it, believing what I had been told, falling in like a mindless soldier.

My throat wouldn't open enough to speak.

"See you later?" Hanna was already jogging to the stairs leading down to the training rooms.

"Yeah." I bobbed my head, nothing else coming out, watching her disappear.

I moved forward, heading to the clinic, but I felt itchy and restless, as if this vast place was too small for me.

"Ah, Ms. Kovacs. Finally." Dr. Karl motioned for me to follow him when I arrived. "General Markos wants me to run every test we can. Not that I made a mistake last time." He pushed his half-moon spectacles up his nose, indignant at the idea he might have failed. "Sit." He motioned to the examining table. "I will make sure every test is done impeccably and we miss nothing."

A handful of nurses joined us in the room, gloved and masked, twisting my stomach.

"Relax and lay back, Ms. Kovacs." Karl scowled at me as he pulled up his mask; the nurses headed for me as if I were a specimen.

I was no longer a person to them.

Chapter 11

I wrapped my arms tighter around my body. My stomach rumbled, but the thought of food made me sick. Being a pincushion at Killian's palace had been a holiday compared to the last three hours with Dr. Karl. After being poked, prodded, and examined in every way possible, I felt violated and exhausted.

I dragged my feet walking to Istvan's office, knowing he wanted me to come as soon as the tests were done. It was well after one p.m., and the offices were quiet as most probably slipped out for some lunch. Even his secretary's desk was empty.

"Hello?" I knocked on the open door, peering into his vacant office, then stepped inside. It was as familiar to me as my own bedroom. I had been in here many times, usually because Caden and I were caught doing something Istvan didn't approve of. But he also would drag us in to teach us lessons about strategy and life. Istvan was tough, but now being older, I understood that some of his teachings were actually for our good. He pushed us to be more, to know more, to see more.

My hand grazed over his bookshelf behind his desk; I had read almost every book in here. The ones he felt were the most important were stacked behind him, always within reach. He even had a tattered first edition of *The Art of War* he bought from some antique auction from the Unified Nations. The binding was so fragile he wouldn't let us touch it. The gold lettering peeled off, notes and odd dot marks fading among the pages and margins inside like some strange code.

Turning to go sit in the chair and wait for him, my gaze paused on the documents atop his desk. My eyes caught on a few words in the open folder, rubbing something in the back of my brain. Stepping closer, my attention flicked to the door, feeling like I was doing something wrong, before my eyes returned to the papers.

The papers were covered in handwritten notes, unfamiliar formulas, and sketches of people's anatomy. Some of the language was in the old Russian, in the dialect before the wall between worlds fell and everything changed. People still spoke Russian, but similar to us, the Western world had invaded so often, the older dialects had mostly disappeared. Istvan had Caden and me learn this old language when most others didn't. He wanted us to be able to speak with Ukrainian leaders and their children with ease. The more we understood them, the better we could spy on them.

Always a chess piece.

My eyebrows creased as I tried to translate the scribbled writing, taking in the date and country which no longer existed, my eyes skimming over the page, reading quickly.

Georgia, 1991

The fae live among us, walk in skins like ours, pretend they fit in. But they want to destroy us, make us their slaves, feed off us, kill us. I will not stand by. I am testing a new formula to take humans to a higher being. In Science, there will be sacrifices, but it is for the greater good.

Fellow scientists laugh and condemn us. But they are the fools. Not us. Without my studies, my experiments, humankind is doomed. Fae are stronger, crueler, soulless. They deceive and use us for food and energy. They cannot die as easily. It is up to me to save mankind from itself. To show I was right all along.

My ideas are far too advanced. I will be heading to America to work on advancing my formulation, while Dr. Novikov will stay here and continue his research into the power of fae food. As of now, no human has lived long on Earth after consuming it, but he has not given up the hope of finding the nectar of life.

I will continue in my experiments to save humans from diseases, birth defects, and weaknesses, but I also believe my formula will eventually eradicate all weaknesses in human DNA completely.

Become better than them.

Fae must be destroyed at all costs.

And I will lead the charge in creating a superior human army.

Dr. Boris Rapava

Formula? What formula?

Like the pills?

Acid coated my tongue, my eyes still running over the page, desperate to believe I had read it wrong. Misinterpreted the old language. That everything in this didn't hint at what Killian suggested about Istvan.

"What. Are. You. Doing?"

A scream jolted inside my head as I jumped back, my attention going to the figure in the door.

Fuck.

Istvan's jaw locked together, his gaze serrated through my body, as though he could cut me in half.

"Ist-Istvan." I gasped, slapping my chest as if it was trying to keep my heart from leaping out.

"I asked you a question." Fury strained his shoulders as he took a step in, his eyes still glued to me, his nose flaring.

"I-I—"

"You know you are never to go behind my desk." He came up and slapped the folder filled with documents closed. "Nor are you allowed to read anything on my desk. Open or not. You know better, *soldier*. You shouldn't even be in here without me. There are highly classified intelligence documents I must look through, which neither you nor Caden have the privilege to see because of your relationship to me."

"Yes, sir." I moved around his desk to the "guest" side. "I was actually just looking at the picture." I reached for one of the frames on his desk near the file, my brain working quickly. "After what I had been through, I miss him. So much." I touched the image, my father's handsome face looking back at me. It was several months before he died. My father had recently come back from a long trip. Istvan, Rebeka, my "uncle" Andris, his wife, Rita, my father, and a few others had a party in the residence.

My father had returned earlier that day from a mission. He came and left all the time, but for some reason, this one really stuck in my memory.

"*Apu!*" I squealed, running to my father, my gangly teenage arms wrapping around him. "*You're back!*"

"*Kicsim!*" *My father's eyes lit up, hugging me so tight.* "*I've missed you so much.*"

"*I've missed you too.*" *I squeezed him harder, my heart feeling complete now that he had returned. Uncle Andris and my father had been gone almost three months this time, traveling to far-off places, but they would never tell me why.* "*Please don't leave again.*"

Dad leaned back, cupping my face. "*You've grown so much. So much like your mother. Smart, strong, fierce, and so special.*"

I saw a sadness in my father's eyes as he searched mine.

"*What?*" *I swallowed nervously.*

"*A battle is coming.*" *He gripped my face tighter.* "*I want you to remember no matter what, if anything happens to me, Andris will protect you.*"

"*Dad...*" *I tried to wiggle away. I hated when he talked about fighting and death. We had this conversation every time he went off to battle. The unrest between humans and fae was constantly flaring up, our country never at rest.*

"*I'm serious, Kicsim.*" *Dad's brown eyes searched mine, making my stomach twist.* "*Andris can find your Uncle Mykel.*" *I had heard very little about my real uncle as my father was cut off after he fell in love with my mother. All I knew was he was a criminal and somewhere in Prague.*

"*Apu, you're scaring me.*"

"*Promise me,*" *he demanded.*

"*I promise.*"

A sad, strange smile tugged on my father's mouth as he kissed my forehead. "*I love you so much, Brex. There's nothing I won't do for you. You are my entire soul.*"

Little did I know then, the battle he spoke of would take his life and Uncle Andris's as well.

That night of this photo, Caden and I had spied on them from the patio while we sipped stolen booze. I always looked at the picture with fondness, seeing my dad's glazed eyes and happy smile, Istvan's arm around my father's shoulders. They looked happy for once. Lifelong friends having a good time. But now, something felt off about the photo, the memory of my father earlier that day shifting the way I looked at it. Something was not right in their expressions. In my father's eyes.

The way he spoke to me.

You're being silly, Brex. Seeing stuff in the shadows now.

Tension shifted along Istvan's shoulders. His hand took the picture from me, his gaze scanning the photo, a faraway glint in his eyes. "Yes. I miss him too. We could have…" Istvan cleared his throat. "We were a great team together. I have no doubt we could have ruled it all, been feared and respected… if…"

"If?"

"If he lived." Istvan set the picture down, his look sliding over the files on his desk. His lips twitched as he closed them, his finger tapping on the folder. "It's good to know about your enemies. What they are thinking. Doing. The more you know, the better you can fight." His voice was even, his regard knowing. "You understand?"

He wasn't stupid; he knew I'd read it.

"Yes, sir." My stomach was still in knots. Seeds of doubt had sprouted in my gut.

I *should* believe and trust Istvan completely. He worked to protect humans. Killian did not.

"I was hoping Dr. Karl's results would be back, but he is making sure they are thoroughly done. No mistakes." He motioned to the chair. "I would like to question you more about your time at Halálház and where you were after. A few things aren't quite clear to me."

I swallowed.

"Skip the part of how you escaped alive and *alone* from Halálház. I'm still confused about how you could have made it to the Savage Lands—so close to us—but it took you over a month to get here."

"I barely made it." I forced my tone to stay level. "They had soldiers out searching for escapees. Walking the wall. So I had to go into hiding."

"Where?"

"Uh… an abandoned house."

"You don't know?"

"Only a shell remained of it."

"You survived with no money for food or water, no weapon to keep you safe?" He sat back, his blue eyes burrowing into me. Istvan was no fool, and he pushed for details most wouldn't think about, making lies so much harder to keep track of. When we were kids, he could tangle Caden and me up in our fibs so easily.

"I did what I had to. It became about survival. Like you taught me." At an early age, I learned no man was immune to having their ego stroked. "I don't think I would have lived if it wasn't for all your lessons growing up. My training, the way to assess a situation. Strategic. Smart. That's how I made it back alive."

"I feel you are keeping something from me." A nerve twitched under his eye; the intensity of his stare dampened the back of my neck, my heart pulsing behind my ear.

"There you are." I turned at the sound of Caden's voice. "I was looking for you everywhere." A flirty smile curled his mouth.

"We are busy right now, Caden." Istvan didn't look away from me.

"Sorry. Just the messenger. Mother sent me to get her. Guess she told you earlier about getting an appointment for Brexley's fitting."

Istvan rolled his eyes. "I'm trying to run a country, defeat our enemy at every turn, but sure, she needs a new party dress."

Caden shrugged, his smile landing on me.

I didn't stand but scooted to the end of my seat, wanting to run out of there.

"Yes. Fine. Go. Actually, I have another meeting soon." He waved me off, and I bounced out of the seat in a blink, heading to Caden. "But, Brexley, we still aren't done here."

"Of course, sir." I bowed my head, then hustled through the door.

"You're welcome." Caden pulled me into him as we walked, his nose brushing against my ear.

"I don't have an appointment?"

"Oh, you do… but it got postponed for another hour." His tawny eyes glistened, his mouth brushing my ear. "How about we grab some lunch? We could take it back to your room instead of sitting with everyone." His kiss down my neck told me he hoped for much more than that. "Spend some time together. Alone."

Anxiety sank into my belly. After my morning, I felt anything but sexual. "I probably should see everyone. They know I'm back now." I wrinkled my nose as if it was the last thing I wanted to do. "Get it over with."

"Yeah." Caden sighed, leaning back, running his hands up and down my arms. "But I get you all to myself tonight."

I pushed a smile onto my mouth.

"What party is the dress for anyway? Another gala?"

Caden's Adam's apple bobbed, his eyes looking away.

"Caden?"

"It's nothing… nothing important." He shook his head, facing me again, a grin on his face. "The only thing important is that you are back. Alive. And with me. That's all we should be celebrating." He twined his fingers with mine, tugging me toward the canteen.

Right as we went down the stairs, a massive outline pulled my attention to the far wall.

95

Leaning against it, a smirk on his face, was Warwick. Rough and feral, he conflicted with every rich fabric, pristine white wall, and elegant furniture piece surrounding him.

"You don't fit here either," he whispered huskily in my ear as if he was right behind me, though he stayed across the room, his mouth never moving. Even as I stayed next to Caden, I was also standing in some dirty alley in the Savage Lands, the smell of trash and feces turning my stomach.

"You don't fucking know me." I spun away from him, anger flaring through me.

"I know you better than anyone here, princess." He growled into my ear.

I turned to tell him off.

He was gone.

The burning sweet taste of Pálinka slid down my throat, scorching my stomach, making me feel solid. As though my body and I were one again and everything made sense.

But nothing did.

The crisp wind, far up on the HDF roof, whipped through my hair and seeped into my coat, pimpling my skin. Lights glistened in the night, dancing across the Danube in soft kaleidoscope designs, but my gaze was locked on the building on the hill. One that no longer felt foreign or filled me with hatred... only confusion.

My ass was numb, but I didn't want to leave. Nor did I want to go back downstairs, where I'd run into people, their mouths full of questions, their minds stuffed with naïve savagery. I'd had enough of that at lunch today. I thought seeing everyone would be good for me, catching up with my friends, grounding me back to earth, to my life here. But their joy at seeing me lasted briefly before their curiosity of Halálház flipped them into frenzied monsters. Quickly they were bragging about how they would have killed every fae in there, cutting and gutting them. In their bloodlust, they seemed to forget what I had gone through was real and traumatizing.

They were all overconfident, ill-prepared, inexperienced, and reckless. All things that would get them killed the moment they stepped out of these gates.

For the rest of the evening, I was positioned in front of a mirror as Rebeka's tailor measured me and complimented me on my "weight loss." I stood there like a robot, despising every silky imported fabric, every sparkly jewel. One small gem on the shoes they chose could feed a family for weeks in the Savage Lands. In the past, I had robbed trains and given to Maja to help her family, but I didn't do it because I had really cared or understood. I had been entitled and arrogant, thinking I was some fucking Robin Hood type, enjoying playing the hero.

But I was nothing more than a snobby rich girl. A *princess*.

I curled my lip at myself, taking another deep swig of the strong liquor. I leaned my arms on the railing, taking in a deep breath of the musty Danube. It felt so odd to be sitting here again, something I had wished for so badly months ago, but now it didn't feel as it should. I expected joy, relief, some complicated emotions at what I'd been through in Halálház. But I hadn't expected the ache in my heart, the feeling I didn't belong, that I shouldn't have come back.

Staring at the fae palace, I tried to pinpoint the room Killian put me in. I knew what it looked like from the inside, how it smelled, what was beneath the fortified walls, what rooms were carved deep underneath the mountain.

My mind was a fountain of knowledge Istvan would kill to know, to cut into and scrape out. I would be considered a traitor for not divulging what I learned. The tunnels, labs, and places I was aware of could possibly bring Killian down.

Still, I couldn't.

Was he standing out on the balcony? Was he thinking of me? Could he feel me across the river, looking back at him right now? And why did I feel guilty for leaving him the way I did? No matter how kindly he treated me, I had still been a prisoner, yet somehow, I felt awful for betraying him.

"Thought I'd find you here." I twisted to find Caden strolling up to me, the wind blowing his rich brown hair, a sexy smile hitching the side of his face. He held a bottle. Everything about him was comfy and warm. Safe. He felt like my only touchstone. The only one who would know where to find me. "Brought back up."

"Good thing." I finished off the first one, setting it to the side.

He snorted, shaking his head and sitting down next to me.

"Should have brought backup for the backup." He nudged me playfully, handing me the new bottle.

"You'd think you would have learned that by now." I took a sip, handing it back to him.

His fingers wrapped around it, watching me for a long silent minute. Then turned his head away, his shoulders rolling forward.

"Caden?"

A strangled choke heaved from deep inside him, stabbing through me like a dagger.

"I thought I lost you—forever." His voice was strangled, his eyes filling with tears. "I never realized how much you are part of me until you were gone." He struggled back a sob. "I fell apart. I couldn't function without you. I didn't give a shit about anything... I didn't care what happened to me or what my future held."

I put a hand on his. "Hey, it's okay."

"No, you don't get it. It's too late. And all I want is you."

"What are you talking about?"

He shook his head. Another few beats passed before he spoke again. "I got Aron killed..." He turned to me.

My throat bobbed at his pain. "No, you didn't."

I did.

"He wouldn't have gotten caught if it wasn't for me." His throat bobbed heavily. "I was on a suicide mission. Everything felt dark, my life over... and he followed."

"He made his own choice."

The guilt Caden felt was nothing compared to what sat on my chest. It might have been Caden's idea that got Aron caught, but he knew the risks. It was my hand that actually killed him. I heard his blood gurgle in his throat and watched the life drain out of him.

"Brex." Caden set the bottle down, cupping my face. "Being up here... it's as if we can we go back in time. Pretend it's that night and change every wrong choice I made, which turned my life into a nightmare. I'm trapped now. My future is no longer mine, and all I want to do is go back and make love to you instead of stupidly pushing you away."

As if fate taunted us, a train whistle bellowed through the night, rolling by, heading for the bridge. The stage was set; the fantasy I had conjured in Halálház was coming true.

"For one night. It's just us." He pulled me into him, his breath skating my parted lips, his forehead pressing into mine. "I love you. I'm *in* love with you. I have been for quite a while."

I sucked in, the words swirling in my head and curling in my chest. How long I had waited for him to say it. I couldn't deny it made me want to forget everything that happened to me, rewind to the last time we were up here together and pretend this was all I wanted and needed.

"Caden, I—"

His mouth came down on mine, snatching up the rest of my sentence. His lips were soft and eager, his tongue curling around mine, deepening the kiss. He gripped me harder, pulling me in, kissing me like I had always envisioned.

Yes. This was right. Caden and me.

"Then why am I here?" A deep voice rumbled.

Oh. Fuck. No. I opened an eye. Warwick sat on the railing behind Caden.

"So many admirers, Kovacs... But you know, I find it odd every time you are kissing one of them, you think of me." Warwick leaned over, his look hungry and dangerous. *"And just think, I haven't even kissed you yet, princess."*

"Fuck off," I seethed, grabbing Caden's face.

"What?" Caden jerked back, his eyebrows furrowing.

"Not talking to you," I growled, climbing onto Caden's lap, straddling him. Glaring up at Warwick, I kissed Caden with everything I had.

Caden groaned, his hands running up my back, pressing me into him, his mouth desperate for more.

"Oh fuck, Brex." He tugged my jacket zipper, his mouth frantic, his hips rolling up into me. "I need to be inside you."

My gaze shot up to Warwick. His attention was locked on Caden, his expression detached, though a nerve along his jaw throbbed.

"Mmmm." I made a sound of agreement, drawing Warwick's eyes back to me. His turquoise eyes darkened, his shoulders tightening.

"You think I care who you fuck?" Warwick snarled. *"You watched me fuck four nymphos last night, so if you think watching you and Captain Quick Pump here will do anything but put me to sleep..."*

"Really?" I snapped back, my eyes flaring with challenge. "Let's see about that." I shoved Caden onto his back, my fingers tearing at his trouser zipper. I could feel his erection throbbing against me.

How many times I had fantasized about this? Imagined every detail of Caden sliding into me, making love for hours?

"Damn..." Caden blinked up at me like he had never seen me before, his fingers greedily tugging at my cargo pants.

"Shhh." I covered his mouth with mine, but I still glared up at Warwick while my hands pushed Caden's pants lower, cupping his cock through his briefs.

A deep growl came from Warwick, the sound vibrating deep into my bones, spiking flames through my veins.

"If you don't like it, leave," I hissed at Warwick.

"No, I like it... I really like it," Caden responded, but I wasn't really listening.

"I'm not the one putting me here. You get that, right?" Warwick pushed off the railing, fury radiating off him. *"You brought me here, princess. You are only fucking him to prove a point... and what are you proving to yourself? That you can force yourself back into a box? Live a life you hate? Good for you."* He tipped his head, his arms folded.

"Fuck you." I seethed, my hand slipping inside Caden's briefs, my fingers wrapping around him.

"Brexley." Caden's hips bucked as I started to work him, his hands pushing underneath my layers, cupping my breasts.

A deep growl came from Warwick, our eyes meeting, making me feel it was really him I was touching, *his* hands gliding over my skin, hardening my nipples. Wetness seeped between my thighs as Caden's hand moved under my sports bra, his fingers kneading my breast. But then I felt an invisible tongue flick at the nipple of my other breast.

A groan scraped my throat, my eyes never leaving Warwick's.

"You like it, don't you?" Warwick sneered as his fantom mouth sucked, my back arching like I had been electrocuted. *"Me watching you... just like you got off watching me fuck those women. Like the night in Halálház... I see you, Kovacs. Know what you want. How dirty you like it. He doesn't. I'm the only one who could handle you. Be honest, it's not him your pussy is dripping for... it's me. You don't even notice he's here."*

I jerked back as if he punched me, inhaling sharply. My attention darted down to Caden, the boy I was supposedly so in love with, and yet now that I had him, I barely even noticed him. The moment Warwick showed up, I became aggressive. Fierce. Confident. Carnal. All things I hadn't ever been with Caden before.

I was no longer the girl who sat up here with him last spring—timid and insecure, desperately waiting for him to give me a scrap of notice. Allowing him to tell me he loved me too much to be with me. What bullshit was that?

My focus went back to the railing where Warwick had sat. Empty. His disappearance caused my chest to squeeze, feeling alone.

"Brexley?" Caden's hand moved up to my face, getting me to look at him. His brown eyes were glassy with desire, his hips pushing up into me, his free hand moving up my tank again. "What's wrong, *bebi?*"

What was wrong?

I searched Caden's eyes. I loved him, I did, but no longer the way I had before. The innocent girl had died on the bridge, and I couldn't go back.

"I'm sorry. I can't." I choked, anguish flooding my eyes and drowning in my chest. Jumping up, I darted down the walkway.

"Brexley! Wait!" Caden's voice carried over the wind, filled with confusion and hurt. "Brex-ley!"

He had no idea walking away from him was one of the most painful things I ever had to do. I wasn't only running from the boy I had been in love with most of my life, but my whole belief system. I had thought myself grown up living through painful times like my father's death. But everything I once understood as truth, as real, and dedicated my life to had tipped over, spilling out on the floor.

Nothing would be the same again.

And I had no idea what that meant for me.

Chapter 12

Soft classical music floated above our heads. The gold and marble sixteen-sided room glinted with candlelight and soft firebulbs. The bright moon peeked through the windows far up in the dome, casting a romantic glow on the vast space.

Glittery ballgowns, twinkling jewels, and crystal goblets danced and twirled around me, creating a world of dreamlike perfection.

Elaborate and over the top, food and drink grotesquely overfilled every table and tray even more than usual. The finest china was set out, suggesting this wasn't a typical party, but a sit-down meal. Istvan only did those when something was of top-level importance.

"Wow! You look gorgeous." Hanna strolled up to me, her mouth open. "I mean... damn."

I scoffed, swiping a glass off a tray. "Thanks."

The deep blood-red dress Rebeka had me wear was the pinnacle of an ostentatious evening, staining my soul. Hundreds of tight hand-stitched roses decorated the huge skirt, while the top was almost pure silk lace. Only my breasts were covered, while the rest of my skin showed through, leaving almost nothing to the imagination. She had Maja straighten my hair until it laid like black glass down my waist, and she painted my lips red while I sat there like a doll. I felt like the Russian dolls my father brought me from his family's homeland—beautiful, wooden, and hollow.

Deep down, I was suffocating. Dying a slow death here.

"How are you holding up?" Hanna rubbed my arm, her head tipping in compassion. "I know this must be difficult." She motioned around with her champagne glass. "I know I'd be in my room with ice cream and Pálinka right now."

A feeling in my gut told me she wasn't just talking about me being back.

"What are you talking about?"

"The celebration." Her brows bunched together.

"What about it?" My throat went dry, and I felt a sinking sensation in my belly.

"You don't know?" Her eyes went wide, her mouth parting. "You mean he didn't tell you?"

"Tell me what?"

"That bastard! That is messed up and cruel. Especially how he was with you at lunch the other day. He couldn't keep his hands off you. Should have known he'd cower out of telling you." She peered around, looking for someone.

"Tell me what is going on, Hanna."

"Oh no, the messenger always gets whacked. He needs to have the balls to tell you himself."

"Tell. Me." I faced her, my teeth gritting together, my voice vibrating with fury. Before Halálház, I would never have raised my voice to her. My defenses rose, and they no longer were patient or nice; they had learned to be cruel. To be the monster Halálház treated you like. "Now."

She swallowed nervously, her skin paling. "Okay. Just please. Don't be mad at me…"

"Hanna…"

"This party. It's… it's an engagement party."

"Whose?"

I knew the moment she spoke, but my head spun with doubt and hope I was wrong.

She bit her lip. "Caden's."

"To who?"

"The Ukrainian princess. She lost her husband two months ago. She's still young, not even thirty. She's beautiful and can bear him children."

Vomit coated my tongue.

"You mean the Ukrainian princess I found Istvan fucking in his office when she was only twenty-two?"

"What?" Hanna exclaimed. "Oh, gross."

The knife of deceit twisted into my chest, ripping the air from my lungs.

"Pretend it's that night, change every wrong choice I made which turned my life into a nightmare. I'm trapped now. My future is no longer mine..."

Caden's words last night came back to me. He'd given me tiny hints he was leaving me, but he didn't have the guts to actually tell me.

Whirling around, my feet started moving, my chest heaving.

"Brexley!" Hanna called after me, but like Rodriguez, the bull-shifter from Halálház, all I saw was red, and I was barreling toward it at full speed.

Istvan, Rebeka, and Caden stood with the Ukrainian leader and his wife. Their stunning widowed daughter stood draped on Caden's arm, staring up at him with stars in her eyes and a perfect smile. Like a good obedient dog.

Caden's eyes flicked up, seeing me, his face turning ghostly white. My gaze tore into him with anger and accusations. His eyes twisted with guilt and apology.

Fuck you, I mouthed, whipped around, and stormed for the closest exit, making it to the hallway.

"Brexley!" Caden's voice followed me. "Brexley, please stop. Let me explain." He ran after me.

"Explain?" I whirled around, seething. "You want to explain to me how you almost fucked me on top of the roof last night?"

"Shhh." He jerked his head around in panic.

"You are engaged!" I shoved into his chest. "All the bullshit you told me last night... How could you do it to me? Haven't I been through enough?"

"Brexley, calm down." He peered around, seeing if anyone heard. I was way past caring.

"I will not calm down. You are a gutless asshole!" I pushed him away again, and anger flared in his eyes.

"Jesus, Brex, you think I want this?" he hissed back, agony and anger cracking his features. "I don't want to be engaged to her. I *want* to be with you. But I don't have a choice."

"You don't have a choice?" A derisive laughed huffed up my throat. "Wow, that's rich coming from you. Wasn't it you who yelled at me that I didn't have to marry Sergiu? Now look at you, lying down like a good boy."

"It's because of you I even have to marry her," he yelled, getting in my face.

"This is my fault?"

"No." He pinched his nose. "Not what I meant. But because your

104

marriage didn't happen with Sergiu, the deal with Romania fell through. They have him set to marry some leader's daughter in China, which is a huge blow to Father since they have some object or substance my father wants."

"Substance?"

"Some special nectar." He waved his hand. "I don't know. That's not important to me right now. You are. I don't care about her."

Nectar. The word triggered something in my memory, but I didn't have time to dwell on it.

"Strange how perfectly timed the princess of Ukraine suddenly became single." I wagged my head.

"*Az istenit!*" Caden ran his hands through his hair, grunting under his breath. "I told you—when I lost you, I didn't give a shit about anything. My life felt gray and cold no matter what I did. Father told me I would be marrying her…" Caden's rage bristled under his skin. "Married to her or some other woman, it didn't make a difference to me." He grabbed my arms, backing me into a wall. "You don't get it. Nothing mattered then. Because I lost you." His brown eyes lifted to mine, full of sorrow and regret. "I love you. *Only* you."

A tear trailed down my cheek, grief digging pins between my ribs. Everything seemed against us, our paths once again forced apart.

He wiped my tear away with his thumb, his face twisting with anguish. "I don't want to lose you again." He pinched my chin, pulling it up. "Please. I can't…"

"You're getting married. She will have your kids. I don't—"

"Don't you dare say you don't belong in my life, because you do. More than *she* ever will. I may have a family with her, but you will always be mine. The one I choose to be with. The one I truly love."

My mouth dropped. "You mean you want me to be your mistress?"

"And I will be your lover." His lips grazed mine, kissing me softly. "We can still live a full life together, no matter who we are married to."

His mouth moved over mine while my brain reeled at the proposition. Not even four months ago, I wouldn't have hesitated. If it meant being with him, I would have taken anything I could get.

"No." The word belted off my tongue.

"What?" He leaned back.

"No." I pushed him back easily, getting distance. "Fuck, no. I'm not going to be your little bit on the side, Caden. Waiting and living for the moments we can secretly meet up, while you go home, kissing your wife and kids." I shook my head. "That is not a life I want."

"Brex." He reached for me.

"No, Caden." I pulled away. "I love you, but I love myself too. I deserve better than that. I've been through too much shit not to be someone's first choice."

"You are my first choice."

"The woman in there is your first choice."

"I don't get to fucking choose!"

"Yes, you do!" I shouted back. "I want a love where nothing can keep us apart."

"Brexley…" Pain lined his face.

"*Nothing.*"

"Caden," Istvan's voice barked from behind me. "Your fiancée is wondering where you went. You do not want to be rude to your future in-laws."

Caden's gaze met mine. Torment, pain, and love flooded his expression as we stared at each other.

"Now, son."

Caden's throat bobbed, and for one second, I thought he would tell his father to fuck off. Choose me. Instead, he sighed deeply, his head dropping as he strolled past me.

My lungs wheezed through the pain stabbing my chest, my eyes watering as I looked to the side. The sound of the door shutting was the final nail in the coffin.

"Brexley." I squeezed my lids together at the sound of Istvan's voice, not wanting to hear anything he said. Wiping away my tears, I took a deep breath and turned around.

He pursed his lips, stepping toward me, his medals and awards clanking.

"I am no fool, nor am I blind. I've seen what you felt for Caden for a long time, what he may feel for you… but you understand, marriage is not about love. It can't be for *either* of you."

I folded my hands in front of me, staying silent.

"This marriage will change everything. Uniting with Ukraine will advance our stance in the world. Hungary will become a formidable capital in the Eastern Bloc. Trade, money, armies, power. Humans will rise to power again. So I can't be sorry for breaking either of your hearts. You are young and naïve and will easily bounce back. You both will soon realize love is a foolish ideal and has no place in the scheme of life. Not for us." He dipped his chin. "Now, clean yourself up, put on a smile, and rejoin the party. The Leopold press are here. It looks bad if you are not there, celebrating with your brotherlike figure on this happy occasion," he ordered and marched back inside.

I watched the door shut after him, a deep rage pinning me to the rug, my fists rolling into balls. To him, I was still the chess piece he had created and had the right to move around. My life was entirely in his hands. All for more power.

My mind flicked to something Caden had said with what I had read on Istvan's desk.

The word nectar…

"…he has not given up the hope of finding the nectar of life." The journal of this Dr. Rapava flashed back.

"They have him set to marry some leader's daughter in China, which is a huge blow to Father since they have some object or substance my father wants. Some special nectar."

"Hungary will become a formidable capital in the Eastern Bloc. Trade, money, armies, power. Humans will find their way to the top again."

"Superior human army."

My lungs squeezed together, the puzzle pieces starting to click together, but I couldn't see the full picture or how deep it went. Istvan was up to something bad, and I would not be used as a pawn, blind and naïve to what was happening around me ever again.

My gaze swung to the hallway where Istvan's office was. A soldier stood there, but he wouldn't think twice about me going down there. Caden and I had the complete run of the place in their eyes. And I'd known where Istvan hid his spare key from the time I was a kid. Adults always thought children were clueless and obtuse. We picked up and saw much more than they thought.

Not having a clue what I would find or if I wanted to discover it, the decision tugged at my gut.

I should go back to the party, smile for pictures, and act like the ward they trained into docility.

I should…

Istvan thought I was a pretty face he could sell off to another country for more power and money. Tamed and obedient. He had no clue. I was more dangerous. I might look like a doll on the outside, but I was savage on the inside.

And I would bend to no man again.

Strolling past the guard on duty, I held my shoulders back and head high, trying to disguise the terror surging through me. Confidence was necessary in the art of deception. If you acted as if you belonged, no one questioned your intentions.

And I belonged here.

At least to them.

"Good evening, Ms. Kovacs." The guard bowed his head.

"Good evening." I kept my chin up, traveling down the hallway, casually peering over my shoulder when I got to Istvan's door. The sentinel looked forward, shoulders relaxed. His job was boring and tedious, probably one of the easiest here, keeping guests from wandering places they shouldn't.

My fingers tapped over the hidden lockbox behind a painting next to Istvan's door, popping the lock open.

One thing with Istvan, he might have been an extremely good general, paranoid when it came to the outside world, always noting every detail, but he had grown lazy and arrogant *inside* his domain. He had not bothered to change the code for the hidden key in years.

As gently as I could, I twisted the key in the lock, holding my dress around the knob to muffle the sound.

Click.

My head swung again down to the guard, my heart throbbing in my ears.

He didn't move.

With care, I opened the door wide enough to slip in, closing and locking it softly behind me.

I exhaled, feeling my pulse beat wildly against my flimsy dress.

You should not be in here, Brexley. My conscience stomped its foot like an uptight preteen. *You're going to get in trouble. Why are you doubting Istvan? What are you even looking for anyway?* All these thoughts tumbled around in my head, racking up my pulse until it pounded in my ears, almost convincing me to slip back out and return to the event pretending this lapse in judgment never happened. *You can no longer pretend you don't know anything. You know something is off. Feel it in your gut. Istvan is lying. You've seen the pills. What they can do. The notes from that Rapava.* The opposing voice slid into my head.

My tongue slid over my dry lips, tilting my ear toward the closed door. I listened for any activity before moving to a shelf with books, which held no interest for anyone, especially an enemy. Books on literature, art, languages. Old and antiquated in times like these. Tugging on the one I knew, feeling for the hook, the hollowed-out design pulled away in a grouping. Fake. Concealing the safe built into the wall.

Caden implied Istvan had more hiding places, but this was the only one I knew about. I had watched him open it from behind a curtain when I wasn't supposed to be using his office in a game of hide-and-seek.

Like the code outside, I hoped Istvan hadn't decided to suddenly change it.

Sucking through my nose, my hands shook, feeling the weight of my conduct. I was purposely breaking in and spying on someone I had thought of as a father figure for years. Someone I had believed and trusted. I could walk out now, step back into my role, become the obedient daughter and soldier.

Perspiration dampened the back of my neck, sliding down my spine, while moisture evaporated from my mouth. I typed in the code, my throat tightening, part of me hoping it wouldn't work, giving me an easy out, an excuse to walk away.

Click.

The lock snapped free, icy weight dropping into the pit of my stomach as the door of the safe swung open. I froze, trying to listen for any sound outside my thumping heart, waiting for Istvan to barrel in and catch me.

Panic lodged in my throat, and fear scraped up my spine as my trembling hands reached for the stack of documents inside. Flipping through them, I knew the third file was the one I had seen the other day. I reached for it, my heart stumbling in my chest, alarm shrilling through my veins like a scream.

A note on the second folder was scribbled in Dr. Karl's handwriting.

Results on Brexley Kovacs. I tested all these three times. We need to talk.

With shaky fingers, I flipped open the file. Most of it was medical lingo I didn't really understand, though I figured out he highlighted things that were not normal. My regard tracked down to a footnote.

Since the first test, her Immunoglobulin M level has tripled the normal rate. The more I tested, the higher her results were, as if each time her body was trying to defend against me. No human can sustain even half of these levels. Ms. Kovacs should be dead. She is not even showing signs of organ failure. If anything, she seems stronger and healthier.

Note: Her fresh wounds from when she arrived have now healed as if they are weeks old.

We must discuss these results in private. There seems to be only one explanation.

Terror punched me in the gut, leaning me over, oxygen gushing from my lungs. My nails dug into the desk as I tried to breathe.

They know you aren't normal. A voice crawled from the depths of my subconscious. It was one thing to let the thought drift across your mind, but to have others say it—it was an accusation.

Did Killian do something to me? Did those pills change me? I pinched my nose, exhaling through my mouth. *Come on, Brex, no one can change human DNA. Right?*

Boxing up my panic before I fully flipped out, I opened the next folder, quickly fanning out the papers on the desk.

Everything stopped. My world tipped on its axis, trying to shove me off.

Icy fingers dragged down my neck, wrapping around my throat. Shock and fear twisted my chest as I took in the dozen pictures staring back at me.

My own image.

A pinched noise rose in my throat, my heart slamming against my ribs. I reached for the first photo.

It was slightly hazy because it was night and at a distance, but there was no denying it was a picture of me—and Killian.

Embracing.

"Oh, gods…" Panic fluttered in my lungs, shadows edging around my vision.

Flicking through the rest, they showed every moment of our kiss. An intimacy and ease between us.

Frantically, I picked up another set. Ones of me standing at the window inside the bedroom Killian gave me. Some alone, some where he stood next to me, our bodies close and in conversation.

My muscles quaked, my mind whirling with justifications about these images when Istvan interrogated me. *He knew the whole time that I had come from Killian's… he knew I was lying.*

My brain rolled with excuses I could tell him—that I had to fake interest in Killian to get away, that I was doing it all to save my life. It could have been feasible… except I had kept the fact I had even been there a secret.

And he kept the fact he knew about my time with Killian from me. He let me walk right into it. It was something he did when trying to trip Caden and me up in a lie. He gave us the rope to do it ourselves.

Terror heaved my lungs.

Istvan *knew.*

Knew from day one I had straight out lied to him while I sat in the chair on the other side of this desk.

And gave nothing away.

Why had he not confronted me? He let me carry on in this house like everything was normal. What was his plan?

Staring down at the table, bile burned up my esophagus. The doctor called me "anomalous," and the pictures proved I lied.

Not just lied, but betrayed and deceived him, my people, and my soldier oath.

Sedition in the eyes of HDF.

Punishable by death.

Istvan would never let my disloyalty go—unless he was planning to use it against me somehow.

Voices coming from down the hall jolted me. Fear and adrenaline chugged through my bloodstream, my heart thudding, palms sweating. My gaze darted desperately down to the evidence of my crimes in front of me. Shuffling all pictures and papers together, I started to shove them back into the safe. But one of them slipped from my grasp and onto the floor. The file with some kind of formula and notes spread out over the rug.

Fuck!

I thrust the other two inside, about to pick up the fallen file.

Footsteps stopped at the door, voices muttering, speeding up my pulse.

Baszd meg!

Forgetting it, I pressed the safe closed, slipping back the false front. The door handle rattled. Panic drove me to sweep up the folder and dart to the curtain I used to hide behind as a young girl. Bunching up my huge skirt to my chest, I tried to flatten myself into the wall, the documents pressing into my skin.

"Come in." Istvan's voice rang through the room, my heart thumping as I noticed the curtain still swaying from my movement. Gritting my teeth, I hoped he either wouldn't notice or think he caused it by stepping in. "Have a seat."

"I'd rather not." Flat and low, the other man's voice tapped at the back of my head. I knew it, but I wasn't sure from where. "I'd prefer to get straight to business."

"Yes, very well," Istvan replied as he moved behind his desk. "Have you found anything more?"

"I have been watching her, trying to find any kind of communication between them, but so far, I have found nothing." The man sounded irritated by this discovery. "Does not mean she won't. She could be waiting until things calm down."

"Yes, she's smart. She wouldn't do anything foolish." Istvan sighed, sounding tired. "I raised her to be clever; now it's coming back to bite me."

I realized they were talking about me. Istvan had someone tracking me, watching my every move.

"Her betrayal has cut deep. I dedicated so much time to her education, hoping she wouldn't turn out like him... but I guess the apple doesn't fall far from the tree." Istvan huffed.

Like him? Did he mean my dad? My father had been his best friend. His faithful general, taken from my side months at a time to serve him, lead his armies, and then eventually taken from my life.

"How would you want me to proceed, sir?"

Istvan inhaled thoughtfully, as if contemplating his options. "My son will lose all focus if anything happens to her right now. He has become weak when it comes to her. Foolish. Plus, I want to watch how this will play out, see if she'll reach out to her fae lover. Otherwise, she is no longer of use to me. She may be stunning, but now with the rumors swirling around about her time in Halálház, no influential noble wants her near their family. My only hope is Prime Minister Leon in Prague, but if he rejects my offer for her, she is useless." Istvan went quiet, the room filling with heavy silence. My heart pounded so loudly I was sure someone would hear it.

"Sir?"

"What I want, Kalaraja..." His name slithered so deeply down into my gut I had to force myself not to gasp aloud or drop to my knees in terror.

Kalaraja. His name meant the Lord of Death.

The name they called him because of his occupation.

He was General Markos' private spy and assassin. I had met him a handful of times in Istvan's office over the years. His eyes were dark and flat. Soulless. Scarred face, bald, and blank of life, he could easily blend into the darkness.

Whenever he had walked by me, chills ran down my body. He was one of the only men I had been truly afraid of. I'd heard stories of his victims—the art and dedication he had, not in merely murdering someone, but torturing them. It was his only passion.

"I'd like—"

"Shh," Kalaraja snipped out.

"What—"

Whatever the assassin did, Istvan shut up.

My lids squeezed together for a moment, petrified. Not a muscle moved as my lungs strained to hold in the last bits of air. And possibly my final moments of life.

Seconds ticked by like hours, dread burning through me. Just a flick of the curtain and I would be exposed.

Tick. Tick. Tick.

My heartbeat struck with the clock.

A woman's squealed laugh from outside reached our ears, followed by a man's murmuring.

"It's only drunk guests outside," Istvan barked. "Calm down, Kalaraja. You are about to attack my plant in the corner." The swish of fabric told me Istvan was moving. The drawer to his desk opened. "I want you to continue to watch her. Report anything you see. I mean everything. Normal or… *abnormal*."

"What do you mean *abnormal*, sir?"

"Qualities you might find odd or different in a human."

A fist drove through my chest, barreling down into my gut, my heart squeezing in pain and fear.

In one sentence, with a shift in his tone, I realized I was no longer the daughter he once considered me.

I was an enemy.

In a world of suspicion, distrust, and hatred, Istvan was always looking for betrayal, but I did not expect how fast he would turn on me.

"And if nothing happens, sir?" Kalaraja replied blankly. "Can I just force her to talk?"

"She may appear like a feeble woman, but I trained her well. She's tougher than most male soldiers. She will not break."

"You underestimate me, sir."

I heard the sound of something hit the surface of the desk. "Here. Your payment for your services so far. When the time comes, there will be a bonus if you make it look as if the fae were the ones to kill her. That will really provoke Caden."

"Yes, sir."

"Now, I must return to my son's engagement," Istvan said. "Her death will burn his hate for the fae even more, and then he will help me lead the new wave of humans to destroy the fae and take back our land. Our world. I know him. Once he learns of her death, he will do it without question. It's amazing how powerful a broken heart can be."

Feet moved to the door, followed by the swish of it opening, footsteps receding, then the door clicking shut.

Shock swelled in my lungs, clogging my throat with emotion, fear, rage, grief, and heartbreak.

A man I thought of as family had so easily ordered my torture and death, turning against me without hesitation. For one moment, I wanted to curl on the ground and let the little girl, who grew up under his care, sob in grief feeling broken and terrified.

Run, my brain screamed at me. *You are no longer safe. Go!*

Instinct kicked me forward, flattening the folder to my chest. I peered around the curtain, searching for a threat before slipping out and heading for the exit. I peered back at his safe, the false front a little askew, then down at my item in my hands. A tiny part of me still wanted to be obedient to Istvan, prove I was the soldier and girl he raised so he would be proud of me.

"Once he learns of her death, he will do it without question. It's amazing how powerful a broken heart can be."

Terror twisted in my soul at his cruelty. Tucking the folder under my gown and wrapping it in the layers of fabric, I slinked out, knowing what I had to do.

And I could never come back from it.

Chapter 13

Music, laughter, and voices hummed from the great hall. Happiness and cheer were everywhere, the guests oblivious to the events playing out under this roof, or even outside these walls. Their ignorance and entitlement only made me walk faster and with greater determination.

With each measured step, I tried to keep my expression blank of emotion, hoping I could slink away down the hall and grab a few things from my room before slipping out into the night.

"Brexley." Istvan's voice came from behind me. Ice frosted my spine, pulling me to a stop, my lungs cinching, my lids crushing together. Deep fear coated my tongue, and I fought back a gasp blooming in my throat. "I have been looking for you."

I lifted my lashes. Instead of seeing the opulent décor of HDF, a dark, seedy bedroom was before me. The smells of sex and sweat drenched the stale chamber. Lit by a dim light from the nightstand, a lone figure sat on the bed, his face lined with frustration, making me strangely want to reach out and brush it away.

Aqua eyes jerked to me. Warwick's scrutiny rolled over me, then beyond as if he could see what was going behind me. Whatever he saw in my face had him bounding off the bed. "Kovacs?"

My mouth parted, my eyes locking with his.

"Brexley?" Istvan's cool voice snapped me back to HDF, abruptly cutting the link to Warwick. "Where have you been?"

Trying to keep my breath even, I twisted to face my guardian.

"I needed some fresh air." I kept my chin up, my eyes directly on him.

His gaze slid from the direction I had come and back to me. His expression did not falter; nothing about him altered. But everything had changed. I could feel the tension of the game I had no idea we were playing. Istvan would never come out and ask me. He would let me hang myself with my lies. The Eastern Bloc was built on power-hungry dictators playing a game of spies like little boys. You couldn't trust anyone, and everyone was a suspect.

All I could do was continue the game. Engage as if everything was the same.

"Rebeka is wondering where you are. Reporters want to take a *family* picture."

He had set down his chess piece, and now it was my move.

"Let me go freshen up, and I will be right in." I motioned to my face.

"You do look flushed, my dear." He tipped his head, his eyes burrowing into me.

"It's warm in there."

"Except you were outside getting fresh air..." He lifted a silvering eyebrow, taking one step closer to me.

"Too much champagne," I said quickly. Keep calm. Keep calm.

The rope was looped around my neck, and I knew if I kept getting defensive, it would strangle me.

Staying silent, we watched each other. The sound of the orchestra music in the main ballroom cheerfully buzzed from the party. It contrasted with the tension mounting between us.

"Well, go ahead, my dear." He forced his lips into a smile. "The powder room is right there. I'll wait for you."

"Please, return to your guests. I'll only be a minute. I'm sure you have so many people to greet." I smiled back, trying to pretend everything was normal.

"Rebeka would be angry if I returned without you." He flicked his head to the door close to me. "Now go on."

I had no other option. If I resisted, he would have no doubt something was wrong. Istvan wanted to keep me close, but I hoped he didn't realize how aware I was of his plan for me. What I had overheard.

If he did... game over.

Pulling my lips into a soft smile, I dipped my head. "I'll be quick." I casually headed for the water closet behind me, my heart choking my throat.

Shutting the door, the panic bubbled up, a small whimper escaping my throat. The feel of the folder against my hip pumped the blood in my veins faster.

My entire world was a house of cards, ready to come tumbling down.

Sucking in gulps of air, I knew the only course I could take was to go along with him, smile for the cameras, pretend to be the ward he shaped and molded.

Fixing my already perfectly styled hair, I tried to calm the fear trembling my limbs and took a deep breath. I pried open the door, schooling my features into serenity, something I'd been doing all my life.

Istvan's attention lasered on me as I stepped out, his lips pursing as if he knew he'd won, giving me no out—unless I was ready to end this pretense and lay down my cards. Stop this game of cat and mouse, where both of us knew I was lying. He didn't yet know that I knew he knew.

He curved his arm, an invitation for me to take it and let him lead me in. Plastering a happy smile on my face, I reached for his arm.

My tall heels caught on the edge of the rug, and I stumbled.

It was a second.

A breath.

A blink in time.

The folder slipped from the knotted layers next to my thigh, the fabric abandoning its hold, as if my dress itself was a conspirator against me.

My stomach plunged through the floor, everything speeding up and slowing down.

The file hit the floor, spreading out the documents across the rich, ornate rug. Dr. Rapava's notes were in full view, the half-concocted formula on top. Istvan's eyes dropped to the pages. His brows furrowed, taking in the papers spread on the ground before his attention snapped up to mine.

His cold blue eyes burned with fury, flaming with another emotion. Not hurt or betrayal. It was confirmation. I had proven myself the traitorous turncoat he decided I was. There would be no explanations or attempts to plead my side. I wouldn't be able to deny I stole them from his vault. No second chances. He didn't work that way.

Our eyes met. Oxygen caught in my throat. A drop of time suspended as we both waited for the other one to act. With a flash in his eyes, a tug of his lip, I shifted from daughter to enemy.

"You foolish girl. I gave you everything." Venom hissed from his mouth. "Guards!" Istvan's voice pierced the air. My survival instincts slammed into me. I bent over, grabbing the top documents, leaving those out of my reach, and flipped around. I had no idea what I was doing; there was no escaping, no getting out of here. I knew where each guard was stationed, the amount covering HPF inside and out, their skill level. They were the best of the best.

It was impossible, but I couldn't fight the feeling in my gut to run, to get outside the walls.

Tucking the pieces of paper into the fabric over my breast, I scrambled toward the stairs. Istvan's shout collided into me as guards came from every direction. The handful of party guests wandering around cried out in disbelief, flooding out from the ballroom.

"Don't let her escape. Traitor!" Istvan no longer kept up his pretense. The walls had been stripped down, showing the bones in our closets.

"Stop!" a guard yelled, his hands grabbing my arm painfully.

The Games at Halálház taught me to look at everything as a possible weapon, even when it seemed like there was nothing.

Hopping out of my heels, I picked one up, swinging it around with all my might. The sharp high heel Rebeka forced me to wear sank into his cheek.

There were sounds of breaking bones, flesh, and veins. A guttural cry howled through the room, and he dropped his grip on me. Guilt and grief warred in my chest. I knew him. I knew all of them, at least by face, but my desperate need to escape rose in me like a cornered beast. My life took precedence over theirs.

The monster of Halálház, who murdered with her own hands, tearing into flesh, who learned to kill or be killed, burst through my conscience, taking over.

Another guard pulled out his rifle, pointing at me.

"No! Don't kill her. She's sick and confused," Istvan ordered. "I want her alive."

Alive so he could torture information from me.

Slamming through the growing throng of guests pouring out to see what was going on, I pushed through to the edge of the stairs. A dozen guards ran up for me like a human wall, blocking my escape. Terror constricted my lungs.

Panic could lock you in place, or it could turn you feral and pitiless.

With a grunt, I leaped over the railing, dropping to the floor at least one story down with a hard thud. My bones creaked and jolted at the impact, but adrenaline kept pain far in the distance as it poured through my veins.

Commotion pounded in my ears, all of it drumming together like

118

white noise. Old friends, both men and women, became enemies as more leaped for me.

Hiking up my puffy dress, I kicked out at one, twisting myself around and slamming my fist into another, using my elbow to slam into the third's nose, smashing it in pieces. Trying to slip away, a woman guard seized the hem of my dress, yanking me back. This dress was the epitome of what not to wear in a fight.

The sound of fabric ripping tore through the air, the delicate silk ripping away, making the soldier stumble. I dove for her stomach, plowing her into the few guards behind her, driving them to the ground.

A fist slammed into my jaw, stealing my breath, and I staggered to the side.

I had no weapon, and more and more soldiers were coming for me, but I knew if I stopped now, my life was over. I was only alive now because Istvan ordered them not to kill me.

Yet.

With a deep growl and my teeth bared, I punched, kicked, and fought everybody who neared me, inching myself closer and closer toward the door. Vibrations of pain volleyed through my bones.

"Kovacs!" A familiar timbre hollered through the noise, halting everyone, including me. "Stop!"

Following the voice, I spotted the man I had idolized for years, craving his teachings like a drug. My mentor, Bakos, kept his eyes locked on me, heading calmly for me. "Ease back, soldier." He kept his shoulders back, his body tight, in defensive mode, but I saw a sadness in his eyes, a heartbreaking confusion.

He and I had a special bond. I had spent so much time trailing after him, asking for extra lessons, always eager to learn more, to advance faster. Fervent to be the best. He loved my tenacious need to work harder and absorb everything.

Now he stood across from me, another enemy.

He lifted his hands like he was easing a rabid animal. "You have nowhere to go. Please. Let us help you. We are not your enemy... We are your family. Your friends."

The way he spoke, I realized he thought I was having a psychotic break. That my mind had snapped after being locked in the House of Death, and I could no longer tell the difference between reality and hallucinations.

Soon he'd know it was not true. Istvan was setting me up while covering his own ass. He was the kind one trying to help a troubled girl. No one would question him. They could easily make me out as crazy.

119

And I fit the part perfectly.

Movement darted my eyes away from him, seeing more and more guards circling me. Most held guns pointed at my head now.

"Don't worry about them. Keep your eyes on me, Kovacs. Just you and me, okay? I won't let anything happen to you." Bakos reached for me.

I wanted to laugh, but my brain whirled with what I could do, the innate knowledge I was screwed. There was no way out of this. Istvan won.

Checkmate.

Bakos traveled to me. Like they were cuffs, his fingers reached for my arms.

Boom! Boom! Boom!

Explosions tore from outside HDF, shaking the building violently and flinging everyone off their feet with a brutal slam. My spine hit the marble floor, punching the oxygen from my lungs, making me gasp for air, my hearing going dim and hazy.

I rolled, covering my head as gold plaster rained down. A chandelier snapped from its tether, smashing to the ground, glass exploding out like bullets. Screams of terror, cries of pain, and shrieks of panic combusted off the walls and ceilings.

Memories threw me back to Halálház, as though I'd stepped back in time, watching the prison crumble around me. I could taste it, hear it, feel it all over again. The shrill screeches of people's panic and terror coated my tongue.

"Get. The. Fuck. Up. Kovacs." As if he were sitting next to me again, trying to make me rise, Warwick's husky voice growled in my ear. *"Run."*

A warm sensation weaved inside me, giving me this unexplainable strength. Pushing up, I gritted my teeth, ignoring all the pain. Blood gushed down my face from the glass cuts and punches, but I felt nothing.

Numb.

Bodies lay everywhere around me. Some guards were already running for the door. No one seemed to notice or care about me anymore. HDF had been attacked. I was not the most critical threat anymore. But it wouldn't be long before attention returned to me.

Without hesitation, I sprinted for the exit, the bottoms of my feet sliced by glass shards, leaving bloody footprints as a trail.

Uproar and disorder spun the guards in circles. HDF had never been attacked before, and no amount of training compared to the real thing.

Soldiers ran toward the explosion, no one paying any thought to me as I scurried the opposite way out the doors, following the tug in my gut into the darkness.

"Brexley!" I paused at the sound of my name, turning back toward HDF.

Caden stood yards away. The flood of lights from HDF both highlighted and shadowed his features. I could see his tux was torn, blood dripping from his cheek, but the agony in his eyes stabbed me in the chest. I couldn't bear the utter anguish as he looked at me, the confusion, the hurt.

I couldn't drag him down with me. I loved him beyond words, but in this moment, I knew my life could never be within these walls. I was now an enemy.

Caden's place was here. This was his home.

I looked back at him, grief batting my lashes as a tear fell down my face. "I'm sorry," I said, not knowing if he heard me before I swung back around and disappeared into the darkness, leaving a piece of my heart behind with him.

"BREXLEY!" A howl of agony came from behind me. The guttural sound hitched a sob up my throat, making me run faster. I fought back my tears, focused on my survival.

As if a tether pulled me forward, I slipped beyond the gates of Leopold, knowing I would never step inside again. Not as a free person.

Deep in the darkness, I spotted a glowing red taillight, a massive silhouette straddling a bike.

His turquoise eyes transcended the dark, raking down me like fingers.

I didn't want to think about how he was here, how he knew I needed a distraction to get out, how I knew where he'd be without even thinking. My senses and mind were already on overload.

"Only you, princess…" He revved the engine as I grappled with the dress, climbing on behind him, wondering how he got a new motorcycle so quickly. They were not easy to get in this country. "Would run from a ball bloody and barefoot."

"Shut up." I wrapped my arms around him.

He snorted, shaking his head, the bike speeding down the street. I turned and looked back, watching the lights of the only place I had ever known become foreign and enemy territory.

Istvan would not let this go. They would come after me. He would send his assassin to track me down.

I sucked in, my head rising, watching the buildings blur past as my old life disappeared behind me.

The problem was, the girl they were going to track had already been destroyed. Beaten, tortured, and buried.

He didn't know he was hunting a monster now.

Like a harbinger riding through the night, my scarlet-red dress streamed behind me, sailing in the wind on a black machine driven by death himself, catching more attention than we wanted. Crested with gems, the finest silk, and expensive lace, the rich, deep color was enough by itself to scream wealth and privilege. Elites wouldn't last long on these streets.

Warwick and I didn't speak as he zigzagged through the lanes, maneuvering around horses and carts, making sure if anyone followed us, they would struggle to keep up.

More and more people strolled the streets the closer we moved to the heart of the Savage Lands. Fires glowed from barrels as groups of people huddled for warmth around them with kids and infants, their faces drawn, dirty, and scarred. But their gazes turned to me, lighting up with awe at my fine dress, then turning quickly to greed.

I knew what a few yards of the rich material could do for them. Fill their bellies for many nights.

Driving into an unlit alley, Warwick turned off the headlights, coasting until he curved us into an even tinier path, stopping the bike. We both sat for a moment in the dark, a sliver of the moon casting an eerie glow on us, only our breaths and distant sounds touching the air. The stench of old urine and garbage attacked my nose, forcing me to breathe through my mouth.

After several moments of no one following us down the lane, my shoulders eased.

He made a sound in his throat, his head turning enough to make out his profile. Without a word, I understood what he wanted. I slid off the bike, brushed debris off my torn dress, and checked that the documents were still pressed securely to my sternum.

Warwick pushed the motorbike behind a dumpster, tossing cardboard boxes over it to help disguise it. He huffed through his nose and jerked his chin for me to follow.

"Keep close," he rumbled, his forehead creasing with irritation, his gaze running down my body. "You're a walking target, especially in Carnal Row."

"Carnal Row?"

"It's what this place is called. It's not hard to figure out why it's called that."

Music, laughter, yelling, and chatter grew louder and louder as we moved onto the main lane, the name fitting the depraved carnival atmosphere. The familiar path packed with figures shocked my system with smells and sights almost as much as the first night I walked through here.

It was a Saturday night, and the place was bursting with sin, greed, lust, and seduction. The festival was alive with sex, gambling, and drinks.

I gasped as a burst of fire flared over my head, drawing my eye up to a woman in knickers and a corset swinging on a hoop, twirling a flaming baton. Hammocks hanging from the ceiling were already filled with naked figures lost in ecstasy, their moans threading into the music coming from each establishment. Roars of what sounded like wild animals bellowed from down the row. Shape-shifters only half shifted mulled around, offering up pills and alcohol. Glittery, cheap costumes sparkled under the firebulbs as barely dressed men and women curled their fingers, enticing people to come closer. Tables were packed with gamblers, fights breaking out as hands were revealed.

As we passed one gambling den, a man shouted, "Cheater!" Pulling out a pistol, he pointed at another man and shot him dead in a blink. The gunfire didn't even make people flinch.

"Hey, beautiful!" A hand touched my face, pulling my attention to a stunning fae woman in front of me. "You look ready to party." Her hand moved down my frame, purring with lust and promises, but her eyes were empty. "I can offer you anything you desire," she said, but her fingers went back to the silk of my dress, her thumb running over the buttery fabric and the gems hand-stitched into the roses. "Oh, my gods…" Her mouth parted. "Is this real? These are real, aren't they?"

Warwick growled, grabbing my hand and yanking me through the throng, away from her.

"We need to get you out of that fuckin' dress. Now," he rasped in my ear, pulling me closer, the heat of his body pressing into me as he herded me toward a familiar building.

Kitty's was lit up, almost every window stuffed with all sexes and types flaunting themselves. The girls were in corsets, robes, and fishnet stockings. The guys were only in tiny briefs showing off their packages, some wearing top hats or leather vests. All of them were in sexual positions putting what they had to offer on display, yelling offers of sex down to those who passed. Young and old, patrons drifted in and out the front door in a steady stream. Grunts from the alley and windows suggested some were already indulging.

"Warwick, baby." They all cooed from the windows. I flicked my attention up, landing on one, my lids narrowing.

"Let me know when you're ready. The girls and I will drop whatever we're doing for you." Nerissa leaned out the window, showing off generous breasts bursting out of her top. Her gaze slid to me, an impish smile curving her lips. Smug. Like she knew exactly how he tasted, what he felt like… and I didn't.

"Oh, looky who's back. Ms. Prude is actually going to lower herself to our kind again?"

"Nerissa," Warwick warned, but her smile turned haughtier.

He leaped up the steps to the door, not even looking back to see if I was behind him. I felt like some nuisance or kid sister he was obligated to come pick up.

Fuck him. Huffing, I clutched the sides of the gown, yanking it up, heading up the stairs, trying not to flinch. The tender pads of my feet burned, leaving partial bloody prints on the steps.

"What? Had nothing else to wear? Just something you threw on, duchess?" Nerissa leaned farther out as she taunted me, the others howling with laughter from their perches.

Snarling, I ignored her, stepping inside the doors.

"*War-wick.*" A lingering, smoky sigh filled with annoyance and love. "I am not some halfway house." The dame herself, Madam Kitty, stood in the large lounge, looking as polished and poised as ever. Her dark skin glowed in the lamplight, highlighting her sharp cheekbones. Tonight, she wore a green sequin-covered dress that fit her body like a glove, her dark hair up in a high sleek ponytail, the ends reaching her waist. I knew the hair wasn't real. Nor were the long lashes and even longer red nails. She was striking, but exceptionally intimidating. Still, something was off, something I couldn't exactly explain.

"Kitty…" Warwick tipped his head to the side, giving her a tiny smile. "I swear nothing will happen."

"My *dear* boy…" Her voice went very low, her hand going to her hip. "The last time you said that, I had to remodel the entire second floor."

"That was one time."

"The time before, it was the living room… The time before I had to replace four beds…"

"That was entirely for a different reason." He held up his hand.

Her curled lashes lowered in a glower before her eyes slowly slid over to me. She always looked displeased, unless she was talking to Warwick, but I couldn't tell at all what she thought about seeing me again.

Her jaw tensed, her attention going back to Warwick. "One of these days you will run out of favors."

Warwick's devastating grin danced over his face cheekily, making me inhale sharply—a genuine smile. His eyes glinted as he took her hand, kissing it. "You are a rare diamond, my friend."

She snorted, taking back her hand and patting his shoulder. "I'm rare, all right." She sighed. "Now get out of my sight before I change my mind." He grinned again, kissing her cheek. "Go!" She batted at him. "Ugh. I don't know why I've put up with you all these years."

Warwick peered back at me, then turned and marched up the stairs, his happy mood dissolving the instant he looked upon me.

Clutching the monstrosity I wore, I headed for the stairs, dipping my head at Kitty. "Thank you."

"Be careful with that one, girl," she said, her reserve and polished appearance back in place, watching customers go in and out the door. "He has a way of pulling you in, drowning you..." She swallowed, and my eyes moved to her neck, noticing the Adam's apple. "And all you do is ask for more."

I paused, my gaze searching her face, seeing the truth behind the mask. "You're in love with him."

Her mouth twisted in a soft derisive scoff, not denying it.

"The love of my life is this place. I have no use for a heart. I learned that lesson long ago." She glanced over at me. "But let me warn you— nothing is worse than loving a man who will never love you back. It's the worst kind of torture because you can grow accustomed to it, long for it, crave it more than life. You wouldn't even know how to stop it. Nor do you want to." She touched my arm, her head tipping, examining me. "But maybe this time, it is he who needs to be careful." Her eyes ran over me before turning away. "I will send up clothes for you."

My eyes tracked her until she was out of view, her warning feeling weighty and potent.

Trudging up the steps, my gaze danced around. I never imagined I'd be back here. It was only a month ago, but it felt like years.

Everything had changed from the first time I walked up these stairs. Then all I wanted was to go home, to my life, to Caden, believing I could easily slip back into that world and be happy. Now I had no home, no place or family to go back to. I was a traitor to my people, no longer welcome.

I was homeless, penniless, and a true orphan.

Sighing, I proceeded to the room Warwick was in.

Whatever this link was between us scared me to death and stroked anger up my spine—because it felt like home. Something my soul clung to, which made me want to sever it more. It wasn't only the fear of the unknown or what I'd lost tonight that played at my emotions, but the certainty of the pull to the room down the hall. I could feel him. See him. Without even being near him, I knew there was a half-empty bottle of Pálinka on the table, takeout cartons in the trash, and a jacket on the chair.

Warwick was not someone you attached yourself to in any way. He was death. A lone wolf. Vicious and cruel.

"It's the worst kind of torture because you can grow accustomed to it, long for it, crave it more than life. You wouldn't even know how to stop. Nor do you want to."

Chapter 14

The wood planks creaked under my bare feet as I stepped into the room. The musty smell was settled so deeply into the walls that no spring day could ever air it out. The indulgences of this room stained the floors and walls; they were imprinted in the furniture and engraved in the very foundation of the building.

Warwick stood with his back to me, staring out the window. His hands were on his hips, his shoulders straining up against his ears. His T-shirt stretched across his back, muscles flexing with every measured breath.

The door clicked closed behind me, leaving us alone in the tiny room. He gobbled up every molecule, every breath, hoarding it and pushing it against me as though he could take up the little space I contained.

I lifted my chin, shoving back against his dominance, denying him from seizing what little I had left. He sniffed in, the silence weaving a palpable weight in the air.

Impulse had my senses reaching out, as if I was right next to him, slithering inside, feeling his anger and resentment like he poured it into my hands, wrapping it around me like a noose.

A deep grunt came from him, his shoulders twitching back. "Stop," he said, so low it almost got lost in the gravel of his voice.

I stood up taller, pushing harder, taking from him what he was trying to claim from me.

"Stop," he growled again, his physique locking up, but at the same time expanding so large he blocked the entire window.

"You can feel that?" It wasn't really a question. I took a step, imagining my fingers trailing down his spine. I could feel the fabric of his shirt, his muscles tense under my touch.

"I. Said. Stop." His head jerked to me, a snarl curling his lip.

"How?" I didn't pause, only moved closer to him, feeling his pulse thump over my imaginary fingertips. I could sense his trepidation and building irritation.

In a flash, a switch seemed to flip.

He sprang forward, wrapping his hand around my neck like a boa, pushing me back into the wall. Sparks charged through my veins, both hate and lust crackling through my core.

"I told you to stop." His luminescent eyes burned through the dark room, his mouth only a breath away from mine, his grip squeezing my throat.

"You don't tell me what to do," I sneered. Every fiber in my body blazed with life, taking in his rich sexy smell, his warmth, his fury.

"Maybe you should listen for once." He pressed into me, the full skirt keeping him from flattening himself against me, but somehow he still invaded my space. His heavy cock was pulsing and hot. "Then maybe I wouldn't have to keep saving your ass, princess."

Anger charred my throat, popping and fizzing like fireworks. A smug grin twitched on his mouth.

"Get the fuck off me." I shoved at his chest, not moving him a hair. "I didn't ask you to save me." I tried to push him again, but he didn't budge an inch. "Nor did I need your help."

"Really?" His free hand grappled for my flailing arms, pinning one back against the wood. "Then what was your little visit here for?"

"I didn't do it on purpose," I seethed, trying to buck against him. "Now let go of me."

"If I actually thought you meant it, I would." He thrust me harder into the wall, his thumb sliding down my throat, his lips skimming my ear. Wetness throbbed between my legs, my nipples hardening at his intensity. A dark chuckle hummed from his throat. My body completely gave me up. "That's what I thought. Whether you like it or not, I know what you enjoy, Kovacs. How dark and dirty you want it. Even if you won't admit it yet."

"Fuck you." I wiggled underneath his grip, and he leaned more heavily on me.

"What do I keep telling you about that?" He grabbed both my arms, trapping them beside my head, his bulk consuming mine. Taking over. Demanding more of my space. *Physically* I was no match; I understood that. But mentally…

In my head, my fingertips skated slowly down his arms. Small bumps rose on his skin in the wake of my ghostly touch. His brow wrinkled, his jaw setting. I swept over his chest, not stopping as I reached the V-line slightly exposed between his shirt and jeans.

He sucked in, and I knew he felt me trace the deep indention as if my hands were actually there.

"Kovacs," he said between gritted teeth.

"What?" I challenged him, staring right into his eyes as he felt my hand slip inside his jeans, grazing the tip of him.

"Fuck." He choked, his body naturally curling into me, seeking more, desiring my touch.

My fingers tingled as if I really were stroking his hot skin, feeling him pulse and grow against my palm. Desire speared through me, my hips opening, wanting.

Gripping him firmer in my mind, my hand could feel every vein, every scalding inch of his skin. But even my imaginary hands were struggling to grasp his width and length.

Fucking hell. This man was indeed a legend.

Air puffed out of my lungs, matching his as I moved up and down his shaft.

He growled and pushed his hips into me, his grip on my arms tightening. His eyes blazed, meeting mine, breathing heavily out of his nose.

In this moment, he was not some myth or cruel beast. We were equal. And I could drop him to his knees as easily as he could me.

Without *actually* touching him.

"Stop." A guttural growl vibrated up his throat.

I pumped him harder in my mind. He inhaled sharply, his eyes glazing for a moment.

"You want to play? Fine," he mumbled. One hand stayed on my wrists while the other clutched the back of my head roughly.

Without warning or ease, two phantom fingers stroked over my lace underwear, pushing the fabric aside, sliding through me while his actual hands stayed exactly where they were. A gasp opened my mouth, a deep groan wanting to escape. I slammed my teeth together to keep it locked inside.

"Someone's wet." Warwick smirked, clearly loving the switch of power.

My body instantly moved to seek out his touch, craving it so badly a jolt of fear almost blinded me. With a feral cry, I thrashed against him, pushing him out of the way. Warwick didn't fight, dropping his hands, letting me bolt to the other side of the room. Not that I could escape him.

"How-how is this possible?" My hand went to my stomach, feeling anxious. "Why is this happening?"

Warwick rubbed his head, moving the farthest he could from me. "Your guess is as good as mine."

Emotion overpowered me. "How do we stop it? I don't understand... Why? How?"

"I. Don't. Fucking. Know!" he roared, anger bursting from him. "Believe me, I wish I did."

I whirled around, glowering at him.

He glared back. "You think I fucking want this?" He motioned between us. "Whatever it is. I *hate* it. I want it gone. Unlike you, it seems," he seethed, looking at me as if it were my fault.

"You think *I* want this?" I stabbed at my chest. "I don't want it either."

"Appears to be working out for you. Twice I've saved you from danger."

"You mean after turning me over to the fae lord? Trading me like cargo?"

"You didn't seem to suffer all that much there. How long did it take to fall into *his* bed?"

My jaw crunched down painfully, fury blasting into him. Instinctually, I knew he could feel my wrath and hate. "You betrayed me."

"That's how it is out here. I told you to only trust yourself. To each his own. That's how it is in the *real* world, princess."

"Bullshit," I yelled. "Look around you, Warwick. You think you're all alone out here? You have a house full of people willing to protect you. *Az istenit!* That woman down there will do anything for you. Hide you at any cost. Are you so blind, or are you okay with using the fact she is in love with you?"

His shoulders rose, a nerve under his eye twitching. A blast of rage hit me in the stomach as he moved to me. "You don't know anything about her, me, or our history. Don't speak about things you know nothing about."

"But you see it, right?"

"It's not what you think. We've been through things your human brain could never fathom. You are nothing but a child."

"Excuse me?" I shouted, closing the last few feet between us, every fiber of my being sizzling. "This fucking *child* lived through Halálház. I have murdered and survived the same as you. Maybe I haven't gone through as much, lived as long, but don't you dare lessen what I have done... what I have lived through and experienced." I pushed his chest. "My hands are stained with blood too."

He exhaled out of his nose, peering down at me through his lashes.

"I think that's what really scares you…"

"Scares me?" He scoffed, leaning over me. "Nothing scares me, sweetheart."

"Except me." The words came out of my mouth without thought.

"You?" He dropped his head back with a dark laugh. "An insignificant human who will not even be a glimmer in my lifetime?"

"Yes, because I see you too, Farkas." I smirked. This time instead of focusing my energy on his skin, I dove underneath, grazing his mind, his soul, reaching for his truth.

I barely slipped under his skin when I felt energy slammed back into me, engulfing me.

Mind-blowing pain.

Blinding pleasure.

A howl echoed through the room at the same time as a cry tore from my lips, the power so penetrating, my knees dipped. Gasping at the intensity, I quickly retreated, not ready for the extreme emotions that overwhelmed every sense.

What the fuck was that?

There was a pause as we stared at each other, not able to speak.

He grabbed me roughly, slamming our bodies into the wall. Untamed madness crackled off him as he flattened into me, the dress not able to withstand the force. The air even seemed to slip out of his way, terrified of the angry wolf. Death flickered in his eyes, his body vibrating. His eyes burrowed into mine.

Demise.

Desire.

Devastation.

Hunger.

Hate.

I felt it all, like a little taste of a drug, and now I wanted more. Needed it.

His fingers dug into my skin, his eyes wild and vicious, ready to tear through the room, my dress, and into my skin, dismantling me until I was nothing. Razing us to the ground until we destroyed each other, leaving nothing but destruction in our wake.

His gaze dropped to my mouth, and he leaned in, the heat of his breath grazing my lips.

"Hello?" A knock sounded on the door, and a woman's accented voice sliced through the room like an ax, cutting through the thick haze between us, jolting us as if someone dumped ice water on us.

The door started to swing open. Warwick moved away from me like I disgusted him, his anger still heavy on my tongue, his sudden absence feeling like a tear in my skin.

Taking a deep breath, I tried to get my legs steady under me.

A squeal came from the door. I twisted my head to the familiar form standing in the doorway.

"Rosie!" A smile burst over my face, my body already moving toward my friend. Wearing exactly what she had when I met her the first time, my faux English rose, with her bright red hair and blue eyes, was even prettier than I recalled. "Oh, my gods!"

"Luv!" She wrapped me up in her arms, her huge bosoms feeling like fluffy pillows. "It's really you." She pulled back, cupping my face, peering at me with utter joy. "When Madam said she needed women's clothes brought up to Warwick's room... I hoped." She pulled me back in for a quick hug again. "I can't believe how happy I am to see you. Ever since you left that evening, my stomach has been all in knots. I had this awful feeling. But then I saw..." Her eyes flicked over to Warwick's, then back to me. "Did I interrupt something?"

"No!" We both shook our heads ardently.

She snorted, winking at me. "You guys keep saying that, and I have yet to believe you."

"It's so good to see you." I took the clothes in Rosie's hands. "Thank you so much."

Her gaze finally took in my gown, her eyes widening. "Bloody hell." Her exaggerated English accent thickened. "Is this real silk?" She touched one of the roses. "Are those authentic jewels?"

"Yes, and they are all yours."

"What?"

"What?"

Both she and Warwick jerked toward me, his shock turning into irritation.

"Sell what you can, make costumes from the rest, do whatever you want. I don't want to look at it again." I squeezed her hand. "The gems are all real, so don't let anyone con you."

Warwick huffed, shaking his head as he grabbed the Pálinka bottle off the table and pounded it back.

"Are you sure? I can tell this thing cost a fortune. You might need the money."

Warwick made a noise in his throat like he agreed with her.

"I'm sure. Pay off your debts, Rosie. Don't be anyone's property. Even Kitty's."

She eyed me suspiciously.

"No strings attached. It's yours."

Tears filled up Rosie's eyes. She batted her thick eyelashes, her head shaking. "I don't know what to say. Kindness without ties... It's not something that happens here."

I didn't understand what it was really like to live in a world so cutthroat that no one did anything without it benefiting them.

Not waiting, I stripped out of the dress, setting the folded documents I stole on the nightstand. I pulled on the loose cami, which did nothing to cover my braless chest, and tugged on the tiny rayon shorts and a shawl. Everything was thin, cheap, and threadbare.

"Here." I handed her the heavy gown, my bones feeling liberated from the weight.

"I will try to find you pants and a more suitable top." She took the gown from me, not quite looking me in the eyes. "If I'd known it was really you, I would have tried harder to find better clothes."

"This is fine."

She nodded, stepping back. "Food is coming. Madam wants me to remind you both not to leave the bedroom. Some of our clientele would be especially keen to find the both of you."

"Got it." I nodded.

"It's not as if you guys couldn't find something to do." She winked at me.

"Night, Rosie." I opened the door for her.

"Night, luv." She grinned mischievously, looking between Warwick and me.

"Brexley," I said, feeling this need to trust her.

"I know." She tilted her head.

"You know?"

"Luv, look at you... Even before I knew your name, I knew you were not one of us. But Anita confirmed it when she smuggled a Leopold paper from one of the soldiers she fucked—you were on the front cover. So stunning and regal. The princess of Leopold."

Warwick chuckled darkly, taking another drink.

"I am not a princess!" I exclaimed, glaring at both.

"You are compared to us, luv. Glad you're back, though." She dipped away, the red harbinger trailing behind her like a stream of blood.

The instant I shut the door, the room collapsed on itself, filling with taut energy. Stuffed and tight against my skin. The energy between us before Rosie interrupted left me feeling like I had a spike in the gut. I couldn't decipher my feelings.

"You gave away a fortune," Warwick grunted. "You realize how stupid that was, right?"

Probably not. Besides my time in Halálház, where money didn't come into play, I had never been without. Never had to worry or think about money. Even our meals in restaurants were taken care of. Markos's assistant handled tabs. I never carried cash.

I was broke now, but I could never regret giving the dress to Rosie. She needed it far more than I did.

Swallowing, I turned around, brushing off his question, my attention on other things. I sat on the bed, the silence stifling the air.

"Both times you rescued me... you knew where to be." I cleared my throat. "How to get me out."

He didn't respond, the chair across the room creaking with his weight as he sat down.

"You know how to make bombs?"

"I have connections." He tipped back in the rickety chair, propping his boot on the bed.

I nodded, twisting my fingers into the duvet. "How do we stop this?"

He sighed, his head tipping back into the cushion, his eyes on the ceiling. "I wish I knew. I'll start asking around, but we need to be careful." His grave expression met mine. "We don't know what this is. And even in the fae world, something unnatural is typically treated with mistrust. Any enemy that finds out you are connected to me... will use it against me and vice-versa."

"Fuck." I pulled my legs up to my chest, laying my forehead on my knees. I hadn't even thought of that. Warwick's list of enemies was probably extensive, and mine was growing every moment.

So much had changed since the last time we were in this room together, but my head kept returning to the moments we sat in these very spots, talking.

I peered up at him. "Why did you give me to Killian?"

He turned his head out the window. "Don't tell me you were *suffering*."

"Screw you," I said evenly. "You have no clue what really went on behind those walls. Don't sit here acting like you did me a favor. You betrayed me, Warwick. *Sold me*."

He downed a hefty gulp of alcohol.

"Was it your plan the whole time?"

I watched him shift slightly in his chair. I tried to reach out and sense any emotions, but as if my hand got slapped, I felt him knock me back. Blocking me.

"Ah." I pursed my lips. "Pretend to save me from Halálház only so you could sell me to him yourself." One leg slipped to the floor, the other curled in front of me. "Well done."

He drank more.

"Why keep me for three days then? Why not trade me right away?"

"Kovacs," he rumbled my name.

"No, I'm curious. Since you find me so physically repulsive, I know you didn't keep me to get a bit of fun."

His head snapped to me.

"It's not like you couldn't get that here any time you wanted anyway."

"You have *no* clue about anything."

"Then tell me. Since I am worth so little to you."

"Shut up, Kovacs." He pushed up from the chair.

"No." I stood with him. "Why bother coming after me tonight? Or saving me from Killian? You made an enemy of Killian now, so what was the point? You hate this connection?" I motioned between us. "At any time, you could have ended it."

He huffed.

"Remember, I'm an insignificant human." I rounded the bed, everything in me calm and controlled. "I'm nothing to you, right?"

His chest vibrated with a growl.

"How much money did you get for me? I hope I was substantial—"

"Shut. Up."

"A prize like me, General Markos's ward, a Leopold elite. I'll bet you got off on how gullible I was, how easy I was to trick—"

"Kovacs," he growled, stepping toward me.

"A stupid, pathetic, feeble human."

"You are anything but stupid, pathetic, and feeble," he snarled. In a blink, he weeded his fingers through my hair, yanking my head painfully. "Or human."

I sucked in, a noise clawing at my throat.

His eyes searched mine like he was trying to peel back every layer to see inside. He pushed off from me, facing the window. "I traded you because I didn't have a choice."

I blinked, motionless on his last words. "What?"

"Killian had something…" He glared back at me. "Something I would trade you for again. I would trade anything for. Even my life. So, no, I won't apologize for your hurt feelings. Because I would do it again." He snapped his fingers in my face. "In a heartbeat. Grow the fuck up. This is not the happy, naïve world you are accustomed to, princess. It's cutthroat and cruel."

Anger bristled up my spine, but I stared at my bare feet; the red polish had matched my dress perfectly. Not the color of love, but of death.

"What did you mean I'm not human?" I struggled over the word, the twist in my gut clawing up my chest.

"Nothing. I didn't mean it." He ran his hand over the back of his neck. "You're human."

"How do you know?"

His head lifted at my inquiry, his brows furrowing.

"I mean, do you smell it on me or see it?"

His eyes tracked me, but he didn't respond.

"What if…" I gulped over the knot in my throat. "What if I'm not?"

"Then what would you be?" His voice was low and tight.

My lashes fluttered. "I don't know, but there is something *different* about me." I folded my arms, needing a barrier, my fears making me vulnerable. "Anomaly. Abnormal. There were other words they called me—but the doctor found things out about me."

"Found what?" His voice was so low, chills ran over my skin. "What did he find?"

Licking my lips nervously, I spoke. "They found my antibodies were beyond normal levels. More to the point, I should be dead from organ failure, but they are even healthier."

"What antibodies?" Warwick prickled with anger.

"Something immune something—ending with an M."

"Immunoglobulin M." His glare drilled into me, his chest moving quicker.

"Yes." I bolted straight, my heart tripping over itself. "How did you know that?"

"Fuck." He swung around, his shoulders quaking with fury. He stalked to the window, smashing his fist into the wall. "FUCK!"

"What? What does that mean? And how do you know?" His violence didn't scare me. If anything, it made me want to calm the beast. "Warwick?" I touched his arm.

He jerked away, his head repeatedly knocking against the window frame.

"Stop." I grabbed him again, not letting him back away. "Talk to me."

He tipped his head to me.

"I have the same thing."

Chapter 15

"This place is magical." A voice hinted at the horizon of my consciousness. "It's like swimming in jelly."

Chirp.

"Ach! Ugh! No, it doesn't taste anything like jelly. Yuck."

Chirp.

"You did not. You told me to try it."

Chirp.

"Why yes, your fingers do slide up easier with it. It actually looks fun."

A strange odor filled my nostrils, yanking me out of the sleep I had finally found, my lashes bursting open.

Bitzy sat in front of me, her fingers wiggling in my nose. Seeing I was awake, she slowly slid them out, trying to look innocent.

"Oh, gods..." I sat up, rubbing my burning nose. "What the hell was that?"

I puffed and wiped at my nostrils, gagging at the texture and smell. My gaze finally took in the scene.

My mouth dropped open, whispering, "*Az istenit...*"

Opie was inside the shallow nightstand drawer, dressed in a leather studded collar and leash he wrapped around himself like a bodysuit. Red, black, and pink pleasure feathers stuck from his back like wings, while his bare feet skated around clear gel... from a lube container.

Chirp.

My attention darted to the imp sitting on my pillow. Bitzy wore the same feathers as wings, with a dart-shaped object strapped on her head.

"Oh, my gods... Is that—?" A groan-laugh heaved from my chest, my hand rubbing my forehead. "I don't even want to tell you where that has probably been."

"Fishy, this place is amazing. Like a giant funland." Opie did running moves through the jelly. "This stuff even warms up. My toes are so toasty."

"My brain can't handle this so early." I couldn't fight the giggle. The post-dawn morning light broke through the curtains. I could tell it was overcast and still early. A chill nipped my skin—the weather grew colder each day.

Without having to look over, I knew the room was empty. I could feel Warwick's absence or presence like an electric shock wave. Warwick still hadn't returned.

After his little reveal, he had basically shut down, told me to stay put, and left. My sleep had been anything but restful. I tossed and turned, waiting for him to return, his revelation rolling over and over in my mind.

Another thing which linked us.

"Look at my spins." Opie twirled like a ballerina.

Chirp.

"My form is fine. My toe *is* pointed."

Chirp.

"Yes, it is."

Chirp.

Opie pointed his large hairy foot. "Oh, you're right. That is better."

"Guys." I waved my hands. "What are you doing here? How did you know I was here?" A flash of fear seared the back of my neck. If they knew, had others learned where I was? Had Istvan or Killian already found me?

"Like how we found you at the last place." Opie did a pirouette. "You smell, Fishy."

"I smell *fishy*?"

"No, you have a smell, Fishy." Opie dropped his arms, climbing out of the drawer. "Thought we went over this."

Chirp.

For some reason, I had the impression Bitzy just called me an idiot.

"But why are you here? Aren't you supposed to be at Killian's?"

Chirp.

Opie shot Bitzy a look as he jumped on the bed, leaving greasy footprints across the duvet.

"See, there was a little *misunderstanding*... a little mishap with an appliance... and well... let's say Master Finn *did not approve*."

Chirp. Chirp. Chirp. Bitzy waggled her middle fingers in the air, her face wrinkling with anger, her large ears lowering.

My eyes widened as I sensed her anger.

"And well, I guess the whole brownie clan had been... not so happy with my 'performance' and the magic-operated corkscrew, which was totally a misunderstanding, by the way. But..." Opie's shoulders slumped in sorrow. "Anyway, Master Finn kicked me out of the clan."

"What?" I exclaimed.

"They had enough of my shenanigans and basically said I was unfit to be a brownie. I was a disgrace to my whole kind." Opie sniffed, his grief tearing at my heart.

"Oh, Opie, I'm so sorry."

He shrugged dejectedly.

I watched him for a moment, my head shaking.

"Well, fuck them!" I hit the bed, both Opie and Bitzy turning toward me. "I say they are a disgrace if they don't see how awesome you are."

Chirp! I agree, fuck 'em!

"Right?" I nodded at Bitzy. Holy shit, was I sort of understanding her?

"Really?" Opie wiped his eyes.

"They are the losers. Boring and predictable. You," I tapped Opie's chest, "are extraordinary. And you will have a life full of adventure."

"Ohhhh, brownies don't have adventures."

"But you are special."

Chirp!

"I don't think she meant that kind of special." Opie huffed at Bitzy, trying to put his hands on his hips, but the pointy spikes from the leather collar dropped them back down awkwardly.

"Finn and those others didn't deserve you in their clan. I want you to be in mine."

"Whhhaaattt?"

Chirpppp!

Both drew back in shock.

Crap... did I say something wrong? "Is it okay?"

"Oh my goodness, Fishy..." Tears filled Opie's eyes. "That is the highest honor you can bestow on a brownie."

Chirp! The gist of that I took to mean: "You sure you want this asshole?"

"Yes." I glowered at her. "And shocking as this is, I want you too, Bitzy. Kind of a package deal."

"We will be honored to be in your clan." Opie dropped to one knee. "Master Fishy!"

Chirp!

I was pretty sure she did not repeat the same sentiments exactly.

"Fuck." A deep growl came from the door. We all jerked toward the beast filling up the doorjamb. "I hope you know what you just did," Warwick snarled, shaking his head as he stepped into the room.

Opie squeaked, diving under the pillow. Bitzy glared, flipping him off, while my body flamed with heat, feeling his aura cover my flesh like a blanket, pressing into my thighs.

"Do you understand you are now the proud owner of two pets... until *death*?" Warwick stomped across the room, his expression heavy with exhaustion.

"They are *not* pets." I twisted, following him to the chair where he sat and yanked off his dirty boots.

Chirp! Bitzy tossed up her middle fingers, sticking her tongue out at him.

"Exactly." I nodded to Bitzy.

Warwick snorted, the light catching the unreal color of his eyes as he glanced up at me. "You do realize you are speaking to something that doesn't talk, right?"

"Doesn't matter. I understand her perfectly." I totally didn't.

Chirp! Chirp!

"Like, I know that was not nice." I clicked my tongue.

Chirp!

"Yeah." I leaned back on my arm, my brow lifting. "She really doesn't like you."

He huffed again, his head wagging.

"Where have you been?"

He blew a sharp exhale. "Needed to take care of something."

"You going to tell me what that something is?"

"No." He stood, tugging off his T-shirt, exposing his broad, tattooed chest, his muscles rippling and moving under his skin, his jeans hanging low on his hips, displaying the deep V-line. I sucked in, darting my eyes to the side.

Chhhiiirrrppp.

"I second that... dammmnnn." Opie's voice tugged my attention back to the pillow. Both sat with their mouths open, staring at Warwick, blinking as if they were in a trance.

Chirp.

"Yeah..." Opie sighed. "He is dreamy."

"Oh no, not you guys too." I ground my teeth. Warwick didn't need a bigger fan club. "Go!" I waved them off.

"But your room needs cleaning, Master Fishy." Opie didn't move, his eyes glossing over. "I could lick—I mean clean—his clothes. Do your jeans need mending while you are still in them?"

Warwick's eyebrows lifted.

"Go," I ordered. "Go explore Madam Kitty's. I'm sure you can find lots of things to make outfits from."

Chirp.

"I think I'm gonna like this outside world too, Bitz." Opie stood up and, in a flash, both disappeared.

Warwick stared after them, his brows crunching together. "Was he wearing a studded collar? And the imp had a butt plug on its head?"

"Yeah. So?" I shrugged as if it was the most normal thing.

"Gods..." He pinched his nose. "And I thought my life was strange before you came into it."

"Where did you go?" Pushing off the covers, I stood up, walking over to him in my barely-there clothes. His neck tensed, his gaze moving away from me.

Grunting, he slipped by me, trying to avoid my touch. He went to the bed, unbuttoning his jeans and tugging them off. His firm ass filled the black boxer briefs. His thick thighs and taut torso were like dangling a gourmet meal in front of the starving. My mouth watered. My body pulsed.

Air stuck in my throat as I watched him crawl onto the mattress, his six-foot-seven frame claiming most of the bed.

"Tell me." My voice came out choppy.

He didn't answer. Rolling over on his back, he stared up at me, tucking my pillow under his head.

"Damn it." I marched to the side of the bed. "Stop being such an asshole. We are in this together, whether we want to be or not."

Hands grabbed my hips, and I was flung down on the mattress. His bulk moved over mine, fitting between my legs. Adrenaline charged up my spine, clipping my air as he pressed down on me, my body instantly reacting.

"Do *not* forget, princess... *I am* an asshole. Actually, I'm worse. I'm death. I crave it like it's air." His thumb slid down my chin to the notch in my throat, a thrill zinging into my veins. "There is a reason I am a legend. Killing and fucking are the only things I enjoy. No one controls me. I control them." He rolled his hips against me. My teeth dug into my lip as my legs automatically widened, craving him as much as it angered me. "There might be a strange link between us, but that doesn't make us *anything*." His hand splayed out over my clavicle, his thumb rubbing over the indention, flames storming through me.

141

Anger and lust.

Desire and hate.

"If I kill you right now, my problem's over." His cock twitched against me, hard and excited.

Death turned him on. And I realized it did me too.

"Then do it." I stared into his eyes. Challenging.

His nose flared, taking me in. I felt the adrenaline course through my veins, the elation.

"All talk, Wolf?" I dared him, my legs wrapping around him, pulling him closer. I could feel my heat and wetness seep into his briefs. A deep groan vibrated up his throat. "Do it now… end this."

His jaw strained, his hand pressing down harder.

"Want this to end? To never have to feel again?" I arched into him, my bones quaking with the intense sensation.

"Kovacs," he growled, tightening his grip. My eyes watered, and my core pulsed with need. "Fuck… You like it," he hissed.

"Go ahead. I won't even fight you." I struggled to speak, pushing my neck against his hold.

"Goddammit," he snarled.

I waited several more beats for him to act, our eyes locked on each other.

My mind focused on his breathing, reaching inside toward him.

"Stop." He huffed, putting his full weight on me.

Again, I was no match physically, but impulse had me reaching deeper inside him. Absorbing. Using. With strength I could not possess myself, my legs squeezed his hips, flipping us over like he weighed nothing. His eyes went wide as I flung him on his back, my body now atop his.

"What the fuck?" he muttered.

Ignoring him, I clutched his neck, leaning into him, dragging my hips over his cock. "Don't forget, Farkas. I can kill too. Death and violence also follow me like a shadow. I am not your minion, pet, or whore. And *no one* controls me either." I pressed into him harder, my lips grazing his ear, trying to ignore his rock-hard erection between my legs, my body aching to ease the need battering against my senses. How easy it would be. Just a tug of fabric, and he would be inside me.

"You had your *one* chance. Don't *ever* threaten to kill me again." I shoved him back into the pillow, crawled off him, and strolled out the door.

I had been in the depths of hell and dragged myself out. Survived.

No one would control me again.

I should have known the serenity of the lukewarm bath would not last long. My life was now tangled with a feral animal's, with no sense of privacy.

Bam!

The door slammed open and Warwick's barely dressed form barreled into the room. He could be silent as a ghost and loud as an angry bear.

"What the fuck is this?" He wiggled sheets of paper at me.

"The spa menu." I closed my lids again, my arms out on the edges, the milky water hardly hiding my naked body, but I no longer cared. "I ordered a deep massage at ten."

"Don't fuck with me. What is this?"

I pried my lashes open, peering at the items he was holding. My stomach sank, seeping slowly down the drain along with the blood and dirt.

"Where did you get these?"

"Why?" I sat up, my wet hair clinging to my breasts.

"Answer me," he growled.

Sighing, I pulled myself out of the tub. Grabbing the thin towel hanging on the hook, I wrapped it around myself and marched past him.

"Kovacs." He caught me in the hall, yanking me back into him.

I could see people in my periphery in the hallway, stopping, watching. Even in a whore house, the sight of Warwick in his boxer briefs and me in a tiny towel seemed to stir up excitement and curiosity.

"Where the fuck did you get these?"

"Why should I tell you?"

"I'm not messing around."

"Neither am I. You withhold information from me. I can do the same." I didn't back down, stepping even closer, my voice going husky. "You know, just looking out for *myself*." I grabbed the papers from his hand, twisted, and took two steps for the bedroom.

"Goddamn it, woman." Arms looped around me, flipping me into the air with a strangled yelp. Warwick tossed me over his shoulder, carrying me to the room. With a bang, he slammed the door behind us and tossed me on the bed, the tiny towel unknotting as I smacked onto the mattress.

Warwick's eyes didn't move from my face, but I still felt his attention move hungrily over my slight curves, making me highly aware of each one. The sensation of fingers trailed up my thigh, hands grazing every surface of my wet skin.

Desire.

Hate.

"Stop it!" I grabbed the towel, wrapping it back over me, though it did nothing to barricade me from Warwick, from this twisted game.

He smirked.

"I don't have to tell you anything. As you don't seem to feel the need to do with me." I got up on my knees on the bed, holding the towel painfully to my chest.

"Fucking hell." He ran both hands through his hair, growling under his breath. "You are the most infuriating person I've ever met."

"Same to you," I snapped.

"Fuck! Fine! I'll tell you everything… what I've eaten and when I piss during the day. But tell me about these first." He pointed to the papers lying next to me.

"How do you even know what they are?" My anger dropped, skepticism straightening out my shoulders.

"Kovacs." He rubbed his forehead roughly.

"I stole them from Istvan." I picked up the documents. "I snuck into his office. He had files on me… on this doctor…"

"Doctor Rapava."

My lungs jilted. "How do you know that name?"

"I will tell you, but continue." He folded his arms.

"When I was with Killian, he was testing the pills I stole the night I got caught and was put into Halálház. For every person he tested, something strange happened. They changed… then they died. Except me. My body fought it off."

"Wait, he was testing you?" Rage gathered on his shoulders.

"I was his first subject, but he tried it on others, and they all got sick and died horrendous deaths." I swallowed, sitting back on my heels. "But I got stronger. Healthier. The more he gave me, the more I became a fortress."

Warwick started to pace, his mind clearly churning.

"When did you stop taking them?"

"I don't know… a week or maybe a few days before you got me out? Why?"

"Because…" He peered up at the ceiling. "I tried to reach for you, but I felt nothing. I thought whatever had been there was gone." He wouldn't look at me. "It wasn't until the night on the veranda at the palace I felt you again."

"You were there. I mean, not just in my head. You were nearby, weren't you?"

He strode to the dresser, yanked open a drawer, pulled out a bottle of brandless liquor, and took a huge gulp. He shook his head with a grunt. He didn't answer, but I didn't need him to. I could feel the truth. He had been there many nights before. Stalking. Watching. Waiting for signs of life. Of me.

"He had a tree fairy try to work her magic on me. I was able to fight it."

"You were able to ignore a siren's advances as well." He gestured out the door to where Nerissa was.

"At least one of us did," I muttered. His eyes darted to me, then lowered.

"Do you think this formula is what makes up the pills you found?" Warwick nodded at the papers.

"Possibly. The similarities I saw with the people at Killian's and what this Dr. Rapava is going for can't be coincidental." I shook my head as the memories attacked me. "It was awful. The test subjects became like machines; they felt no pain. They grew stronger, tougher, and had no other thought than doing someone's bidding. But when they died, their brains pretty much melted." Images of the way the girl died caused me to shiver. I had no doubt the first lady I met was probably one of those mindless creatures by now. "Istvan... I think he's trying to make a super-human army. And now Killian has it. He could do the same. I know the pills Killian found have fae essence in them."

"*Nyasgem!*" Warwick slammed his fists into the dresser, taking a few deep breaths. "Get dressed."

"What? Where are we going?"

"You wanted me to tell you what I've been doing?" He grabbed his jeans off the floor. "I'm going to show you instead."

Chapter 16

Deep in the hooded jacket I took from the box full of lost garments and items left from clients at Kitty's, I ducked farther into Warwick's back, the motorcycle speeding over the bumpy streets. The rain pelted at my exposed skin as the wind whipped brutally against my face.

It was late morning, the weather keeping most people off the streets, but it was still dangerous to be this exposed.

Warwick tried to shroud himself under a hat and driving goggles, pebbles and rain kicking up into his face, but the man drew attention no matter how much he tried to hide. His entire presence demanded it, even if he were asleep.

Probably even dead.

Heading northeast, Warwick turned down a grand lane that I had never seen before. The lines dividing the street were no longer there, but it stretched at least six lanes across, as if they wanted the whole city to fit here. Sitting back on wide crumbling sidewalks were large decrepit buildings. Relics of a time long past. Stylish large homes, neglected museums, theaters, cafes, and shops were boarded up and falling apart, but they still showed their elegance, the desolated structures screaming old money.

I had heard of this area. It was where a lot of the elite living in Leopold came from. Most abandoned their grand mansions and elaborate townhomes on the illustrious Andrássy Avenue to hide in the protective walls under Istvan's protection, while the rest of the world fell apart and was overtaken by nature and poverty.

Graffiti covered walls, trash was everywhere, and campfires burned in front of long-abandoned designer stores and pricy cafes. Some mansions were burned out or on the precipice of tumbling down. People built makeshift camps in gardens, using the overgrown plants for shelter. The prestigious area was now no more than a campground for the underprivileged, the destitute, and abused.

Warwick whisked the bike down a lane where groups of savages peered at us with interest, their eyes tracking us through the rain, ready to take or attack. Guns and knives were pulled out as we passed, their bodies threatening and defensive.

Warwick pressed into me as if to say, "Stay alert and close."

Weaving the bike down another lane, he slowed to a stop.

"On foot from here." He waited for me to climb off before he followed, tucking the bike under some overgrown foliage. "Keep on guard."

Nodding, silently I followed, knowing it was pointless to ask him where we were going. The gun he gave me before we took off was kept cocked and ready to use. Still not accustomed to a place so lawless, I had to remember out here no civility existed.

Warwick pulled me into buildings and out, his head constantly snapping around, the tension in his body tangible. I could feel his nerves licking against mine as if they were crawling through me as well.

We stepped into a building that had been burned, black soot painting the walls, the rainy sky darkening the chilly space to almost blackness.

Click.

The muzzle of a gun rammed into my temple, silent as the dead. Two huge outlines appeared from a burned-out hallway, moving in on us from either side.

Terror dropped my stomach and stole the air in my lungs.

"Drop your weapons. Both of you." The voice was low and cold. Detached.

"No," Warwick growled.

"You have two seconds to drop it, or I will shoot her in the fuckin' head. Your pretty girlfriend's brains will be all over the floor."

My chest struggled to move as I lifted my gun, showing I would cooperate, moving slowly to place it down.

"It's me, you fucking morons." Warwick turned his head to the speaker. "And if you touch her, I will use your entrails as wall art."

The figures moved in closer. My head swung between them. Identical, the guys were almost as tall as Warwick, built with thick necks and longer noses. Compared to anyone other than Warwick, they'd be intimidating. Handsome in a unique way, their eyes were so dark brown they appeared black. They had pure white hair that looked like fur and only appeared to be in their twenties. The way they moved, stalking and ready to strike, reminded me of bears, giving me little doubt they were shape-shifters.

Polar bears.

"Then you know how it goes," the same guy replied. He seemed to be the leader of the two, the other one keeping his gun aimed at us. "Never can be too careful."

Warwick scoffed. "You think anyone could pass as me?"

The first twin simply shrugged. "The lieutenant still doesn't trust you after the stunt you pulled."

Finally, Warwick huffed, handing his gun to the second guy, the first one taking mine.

"This way, legend. Keep your hands where I can see them." The first one sneered, sticking his pistol into Warwick's back, pushing him forward. The other one got behind me, doing the same, trailing after the other two.

Trust was something I had been low on lately, but all I could do was go forward and believe Warwick knew what the fuck he was doing.

"It'll be fine, princess." Warwick's voice rose into my ear, the feel of him next to me making me jump. My eyes darted around, knowing I wouldn't see what my brain was sure of.

Him behind me.

In front of me, Warwick curved his head enough to smirk at me.

"Bastard," I whispered under my breath, producing a low chuckle from him.

The guard grunted behind me, pushing me forward. We went through several guarded gates, upstairs and down, twisting and turning down various hallways. A perfect maze to confuse or trap any intruder.

"Warwick to see the lieutenant." One of the guards spoke into one of those rare high-tech walkie-talkies, which surprised me. They were very expensive and hard to get. I would think only the elite would have technology from the Unified Nations.

Where were we? Who could get access to those in the Savage Lands?

We climbed up some wide curving stairs of the dilapidated mansion to the second floor. Timeworn, wooden floors creaked under my feet as the guards stopped us at what looked like an old receiving room. Thick boards covered the windows, cutting off any light or exposure to the outside world.

Firebulbs bathed the bare room in shadowy light, which glittered off the flaking gold-leaf trim, softening the peeling wallpaper and paint. If you squinted and really used your imagination, you could almost picture this place as it might have been.

We stood for a few moments, tension strung tightly across my shoulders, before we heard footsteps pound up the stairs. A tall, lean figure emerged into the room, dressed in plain brown military pants, a jacket, hat, black boots, and a belt, with three guards behind him.

A sharp gasp ripped through my lungs, my feet stumbling back, not believing it could really be the familiar face that lingered in my childhood memories. His hair was peppered with salt now, but I knew his sharp features, dark bushy eyebrows that had always been in contrast to his lighter hair, and the deep scar that twisted the side of his face. He'd gotten the wound in battle, saving my father's life. He'd been a constant at my father's side—his right-hand man—who I'd believed died in the same battle my father did over five years earlier.

Lieutenant General Takacs.

"Un-Uncle Andris?" I stared at the ghost before me. His "remains" had been buried near my father. I had attended his funeral.

The man's head jerked to me, his light blue eyes finding mine. Shock parted his lips.

"Brexley?" He stared at me as if *I* was the manifestation, slowly moving toward me. "*Drágám…*" *My dear.*

"How-how is this possible?" He was really here. In the flesh. "You are dead… I-I went to your funeral."

His boots hit my borrowed ones, his slender frame standing over me. "You shouldn't be here, *drágám*." His head snapped to Warwick. "Why did you bring her? She shouldn't be here. Involved with this…"

"*I* shouldn't be here?" I exclaimed, my brain ready to explode. "You're supposed to be dead. I stood next to your wife and cried with her."

"For all intents and purposes, I am dead," he said softly, cupping my face tenderly. The man was a strange contradiction. He looked foreboding and intimidating, almost cruel. But he was the opposite, at least with me. He always brought me gifts and treated me like the daughter he and his wife never had.

"*Nagybacsi.*" *Uncle.* Tears batted at my eyes. I'd called him uncle since I was six, even though he was not a blood relation. Never knowing my father's mother or my real uncle, Mykel, my father did his best to create a family for me.

Andris and Rita Takacs had been that family to me. She had died two years ago of a lung disease when a virus swept through our country and she couldn't fight it. Losing her had felt like losing the last bit of my father. Of my family.

"I don't understand. How is this possible?" I stared up at him in disbelief.

"No... No, this can't be. He would not want you to be part of this." He shook his head vehemently, ignoring my questions, his eyes watering, his hands clutching my arms, pulling me into a tight embrace. Holding me so tightly. It was like I stepped back in time, and I was a little girl again, surrounded by love and people who cared about me. Protected.

Nagybacsi held me as if he never wanted to let go, rocking me back and forth. "I promised him, *dragam*... I made a vow to protect you the best way I could. I tried... You shouldn't be here." He leaned back, anguish filling his eyes.

"Who?" Though I already knew who. It was written all over his face. The only man Andris had ever shown any affection to.

My father.

"Is he... Is he still alive?" A bubble of hope floated up my chest but was quickly popped as soon as I looked into Andris's eyes.

"No, *dragam*... he's not. He died that night."

Nodding, I tried to hold back a wave of tears. It was something I already knew, but for a brief moment, I wanted to hope. Believe.

Andris and my father were as close as brothers. My father had told me they could read each other from hundreds of feet away, know the other's move without speaking. It made them great partners in war. Andris was my father's second on the battlefield. My dad was passionate and would run toward danger in a blink, while Andris was a planner, followed the rules. They had a perfect balance, saving each other's lives countless times.

"She was supposed to be returned." Andris's gaze flicked to Warwick again angrily, stepping away from me. "She was supposed to stay in Leopold."

"Don't look at me. This girl can't stay out of trouble." Warwick moved in next to me, folding his arms. He towered over Andris.

"You were *supposed* to make sure. Protect her! After what you did..." Andris puffed up, his face turning red with fury, moving to Warwick. "Why did you bring her here?"

"I can't force her to do anything." Warwick challenged back. "If you haven't noticed, she's got a mind of her own and a will more stubborn than anyone I've ever met." He stepped into Andris. "Plus, she doesn't need anyone to protect her. She's stronger and a better fighter than most. She survived Halálház… got through the Games, which is far more than anyone else in this room right now."

Andris took a breath, rubbing at his dark eyebrows. "This was not how this was meant to go."

"Tell me about it." Warwick snorted.

"Wait, what do you mean? What the fuck is going on?" My head snapped back and forth between the two, my heart speeding up.

Andris tilted his head at me, a deep sigh exhaling from his lungs. "First, tell me, why did you leave Leopold?"

I licked my lips nervously.

"It's okay, Kovacs, you can tell him." Warwick stood next to me. Though his mouth did not move, a copy of him stood on the other side of me, growling in my ear. It should have freaked me out, but strangely it didn't. I was growing used to it. It calmed me, as if we could have a private moment without anyone knowing whenever we needed one.

"I had to." Swallowing, I looked up at Andris. "I was no longer safe there."

"Why?"

"Because Istvan thought I was spying for Killian… and because… because…" I couldn't say it out loud, the fear gutting my stomach.

Andris's eyes rolled over me, his jaw twitching, a deep sigh coming from him. "Because he *knows* the truth about you…"

The truth about you.

The words poured over my skin, scorching my throat.

"Wha-what?" My voice came out in a breath of fear.

"Dragam." Andris touched my arm. "There is so much to tell you… I just wish it wasn't under these circumstances. This is not what your father wanted."

At the mention of my father, tears filled my eyes, my lashes batting them away. "What didn't he want? What does Istvan know?" I nipped my lip, daring to ask the question sitting on my chest for a while. "What is wrong with me?"

Andris peered around at the room at his guards. "Please go back to your stations."

The blond polar bear twins, along with the other guards, nodded and quickly headed out as Andris steered me toward what looked like a bookcase. The shelf slid to the side, revealing a room behind, decorated with a desk, chairs, and a map of Budapest open on the surface of the desk.

"Please sit. Can I get you anything to drink? Some tea?" Andris walked around the desk, tapping at the walkie-talkie on his belt, ready to direct an order to someone. "We don't have much here, but I can offer you at least a refreshment."

I stared at him. A cup of tea was the last thing on my mind.

"I think we need something stronger for this conversation," Warwick muttered, his palm touching my lower back, pushing me farther into the room, shutting the door/shelf behind us.

Andris bobbed his head, opened the desk drawer, and pulled out a bottle of Unicum. My nose wrinkled automatically. It was a Hungarian staple—a liqueur with a bitter herbal taste I had yet to acquire a palate for. It used to be typically drunk as a digestif and aperitif, but times and scarcity made it an any time liquor. Anything to ease the starkness of reality.

Pulling three small glasses out from the same drawer, Andris poured the amber liquid and shoved two glasses toward us. Warwick drank his down.

"Sit." Andris nodded to the seats, but I didn't move, my body wound up tightly.

"Fuck the drink. Tell me what's going on." I folded my arms, frowning at him.

Andris shot back his drink in one gulp, his face puckering for a moment before he sat down in the office chair.

"When I left, you were just a young girl… now look at you. All grown up."

"Uncle Andris…" I warned, my patience thin.

He took another drink, letting out a breath.

"You know you were born in… unusual times." Andris's dark brown eyes met mine. His mother had been Armenian, while his father was French, giving him such contrasting but striking features.

"Yes, but it doesn't tell me how you are still alive, how you two know each other." I motioned between him and Warwick. "And what you seem to know about me."

Andris chuckled softly. "Patience was never one of your strengths. The same as your father. Jump in and go. You wanted to know everything, do everything yourself, even as a baby."

"Andris." My teeth gritted.

He breathed out slowly. "Losing your mother, raising a baby, and still in charge of protecting Leopold, your father didn't notice anything was unusual until you were much older. I think you were four or five when you climbed up on a banister in HDF and fell off." The memory was so distant and hazy; it felt as if I heard the story, not actually experienced it. "God, blood was everywhere. We were sure you were dead. But you popped right up, wanting to climb back again."

"You know the patience you were speaking of?" I grumbled. The sensation of Warwick brushed my back like a calming balm while his form leaned against the wall several feet away from me. My eyes darted to him, glaring. His lips lifted in a grin.

"You fell farther than two stories, *dragam*, onto a marble floor." He clasped his hands. "When your father rushed you to the clinic, they checked you out, gave you one stitch, and let you go."

"So? I was lucky."

"It was then we started to notice little things. Other kids would get hurt and take weeks to heal, yet you did in just a few days."

My mind flashed to how many times I had been beaten and then taken to the HDF clinic after training, and after a couple of hours, I headed back for more, feeling fine.

"The healing around them appears to be at least three years old. Much longer than her time away." Dr. Karl's words flared back through my mind.

"So I heal fast." I folded my arms, glancing off to the side.

"You have never been sick. Have you?" Andris asked. "Caden got colds, flu, chickenpox, pink eye… and you got nothing. He almost died of scarlet fever. Do you remember? Very contagious. While you never even got the sniffles."

"I have a strong immune system." According to Dr. Karl, I had off the charts, abnormally strong immunity.

"I recall a time I was playing with you, and you moved so quickly I didn't even see it… even though you stood right in front of me."

I swallowed, my throat closing in on me.

"Only three people know this story, and two of them are dead." Andris took another drink. "Do you remember our cat?"

"Aggie." I had loved that sweet, old cat.

"You found it dead in the garden. You were so distraught." He rubbed at his head. "If I wasn't standing there, if your father hadn't seen it also, I would have thought it was a trick of my brain."

I sucked in. The memory was spotty and muddled. I had only been six, but I was sure the cat was still alive when I found it. It died on my lap.

"You were sobbing and went to pet it." Andris shook his head. "The cat came back to life."

"What?" I stepped back, feeling the wall press into my spine.

"It climbed in your lap and meowed. You were so scared you jerked your hand away. It instantly went limp. Dead."

"Maybe it wasn't dead before," I whispered.

"*Rigor mortis* had already set in." Andris sat back. "Believe me, we tried to come up with every excuse possible. But that moment set your father on a trek, a quest for answers."

"Answers?"

"Answers to what you were."

"So, what are you saying? I'm fae?" I let my fear slide off my tongue, my chest clamping down in terror.

"You're not fae." Warwick shook his head, his forehead rumpling, his eyes digging in as if he were trying to see past my shell, poke in and find a reason.

"How do you know?"

"Your parents were both human and mortal," Andris replied.

"You knew my mother?"

"Met her once." He nodded. "Eabha was stunning." My mother's name drove into my chest, hearing the lyrical AY-va sing from his lips. My father used it so little, always saying *your mother*, I almost forgot she was a person, with a name. A woman with hopes and dreams. Not some fairytale I made up in my head. "Your father was devastated when he returned from the war to find she had died the night of the Fae War. Between your birth and the magic from the Otherworld crashing into Earth, her body couldn't take it... He never even got to say goodbye."

I licked my bottom lip, peering at the ground, the guilt of her death on my conscience. I understood his subtle meaning; if she had been secretly fae, she wouldn't have died in childbirth or from the magic. Humans succumbed to that.

"Then there is no way I could have brought the cat back to life." I could hear the hope in my voice, the need to counter the sickening squeeze deep in my soul.

"As far as I know, only necromancers can raise the dead." Warwick's focus trailed up and down me. "You are not that."

A picture I saw once of a necromancer scared the crap out of me. Skin and bones, hooded in robes, ghostly looking monsters.

They were the origin of the image of death with a scythe.

"What about a natural obscurer? Isn't Queen Kennedy rumored to be one... that she can raise the dead?"

"You'd have to be a Druid." Uncle Andris shook his head. "A *very* powerful one."

Right.

A natural obscurer came from the most dominant Druid line. Their mothers purposely worked with black magic while pregnant, wanting the power to seep into the unborn child. And yet, it was still a long shot the baby would become one. The leader of the Unified Nations was exceptional and queen for a reason. Her roots came from the most top-tier Druid.

"Then what am I?"

"We don't know." A pained expression settled on Andris's face. "At least, I don't think your father ever learned. He grew more and more withdrawn. Slipping out, leaving for days. He stopped telling me anything, saying it was for Rita's and my protection. If Istvan found out what he knew…" Andris choked over the last few words. "All he made me promise was to keep you safe. Make sure Istvan never learned what we suspected."

"By putting him as my guardian?" I tossed my arms out.

"I was supposed to be your guardian." Andris tipped his head. "But it could not be. I talked your father into making Istvan your caretaker."

"Why? Then I'd be right under Istvan's nose."

"Exactly." Andris's gaze snapped to mine.

"Keep your enemies so close they become family," Warwick stated, nodding in understanding. "Blind them to suspicion."

"It worked too." Andris folded his hand on his lap. "For the last five years, you have been hidden right in the open. Your father and I knew that the closer you were to the Markos family, the safer you were. Until…" He shook his head at me.

Until I landed my ass in Halálház.

"*Baszd meg.*" I swiped the liquor off the table and slammed it back, the pungent taste burning my throat. I banged the glass back down on the table and glared at Andris. He filled all three cups without hesitation, watching me down the second.

"You have grown up so much, Brexley. The pictures of you don't do you justice."

"Pictures of me?" I tapped my glass for another. I hated the taste of Unicum, but the burn grounded me. "You've been watching me this whole time?"

"Of course."

"You owe me answers. What is this place? Why are you hiding here, and why did you fake your own death? Also, how do you know each other?" I motioned between the two men.

"My 'death' was necessary. I knew too much… had seen too much. I could no longer carry out Markos's orders. It was only me who was supposed to *die* the night of that battle, slip away into the night. Your father would have never left you. Ever. But things went wrong. I don't even know what exactly; everything was going to plan. But we got separated. It was too late by the time I found him." Grief flashed over Andris's face. "I failed him…"

My head bowed, clearing my throat. "Why was your death necessary?"

"We'll get to that." Andris stood up, finishing his second drink. "As for this place, it is one of the hideouts for the Resistance…"

"Resistance?" My mouth parted in shock, another puzzle piece clicking in. I knew of only one Resistance party in this area. "Y-you're part of Sarkis's Army?"

"*Dragam.*" He smirked, his arms behind his back. "*I am* Sarkis."

I blinked at him. "Oh, my gods…"

It was like I was hit with a bat, and memories and pieces all fell into place. The stuffed puppy he had given me was named Sarkis. It didn't click until now. The signs were right under my nose.

Sarkis was an Armenian word meaning *protector, shepherd.* He had named his army the same as the toy that kept me feeling safe and protected as a child when they left on missions, like a clue. I may have stopped cuddling with the toy so long ago I had almost forgotten him, but my shepherd never stopped protecting, guiding, and watching over me.

Chapter 17

I gripped my head and plunked down in the chair, my head spinning.

Andris Takacs, the man I thought was dead, was not only alive, but leading the Resistance army.

"Breathe," Warwick's husky voice slithered up my spine, the feel of him at my side, even though I knew he still leaned against the other wall, sipping Unicum.

I inhaled, letting out a slow breath, not fighting his instruction and the soothing effect his voice had on me.

"I know it's a lot to take in." Andris stood stiffly behind his desk, watching me. I didn't sense any emotion in his voice, but deep in his eyes, I saw his love.

"A lot to take in?" I huffed. "I can barely handle the fact you are still alive and that you could leave Rita like you did."

"It was her idea."

"What?" I jolted.

"She knew my time was running out." He licked his lips nervously. "Brexley, Rita and I loved each other, but not the way you thought. We weren't in love with each other. She was a wonderful woman. She meant everything to me. But she knew I was in love with another."

"What?" I bolted up. "You were cheating on Rita?"

"She knew and was fine with it. Our marriage was never one of romantic love. It grew into deep respect and friendship. When I heard of her passing, part of me died with her. She knew her life was better where it was, and that mine was here."

"How did you fake your own death? Why did you?" I exclaimed. "What made you leave… her? Me?"

He flinched at the last part, sorrow wrinkling his brow. "I had to leave."

"Why?"

"I fell in love with a fae."

I choked, sensing a hand I knew wasn't actually there rubbing my back. "Fae?"

"We met on one of your father's quests, many, many years ago, in China." A smile I had never seen before hinted on his face. "She halted me in my steps. She overwhelmed me. I tried to fight it, deny it. I hated myself, accused her of glamouring me. But no, it was just her." He chuckled lightly. "Benet used those trips as cover, telling Istvan we were gathering information on our enemy while trying to find any information he could about you. Those months traveling, we saw the worst and best of humanity. And I realized HDF's teachings were wrong. There was kindness, family, beauty, compassion, and love among the fae. They laughed like us, teased like us, loved like us. They were not the monsters we were told they were. *We were.*

"While Istvan's path was set on greed and hate, my path, your father's path, changed. I fell in love with a beautiful soul. A shape-shifter. She showed me the injustice out there. Opened my eyes to the inequality and prejudice on both sides. Once my eyes were open, I could no longer be the soldier Istvan demanded. He wanted me to kill without question, slaughter fae children and women, while I wanted to fight for those who couldn't fight for themselves." He let his arms drop. "Istvan knew something was wrong and that I was changing allegiances. He started to have me followed. I knew it wouldn't be long before they found out my secret. If they found her, they would have tortured and killed her. And me. Possibly Rita."

My chin hit my chest thinking of how quickly Istvan had turned on me. Killing a traitor's fae lover would not even be a blip on his radar.

"Rita was the one to come up with the plan, fearing at any moment Istvan would find me out. It was me who was supposed to 'die' on the battlefield. But like I said that night, everything went wrong." Andris's jaw twitched with emotion. "I am so sorry, *dragam*, that I couldn't save your father. I was never able to tell you that. I miss him every day too. He was a wonderful man. And he loved you more than life."

I peered down at my hands, fighting back tears.

"I've been trying to watch you as best I could to follow his wishes. I had hoped you would live a safe and comfortable within the walls of Leopold, never knowing the difference."

My head shot up. "You think living in ignorance and hate is better? To be stifled and miserable? Married to an abusive man who would beat me for fun, my days spent learning how to cover my bruises for parties? Being no more than a doll? You think that's the life I wanted?"

Andris dropped his head. "But at least it would have been safe."

"Safe?" I stood. "That's not safe. And it's not the life I want. My eyes are opened now as well. I felt it the moment I came back to HDF. I no longer fit—if I ever did. I can never go back." I rolled my shoulders back. "People have tried to control me my whole life, out of love or power. No more. I'm in this fight now."

Andris watched me for a moment, his eyes softening. "You are so much like your father."

"Thank you." My chin lifted.

"I see danger and violence still surround you." A quiet but strong woman's voice spoke behind me. I hadn't even heard the door slide open.

I recognized the tone, one I never thought I'd hear again. Especially here.

I whirled around, my eyes taking in the figure, but my brain struggled to understand.

The tiny girl I'd been forced to whip in Halálház, the girl who saved my ass and protected me, stood before me.

"Ly-Lynx?" My brain could not understand her presence.

A gentle smile pulled up her pretty round face, which was framed by long, shiny straight hair hanging down loosely. Out of the prison uniform, in tighter fitting clothes, she appeared a little older but still young and sweet. She strolled past me to Andris. My mouth dropped as she rose on her toes, kissing him.

What. The. Fuck?

"*Szerelmem.*" *My love.* Andris grinned blissfully down at her, wrapping his arm around her waist, kissing her softly again. "Everything proceeding as planned?"

"There are some complications." She lowered back down, handing him a file.

"What the hell is happening right now?" I pressed my palm to my head, my mind twisting and turning, trying to keep up.

Lynx was the woman he fell in love with so long ago? She looked barely more than sixteen, but being fae, she could be centuries older.

"I'm so confused."

"I can imagine." Andris dropped his arm from Lynx. "Istvan thought you were dead, and Killian didn't have a clue who he had captured until that little comrade had to share it with everyone. But I always knew where you were the whole time. Had eyes everywhere. Tried to watch out for you in any way I could."

"Oh, gods…" My mind flashed back to the times Lynx helped me. *Protected* me.

"But she was in there before me… how?"

"She was caught on another mission, but through a guard, I was able to stay in contact. I got a message to Ling to watch over you." He nodded down to the girl I knew as Lynx. Of course, she wouldn't use her real name in there. His gaze flicked to the corner. "I acquired alliances I never thought I'd find."

"Enemy of your enemy hardly makes us allies," Warwick muttered.

"It does in this world." Andris moved away from Ling, dropping the file on his desk.

I jerked to face Warwick.

"You knew who I was the whole time?"

"Not the *whole* time, but soon after." He smirked, his cerulean eyes focusing on me.

I felt tricked. Stupid. As if I was the only one not let in on a joke.

"My plan to get Ling and you out had to be bumped up when your identity was discovered and you went into the Games." Andris scanned some papers. "We blew up Halálház, freed you, helped Warwick bomb Lord Killian's to help you escape… and now I'm guessing from HDF as well."

"I had some left over." Warwick shrugged.

I barked a derisive laugh before downing the rest of the herb liquor. My head spun like a carousel with all the revelations.

"This isn't enough to go on." Andris shut the folder, looking over at Ling. She was so pretty, tiny and delicate, but something told me not to underestimate her.

Ling shook her head. "I'll keep trying, but we are fighting against an exceptionally complicated magic firewall."

"Magic firewall?" I repeated.

"Metaphorically." Andris leaned back on his heels, staring at her with pride. "Ling is what you call a hacker."

"Hacker? What the hell is that?"

"Before you were born, our entire world was run on computers. All information could be found online. Money was handled and transferred digitally, as well. But when the wall fell, magic destroyed technology as we knew it. The King in the Unified Nations has established a new internet that's even more powerful. But here, only the elite can even afford a computer. The problem is this new system is even harder to break into. It's protected by magic. Ling is a Kitsune, a fox-shifter who can deceive and trick magic spells. Sneak in and out of places, virtual or real. Her father was one of the top hackers in her homeland, and he taught her everything. She helped break down the spells guarding Halálház so you all could escape. She is the best out there."

Ling kept her expression even, not responding to his praise.

"A Kitsune who calls herself Lynx?" I lifted an eyebrow.

"Ling-ks." Andris grinned. "The *KS* stands for Kitsune."

"My brain hurts." A laugh barked up my throat. So many puzzle pieces to try to put together.

"I will try another backdoor in." Ling leaned in, kissing Andris again. She nodded at me before turning for the door. I watched the woman who took a whipping from me. Now I understood why she helped me, protected me. Why she was so nice to me.

Because she was asked to.

The moment her footsteps retreated down the stairs, Warwick strode to the desk.

"Can we get to why we're here since she's all caught up?" Warwick tossed down the folded sheets of paper.

"What the hell?" I grappled inside my coat, where I had kept the documents, finding the inside pocket empty. "How did you do that?"

He curved his face, his mouth only a few inches from mine. "You're not the only one who can move without being seen."

Air caught in my throat at his proximity. I couldn't seem to acclimate to him. To not respond to the carnal intensity he carried.

Andris's finger pinched the papers and picked them up, his pupils tracking over the documents, the color draining from his face. "Where did you get this?" His gaze darted to Warwick, then me. "How did you come by this? Is this real?"

"It's real." Warwick nodded at me. "Ask her."

"Where did you get it?" Agitation rose in his voice.

"I-I…" I swallowed. "I stole it from Istvan. It was in his safe."

"And he knows you have it?" Andris lowered the papers to look at me fully.

"Yes."

Andris whispered, almost to himself, before his hand hit the desk.

"*Szar.*" *Shit.* He hissed through his teeth. "He found it… what your farther and I were afraid of."

"What do you mean?"

"This document was one of the things Markos had your father and me searching for. It was during those trips we were trying to find anything out about you." Andris flipped between the two pages I was able to steal. "He had read about this scientist, Dr. Rapava. The more he learned about him, the more obsessed he became with this man's work. He liked the idea of humans becoming the superior race again. He wanted to destroy fae and take back what he felt was rightfully ours. It didn't seem to occur to him that it was technically their land first. *We* sent *them* into hiding. Humans have invaded, massacred, and taken over territory since the beginning of time, but all he could see was what they had taken from us.

"Markos is obsessed with power. Every battle we lost, he got more possessed with this idea. Of humans advancing, become stronger, be unbeatable in a war against the fae." Andris shook the pages. "Using Rapava's work was how he wanted to do it. Replicate his formula in powder form. The problem was, the doctor went to the States in the far West, where all his advanced work was said to be destroyed. We knew some of his early experimental notes survived. Another scientist had some of them and Rapava's first experiment journals. We continued to tell Istvan that it was merely a rumor, but it looks like he continued looking and discovered it since." Andris slapped the documents down. "Damn it. This is bad…"

"About to get worse." I cringed. "Istvan not only found Rapava's formula but is copying and producing it. I don't know how, but he is. He's sending it to other countries, probably building an alliance with all top leaders there are while lining their pockets." A pang hit my chest, as I still mourned the man I thought I knew, the man who spent hours teaching me chess. Istvan had been aloof, but I never thought of him as a monster. "He has been shipping pills to the Czech Republic." To the leader he wanted to sell me off to as a wife. "And I have no doubt to Ukraine and beyond now."

Now I realized how sinister Caden's marriage was. It was part of Istvan's power grab, to become the ruler of all, eventually becoming more powerful than the strongest leaders in the Eastern Bloc.

"He's producing pills? He's been able to procure *fae essence*?" Andris exhaled harshly. The two words sounded like a weight hitting the floor. "How?"

"I don't know." I wagged my head.

"How do you know this? How do you know Istvan is producing them?"

"Because they were the reason I was caught and put into Halálház. I stole them from a shipment heading to Prague."

"Stole them?" His dark eyes carved into me. "Do you still have them?"

My stomach laced together in knots, fear riding up my spine.

"No." I pinched my lips. "Killian has them."

Andris went still, his ribs pushing against the fabric of his jacket.

"The fae leader has these pills?"

I nodded.

"You have seen them?"

"Yes, I saw his test subjects." I licked my lips. "And I am one of them."

It was like I'd dropped a bomb in the room. The silence burst into the space, choking and expanding.

"You. Are. One?" Andris's nose flared, his eyes wide.

"He tested them on me first, but nothing happened to me." A bead of sweat dotted the back of my neck, the significance of my revelation hitting me.

Nothing happened to me.

Because I wasn't normal.

"No one else survived." I unzipped my jacket, heat enveloping my skin.

"What happened to them?"

"They all died. Painfully. But there was a stage where they turned machinelike and became aggressive and easy to control. They attacked on command and had an extremely high pain tolerance."

"But not you?"

"No."

"Her body fought it." Warwick leaned back against the wall, arms folded. "Became stronger, just like me."

"What do you mean?" I glanced at him.

"You think no one's tried to kill me in other ways besides coming straight for me? Poison my food and drink?" He tilted his head. "But my body fought it off, growing stronger instead."

Because of his increased Immunoglobulin M levels protecting him...

Like mine.

That couldn't be a coincidence. I just didn't know what it meant.

Andris started to pace, his hands on his hips.

"How long were you tested? When did they start changing?"

"Killian tested me for about two weeks. I stopped taking the pills about a week ago. Nothing ever happened to me, but when I was down in his labs,

I saw what happened to people on them. It took about twenty-four hours before they started to go mad. I think it was around day four or five they went into the catatonic state. He had one try to attack me."

"What?" Warwick pushed off the wall.

"She was behind bars. I was fine." I waved him off. "But I had never seen anything like it. They were robots, then they flipped, turning into feral animals. The only thing she wanted to do was kill me until he ordered her to stop. She had been like that for a few days. After that..." I shook my head. "They start dying—their brain basically melts."

Andris continued to pace behind his desk. "As if we didn't have a big enough battle to fight, now both our enemies have the formula and are using it."

"I don't think Killian wants to use it against us. I think he wanted to know what Istvan was planning."

Andris's head snapped to me. "Don't be naïve. Killian is ruthless. He is going to use this against us."

"I don't believe Killian would do that."

"Why are you defending him?" Warwick sneered.

"I'm not." I switched weight to my other leg. "I just don't believe he feels threatened by humans. He seemed more disconcerted by what they did."

"Disconcerted?" Andris left out a harsh laugh. "The man is merciless and cruel. Mark my words, he will use this against us."

"That wasn't what I saw."

Andris halted, his eyes wide on me. "You like him..."

"No—"

Warwick snorted, his eyes flashing at the knowledge of how he'd found me with Killian.

"Don't be a fool, girl. He was playing you. He will slaughter us without a thought. You cannot trust him," Andris stated.

My mouth opened to respond, but footsteps outside the door interrupted us. I twisted to see a man dressed in all dark clothes, boots, and hat.

"Lieutenant, here to report in." He lifted his head, showing me his profile.

Holy shit.

My room tipped, shock almost dipping my legs, another blow hitting me.

Soft brown eyes, silky brown hair, his tall stature proud and graceful.

"Za-Zander?" My mouth dropped, eyes running over the horse-shifter. What the hell was going on?

"Brexley? Oh, my gods." His eyes widened with disbelief, moving instantly to me, his arms wrapping around me, pulling me into his warm chest. "What are *you* doing here?"

"I was about to ask you the same thing." Though Andris's earlier words already came back to me.

"But through a guard, I was able to stay in contact."

"Oh, gods, you're *the* guard." I leaned back, pointing to him, then to Andris. "He's with you."

Uncle Andris's head bowed in confirmation.

Zander's assistance, helping me escape both Halálház and at Killian's palace, became crystal clear. He was part of the Resistance.

A spy.

"What happened? I thought you were back at HDF?" Zander reached out, touching my face, his eyes searching mine, his thumb swiping gently over my cheek. "Though I won't lie... It is *so* good to see you."

A growl pulsated through the room. I felt a flash of anger at my back as I sensed Warwick's presence strolling around Zander like he was hunting a gazelle, his lips curled. I looked to the massive form behind me who hadn't moved from his spot. *Stop.* I glowered at him. Warwick's mouth twisted, shifting against the wall.

"You!" Zander's gaze darted over my shoulder, lowering into a glower. "What the hell did you do, Farkas? You were supposed to get her home. Safe." Zander's hand dropped away, stepping closer to the Wolf. "I knew we shouldn't have trusted you." Zander charged for Warwick, his hands shifting into hooves as he smashed them into Warwick's chest. The Wolf only took a small step backward. "*Lófasz a seggedbe!*" *Fuck you! A horse dick into your ass!*

"And here I thought it was her ass you wanted in." Warwick scoffed.

"Fuck you!" Zander shoved him again.

The switch in Warwick was instant.

"Back off, pony." Warwick reclaimed the step, puffing out his chest, his aqua eyes darkening with anger. "You get only *one* warning."

"You are the reason she was even with Killian. Why the lieutenant ever thought we could trust you again, I don't know. Who are you going to sell her to now, Farkas? She's nothing more than a profit for you, isn't she?" Zander bared his teeth, his hooves striking Warwick in his torso.

A powerful rage filled the room and rushed violently over to me.

"Warwick, no!" I belted out but was too late. Warwick's hands clutched Zander's collar as he lifted the horse-shifter and slammed him brutally against the wall, shaking the foundation. Zander's head banged against the wood with a crack.

"You fuckin' touch or threaten me again, I don't care what side you are on… I *will* kill you." Warwick squeezed Zander's neck more tightly, getting close to his face. "Stop thinking you're some hero, coming to save the damsel. She could gut you and wash her hands in your blood before you could even blink, donkey."

Was it sick I found his threat to Zander hot? That he thought me capable of doing that? Fuck… what was wrong with me?

"Warwick, let him down," Andris ordered.

Warwick didn't respond, locked on his prey, fury flexing every muscle.

Not moving from my spot, I felt my ghost self near him, my hand brushing his back, gliding up his enormous arm with fingertips only he could feel. He tensed under my illusory touch, his gaze darting to where he felt my fingertips.

"Let him go," I said calmly from my spot. I knew he could hear me whisper the same words into his ear.

He inhaled sharply, clenched his jaw, and dropped him. Zander slid down the wall, crashing to the ground, gasping and coughing.

"You're lucky she has your back this time, pony boy. Next time you come at me, you better be ready. There won't be anyone to stop me." He stepped back; his eyes still lowered on the horse-shifter.

Zander got to his feet, straightening his clothes, his expression cut with fury and humiliation.

"We have *enough* enemies we're fighting out there," Andris barked, motioning beyond us. "We don't need it in here too." He inhaled and blew out a breath. "Zander, your report."

Zander pushed back his shoulders, his cheeks red, his eyes blazing. "Killian wants her back, is threatening action on HDF. A bounty is on Warwick's head." Zander's eyes darted to us, then back to Andris. "He has been in a rage since her escape. Cleaned house of anyone he suspected of being involved or failing to stop them."

"But he still doesn't suspect you?"

"No." His throat bobbed. "He doesn't. And the one person who did… she's in a healing coma. She can't say anything."

My spine straightened like a rod. "Nyx?" My mouth parted. "She's still alive?"

Zander gave me a firm nod. "Yes, severely injured. The healer thinks she will be in a coma for at least two or three more weeks."

Jamming a hand through my hair, I paced in a circle. If Nyx fully recovered, she would come after me. Nothing would stop her. Not even Killian. I took her lover, and Warwick almost took her life.

"The moment you feel you've been compromised..." Andris left off the rest.

"I know." Zander dipped his head in gratitude. "I'm still of value to you and him if I stay."

"What is he doing in pursuit of her?" Andris flicked his chin at me.

"He still thinks she is at HDF, but since the explosions last night, he's even more frantic to find her. He's connected the bombing at Halálház, the palace, and HDF as the same."

"*Szar!*" Andris thumped his hands on the desk, leaning over. "Has he linked it to us then?"

"Not yet, but he's starting to suspect. He didn't think the Resistance was anything more than a few scattered hoodlums stirring up trouble, but now he's starting to put a few spies out." Zander said. "He ordered a few soldiers to retrieve any bomb materials left from Halálház. He will see the high-grade quality, notice it's the same from the bombing of the night she escaped. He'll know it's more than some homemade bombs."

Andris stared off as if trying to figure out his next step.

"Okay. Thank you, Zander. You can go. We don't need anyone to notice your absence as well right now."

"Thank you, sir." Zander bowed, stepping back, his attention shooting over to me, a smile curling his lips. "Brexley."

"Zander." I grinned back.

"Hope to see you again soon."

"Same."

Zander winked, turned, and marched out of the room.

A growl only I could hear bit at the back of my neck. I curved toward Warwick, lifting an eyebrow.

Blank of emotion, he stared back at me, challenging. I met his stare, folding my arms to match his. The connection between us tightened around my ribs, filling the room with hostility and intensity.

Hate.

Rage.

Dominance.

I could feel him move around me, hinting at my edges, but I shoved back, not wanting the intimacy, wishing the shivers that ran down my frame would go away.

A forced cough drew both of us to the figure staring at us, Andris, whose gaze darted between us as if he could see the webs between us, a frown pulling at his forehead.

"Do you want a tour of the base?" Andris motioned out the doors, speaking to me. "It might be better if you stay here with us now."

"No." Warwick's response barely sounded like a word but was more like a bark.

"It would be safer for her, Farkas." Andris walked toward me, putting himself between us. "It wasn't so long ago you betrayed us, turned her over to Killian. I would rather have her here. Know she's secure. Plus, Killian's men and Markos are out hunting for her and *you*."

Feral and dominant, Warwick's entire body strained.

"Yes, I agree." I grabbed my uncle's arm, my attention locked on Warwick. "I think it would be best. I'd be much safer here. Plus, you are finally free of me."

"Free of you." He scoffed low like it was a joke, the vibration traveling straight between my legs.

"You don't control me." The version of me only Warwick could see strolled around him. *"You might think you are some badass legend everyone bows down to, but not me."*

"Fuck, princess... You are going to be begging for me to control you... to do things with you no one could dream of." His husky breath trailed down my neck, and despite myself, my lashes fluttered, my breath hitching. I was overwhelmed at the sensation of his hands running up my thighs, his physique pressing into me from behind, curving my spine toward him. Heat pounded through my veins, and I struggled to swallow. *"Not only will you bow, but I will have you on your knees pleading for more."* His fingers traced along the band of my pants, slipping under the fabric. I felt like I'd taken the biggest hit of a drug. *"Yeah. You like that, Kovacs?"*

Fuck... I did... too much. A groan sat in my throat, my teeth sawing together. His hand pushed lower.

"Well, thank you, Farkas, for saving Brexley." Andris's voice sliced through the link, snapping me back to reality with a brutal drop. My body twitched at the sudden absence of him. "She means everything to me. I will always be grateful for what you did."

I realized I could so easily slip into my little bubble with Farkas and disregard anything else. Forget reality. Forget he wasn't actually touching me.

"I'm sure you know your way out. You know how to contact me in the future."

"Yes," Warwick responded to Andris, but his smug expression stayed on me, weighty and penetrating.

My uncle, my *nagybacsi,* nodded, patting my arm, pulling me toward the door.

Rotating my neck, I looked at him. "Goodbye."

"Yeah. See you, princess." He didn't even hesitate, strolling past me and down the stairs, not even looking back once, as though I'd finally released him from a cage.

It was for the best. We needed to sever this link between us. Maybe time and distance could at least mute it. Neither of us wanted it, nor did we even like each other.

If it was for the best…

Why did I feel so empty?

Chapter 18

Two levels below the boarded-up mansion, life buzzed and moved around the windowless rooms. The large bunkers were taller than I figured, making it possible to almost forget you were buried in the earth. Not that I could. I despised being underground after months of being without the sun or stars, no fresh air, living in a tomb at Halálház. Being down here prickled at me with deep-seated fear, like being covered with ants.

More than sixty people milled around the base, all dressed in dark clothes, but nothing that screamed "uniform." A collection of shapes, colors, races, and species, most seemed to be in their twenties to thirties, but with fae, you never knew.

The modern underground bunker was larger than the square footage upstairs, telling me it was constructed well after the homes were built above. The large area was broken up into a training room, mess hall, computer room, offices and bathrooms, and bunk rooms were down a hallway.

"This is only some of us. Some choose not to live here. We have over a thousand fighters to our cause, but only about a hundred live here. Nothing compared to Povstat in Prague, but every day more join us." Andris guided me through the bunker.

"This is what we call the hub or the brains of the operation." Andris pulled me to a room where Ling sat, motioning us inside. The space was packed with screens, machines, and other equipment I had no clue about.

The monitors displayed numbers and letters, maps, and what looked to be bomb materials. "Intel, hacking, coding, buying black market items, researching for missions. This room is the crux and where we plan everything." Andris pointed to the screens.

Ling tapped on a keyboard, along with several other people, none of whom even looked up when we entered.

"Wow." I didn't have to know a lot about computers to know this equipment was not only imported, but probably extremely expensive.

"This way is the training room." Andris moved quickly, peering into the room. About twenty people worked out on the mats, perfecting moves. It reminded me a lot of my training at HDF, but here they looked more to be self-training, and there didn't appear to be one lead instructor.

A huge guy darted for a girl only about five foot two on a mat. In two moves, the girl twisted his arm and flipped him over on his back.

Damn.

"Birdie?" Andris called to her. "Come here for a moment."

She blew a piece of loose hair from her face as she strolled over, regarding me with annoyance. She looked to be about my age, short, thin, but had a solid frame, with heavily lined light blue eyes and white-blonde hair, which hung to her ass even in a ponytail. She had a nose ring and piercings up each ear. Wearing all black, her entire persona was defensive and challenging. Ready to fight you, as if she had spent her life proving she wasn't weak, and being a pretty girl didn't make her a target.

Something I understood. It didn't make me like her, though.

"Birdie, Brexley." He introduced us. The fastest forced smile slipped on and off her lips like water.

"Hi." She placed her palms on her hips, then tilted her head. "Wait... Brexley as in *the* Brexley Kovacs?"

"One and the same," I replied dryly.

"She'll be staying here, and I thought you two could room together." He seemed to ignore the tension between us. "She could follow your schedule."

"What?" she exclaimed, already shaking her head. "Oh, hell no. I finally have a single room."

"Birdie." His tone was filled with the warning I remembered so well from my childhood.

"You know I don't get along with people." She glowered at him. "I'm not roommate material."

"Neither am I." I stared her down.

"I think you two have far more in common than you think." He patted our arms. "Brexley, will you be okay? I have a few things to deal with."

"Sure," I replied. Birdie and I continued to glare at each other.

"Okay, I'll check in with you later." He rubbed my arm before strolling off.

Birdie crossed her arms, sizing me up. "Guess I thought you'd be... I don't know... more. The illusive Brexley Kovacs seems a bit of a letdown." She shrugged. "What kind of name is Brexley anyway?"

"What kind of name is Birdie?"

"It's not my real name, but it fits me." She took a step closer, testing me. "While people are busy cooing about how cute and small I am, wanting to stroke my feathers, I swoop in and kick their ass. Want me to show you?" She gave me a pointed look before swiveling back to the mats, shoving a guy out of her way.

I changed my mind. I think I liked her.

An hour later, sweat dripped down my back as I reached over and grabbed a cup of water. I had jumped into training, peeling off my top layers, leaving me just in pants and a tank.

It felt good to work out at that level of intensity. It had been a while. And Andris had made sure everyone here drilled at a high level, even more seriously than HDF. They were not fooling around.

"You already done, X?" Birdie bounced on the mat, her face dripping with sweat. Somehow her eyeliner still held in place, but her hair stuck to her face. She had taken to calling me "X" for some reason. The fae believed names held power and intimacy, and it had leaked into our generation. Plus, it would have been stupid to link your real name to a radical group. I doubted anyone here used their given name.

"Not at all." I wiped my forehead. My muscles burned with fatigue, and I loved it. Birdie was small, but damn, the girl could fight. I knew she was fae, which made her faster and stronger, but I did my best to keep up.

"Have to say, you're better than I thought." She moved back on the mat, making room for me. "Especially for a human."

"Thanks," I replied dryly. "You too."

She smirked.

"What are you anyway?"

"Don't you know it's rude to ask?" We started circling each other.

"Do I look like I care?" I shrugged.

"Well, you look like one of those girls raised with perfect social etiquette. A cloth napkin in her lap and separate play shoes."

All fucking true.

"I was never really good at being that girl." I stepped sideways, keeping the same distance away from her as we learned each other's weaknesses. "And you look like someone who doesn't give a shit about etiquette or what's rude."

She snorted. "I'm the lowest fairy you can get and still be considered fae."

"Parents?"

"Strung out on fae-cocaine. The only thing they cared about was their next hit or beating me when they couldn't get it. I left when I was about ten and never looked back." We orbited each other, her strikes for me fast, but I dodged everyone. "Since I already know about your tragic orphan tale, I say sharing time is over. Not that anyone here would feel a bit sorry for you. You had food and a warm bed, which is a hell of a lot more than most of us." She darted in, her fist clipping my hip as I swiveled out of the way. Her lids narrowed, her jaw rolling. She tried again as I dropped to the ground, kicking up. My heel smacked her in the gut, flinging her back, thumping her hard to the ground. Her eyes widened in horror.

I moved faster than she expected. "You don't move like a human."

The other trainees stopped, their eyes on us, and their mouths dropped open in shock, then darted to me in bewilderment. The response had me thinking this had never happened to Birdie. She was clearly used to being the one who dropped people.

She bounded up quickly, her expression straining with fury. She moved in, her anger blinding her to the obviousness of her move. I leaped out of the way, my elbow ramming into her shoulder blade, my other hand striking her chin as I spun. She didn't fall, but heaved a grunt from her chest, whipping around to face me.

Murmurs and movement surrounded us as figures encircled us, their full attention on our fight. My focus drifted for a second, and she leaped for me, her fist cracking across my cheek. I stumbled back. Fire scorched up my face, the side of my mouth split. A trickle of liquid rolled down my chin.

Touching it, my fingers came away red.

Oh, hell no.

Diving for her, my hand struck fast, colliding with her kidneys, forcing her to bend over, a cry breaking from her lips.

"Damn, no one has ever taken Birdie down," a man commented. "Five hundred forint on the new girl."

"Six hundred on Birdie."

Bets hurled around us, but their voices were distant, my focus on her.

She was scrappy. Someone who grew up fighting dirty. I had been trained properly, but my time in the Games proved I could be as filthy.

Sweeping her leg, her boot sank into the back of my knee, my face slamming into the mat with a crack. I would feel the pain later, but adrenaline shoved it aside as Birdie jumped on me.

The crowd cheered and yelled, stirring intensity in the room.

Blood gushed from my nose, my insides festering with anger as her punch came down on the back of my neck. With a violent flip, I rolled and tossed her off. Birdie tried to bounce up, but I grabbed and flipped her before springing on her, pinning her. My arm curved back, ready to deliver the final strike.

Her eyes blazed with resentment, blood drizzling across her chin. You could tell she was not used to being the loser.

She growled at me and would have come again, but an older woman stepped into the room and clapped. The room burst with commotion.

"All right. That's enough," the woman said. "Chow time!"

Begrudgingly, figures begin to step away. I let my attention wander.

Stupid rookie mistake.

Crack!

Birdie's knuckles plowed into the side of my jaw, hurling me back onto the mat, agony exploding in my brain as I grappled for air. Tumbling onto the ground, I clutched my face, bracing for her to come after me again. But she just laid there. Both of us were flat on our backs, wheezing and bleeding. And I was seriously contemplating throwing up. But sick as I was, I loved it.

A half cough, half laugh rattled from my lungs. I was too exhausted to move.

Her head fell in my direction, and I turned to look at her. A smile curved over her mouth, and then laughter burst from her too. We stared up at the ceiling, laughing like insane people.

I could feel the curious looks, but it only made us laugh more.

My uncle was right; we seemed to have more in common than I thought.

We both got a buzz from fighting, even if our asses were the ones to get tossed.

Ten minutes later, I was following Birdie to a table in the canteen. A bowl of stew and bread in one hand and hot *Alföldi kamillavirágzat*, a wild chamomile tea known for its medicinal purposes, in the other. The way my face ached, I was ready to drink the whole pot.

"Did the little birdie get her wings clipped?" A guy with chiseled cheekbones and tattoos covering his neck, arms, and hands smirked, then shoveled a huge spoonful of stew into his mouth. His dark eyes glinted at her. His black hair was shaved on the sides and long on top, which he had knotted up. He appeared to be of Asian descent.

"Shut the fuck up, Maddox," Birdie snarled, plopping down on a bench across from him. "I could still take you."

He scoffed but kept shoveling in more stew.

"Guys, X." She motioned to me. "X, this is Maddox, Wesley, Zuz, and Scorpion." She gestured around the group, but her attention was already on her food.

"Hey." I nodded, sitting at the end of the bench next to her. They all looked to be around my age, and extremely beautiful, fit, and so different from the group in HDF. There the boys were always shaved, all of us clean and changed for dinner, boots polished. Our dinners were steaks and gourmet food. Here they were brash, wild, and untamed. Dirty, tattooed, scruffy, with ripped and worn clothes. They scarfed down watery stew like it would disappear.

I scanned the assembly, my gaze landing on the guy sitting across from me, a strange feeling twisting in my gut, a tap at the back of my neck causing me to peer at him through my lashes.

Scorpion blatantly stared at me, his look penetrating, his face blank. His hazel eyes were so intense, I felt uncomfortable staring at him for long. They held a power, a feeling of death, like he would just slit my throat right here. He reminded me of Warwick. His look was severe, with tattoos covering every bit of visible skin below his head. His longer brown hair was tied back in a messy knot, and he wore thick rings, piercings in his brow. He had on a tattered T-shirt and ripped cargo pants with boots, like he didn't give a fuck and only put on these items because he was forced to. Even sitting, I could tell he was at least six feet with broad shoulders.

"Wow." The other female at the table, Zuz, spoke, yanking my attention to her. Her expression was twisted like she smelled something bad. Tall, lean, fit, and stunning, her dark blonde hair hung in a braid down her back, showing off her porcelain skin, full lips, and pert nose. She had a large gap between her front teeth, but on her, it worked. "So, you do exist. The infamous Brexley Kovacs," she said in a thick Polish accent, her meaning clear.

"Not a fan, I'm gathering." I took a bite of my bland stew then stared back at her, not in the least intimidated by her haughty tone, trying to ignore the feel of Scorpion's eyes still on me.

"I've just heard so much about you, and…"

"Expected more," I replied, lifting an eyebrow. I heard Birdie snort under her breath. "Good thing I don't give a shit about what you think." *Bitch, please. I made it through Halálház; you do not scare me.*

Wesley choked on his soup. "Damn, Zuz, someone who doesn't fear you."

She snarled at him, his brown eyes meeting mine with a cheeky grin and a wink. Wesley was handsome, but the most understated of the guys. His dark brown hair was short, and he had no visible tattoos. His energy was lighter and playful. You could see he was the "charmer" of the group.

"Let me say, I was impressed with your moves in there." His lips hitched up. "I have never seen anyone challenge Birdie like you did."

"It was a one-time thing." Birdie sounded defensive. "I didn't sleep last night."

Wesley and Maddox laughed, shaking their heads.

"Sure." Wesley patted her arm.

"I'm up for a repeat tomorrow if you need me to kick your ass again." *Please say no, please say no.*

The guys howled as Birdie turned to me, her lids narrowing. "First, you didn't kick my ass. If I recall, I knocked you on yours."

"After she pinned you!" Wesley exclaimed.

"So?" she retaliated, her voice rising. "There is no timeout when you're on the mat. Just like when you are out there, you take any opportunity you can."

"I think Birdie can take her, no problem." Zuz grinned acerbically at me.

Their banter bounced back and forth, but it hazed into white noise as my awareness of Scorpion grew stronger. He hadn't spoken a word. He had barely moved, but I couldn't get over the heavy sensation coating my skin. The urge to look up like he was calling to me stirred me in my seat. It wasn't necessarily sexual, but I felt overly aware of him. My leg bobbed with uneasy energy.

"I'm gonna go to the bathroom," I muttered, getting up, not even looking or waiting for a response as I darted out of the canteen. People moved around me, staring openly, probably having heard the rumors I was here. I shoved past them, locking myself in a stall.

Leaning back against it, I dropped my head in my hands, breathing deeply.

"This is what you call me being free of you? Miss me already, princess?" My body reacted instantly to his voice, pissing me off.

Fuck.

I lifted my head to see Warwick sitting on the top of the toilet, his lips twisted with arrogance.

"No, you just come to mind when I think of shit." I folded my arms.

A ghost of a grin hinted on his mouth. His eyes on me shattered the feeling that Scorpion had left me with a moment before. Even in my mind, Warwick was a force I could not guard myself against. He took over. Controlled me. Demanded my attention.

Climbing off the toilet, his piercing gaze moved over my face. I inhaled, pinning myself to the door, feeling the heat of his tall frame collide against mine.

"Leave you alone for an hour, and you've already been in a fight?" He lifted his hand, his knuckles trailing down the cut on my mouth, along the pulsing bruise on my jawline.

Inhaling, I waited for pain, but none came, only the zing of his touch, igniting me from the inside out.

"How do I feel you? It's like you are really here." My voice was barely above a whisper, my throat struggling to swallow. I craved more of his touch. His full lips hovered only centimeters from mine.

"Fuck if I know," he rumbled, stepping in closer, his breath seeping down my neck. Every muscle, the texture of his clothes, his loose hair tickling my cheek. It felt real. "But *I will* find someone who can break it. End this."

My eyes darted to his, my chin pulling from his grasp, repelling the harshness of his words.

"Yeah. That would be good." I moved in the tiny space, trying to get away from him, my back to him. "The sooner, the better."

His hands clamped down on my arms, flipping me around. He shoved me back into the divider wall, his body taking up far more than the space in the stall.

His thumb brushed over my cuts and bruises, stopping on my mouth. "Love to see how the other person looks." His eyes glinted with heat and what looked like pride. His finger dragged down my lips, parting them. Desire raged through my body, my mouth wanting to nip his thumb. He huffed as if he could feel my need, moving in closer.

Bam.

The main door to the bathroom slammed open, causing me to jump, breaking the link. Warwick vanished in an instant.

"Hey?" Birdie's voice echoed off the tile. "You hiding in the bathroom? Don't take Zuz personally."

"I'm not hiding." I opened the door, stepping out, going to the sink.

At least not from what you think I am.

"Well, I was going to head back to the room." She thumbed behind her. Awkward. Stiff. "If you wanted to go with me."

I had the feeling she didn't have a lot of girlfriends or even close friends. Every word sounded foreign and forced.

"Sure."

"Let me state again: I think this is an awful idea, like the worst. I don't mesh with people. My last roommate would concur."

"They moved out?" I followed her out of the restroom.

"No." Birdie glanced over her shoulder. "She's dead."

O-kay then.

As we turned down the hall, something I couldn't even name had me looking back toward the canteen.

Leaning against the wall, his arms folded, Scorpion stared at me.

Like cobwebs interlacing the space between us and wrapping around some deep instinct in me, a shiver ran down my spine.

Not because I was scared of him, but because in my gut I knew he was experiencing the same thing I was, like a magic drew us to each other.

Chapter 19

The rooms were small and basic, very similar to some of the soldiers' barracks in Leopold. Two metal beds on either side, one nightstand between them with lockers at the ends of the beds for personal storage. A towel, nightclothes, bathroom kit, black cargo pants, and top were waiting on my bed. Folded with a note signed *My heart feels full again—Nagybacsi.*

"Look who is already Lieutenant's pet." Birdie rolled her eyes at the note.

"He's family to me."

"Don't we all know it." She huffed, opening her locker and pulling out a towel and bathroom kit. "Sometimes *your* well-being dictated his actions even ahead of our mission. *Brexley, Brexley, Brexley.*" Her lips curled as she stood up.

It felt strange to know the Resistance knew about me this whole time, had been watching me, and I had no clue.

"I have never seen him lose his shit like he did when he found out you were in Halálház. Not even when Ling was caught." Looking ready to head off to the shower with a towel in her hand, she sat on her bed instead. "She was trained for something like that. Prepared. He knew she would be okay. But you... fuck. He flipped out. Almost blew our cover."

I glanced down at the note in my hand, placing it on the nightstand. Andris was better at expressing his emotions in writing than saying them out loud. My birthday cards were always full of love, but I heard it very seldom from his mouth.

"I don't think he thought you would make it out. Honestly, none of us here did. We had bets."

"On whether I would die or not?" I tucked hair behind my ear.

Birdie shrugged. "You're human. No human lives long in there."

"Yeah…" *Human. Was I?* Shoving away the thought, I looked at her defensively. "Well, I did."

"I heard you were in the Games. Ling told us you killed two people at once, one being fae." The first sign of excitement lit up her eyes.

I didn't respond.

"That you were beaten, tortured, starved, and still even fought against the *Wolf.*" Birdie rolled over his name in a hushed whisper, like she was afraid to summon the devil. Not far from the truth, actually. "Ling says he's real, but come on. Warwick Farkas? The legend known to kill a dozen fae at once without a weapon? There's no way you could fight against him."

I kept my mouth shut. It was clear Andris kept his association with Warwick secret. Little did she know he had been right above her head just hours ago… or in the bathroom with me only minutes prior.

"I guess if I did all those things, it's probably wise not to underestimate me." I tilted my head, lifting an eyebrow. "Though it is fun when people do."

A knowing smile quirked her mouth, and she nodded. She understood all too well. Fae were far less sexist than humans, but it still seeped in, tainted the land here, going back generations.

"I'm gonna go jump in the shower." She rose from the squeaky bed, traveling for the door.

"Um, hey." I cleared my throat. "I was wondering… What is Scorpion's deal?"

"Oh?" I heard a strangle in the vowel in that single word, instantly having me curious if she and Scorpion were a thing.

"Just got a strange vibe off him. He looked as if he wanted to kill me."

She chuckled. "That's how Scorpion is with everyone. A man of few words, and most of those are one syllable. But when you see him fight, it's like poetry. Harsh, vicious, cruel poetry. But damn, I can only imagine the way he fucks."

"So, you two…?"

"No." She frowned. "He won't touch any girl here, but he goes on a lot of missions, and I'm thinking he finds someone to get him off. No person with so much rage and death can go long without releasing it somewhere." She bit down on her lip. "I'd be more than willing to work out his anger with him."

"What's happened to him?"

"What hasn't?" She scoffed, her eyes rolling back. "Like most of here, he has a real fucked up past. But he was in the Fae War twenty years ago and has some real PTSD shit going on. He and Maddox were Unseelie soldiers together. Maddox knew him since they were kids and said the man who went into war was vastly different from the man who walked out." A tendril of dread slunk around my stomach. "Drunk one night, Maddox started confessing all this shit... told me he saw Scorpion get killed. Like completely gutted and cut in half."

"What?" My spine straightened.

"I mean, I doubt it. They were in the middle of a fucking war at night. Maddox probably thought he saw him get axed." She shook her head, grabbing for the door handle. "Though it freaked me out how persistent Maddox was. He looked me dead in the eyes, and I had never seen him look frantic or scared before. He swore he saw..."

"Saw what?" My throat strangled, barely letting the question out.

She stepped through the doorway, looking back at me.

"That he had watched his friend die then come back to life that night."

The clock glowed three a.m. in the pitch-black room, sleep dodging me at every turn. Birdie's heavy breathing was a constant taunt of what my mind denied me.

After my shower, I had climbed into bed, hoping my fatigue would pull me instantly into a slumber. Nope. My mind tossed and turned over thoughts and questions, not able to stop the nagging sensation in my gut.

Thoughts of Scorpion nipped at the back of my head. It was a coincidence. Lots of people died that night. Probably a lot who were close to death ended up surviving. Maddox probably thought he saw something different from what happened. In times of war, memories could twist in your mind.

I had heard countless stories of how brutal and horrendous the war had been, but I couldn't fully imagine it. Millions of humans had died from the influx of magic. The loss of fae from the battles stretching across the globes was also great.

When I was six or seven, a violent thunderstorm hit Budapest, and my father hid behind our sofa, yelling out orders, screaming to attack, talking to people I knew were no longer alive. I got so scared I started to cry. My tears brought him back to himself. He wrapped me in his arms and started to sob.

"I'm sorry. I'm so sorry. It's okay, kicsim." He rocked me in his arms. *"Daddy just gets confused sometimes. Thinks he's somewhere else."*

"Where?" I clutched a stuffed dog to my chest, digging my head into my father's shoulder.

"To a place where I lost more than my friends. I lost my heart that night."

"Mommy?"

"Yes, kicsim. I wasn't there when she left this world. Never got to say goodbye. But I gained you... It makes it worth it." He kissed my forehead. *"Because you, my little one, you are my soul."*

We stayed this way for a moment before he spoke softly. "Know if anything happens, I will always look out for you. There is nothing I won't do to keep you safe. Your uncle is watching over you too. We will all protect you."

Little did I know the real significance of those words. He wasn't talking in general; he knew then something was different about me.

Itching in my skin, I tossed off my covers, needing to move. In sweats and a T-shirt issued to me, I slipped on my boots and sports bra, heading to the workout room to focus my energy.

The hallways were dimmed for the night, and all the rooms were dark, but the people on night watch nodded at me as I passed.

Turning on the training room lights, I went straight to the hanging punching bags, diving straight into a warmup Bakos had us do a lot. Ten minutes in, sweat trickling down my brow, I felt a prickling at the back of my neck, and with a swish of awareness, I sensed someone in the room.

I was not alone. Spinning around, my body jerked with alarm.

Scorpion leaned against the wall, watching me. Dressed as if he never went to bed, his penetrating hazel eyes trapped me in their gaze.

Swallowing, I schooled my expression into composure, but my heart thumped wildly in my chest, and not from exercise.

"Did you need something?" I reached over to grab some water.

He didn't move or speak.

"Nice talking to you." I started to turn back for the bag.

"You can cut the crap." His deep voice fit him perfectly. Raspy and irritated.

"Cut what crap?" I tightened my ponytail.

Scorpion pushed off the wall, his six-foot frame heading for me. He had a lean build, though I could tell what body mass he did have was pure muscle.

"You know what the fuck I'm talking about." His boots hit mine, driving me back until I hit the bag, his cankerous tone spitting out like nails.

I stared back at him, my jaw clenching down. My entire world was about to crumble around me. Warwick was hard enough to explain, but Scorpion would push me over. There would be no rationalizing it away.

"I don't know what you mean." My throat bobbed, my eyes going to the side with anxiety.

He scoffed, moving in closer. "I can fucking feel your panic. I can taste it." He snarled, getting into my face. "How the fuck is that possible? How did I know where you were without even looking? How can I feel you like a goddamn ghost tramping over my grave?"

"And here Birdie says you don't talk much." I glared, my defenses rising like a fortress.

His hand grabbed my chin, fury bursting through him. "Don't fuck with me. What the hell are you? How are you doing this? Aren't you human?"

Ripping my face from his grip, I moved away from him.

"Tell me."

"I don't know."

"Don't fuckin' lie to me."

"I'm not!" I tossed out my arms. "I don't understand this any more than you do."

He tilted his head. I could feel his distrust, his anger brushing against my skin.

"You doubt me. Fine. You say you can feel me? Reach out. See if you can detect any lies." I motioned to myself, then dropping my arms to my sides, opening myself to him, which felt like brushing my hair the wrong way. I wanted to close down, push away, fight the obtrusive connection slinking over me like webs.

His chest rose and fell as he stood still, as if he weren't quite sure what I was suggesting. But after a few moments, I could sense his presence flutter around me.

Fuck.

Still hopeful this wasn't what I thought, I pushed out my thoughts to him. A glimmer of myself circled him while I stood feet away. Doing this with Scorpion felt much harder, as if I had to actively focus on doing it, where with the other asshole... it seemed to happen without even trying.

"Am I lying?" My vision whispered in his ear, though I hadn't moved.

183

His head yanked to the side with a yelp, and he jumped backward. "Fuck," he bellowed, his head snapping back to where I still stood a dozen feet away. "H-how?"

"Again, I don't know." I folded my arms, cutting off the connection, glancing at my boots. "Trying to figure it out. You aren't the first. Hoping to find a way to break it."

"You know about this? There's another like me?"

"Hey. This is a two-way street, buddy." I put my hands on my hips.

"I had no fuckin' streets until you showed up... *buddy*," he snapped back.

His tone made me want to kick the crap out of him, and not in the sexy way.

"Yes. There is another." Yeah, lucky me—linked with a freaking myth. A terrifying, sadistic one. And now it appeared I had another violent asshole to add to the list. "I thought it was just him."

"*Kovacs!*" As if I summoned the devil himself, Warwick was in the room, his gaze wild, voice demanding. "*They're coming! Run!*"

"What?" Terror iced up my spine. Without trying, I was outside the rebel base next to Warwick, who appeared to be hiding in some overgrown bushes. The streets were quiet and dark, but my gut screamed something was wrong. In the distance, I saw hazy silhouettes. Sounds of horse hooves and boots clipped the street. Several hundred of them marched this way.

"They're almost here." Warwick barked, his hands gripping my shoulders. "Get the fuck out! Now!"

The link snapped, and I was back in the belly of the Resistance, Scorpion staring at me wearily and confused, his form taut.

"What?" His head darted around, sensing the utter panic coming off me, but he clearly couldn't see, hear, or feel Warwick.

"They're here..." I repeated.

"Who's here?"

Again, I somehow knew. A gut response.

"HDF." I looked into Scorpion's eyes. "They found us."

A shrill alarm rang through the bunker as figures darted every which way, the air stinking of panic.

Scorpion hadn't questioned me, immediately darting for the night watch and sounding the alarm, probably feeling how deadly serious I was. It wasn't long until the outside camera picked up on the soldiers coming down the lane with an arsenal that could destroy the entire block. They weren't even trying to be secretive about it. They were coming at this base with the full power of the guard, wanting to obliterate us. These were soldiers I knew personally, a group I would have been a part of just a few months ago, invading the "thug" rebel base without a question.

Now I was among the hunted.

Scorpion had run off with Wesley and Maddox, taking point on the roof to give us all more time to escape.

"Brexley!" Andris trampled down the stairs, yelling my name, frantically searching for me.

"*Nagybacsi!*" I called after him, pushing through the handful of people packing up equipment in the lab, feeling his arms wrap around me tightly.

"You need to go, *dragam*." He pulled away, his usually stoic face full of dread.

"What about you?"

"Don't worry about me. This is not a time for us to fight. We cannot win here. It's like shooting fish in a pond. Our fight is the long game. Everyone knows how to get out, and when it's safe, I will get in contact and reestablish headquarters. Istvan has been itching to find me... or rather *Sarkis's* hideout and destroy it. I will let him think he has this win. But you need to get to safety."

I nodded, watching how only the computer room was being cleaned out, taking vital information. Ling shoved laptops, files, and maps into a bag, tossing it to Andris as she filled another, pulling one over her shoulder.

Gunshots and yells boomed through the room upstairs, intensifying the rush of the thinning crowds.

"Birdie!" Andris pushed me toward her. "Get her out of here!"

"Come with me," I yelled back at Andris, the chaos above and in the bunker growing louder. I had scarcely gotten him back; I didn't want to lose him again.

He cupped my face. "I will make contact once we are all safe, *dragam*." He hurriedly kissed my forehead, shoving me back into Birdie. "Stay safe. I love you. Now go! Get her away from here," he commanded Birdie again and slipped away in the crowd with Ling.

"Come on!" Birdie grabbed my arm, tugging me the opposite way. As if they had rehearsed an outcome like this, people divided up around the bunker.

"There are multiple exits," Birdie explained, jogging down the hall. "So as to not gridlock our own escape and get ourselves killed in the panic.

We each have a certain exit. Smooth, efficient, and brings us up on all different sides of the block."

This strategy was pretty genius. It must have taken a lot of planning and secret construction.

"How long has this been your base?"

"Since I joined. Which was about four years ago." She skirted us around the corner and into a water heater closet. A path behind the heater had already been opened, and a few people were running down the dark tunnel. "Why, after all this time, did they find us today?"

Guilt twanged me like a guitar string being plucked. Seemed a little too coincidental. The day I arrive here, the location is found…?

It was no fluke.

We ran several yards in the tunnel before we hit stairs, which clanged beneath us as a handful of us jogged up. It returned me to my escape at Halálház, constricting my lungs and spinning my head. The memories mixing with my present, making it hard for me to breathe.

Everything was a haze when I reached the top and plunged out into a dim alley, dawn only a hint on the horizon. Voices and gunshots rang through the dark streets. A mist of damp air shivered my bare arms. The smells of rotting garbage, wet stone, and urine burned my nose.

Bang! Bang!

Bullets zipped close by us, ricocheting off buildings.

"Shit." Birdie hunkered close to the wall, pulling out a gun.

"You don't happen to have an extra one?" I thought I was joking until she pulled out three more from her clothes.

"Take your pick." All of them were top of the line, expensive, badass weapons.

"Damn." My mouth fell open. We hadn't been issued anything this nice as soldiers at HDF.

"Little hobby of mine."

"What? Being the most badass gunslinger in the Savage Lands?"

"I love to *collect* pretty things." She let the safety off with a wicked grin. "No one suspects the cute, doe-eyed blonde girl to rob them blind while they are busy gambling." She winked, handing me two while double-fisting the other. Tucking one in my waistband and keeping the other in my hand, we scuttled closer to the end of the alley, peering out.

"Fuck," she exhaled.

"Yeah…"

The six-lane avenue teemed with HDF soldiers, motorcycles, and horses. My gaze took in their configuration, assessing and recognizing battle formations. I was one of the only people here, besides Andris, who knew their style intimately, had insight into how they fought.

"Come on." Birdie started to move, more people from below joining us in the alley.

"No." I grabbed her shoulder, pulling her back.

"What?" She looked around, then glared at me.

"They will have soldiers in the back facing out, looking for threats from behind, ready to shoot anything that moves." Fae were a lot harder to kill, but since the wall fell and magic- and iron-laced bullets were standard now, it wasn't as hard if you were a really good shot.

"Please, I move faster than they could even blink." A girl looking no more than sixteen came beside us. "I'm not hiding from some douchebag humans." She rolled her eyes, inching forward.

"No!" I tried to grab for her, but she flew out of the alley.

Pop! Pop! Pop!

Guns went off at her. She darted through them, her speed impressive, and my hopes soared as she got closer to the other side.

Pop!

Her body hit the ground with a slap.

"Gigi." Birdie gasped as we watched blood pour onto the cobbled street, the entire side of her face gone. "Fuck!" Birdie growled, hitting the wall. "That stupid fucking bitch! Why didn't she listen?"

Another thing Birdie and I had in common, turning heartache and fear into anger.

I rubbed my head.

"What now?" someone asked, a handful of Resistance fighters now gathered in the alleyway.

I searched around the dead-end passage and noticed a dumpster against the far wall.

"We go up." I motioned to the dumpster. It was a climb, but if we got to the roof, we could cross over to the back and bleed into the night. "Go!" I ordered.

All of them reacted instantly, rushing to the dumpster and climbing up. The top was gone, so only two at a time could use the edge to jump up to the window and then climb to the roof.

I kept on guard, only turning to help Birdie get up, preparing to climb up myself.

"Stop!" A voice rang out, dropping lead in my stomach. *Shit, shit, shit.* Turning slowly around, three soldiers stood at the entrance. I hoped I could distract them enough to let them all reach the top.

"Brexley?" A man's voice strained in surprise. Through the haze of my panic, I focused on the group. I knew all of them. They had been in Caden's class. Elek, Joska, and Samu.

"*Szar!*" *Shit!* Elek spat, his hand going to a crude walkie-talkie soldiers were issued once they were put in the field.

"No!" I lurched forward.

"Don't move!" Joska's beefy hands regripped his gun, pointing it at my head. He was a big dude who I remembered had the extremist attitude that if you weren't pure human, you shouldn't be alive. And women shouldn't be soldiers. Bigoted, sexist, and righteous. A new crop of what they called *pure human nationalists*. "Drop your weapon!"

The third guy, Samu, stayed quiet. He always let the dominant person lead, following like a sheep, regurgitating whatever they said without one thought of his own. He had trailed after Caden for six years like a puppy. Caden had been too nice to say anything, but the guy gave me the creeps.

"Captain, we have her. We have Brexley Kovacs," Elek spoke into the device. He was the only one I had once liked. He and Caden had been pretty close, so I got to know him. He teased me and hinted about us hanging out together, just the two of us.

Now everyone was my enemy.

"I said drop your weapon or I will shoot you. I don't care what Markos wants. You are a disgusting fae traitor." Joska took a step closer, flicking his gun to the middle of my forehead. "You should be hung as the turncoat and spy you are, but I will blow your fucking brains out right here. Now get on your knees."

My eyes lit into him, the fighter underneath my skin itching for release.

"Now!" He shoved the barrel into my skull.

He was not someone who would give empty threats.

But neither was I.

Lowering, I placed my gun on the ground, slowly raising my hands, my gaze shifting around for objects I could use.

"Don't move." Joska and Samu descended on me, kicking my gun out of my reach. The metal scraped the pavement and hit the wall.

"Search her," he ordered Samu. Samu patted me down, found the other gun, and tucked it into his pants with a lingering stare.

At least the others got away.

"Handcuff her. I want to personally take her to the general." Joska sneered, motioning for Samu to do the dirty work again.

If they took me to Istvan, I was done.

But that wasn't in my plans.

My fists rolled up, the bitter taste of adrenaline on my tongue, my muscles flexing, ready to react at my command.

Three against one. All of them with multiple weapons. Most likely, I would die here, but I wasn't going without a fight.

A vein twitched in my neck at the sound of the metal cuffs opening, heading for my wrists. My patience scraped my bones, priming me for action.

Out of my periphery, I noticed a flutter of movement, a figure swooping down, more like an angel of death than a bird.

Birdie landed right beside Samu, slamming her fist into his kidney. He swung around, Birdie kicking the gun out of his grip.

With her arrival, chaos burst into the tight alley, and I seized my opportunity. Grabbing the barrel of Joska's gun, I twisted it out of his grip as we had both been taught by Bakos.

My leg swept and kicked the tendons in his knee. He grunted but didn't budge, his knuckles slamming into my face. I stumbled back. Pain crackled through my already sore jaw, raising my anger.

The girl who survived the Games growled from my chest.

I went for the tender part of his throat, my fist punching his larynx. Gasping, he clutched his neck as I nailed him in the eye socket, a loud cry bolting from his lips.

Tough guy wasn't so tough now.

"You bitch," he choked out, his teeth bared. I'd heard enough of his misogynistic comments to the girls in his class to know how he felt about women training next to him. I knew he couldn't stand the thought of one beating him up.

This would be fun.

Samu and Birdie were fighting right next to me as Elek ran for my gun on the ground.

Joska barreled for me. While the tiny alley didn't give me much room, I twisted just out of the way, so he only nipped my hip. Pain raced up my nerves, and I looked down. Blood seeped out, soaking my pants red. Darting my attention back to him, I saw the dagger in his hand, a smug grin on his face. The fucker stabbed me.

Little did he know a fight like this was a morning ritual in the mess hall at Halálház.

He lunged for me again, his knife darting for my chest. Fury raised the monster inside me, my vision hazing over as I twirled, kicked, and punched. My senses were on high alert, but at the same time lost in a cloud

189

of violence. I relished the sound of cartilage breaking and muscles tearing, the strike of flesh and bone being hit. An agonized cry erupted from him as I slammed my elbow into his spine, cracking a vertebra and dropping him to the pavement with a thump.

Right then, Samu went flying back onto the pavement. Out cold, drawing a quick glance to Birdie, I saw a contented smile on her face. She fucking loved it too.

"Stop!" Elek's voice bellowed, the blast of gun halting us. Elek lowered the gun from the air to us swinging it between Birdie and me as he stepped forward. "There's no point, Brexley. They know you are here. Markos is coming." A slice of regret cut across his brows. "I wish it wasn't this way, but you gave us no choice."

"You could let us go," Birdie replied, shrugging. "That's a choice."

He shook his head. The fight to be a good soldier was too powerful. It was embedded in you at an early age. Obey. Take orders. Fight for your cause. Except the cause was a lie, and the reasons were all bullshit. There was only Istvan and his need for power.

"I'm sorry, Brexley. You will come with me. All others are to be shot on sight." He switched to pointing at Birdie.

"Elek, no." I reached out, my steps slow. Cautious.

"Sorry…" His finger squeezed down.

Boom! The shot thundered in the alleyway, making me jump and scream.

Birdie's eyes went wide, full of torment, but then her brows furrowed in confusion, her eyes dropping to where she should have been shot.

Elek's body fell forward, slamming face-first onto the cement. Dead. A huge silhouette stood behind him, gun still pointing at the spot Elek had been.

"Warwick." Relief heaved in my lungs at the sight of him. Our eyes met, and I could feel his familiar touch along every inch of my skin, though this time it seemed to be checking me for injury. Furious and pugnacious.

"Let's go," he grumbled.

I scrambled forward, the noises of battle sounding right on top of us. Swooping down, I got the two guns I had been relieved of. I stopped at Elek's figure, crouching down, my hand reaching out to close the eyes of my old acquaintance.

Sorrow filled my heart like a tsunami. He was a good guy. He didn't deserve to die like that. No matter what we were told about it being an honor to die for HDF, the reality was utter crap.

My hand brushed over his face, recalling the times Caden and I had hung out in his room with the rest of their class, getting drunk. He would find reasons to get close to me, flirt with me, but because of Caden, he never crossed the line or asked me out.

"Kovacs," Warwick called to me, but I couldn't tear myself away from Elek. One moment alive, now he was dead... because of me. I knew his mother and father. They would be devastated. Emotion swirled inside me, bursting at the seams, wanting to change his story.

Under my palm, a nerve twitched in his face, a spasm in his body, his lids fluttered.

"Kovacs, now." Warwick grabbed my hand, yanking me back onto my feet, his nose flaring, his gaze darting between Elek and me, his brow crunching together.

Numb, yet alive, the vast emotions swirled inside, my brain not wanting to land on what I had been doing. What I might be capable of.

"We need to go." He released me, stepping away.

I dipped my head in agreement and looked back at Birdie.

She watched us, her expression awed, her blue eyes wide.

"You're fucking Warwick Farkas..." Her mouth parted. *"The Wolf."*

He grunted, inching to the lip of the alley.

"He is, isn't he?" She faced me. "Holy shit. He's so... Is there even a word for him?"

"Asshole?" I replied, getting a glower from Warwick.

"No, seriously, this is really Warwick Farkas?" She said his name like he was a god.

"Birdie..."

"He's real? The actual legend is standing in front of me? The guy who came back to life? And you knew and didn't tell me?" She punched my arm.

"Ow." I rubbed my shoulder.

"That's for not telling me you were sleeping with a myth. Is the sex astronomical? Mythical status?"

"Yes," he grunted.

"No," I responded.

"I can't believe you didn't tell me earlier. I was totally going on about him... and you're fucking him?" Birdie's mouth dropped open.

"No. No, it's not like that. W-we're not... No... We aren't." I shook my head, unable to stop babbling. "He wasn't talking about sex *with me.*"

Warwick grunted even louder, his irritation curling up the back of my neck.

"Can we focus here?" It was freezing outside, and my body was in pain.

"Right." Birdie gripped both of her guns. "Kill first, talk later about how you are *sooooo* fucking him. And if you aren't, you really should be. Or I volunteer."

"She really thinks you should be, princess." Warwick's voice rumbled in my ear, his presence up close, while the real man stood a few feet away, his eyes on the battle on the street.

"No," I growled under my breath, and I could see the real man smirk.

"Well, as you know, fucking me is a mythical experience. Most never recover."

He switched to the other ear, the trace of his fingers sliding across my lower back.

"You mean it's fictional?" I replied just to him.

The real Warwick let out a gruff laugh, his eyes darting back to me, making Birdie look between us again with skepticism.

"Sergeant Gabor, state your location. Markos is moving in." A crackling voice rose from Elek's walkie-talkie device, and fear compressed my lungs.

Markos. He was here. He rarely came to battles personally, dictating from the safety of HDF. But I was personal to him.

"Shit, how do we get out of here?" Birdie motioned around, the lanes filling with more and more soldiers.

"Distraction." Warwick's eyes slid to me, and a smile spread across my face because I knew exactly what he meant.

"Distraction?" Birdie peered up at him, then to me.

BOOOOOOOM!

An entire building across the street from the base exploded, shaking the ground. Clouds of debris and glass mushroomed out, raining down on us like hail.

All of us ducked, Warwick's form looming over us like an umbrella until the worst of the blast was over.

He glanced at Birdie, one eyebrow lifting. "Distraction."

Chapter 20

The air was thick and heavy, choking my lungs. I yanked my shirt over my mouth as we darted across the vast avenue congested with chunks of rubble, dead bodies, and overturned wagons. The thunderous sounds of screaming, confusion, gunfire, and tumbling wreckage cracked the pavement like mini bombs, all creating a deafening sound.

Warwick took the lead, weaving through the destruction, pausing behind an overturned cart midway. Birdie and I kept on his tail, our weapons up and pointed. Alert and on guard for any trouble.

"I have to say…" Birdie pushed her back into the cart as she slid in next to us, pointing her gun behind us, the piercing sounds of gunshots filling the atmosphere. "For a distraction, that was pretty good."

Warwick didn't respond, his eyes forward, while mine watched for any danger coming from other directions. The gray skies didn't help with the smoky air. It was hard to see more than a few yards in front of us.

"You'll find a lot of things blow up around Warwick," I replied.

"Like my ovaries," Birdie muttered under her breath loud enough I could hear her. I shot her a look. "What?" She shrugged. "Like you weren't thinking the same thing."

Yep… No! No, Brexley, you were not.

"Shit," Warwick grumbled, ducking back behind the wagon, his fury knocking against my bones.

"What?" Anxiety darted my head around. I could feel he was pissed, but not why.

193

"The explosion was supposed to take out that thing." He motioned to the street.

"What thing?" I peered over, my eyes assessing every movement and shape through the hazy air.

"That," he grunted, pointing to a huge object being rolled out into the middle of the boulevard.

"*Ó, hogy baszd meg egy talicska apró majom!*" *Oh, may a wheelbarrow of small monkeys fuck it,* Birdie hissed, her head shaking. Many old Hungarian phrases had survived and seemed even more relevant now in this crazy world.

My throat tightened as I gazed upon the object. I knew exactly what it was. I had loaded it many times in a drill. Made from iron, cannons had survived the fall of the wall unscathed, highly sought after in the Eastern Bloc countries. Especially in fighting fairies since iron was their weakness.

"Fuck." My stomach dropped at the sight of the cannon being set in position, pointing right at the rundown mansion that held the rebel headquarters, a soldier lighting the fuse.

Please be gone already. Please. The fear was instinctual. My thoughts went directly to him, pulling me to his location.

Shit. I stood on the roof, looking at Scorpion's back alongside Maddox, Wesley, and the twin guards I met when I first arrived here. They were hiding behind a partial wall, firing down on the HDF soldiers. The haze was still thick, and a massive chunk of fallen debris blocked their view of what was really happening below—and the peril coming for them.

Terror plunged through me, and I saw Scorpion jerk, his body whipping around, sensing me, his eyes finding mine.

"Scorpion! Run!" I yelled through our bond. Down on the ground, I heard the sizzle of the fuse about to run out. "NOW!"

His eyes widened and he instantly reacted.

"Go! Go!" he bellowed at his group, waving them toward the stairs. Maddox instinctually responded to his friend, scrambling across the roof, the others moving slower, questioning his reaction. I knew they didn't have time to get all the way down the stairs, anxiety shooting through me at the thought. I couldn't do anything.

"What? What's going on?" Wesley curved back to Scorpion.

"Just fuckin' move!" Scorpion yelled, his arm waving for them. The five of them hustled for the far side, but the me on the ground heard the crackle fizzle out in a way that meant they were out of time.

"Hurry!" I pleaded and motioned for them to rush, knowing only Scorpion could hear and see me.

"Cannon..."

BOOOOOM!

The iron ball sliced through the top of the building, directed at the shooters on the roof. Brick, wood, plaster, and metal shredded, exploding into chunks as the guys raced for an escape. It flung them forward like paper in the wind. Their figures soared off the five-story building as rubble raced them to the ground.

"Scorpion!" I screamed as I watched his body plummet.

The link between Scorpion and me was severed with a harsh snap, forcing me to suck in violently.

"What? What's wrong?" Birdie said. She and Warwick both turned to me, my hand on my chest, trying to stabilize myself.

Were they dead? Did I not warn them in time?

"X?" Birdie called to me, but I couldn't stop trying to reach back out. My heart thudded in my chest, grief knifing me. I barely knew him, any of them, but the link to Scorpion made all that unimportant. We were tied together. It felt like losing a family member.

Suddenly I was back behind the building, Maddox and Wesley stirring, but I searched for the other. For the guy who had suddenly become so much to me.

I spotted a figure crushed under a huge chunk of cement, blood and gore splattered everywhere.

No... please, no... Vomit churned up my throat.

A groan shifted my view to another figure in the debris

"Scorpion!" Lying on his back covered in dust, rubble, and blood, his eyes bolted open, sucking in a gulp of air. His head turned, our eyes meeting.

"Kovacs?" Warwick's voice yanked me from the link with Scorpion, swiveling my head to him. His aqua eyes narrowed on me, like *what the hell is going on with you*?

"They're okay." I breathed, my spine curling into the cart with relief. "He made it out alive."

"Who made it out?" Birdie asked.

"The guys... Maddox, Wesley, and Scorpion." I knew at least one of the twins had been killed, but I could not deny the relief the others were okay.

"How do you know?" Birdie looked puzzled.

I could feel Warwick's eyes probing into me, but I wouldn't meet them.

"Reload," a man yelled, shifting our focus to the soldiers. "Level it!"

"We have to get out of here." Warwick motioned for us to follow. "I hid my bike in the bushes, there." He pointed to overgrown shrubbery on the main road.

"Right there?"

"I didn't have time to find a better spot, princess," he snapped at me. "If I remember, I was warning your ass instead."

We inched our way to the other side of the street, hiding every few feet, making sure we weren't followed or seen. We gathered into an alleyway, Warwick's bike only a few yards away now.

"Well, this is where we part ways." Birdie reloaded her gun, her voice emotionless.

"What?" I was surprised at how I had bonded to this group in only a day.

"Yeah, I have a place to hole up for a bit." She shrugged. "Plus, I'm better on my own." I totally understood that.

"I have no doubt our paths will cross again, X." She pulled her hood higher over her white-blonde hair. "Trouble seems to follow you."

I snorted. "Yeah, I get that a lot."

"Something tells me you will be in the middle of whatever is coming." She nodded at me, then did the same to Warwick. "Legend."

She was gone, running down the open-ended passage, away from the chaos with no sentiment or "take care." It made me like her more.

Booooom!

Jumping, I swung around as another cannonball ripped through the mansion, completely demolishing the top of it.

"Come on." Warwick stepped out, slipping against a wall, creeping toward the bushes.

I kept my gun up, eyes focused behind us while my heart slammed in my chest. The noise and pandemonium reached piercing levels, tearing at my security and sanity. Every moment felt like my last.

I had never been in a war, but this was what it was like in my mind. The dead bodies of young soldiers dotted the ground, the air thick with the smell of terror, hate, and death.

Screams and orders. Bullets and bombs.

Destruction. Bedlam.

Battle was not something you could truly understand until you experienced it. It triggered the basest responses in people. Survival. Forgoing friendships and ideals.

I was stunned, gutted, and horrified… because I was no different. This wasn't the first time I killed fellow comrades to survive.

Kill or be killed.

"Corporal Markos!" The name cut through the commotion, peeling away all the layers, yanking my head to the boulevard, my stomach a nauseated swirl.

Everything stopped.

My eyes fastened on my former best friend. The man I loved for half of my life. Only about twenty yards away, dressed in his soldier gear, his rank far above what it should have been for a new graduate. Istvan was all about nepotism if it kept power in his family, and having only one son put all that on Caden's shoulders.

Caden's chest puffed, jaw tight. "Report."

"We found Gabor dead and Sergeants Anto and Joost unconscious and in serious condition." The soldier swallowed nervously. He was talking about Elek, Joska, and Sam. "Private Kovacs was gone. But we are searching everywhere, sir."

I was right here. Only about 60 feet away from them.

"If you find her, come straight to me, do you understand? Not to my father or Kalaraja. Me."

Kalaraja. *Fuck.* Should have figured the Lord of Death was near. No doubt he was the one who tracked me here.

"Kovacs." Warwick had pulled out his motorcycle, flinging his leg over it. "Come on."

Click. Click.

The sound of a gun being cocked froze me in place. I felt the barrel press into my temple as a figure stepped out of a dark, empty doorway.

Warwick pulled out his gun in a blink, pointing it at the man in a standoff.

"I can shoot her faster than you can shoot me." Kalaraja's familiar nasal tone sent shivers up my spine.

Every cell in my body was frozen, guttural terror freezing me in place. My gaze locked with Warwick's.

How stupid and novice for neither of us to have considered a snake would be lying in the grass waiting for us.

"I think Ms. Kovacs is coming with me." Kalaraja took the gun from me, unaware of the one I still had tucked into my pants.

It would be only a moment before he found it.

"You are not going to shoot me. Her life means too much to you, doesn't it?" He sneered at Warwick. "And here I thought the mythical Warwick Farkas, who is said to kill without thought or emotion, would be worthy of such praise. I believed we were alike in that way. How sad.

197

Stacey Marie Brown

Sentiment takes down another legend." He jammed the gun into my head, trying to get me to budge. "Move."

I knew Kalaraja wouldn't leave Warwick alive. He'd probably shoot him in the head the moment I started to walk while Warwick was distracted by me.

"Warwick..." I stood next to him, though I hadn't moved. *"Shoot him."*

"He'll kill you."

"Why, yes, I will." Kalaraja answered Warwick's response to me.

"He's going to kill me anyway. And if you don't shoot first, he will kill you as well." I touched his arm.

"Think I'd go down so easy, princess?" He winked at me. "Not the fuckin' *legend* for nothing."

"Don't."

"Too late." A mischievous grin tugged the side of his mouth.

The pain of the barrel in my temple was sharp. Warwick's spirit moved beside me now, while his body still sat on the bike, holding the gun on Kalaraja.

"I know you can fight," Warwick rumbled in my ear. *"But this guy isn't fully human. Take what you need, princess."*

"What?" My mouth parted. That made no sense. He worked for Istvan. He was part of HDF. "Not fully human?" My gaze snapped to Kalaraja.

Kalaraja's eyes widened. "What did you say?" I could see a wild fear darting his eyes back and forth between mine as if someone just revealed his secret. His thumb pushed down on the trigger.

Our time was up.

"Now," Warwick yelled at me.

A flood of adrenaline whisked through me. My body moved with speed, power, and strength I couldn't even fathom, as if Kalaraja was suddenly in slow motion. Ducking, I shoved his arm in the air. The ring of the gun discharging sounded far away. Turning into him, I punched his throat, my knee cracking into his pelvis, bending him over. My elbow hit his spine, dropping him to the ground, his gun tumbling to my feet.

Swiping it up, I sprinted for Warwick, the engine revving. I was about to climb on when angry voices turned my head to the side, colliding with the one I knew better than my own.

Caden stood rigid with the three soldiers he had been talking to, our eyes locking.

It was only a second of time, but I felt all the emotions in his eyes, like a tragic novel. Agony, grief, betrayal, hurt, confusion, and worst of all...

198

love. I knew him so well, I understood he was trying to say: *Come back to me, I'll protect you, keep you safe. We'll fix it together. Don't do this… because if you do… you can never come back. I love you.*

A part of me wanted to. Wanted to run into his arms and hope we could work it all out.

But I was no longer the girl who believed in fairytales.

He had yet to understand I was already past the point of no return. There was no redemption for me. No fixing it.

Sorrow flickered over my features. *I'm sorry, Caden.* I clamped my jaw and swung my leg over the back of Warwick's motorcycle.

I could see the utter devastation in his eyes. The betrayal. The realization I picked the world with fae, a life on the run, over him. But like me, he was also a well-trained HDF soldier. Even though he knew Istvan would probably kill me if I returned, Caden was quick to shove the sadness back. He lifted his head, his eyes narrowing in on me with disgust and hate as he barked orders to men around him. "Get her!"

He'd just declared us enemies.

Warwick gunned the bike, spinning us away from the battle.

Gunshots zinged by, ticking the ground near us.

I turned back to see Kalaraja climbing to his feet, motioning and yelling at the few soldiers Caden had ordered after me. They ran for motorcycles sitting in wait down the street. They jumped on, tearing after us. Kalaraja leading them.

"Hurry." I gripped Warwick tighter. "We're about to have company."

Warwick punched the gas, the bike lurching forward, swerving sharply around objects, bodies, and debris, leading us away from the battle. Glancing back, the four bikes were closing in.

Bang! Bullets licked our skin.

I curved around, firing back, my arm trembling from adrenaline and the harsh movement of the bike, no shot hitting its target. It would only take *one* of theirs to end this.

"Shit!" Warwick muttered. I looked to see carts and horses up ahead, people preparing for morning market, unaware or not caring about the fight happening down the street. Not when they still had bellies to feed. "Hold on!"

I tightened my hold as the bike squealed, and he detoured down an alley, the bike tires scrambling to keep up. Warwick's boot planted on the damp ground to hold us from flattening into the cobblestones while pointing us down the slim passage.

Bang! Bang!

Slugs clipped the bike, the alley making us an easy target. This was so much like the night the gang attacked us. Unlike them, Kalaraja was a trained, lethal soldier. His bullet would hit the mark.

I couldn't let that happen.

The bike tore out of the alley and back onto a smoother street while gunshots rang out behind us, hitting the tailpipe and fender.

"Hold on to me," I screamed over the engine as another shot pinged off the taillight, blowing it out.

"What?" Warwick peered over his shoulder, eyebrows wrinkling.

I grabbed one of his arms, curling it around my torso. "Hold on."

Not second-guessing my plan, convinced the next bullet would be embedded in my spine or the back of his head, I pulled one leg up to my chest. Sitting back on my tailbone and twisting, I flung my other leg over, flipping me around with a slight wobble, facing out toward the strife.

"Shit, Kovacs." Warwick's grip clutched down on my hip. "You're fucking nuts!"

"Thought you knew that!" I yanked out my second gun from the back of my pants, the figures chasing us in full view now. "Come on, assholes…"

I lifted both arms and shot. The blasts rang out through the abandoned streets, one hitting the tire of a soldier's bike. The damp street caused it to slip out of his control, the sound of metal squealing across the ground, his body slamming into an old fire hydrant with a fatal blow. The other soldier peered back at him, but Kalaraja didn't take his eyes off me.

I was his target. Nothing else mattered. I doubted he had ever failed to get his mark.

He's not fully human.

His gun rose, pointed at me.

Bang!

"Warwick!" I yelled in warning, my emotions plunging into him. He snapped the bike to the side, but it was too late.

Pain burst through me as the bullet drove into my stomach, tearing through flesh and bone.

In shock, I looked down at my hip. Red painted my white T-shirt. The hole in my side was near where Joska knifed me.

Fuck.

This was not how I wanted to die. Just another kill for the Lord of Death. I could see Istvan learning the news with a false breath of sadness, but then he'd nod his head unemotionally and thank him for a job well done. No longer a problem, he'd tell himself it had to be done.

Anger curled my lip, adrenaline pouring into my veins, numbing any pain

I might have felt and helping me ignore the warm blood absorbing into my T-shirt, and the sense that my insides were splintering and dying. All my agony vibrated under the surface until I felt nothing but rage and vengeance.

Warwick raced across the Savage Lands, weaving and zigzagging us through the dilapidated and falling buildings, wind and loose hair striking at my face like whips.

I pointed the guns at my targets. I fired both guns, bullets recoiling from the chamber in repetition as I narrowed my attention on the three left.

My bullet went straight through the head of one guard who tipped off his bike, the machine skidding across the pavement, creating sparks in the dull morning light. His limp form rolled into the middle of the street, where he'd be left to be picked apart by scavengers, both animal and human.

Bang!

Another blast of pain wrenched through me, my lungs wheezing for air, but I didn't look down. It didn't matter. I knew I was going to die, but I was going to take Kalaraja with me.

The guttural need to protect Warwick, keep him safe and alive, helped me bring my weak arms up again. They did not tremble. My hatred and wrath fueled me from deep within.

Bang! Bang! Bang!

A bullet hit Kalaraja's shoulder, jerking him back, but it only seemed to piss him off. He snarled at me.

Yeah, fucker, the feeling is mutual.

A bullet clipped the ridge of Warwick's bicep from the final guard.

Hell no. A cry of fury burst from my mouth, sounding like a madwoman. I killed the final guard, bullets also spraying into Kalaraja, his body slipping off his bike and tumbling to the ground. The last two targets neutralized.

With relief, I eased back into Warwick, my arms dropping, feeling a heavy sigh trying to come up my throat. It was raspy, and I knew liquid was filling my lungs.

Rain clouds covered the sky, but it felt as if it was getting darker, not lighter, as the morning grew older.

"Kovacs?" Warwick's head turned to me, the rumble of his voice against my back. I felt cold, terribly cold, except where he touched me. I wanted to curl into his heat, let his body wrap around me. "Hey."

My mouth didn't want to work.

So cold...

"Kovacs?" His voice rose, his bulk turning more, his hand gripping my side tighter. Blood resembling strawberry jam began to drench us both.

"Holy fuck!" He yanked his hand away, looked at it, then back to me. So, so cold and tired. I just wanted to sleep.

"Fuck. No! Kovacs, you hold on. I need you to hold on for a little longer." A long string of swear words hissed under his breath, the bike revving higher, the vibration only lowering my lids. I could not keep my eyes open.

"Stay with me." He wrapped his arm back around me tighter.

Everything started to feel like a dream. Was I awake? Was I sleeping? I no longer knew.

But the call to close my eyes and let the darkness take me warred with the cries of my name.

"Kovacs!" His voice made me want to hold on, to reach out and let him take my hand, pull me back, but a strong force tugged me down a river. I could no longer fight the current. "Don't you fucking give up on me now. I won't let you." His voice sounded closer. "You survived Halálház, you endured torture and the Games... You can survive this..."

I sank further down into the abyss.

"Brexley." The sound of my first name circled around my heart, the slice of pain I could hear in it. "Please..."

I wanted to obey, but the tide carried me away, breaking up his words and drifting them away from me.

I let myself go under.

No longer cold.

Chapter 21

If I found peace, it didn't let me stay long. A swirl of harsh voices, nausea, pain, and confusion jarred me awake. Time, space, and even my thoughts didn't feel tangible. Everything was abstract and confusing. I felt my lids flutter. Fire burned across my torso, and I heard a guttural scream crash against the walls.

"Hold her down! I have to clean it," a sensual, clear voice commanded.

"I'm trying." A deep gravelly voice raked over me, followed by a pressure on my arms that instantly calmed me. But I could hear him suck in as if he were in pain now.

There was a pause.

"What?" The husky voice helped my muscles unwind, even dulled the fire raging across my torso.

"Nothing," the other guy responded, skepticism floating over the two syllables. "She is going to react violently to this."

"I don't give a shit! Just fucking heal her now, Ash."

"*Az istenit*, Warwick. I'm doing my best with what I have here. This girl has multiple fatal wounds. Stabbed, shot. Her lungs are full of blood. Her kidneys resemble shredded cheese, and her pulse is barely there. I'm trying my best."

"Try harder." A low growl sounded. A threat. I could taste it like the bitterness of adrenaline. "Fucking fix her."

The other guy made a noise but didn't respond. I heard the sound of movement, glass and metal clanging, then felt compression on my stomach. I could feel my body twitch, but the pain never fully reached me.

I heard a long, deep grunt, fingers digging into my arms, a snorted, choked breath.

"What the hell?" the first man asked. "Warwick?"

"It's nothing. Keep going," he seethed through his teeth, his tone filled with torture.

"It's not nothing. What is going on? Why are you acting like the one getting a bullet dug out of your kidney while she lays here calmly?"

"I. Said. It's. Nothing." He breathed heavily, close to my ear. "Keep going."

"She probably won't live. I want you to be prepared. Her system will most likely shut down with shock."

"Just do it!"

There was a beat…

Flames burst inside me, my spine jackknifing. But it was his deep roar that shook the room, tearing through me and filling me with excruciating agony.

It was too much.

I slipped back into endless blackness.

The murmur of voices, though soothing, tugged me from the blackness. My lashes fluttered, trying to open. Bile clung to the walls of my esophagus, and though I couldn't pinpoint the pain, nausea rolled through me as though I was on a stormy ocean.

Weakly, my lids cracked open to an old wood ceiling made of tree branches. The room was dark and dim, the only light coming from a fire crackling across the room, but I still flinched at the brightness. Peering at my outstretched body, a soft blanket lay over me, a pillow under my head, and I looked to be lying on a wooden dining table.

"I've known you a long time. Fought at your side." The smooth, seductive voice drifted sensually to me, coming from near the large fireplace. "Janos and I were the ones to find you on the field…"

A chair creaked. My head dropped to look over. In two homemade-looking wood chairs in front of the fire, Warwick and a man I didn't know sat drinking.

Warwick's shirt was still caked with dried blood, a bandage on his arm, his pants stained with grease, dirt, and more blood.

The other guy wore dark green, loose cotton pants and a lighter green shirt, his feet bare.

From what I could see of the unknown guy's profile, he was seriously gorgeous: chiseled jaw, full lips, stubble, and wavy, dark blond hair tumbling to his shoulders. Pretty compared to Warwick. Shorter and less broad. But almost all men were slight compared to the Wolf. Warwick had a way of making everyone else appear small. Insignificant. Though sitting, I could tell this man still was tall and fit, looking to be in his late twenties to humans.

"I'm putting a lot on the line having you here. If Killian or any of his men found you... I'm still tied to him. A debt I have to work through." The guy frowned.

Warwick rubbed his face, staring back at the fire.

"You really have issues trusting people. Even me... after all we've been through." The pretty man took a drink of whatever was in his wooden cup. "At least tell me what she is to you."

"She's nothing." Warwick's voice came out low.

"Yeah, that's why you brought her here, knowing the risk, and threatened my life multiple times if she didn't live." The guy snorted, refilling his glass from a bottle on a side table. "You are a lot of things... The one thing you are not, my friend, is a good liar. Nor do you take risks for people who are *nothing* to you."

Warwick's eyebrows furrowed.

"You don't care enough to lie. You are a tsunami—brutal, overwhelming, devastating, harsh, but never false."

Warwick slunk back farther in his chair, scouring his face. He dropped his head back for a moment, taking a breath. "I don't know what she is..."

"In general or to you?" His friend's question stirred him in his seat.

"Fuck, I don't miss this." Warwick motioned to him. "This insightful shit."

"Comes with my nature." The guy chuckled. "It's why I am so good at healing people."

"If there's a wound, you want to fix it."

The guy snorted. "Some wounds are not on the outside."

Warwick grunted in annoyance, making his friend shake his head.

"She has no aura. I can sense nothing there." The guy tapped his hand on his knee. "Like you."

"Don't."

"Don't what? I'm simply stating facts. Seems odd neither of you have auras…"

"What are you getting at, Ash?" Warwick leaned forward on his knees. "The one thing you are not, *my friend*, is subtle."

"You're going to tell me when you held her down earlier… you weren't taking on her pain?" The man, Ash, tilted his head. "It will be very awkward to watch you lie again, so why don't you get straight to the truth?"

Warwick got up, his large boots hitting the creaky floor, his head almost touching the ceiling. Exhaustion started to tug at me, but my curiosity forced my lids to stay up.

"I don't know."

"You don't know what?"

Warwick rumbled, resembling a wild beast.

"What the fuck this is!" His arm waved off in my direction. "The moment she walked into Halálház… I've felt… It's like…" He huffed, giving up.

"Jesus, you are even worse at admitting any emotion."

"That's not who I am."

"No, you're right. But I think you need to tell me about this."

Warwick pinched his nose.

"We are connected." He breathed heavily. "Like I can fucking be in the same room as her and be across town at the same time."

"What?" Ash bolted up. "Like a dream? There's no way you could dreamscape or dream walk. You're not fairy. And neither is she."

"No, it's nothing like that. It's not a dream. We aren't sleeping… it's real. I can touch her, smell her, see everything happening around her, and she can with me. It's as if we're both really there. Wide awake. But no one else can see the other."

"That's not possible."

Warwick let out a strained laugh.

"Well, tell the universe that."

"So, you guys can visit each other and also take each other's pain away?"

"Not totally away, but some of it. Like a painkiller. It happened at Halálház, but the first time I really acknowledged it, I was digging a bullet out of the back of her leg. My calf burned as if I were cutting into mine, while she seemed to ease. I think she did it to me when I was shot helping her escape from Killian's."

"How many times have you both been shot?"

"Counting today?" He snorted sardonically. "A lot."

There was a pause.

"I had been hurt, really bad. I should have died. Instead, I healed. Fast. Quicker than I should have. Even for me."

"Just like she shouldn't be alive right now. Healing," Ash said numbly. "*Szent szar.* I knew something was happening. I could feel it, but I didn't expect this."

"Neither did I."

After a moment of quiet, my lids shut on their own, oblivion clawing and tugging on me, dragging me down. I wanted to listen, fighting tooth and nail to stay conscious.

"This is unbelievable. I mean, I've heard of some crazy shit. Intense bonds between mates, dream-sharing, soul touching…"

"We're not fucking bonded. She's not my mate, and I'm certainly not hers. I'm not anybody's."

"Then what the fuck do you call this?"

"Something that needs to end." Warwick's words reached deep inside, making me flinch. "I told you because I hoped you might be able to help me."

"Help you?"

"Help me break it. You are a powerful tree fairy. Who better than you?"

"I don't think I can."

"Ash…"

"Look at her, Warwick. You'd be a lucky fuckin' bastard to be linked to her."

"No." His words started to break apart, drifting away from me. "I'm not capable of that. She deserves somebody better. Someone who wants her."

Ouch.

I began to slip away, but I swore I heard Ash laugh.

"The only person you're lying to is yourself."

"I don't know if you should eat that…"

Chirp.

"I know I'm not your mother, but you can't just put anything into your mouth."

Chirp!

"Hey! Leave me out of it. Plus, that was *also* a total misunderstanding."

Murmurings dragged me out the delicious depths of nonbeing, where nothing could touch me. An irritation tickled my nose, made my head wiggle.

Chirp.

"No, she doesn't seem to like it any better."

Chirp.

"I don't know. People are weird."

The familiar voices dropped me roughly back into my body. Awareness and understanding seeped slowly back into my mind, along with shooting pain and memories.

Attack.

Escape.

Shot.

Agony.

After that was all a blurry mess of clips, nothing fitting together.

A groan started in my raw throat, but the soreness forced me to swallow it back; my esophagus felt like it had been shredded with razor blades.

As if I were swimming through mud, I struggled to pry my lids apart. Another moan slammed my lashes together again, my head slicing in half from the light pooling into the room.

"Master Fishy! You are awake." Opie's voice drew my eyes open again.

He went onto his toes, peering right in my eyeball. "Oh, you look like crap."

I felt like it too.

Chiirrp.

Bitzy was in the backpack on the pillow next to my head, her ears lowered down, an odd smile on her face.

Adorable, but disturbing.

Speaking of disturbing…

Today, Opie was in a bodysuit made of fishnet stockings, pleasure beads for a belt, and a leopard-print pasty covering his lower half, while Bitzy wore a matching leopard choker.

"You okay, Fishy?"

Not having enough energy to even speak, I tried to sit up a little more, the room spinning. I swallowed back the vomit in my throat, breathing through my nose. My gaze traveled down my body, which was when I realized I was naked except for my knickers and a bandage covering most of my torso, which wrapped me from my breasts to my hips. The tan bandages were spotted dark red in places.

A blanket covered me, and a pillow rested under my head, but I lay on a hard wooden table, where I was sure Warwick's friend had operated on me. Herbs, potions, bowls of liquid, medical instruments, bloody rags, and gauze were scattered everywhere near me. Slowly looking around, I took in the shadowy room. The only light was from the two windows above letting in a dull morning glow.

The entire home was made from wood. The ceilings were low and the windows small, like we were partially underground, but the room had a cozy, reclusive feel. The space might have been considered roomy, but it had beam posts and large furniture pieces. Every wall had a different style bookcase, shelf, and table loaded with stacks of books, plants, jars, bowls, and various clutter, which cramped the space.

A soft snore drew my head toward the stone fireplace. The fire was gone, but Warwick filled one of the chairs, slunk in deep, his legs outstretched and head tipped back, sound asleep. It took a moment to take him in. Even in sleep, I could feel his guard was up. Ready to respond if something happened.

Past him, on the far side of the fireplace, I saw a curtained-off doorway where the owner of the house might be. My mind flickered over a memory. I couldn't quite remember much except his voice. Smooth. Sexual.

I turned, spotting another doorway near me, opening to a small messy kitchen. The entire place was probably the size of my bedroom and bathroom back at HDF.

"This place is so... lived in." Opie pulled my attention his way, his body wiggling like his skin itched. "I mean, I don't want to clean it or anything." His face looked as if he wanted to do just that. "It's so untidy and dirty. Not that I have anything against it. To each his own, right? But..." He blew out, running his hands through his brown beard. "What do I care if he likes to live in filth?" He rolled his eyes. "Tree fairies." He shook his head like that explained it all.

A stronger memory of the man who lived here flickered in my head, the one who saved me, with his crystal green eyes, honey-colored hair, and a striking face.

"You must really enjoy almost dying, Fishy." Opie moved down the table, organizing the items in categories, not able to fight his nature. "I could smell the blood miles away."

I stared at my friends, not even bothering to ask how they found me.

209

Seemed they could follow my "smell," no matter where I was. But by their outfits, they had come from Kitty's.

Bitzy made a happy chirp, her fingers touching my face, still smiling at me, freaking me the fuck out.

"What the hell is wrong with her?" I grunted, every word and movement anguish. Every second that passed, more pain gnawed on my nerves.

"Wrong?" Opie tilted his head over to us.

"She's smiling at me... and not flipping me off." I blinked as she sighed happily, her blissful grin not leaving her face, her long fingers curling in the air as if she could touch it. "Is... is she high?"

"Oh. Right. She might have eaten something from one of these jars." Opie went back to straightening items on the table.

I snorted as Bitzy tried to snatch at nothing.

"Great, you're awake."

At the sound of a sultry voice, I turned and propped up on my elbow, seeing a stunning man saunter out from the back room. His unbrushed, wavy, shoulder-length, blond hair framed his bright green eyes and prominent cheekbones.

Damn. He was sooooo pretty.

Warwick bolted up, pulling a gun from his belt, pointing it at the source.

"Fuck, Warwick. Don't shoot me before I've had my tea." The man yawned, holding up an arm. "Damn, you are wound tightly."

Warwick peered at his friend, then at me, muttering something before he stomped through the doorway his friend had just come from.

"Sadly, can't even blame it on him not being a morning person." The guy winked at me, his sexual energy slamming into me.

"Tree fairies," I muttered to myself as if that did explain it all. My experience with them at Killian's suggested it was their nature. Still, it was hard to brace yourself against the intensity they released into the air, especially now when he was only dressed in a pair of light brown cotton pants. He rubbed at his bare, pristine ripped chest, a sexy smile on his lips.

"Glad to see you are awake. Though a little surprised."

"Surprised?" My voice croaked.

He stopped in front of me. "After what you went through? Even a fae wouldn't wake up for weeks." His brows furrowed, looking over me critically. "To be honest, I didn't think you were going to make it through the night."

"I'm hard to kill, it seems."

"So it seems." The side of his mouth crooked up, his bright green eyes landing on me. "I'm Ash."

"Brexley."

"Oh, I know." A suggestive grin pulled on his face before his attention went to the end of the table, his eyebrows popping up. Following his gaze, I saw Opie shoving his feet into puffy cotton balls, peering down at them like they were the latest fashion.

"Did I just inherit a cross-dressing housecleaner?"

Opie's head swirled to Ash, his mouth opened then closed, his chest puffing up, his cheeks turning a shade of purple.

Uh-oh.

"How dare you, sir." Opie huffed indignantly, his arms folding slightly above the pleasure beads. "I am no housecleaner!"

I tried to hide my smile. I loved that that was the part he was insulted by.

"You're a brownie." Ash motioned to him. "Though brownies don't normally show themselves or wear outfits as though they work in a whore house."

"First, I do not work there. And second, do I have the look of a normal brownie to you, sir?" Opie's newly acquired cotton ball slippers stomped down with a puff.

Even through my nausea, I had to hold back my giggle. Opie glared up at me, and I forced my face to be serious.

"How dare you call him normal," I chided Ash. "Shame on you." I could see Ash's mouth twitching with humor, but he nodded.

"Sorry, my friend. You clearly are something... *else*."

"Something magnificent." I nodded at Opie. "Right?"

Opie wiggled with coyness until a full smile pulled on his lips. "Do you like it? Mistress Kitty left out a box of stuff I could use." He motioned down to himself.

"I love it."

"Madam Kitty?" Ash's head jerked back to Opie, his eyes narrowing. "You were at her place?"

"They followed *her* there..." Warwick's husky voice jolted against my spine with energy. My heart thumped as I twisted to see him standing there, his chin jerking in my direction. Fresh from a shower, his hair dripped, water trailing down his marred and inked skin. Only a towel covered his lower half. Every inch of my body heated, my throat tightening as I tried to swallow. "I've been hiding out there. Well, I was until..." Warwick's sharp glance pierced me.

"You've stayed in touch?" Ash's tone sounded strained, but I couldn't pick out any particular sentiment.

"I'm not getting in the middle." Warwick ran a hand through his hair, irritation radiating off him. "Anything here I can wear?"

"There should be something in the far closet. Though nothing is gonna really fit *you*. You sure you're not half ogre?"

Warwick huffed and went back into the room, his gruffness on high today.

"He has the personality of one." Ash winked at me, making me laugh.

"Heard that, asshole," Warwick yelled.

"I know!" Ash shouted back. His easy smile made me smile. "Can I?" He motioned to the bandages. I nodded, too tired and in pain to care about modesty around a stranger. That ship had sailed back in Halálház.

He helped me sit up, slowly unwrapping the dressing, leaving the ones over my breasts in place. He inspected the wounds he had stitched up. One close to my right lung and the other around my kidneys.

"They're actually healing remarkably well." He looked up at me. I could see the question in his eyes as he grabbed a bottle full of clear liquid and started dabbing around the lacerations. *What are you? You aren't human.*

"You guys have known each other for a long time?" I asked, needing to distract myself from his curiosity and the agony from the wounds. Their back-and-forth banter reminded me of old friends or brothers.

"Me and Warwick?" Ash continued to work. "Fucking forever. Knew him when he was actually somewhat of a nice guy. One you didn't want to punch all the time."

"Heard that too," a muffled voice cried from the back room.

Ash glanced up at me, his sassy grin warming my stomach. His laidback, carefree personality laced with sexual cheekiness was easy to connect with. And it didn't hurt that the guy was unnervingly gorgeous.

"We used to be part of the Unseelie fighters here in Hungary."

"You fought in the war?" I inhaled, pain sizzling up my throat, the smell of turmeric tickling my nose.

"Yes." He nodded, a frown furrowing his brow. "Most did, from farmers to breadmakers… It was a fight for life, for freedom."

"For the humans."

Ash exhaled, grabbing clean bindings. "Technically, humans had more to lose, but so did anyone who believed in liberty, in the power of balance. Earth is a magical creation; everything depends on everything else to survive. Humans, fae, animals, insects, plants, oceans, rivers… One thing gets removed, and it causes a ripple effect for everything else.

Humans are a source of 'food' to a lot of dark fae. Along with that, the previous queen was controlling us as well." He fastened the fresh gauze up. "Plus, the woman was out of her tree. Nuts." He winked.

"Cute." I shook my head. "Saw what you did there."

"Little tree fairy humor." He stood up, leaning against the table, and looked at my wound. "I will need to check it later today. Can I get you some tea?" He trailed off, his head lowering to the table, where a drugged-up imp rubbed her long fingers and head over his soft pants like she was in heaven, a purr emanating from her tiny body. Now out of the bag, I saw she also had leopard pasties on. "What the hell? Is that an *imp*?" He moved back, his eyes wide.

Bitzy held up her hand, wiggling her three fingers in a flirty wave, but her eyes darted to her hand, her mouth opening like the movement was mind-blowing.

"Wow, another brainiac in the group," Opie huffed, rolling his eyes.

"They're supposed to be extinct." Ash stared at Bitzy with awe.

"Extinct?" I frowned.

"The body fluids of imps supposedly have magical healing qualities. The old Seelie queen made it legal to hunt them. They were caught by the millions, killed, and turned into healing potions to sell at market. Their numbers declined to the point they were assumed extinct."

"I guess not totally. And you are not touching Bitzy, tree man." Opie marched over to Bitzy, patting her on the head. "She's no healing potion."

"Bitzy?" Ash chuckled, looking between them in bemusement. "And is Bitzy the imp wearing a dog collar and pasties?"

"Those labels are so antiquated." Opie motioned to her throat. "This is a choker. And instead of pasties, I prefer to call them *fashion boosters*. It's my design."

Ash blinked at the brownie and imp.

"Yeah, I don't think he's ready for your fabulousness," I stage whispered to Opie. I could feel my eyes growing heavy, exhaustion creeping back in.

"Clearly." Opie sighed. "But what do I expect from a tree fairy?"

"What does that mean?" Ash folded his arms.

"I'll bet your entire closet is filled with the same colored shirt and hemp pants."

Warwick picked the perfect moment to step out wearing forest green pants and T-shirt, matching the ones Ash wore, the fabric stretching over his chest on the verge of ripping. The pants fit tight and came down only to his calves.

I clapped a hand to my mouth, trying not to laugh.

"Shut up," he grumbled, moving our way. "I need to run back to Kitty's anyway and get a few things."

I noticed Ash shift on his feet at the mention of her name. What was between him and Kitty?

Warwick strolled up to the table, his eyes dropping to Bitzy. She twirled one finger around her ear, the other hand wiggling flirtatiously at Warwick.

"What the fuck is wrong with her?" he grumbled.

"She ate something." Opie tried to grab her hands, but she kept moving them out of his way, reaching out to caress Warwick's leg.

"Ate?" Ash's spine straightened. "Shit. She got into my mushrooms?" Ash darted to a jar on the table.

"I told her not to put things into her mouth she doesn't recognize." Opie shrugged.

Chhhiiirrrppp.

"Shush. No one was asking you." Opie looked away. "Told you it was a misunderstanding."

Bitzy let out a squeak, then leaped onto Warwick's arm.

"Bitzy, no! He'll probably eat you." Opie tried to stop his friend as she crawled up to Warwick's shoulder.

Warwick turned his head to look at her, his eyes darting to Opie for a second before his head lurched forward, his teeth snapping together a hair away from Bitzy. Opie shrieked, his hands flying like a windmill, falling onto the ground dramatically.

Bitzy let out a sound resembling a giggle, tapping Warwick's mouth as if he was being silly.

"You are such a bastard," I snorted.

Warwick grinned wickedly at me. "She liked it."

"Oh, gods... my heart." Opie patted his chest theatrically. "I just lost eight of my nine lives."

"You're not a cat." I scrubbed at the space between my brows, my head starting to pound.

"What? I'm not?" Opie sat up, patting down his body like he was now discovering it.

"Drama queen," I muttered.

Bitzy's happy chirps drew my heavy head up again. She wiggled through Warwick's long damp hair, squealing.

Chhhiiirrrppp. Bitzy's fingers held on to Warwick's hair as she swayed back and forth like she was dancing to music. Warwick didn't even seem to be fazed by her.

"Damn. I think I'm the one hallucinating." I let my head drop back down, staring at my bare knees, my grip on the table the only thing keeping me upright. Sleep was creeping up on me again. The rocking in my head made me feel uneasy, my bones growing dense.

"You?" Ash snorted. "I have a cross-dressing brownie, a hallucinating imp, a folklore wearing my pants, and a naked girl on my dining table who should be dead."

I inhaled sharply at his words.

Ash shook his head, staring at our strange little group. "It is way too early for this." He turned for the kitchen. "I'm making tea."

I blinked after him, my lids growing heavy.

"Kovacs." My name rolled from Warwick's chest, sending shivers all through me. "Sleep."

We had so much to discuss and figure out.

"Rest. We'll talk later." He grabbed my head gently, trying to help me lay down again. The moment he touched me, I felt heat and sparks sizzle through my abdomen, numbness crashing in, relieving the pain. A smile curled on my mouth as he eased me back onto the pillow, the dreamworld calling for me.

"You take my pain away," I muttered. A flash of two men by the fire came into my mind, their words sounding important and urgent. But before I could pull them in, make sense of them, darkness dragged me under.

Chapter 22

"Stop trying to help. I won't be able to find anything."

My lashes fluttered open at the man's low, silky tone muffled through a curtain. Gazing around, I found myself in a bedroom, covered in blankets and fur, instead of on the table in the main room. A tiny window let in early evening light, allowing me to see the small chamber. The bed was a feather mattress on the floor piled with blankets and pillows, making you want to burrow into them and stay until next spring. Two areas across from each other were sectioned off with shelves stacked with clothes and household items. More ledges were stuffed with books, plants, and personal items.

"I don't know how you find anything *now*." Opie's small but clear voice flittered in.

"I thought you said you didn't clean," Ash huffed.

"I'm not cleaning… I'm consciously uncluttering."

A smile grew over my face, and I slowly pushed myself up. I still felt like crap, my body throbbing, but good enough to head to the bathroom and go on the hunt for food. The last thing I ate was a little stew at the Resistance base.

My heart instantly tugged at the thought of my new friends. I wondered how Andris, Ling, Birdie, Maddox, Wesley, and especially Scorpion were. Shutting my eyes, I thought of Scorpion, trying to grasp the link between us.

I could sense him, a thread, but I couldn't seem to reach him. Either he was sleeping, or I just didn't have enough energy yet, but I knew in my

216

gut he wasn't dead, which eased me some. It still didn't make me any less worried about him and the others.

How strange I had become so quickly bonded to a group of people I barely knew, while I had attacked others I had known almost all my life.

With a strangled exhale, I pulled myself onto my feet, pressing my hand to my wounds. My fingers rubbed a man's soft dark green T-shirt, which I now wore, the bottom scarcely hitting the tops of my thighs.

Taking a few steps toward the bathroom, I chomped down on my lip. Beads of perspiration from the pain dampened my lower back, but I finally shuffled into the water closet like an old woman.

Built almost entirely out of wood, it was small but beautiful. As if built into a tree, the back wall was an enormous tree trunk. A spout emerged from the wall, like a showerhead, and stone covered the floor. The sink was stone with wood cabinetry for storage and a sitting bench with a hole in it, similar to an outhouse. Ferns and plants filled the room, making it feel as though I'd stepped into a forest, not the latrine.

After peeing, I washed my hands, shocked at my reflection gaping back at me. I flinched at the mess staring in the glass. I had forgotten I'd been in a fight with Joska before I was shot. The cuts were healing, but my face was still swollen and black and blue. I brushed crusty and tangled strands of knotted, dirty hair off my face, gummy with dried blood. Everything on me was sweaty, grimy, sticky, and disgusting.

This seemed to be my new normal.

Wanting a shower but not sure if my wounds could get wet, I ambled out to the main room, the fire crackling in the hearth, the room quiet and calm. Without even looking, I knew Warwick wasn't there. His presence filled the air when he was around, and when he was gone, he seemed to leave something missing.

Ash sat at the table I had been on earlier, hunched over a slew of old books, a strange energy coming off them. Opie was quietly organizing his jars, while Bitzy was passed out in the backpack on his shoulders, mouth wide open.

"Fishy!" Opie waved, sensing me first.

"Hey, you're awake." Ash looked up, curving toward me. His smile expanded over his face, making my insides giggle. His energy was intense, tingling around my thighs.

"Yeah." I nodded, running my fingers through my tresses. "Thanks for letting me sleep in your bed."

"Of course. Though I was going to move you myself, Warwick was the one who carried you there the moment your eyes shut."

"Oh." I shifted on my toes. "Where is he?"

Ash shrugged. "Took off after he got you settled and hasn't been back. That was," Ash peered up at a clock ticking softly on the wall, "seven hours ago?"

"I slept for seven hours?"

"You needed it." He pushed off the bench. "You hungry? Thirsty? We'll start you off with something small and bland first."

"Sure."

He headed to the kitchen, and I went to the bench he deserted, easing myself down. Magic hummed down my arm, and I was drawn to the books laid out on the table. A strange buzz, like a whisper on the wind, drew me to touch it.

My hand lifted, my finger itching to run over the pages.

"Oh, be careful with that one," Ash spoke over his shoulder as he poured me a cup of tea. "It's very, very old, kind of cranky, and needs a lot of coercion to get it to open up to you."

"What?"

Ash picked up the mug and a slice of homemade bread, walking back over to me.

"Right. I forget you humans don't know much about fae books." He sat beside me, placing the food in front of me. "A lot of them died out when the wall fell. The abundance of magic wiped some of them clean."

"What do you mean died out? Like got lost?"

"No." Ash shook his head. "Our books in the Otherworld, the fae realm, are alive, so to speak."

"Alive?" I took a sip of the warm tea, the taste of calendula coating my tongue. It was a potent healing herb.

"They hold information the same as any other book, but if you treat them well, they will show you, tell you stories not written in their pages. This one holds a history of the past back to when there were fae god kings and witches. This old book was powerful enough to survive the merging of our worlds. But time has also made it crotchety. Not a fan of the new ways."

I stared at Ash, and my mouth parted. This was information I had never learned or heard about, something that got lost in the human side of history in this new world.

"Does it work on humans?" I swallowed nervously. "Can they feel it?"

Please say yes. Please say yes... I'm not a freak.

"Do you feel it?" He eyed me as I tried to swallow some bread.

"Don't worry." Ash smiled. "Humans could probably sense the magic coming off it, but the book wouldn't talk to them. They wouldn't be able to read it no matter how hard they tried. Fae books can sense if you have even a drop of fae blood in your veins. Though it is particular to whom it fully opens to. Some fae would only be able to read the surface level of this book, while others would never find the end."

"And where do you fall?" I whispered.

His eyes met mine. The gaze felt intense. Intimate. "I have yet to find the end. But it took years for it to fully let me in."

"What were you looking for?" I forgot all about the tea and bread, my attention drawn to both Ash and the book. Even Opie bobbing around, noisily investigating the jars he organized, didn't detract my focus. I had a strange feeling I already knew the answer without really knowing how—a flutter of voices talking, a fire, Warwick...

"You." Ash held my gaze.

I gulped. That was what I thought. "What about me?"

"You and Warwick." His head wagged. "The connection you have shouldn't be possible."

"Why assume it's me? It could be him." Trepidation stumbled out of my airwaves.

"He's definitely part of it, but I think it is you." Ash's voice dropped lower, sending a shiver through my body, tears building under my lids.

"How do you know?"

"Because I feel it too." He licked at his lower lip, rubbing at his brow, his intensity cranking up. "The pull toward you."

"What?" The word barely made it out of my throat.

"Tree fairies are good at healing and creating potions because we are connected to the earth, like the roots of a tree. We understand things you can't put into words—we feel everything. Life and death."

A nerve along my neck twitched, my breathing becoming more erratic.

"I can't see auras like Druids do, but I feel them and can sense energy in every living being." He leaned in closer. "And you, Brexley, are both life and death. Nothing and everything."

A sharp inhale sucked through my nose, my form going still. "What do you mean?"

Ash tucked his wavy hair behind his ear. "You already know, don't you?"

Just because Andris said I brought a cat back to life didn't mean it was true.

Or Aron, Mo, Rodriguez, the woman dying in the cage... and Elek, yesterday.

Fighting back the terror and tears, I gulped, "What does it mean? What am I?"

"I don't know." His forehead wrinkled sympathetically. "From what Warwick has told me so far, I know of nothing that can create what exists between you two. It's unnatural, even in the fae world. I can feel the energy coursing between you two, but I don't understand it. It's like a language I don't recognize. I'm also not sure it's something that can be broken as much as you and Warwick might want it to be."

His statement slammed fevered memories from the night before. Warwick demanding Ash to find a way to break the connection. *"I'm not capable of that. She deserves somebody better. Someone who wants her."*

"Are you sure?"

"I can keep looking…" He trailed off, nipping his bottom lip.

"What?"

"I want to try something."

"Try what?"

Ash stared at me. Reaching over, his fingers wrapped around mine, slowly moving them toward the book.

Trepidation hammered at my pulse, and my mouth went dry as our fingers hovered a breath away from the pages. Magic pumped off it, tickling my skin. I trembled with both the fear of finding an answer, but also of not discovering anything.

"Breathe, Brex." Ash's voice was soothing and calm. "Close your eyes. Relax. It will resist if you come up defensive and guarded. Take another breath."

"What's going to happen?"

"If you're human, nothing. But if you're not…" He brushed his thumb over my fingers. *If you're not.* "Guess we'll see, won't we?"

Inhaling and exhaling slowly, I tried to ease the tension in my shoulders. I let my lids close.

"Open yourself to it. Remember, it can't actually physically hurt you. Everything you experience is in your mind, like watching a movie. The events have already happened, and you are just watching them. Can't interact." Our fingers hovered over the pages. "In your head, introduce yourself, show it respect."

Introduce myself to a book? Seriously?

As the thought went through my head, I felt zaps of magic. Angry. Insulted.

"Brexley," Ash warned.

Rolling back my shoulders, relaxing my face, I let go.

Hello, I'm Brexley Kovacs.

Ash pressed our fingertips into the pages.

As if an explosion went off in my body, every nerve in me froze as the electrical current burst inside my veins, my heart pumping like it was going to explode. Images I couldn't grasp flew through my head as a deep, inhuman voice repeated my name as if he were tasting me, learning me, flipping through my memories so fast I was about to throw up.

When it stopped, I stood on a field. No moon was out, but the sky glowed with vibrant colors, swirling and weaving like the aurora borealis. The air snapped with magic; the countryside was stuffed full of figures battling. Screams and sounds of metal clanking shredded the night sky. I whipped around to take in the chaos, fear shooting up into my chest.

Creatures I had never even seen before tore into each other, and birds the size of planes flew in the sky. Creatures as little as brownies and as huge as giants dotted the landscape. The night rang with death, the field drenched in blood.

In the distance, it looked as if there was a curtain of energy that crackled and sputtered with light, holes forming in it. Behind it I saw an outline of a castle. It looked exactly the same as some of the drawings and pictures I had seen in books of the Fae War, of Queen Aneira's castle, the Seelie leader before the wall between the worlds fell twenty years ago.

I was there. The night Earth and the Otherworld became one.

The night I was born.

I could feel guts squishing between my toes, smell the bitter odors of blood and fear, hear every clank of metal, every shriek of death. People were dying right in front of me. Everything was so real. So vivid, overwhelming me.

"Let me out," I spoke to the book, but nothing happened. "I want out!"

Why would it bring me here?

"Warwick?" a man boomed, spinning me around. I gasped, my gaze landing on a familiar figure.

Ash.

Dressed in layers of dark clothes, his hair was longer than he wore it now and tied up in a knot. Most of his face was covered in blood. Carrying a sword, his belt dripped with more knives and guns.

The guy next to him was tall, lean, dark-skinned, wearing the same outfit, with sharp but pretty features. There was something familiar about him I couldn't quite place.

"Where the fuck did he go? What did he tell you?" Ash asked his comrade, but the guy didn't seem to hear him, his eyes moving frantically over the terrain. "Janos? Hey!"

Janos's head whipped to Ash. In a gesture I wasn't expecting, Ash reached out, touching the man's cheek gently. "It's okay, we'll find him."

"Don't lie to me, Ash," he muttered. "I can read your face. They caught him, didn't they? How could he just run off without us? If they finally found him, they will show him no mercy."

"Come on, this is Warwick we're talking about." I could sense a deep intimacy in the way Ash's fingers rubbed the other man's cheek. "The guy is tougher than anyone I know. He'll be fine. We'll find him. Okay?"

Janos nodded, pulling away from his touch, his Adam's apple bobbing. He sniffed in and pulled his chin up high, readying himself to go forward. Looking regal. Refined.

Holy fuck.

In one action, I saw someone else in Janos's face. My jaw dropped in shock.

Madam Kitty.

There were rumors of transgender people in the Savage Lands. But in Leopold? There weren't even whispers of them. I hadn't even known what the word meant until my late teens. When I met Ms. Kitty, I didn't even consider she was trans.

I had been so sheltered within the walls of HDF.

"Come on!" Ash tugged on Janos's arm, giving me no time to think more about it as I followed them through the combat. They sliced into bodies and fought as they moved over the field swiftly.

Gunshots volleyed past, and small bombs dropped from the giant birds in the air, spurting dirt and flesh into the sky, landing on me like hail. Ash and Janos moved with skill and partnership through the battle, ascending a small hill. They came to a stumbling stop, my feet slowing next to them, their eyes latched on to something below.

"Warwick!" Janos screamed before he took off, running to a large object lumped on the grass. Janos's legs gave out, and he dumped himself onto the damp earth next to the form, his body curling over the burned mess, a sliver of a face showing through the scorched blackness. "Noooo!"

It took me a moment to put the pieces together. To recognize what I was seeing. Acid tore up my throat, and I covered my mouth, emotion punching me in the chest as vomit burned my esophagus.

Warwick was that object. He told me the night at Kitty's how he died, but to see it was a wholly different thing. The larger-than-life man was a distorted pile of vulture fodder. His neck twisted unnaturally, his huge build had mostly been burned down to the bone, clothes still smoldering, stabbed so many times his entire torso looked like he had been flayed open. The one eye that wasn't charred stared emptily up at the sky.

Dead.

"Oh, gods." I swallowed back more bile.

Ash stood there, agony etched on his features, his frame swaying as if he was about to pass out.

Janos sobbed in grief, bending over the corpse. "I'm so sorry. I failed you…" Touching Warwick's face gently, he closed the one unburned lid. Janos's fingers shook violently, lingering on the slice of Warwick's face that still somewhat resembled a man.

Like a zombie, Ash staggered up, dragging his weapon behind him and staring down at the remains of his friend.

"*Baszd meg,*" he uttered, his expression twisting. "*BASZD MEG!*" A guttural bellow howled into the night, screamed up at the sky in sheer agony, burning my eyes with tears at his heartbreak.

The atmosphere crackled and popped, the holes in the atmosphere growing bigger, and the castle no longer looked like it was being seen through a film as fairies, trolls, ogres, and other figures battled everywhere. Only a sliver of the wall was left between the two worlds.

A pack of wolf-shifters came tearing over the land, snapping and ripping into everything it passed, getting closer to Ash and Janos.

"Come on!" Ash yelled for Janos to move and fight, but Janos continued to weep over Warwick. Ash stomped over, yanking Janos up, bringing their faces close together.

"He wouldn't want us to die tonight too." Ash held Janos's face, their noses touching. "If you can't fight for that, fight for *him*. We owe it to Warwick to track those fuckers down. Kill each and every one. Do what they did to him. I need you, Janos. I can't avenge him without you."

Janos sucked in, nodding. They stepped away from each other, pulling out weapons, and turned straight into the mass of wolves, hacking and slicing at them, dissipating into the endless enemies coming.

I didn't follow, my feet timidly moving closer to the man on the ground. The brutal way he was murdered showed even more prominently up close.

I bit my lip until I tasted blood, lowering myself down next to him. Even if I knew he was alive in my reality, seeing him here was gutting. Heart-wrenching. Wrong. Supposedly the half-breed fae died this night, and the legend rose from his ashes. I couldn't imagine how he could come back from this. How was he alive now? There seemed no way.

He had been burned to nothing, gutted, had his neck broken.

No one came back from that.

Not even fae.

A deep panic at the idea he wouldn't wake up this time drove into my gut like a drill. The terror of losing him trailed a tear down my cheek, building energy in my chest. The air hissed and sizzled, magic sparking at my skin.

I couldn't stop myself; my hand reached out for his cheek.

My palm touched his singed skin as a loud crack filled the night. A lightning bolt struck the earth; earsplitting shouts and yowls echoed throughout the battlefield while blinding lights exploded near the castle.

The last strands of the wall were falling.

A whoosh of magic slammed through me like a tidal wave, the power shredding me so brutally, a gut-wrenching scream tore from my lungs. Tumbling me over Warwick, the energy plunged into me felt as though I was going to combust, my muscles shuddering violently.

There was so much pain.

I thought the book couldn't hurt me.

It whipped through me like spiked tails, lashing and spearing my insides, leaving me heaving for air and twitching as if I'd been electrocuted.

Under my palms, Warwick's lids burst open, and he heaved in a violent breath of life, his body convulsing. His blazing aqua eyes went straight on me.

Looking directly into my eyes.

Seeing me.

Chapter 23

With a shove, I felt myself being tossed back, the book yanking me out with a cry as blackness enveloped me.

"Brexley?" I heard my name called from afar. "Brexley!"

With a gasp, I opened my eyes, my lungs sucking in gulps of oxygen. Irises the color of moss peered down at me. Ash bent over me, his face filled with worry and awe.

Blinking, it took me a few moments to realize where I was, my mind feeling like scrambled eggs. I laid on the ground, having fallen backward off the bench.

"Are you okay?" Ash asked, his gaze searching me, making sure I was physically all right.

"Damn, Fishy, you hit the ground like a wet sponge." Opie leaped down next to me, Bitzy's head bobbing around in the backpack, her tongue hanging out even more. "Splat!" He hit his hands together. "For a back dive, though, I can only give you a two. Your form sucked."

"Thanks," I grumbled, trying to sit up, still grappling for air. Ash wrapped his hands around my arms and back, helping me sit.

"You hurt anywhere? Anything feel torn?" He nodded at my wounds.

"I don't know." My brain felt scattered, my skin still buzzing from the experience in the book, as if it really happened.

He moved in closer to me, his fingers reaching for the T-shirt. "Do you mind?"

"I was stripped and beaten in Halálház, used as a lab rat for both Killian and Istvan... so no, I don't care."

Ash's mossy eyes met mine, a sadness flicking through them.

"Even more reason to ask." His sentiment stirred emotion in my chest. Gently he lifted the shirt, frowning at the fresh bloodstains. "You pulled your stitches. Though this other one is healing remarkably fast." His hand brushed the one in the middle of my chest. "Don't move." He got up, grabbed supplies off the table, and returned to me. With a light touch, he unwrapped the old dressing, cleaning the blood away.

"What happened? The book showed you something, didn't it? I've never seen it take to someone instantly. What did it show you?" His question brushed at my skin, his body really close to mine as he doctored up my wounds.

Opie had moved to his side, rifling through the jars he pulled down, inspecting the swabs and cotton balls like he was already turning them into future outfits.

"It kept me out today. It wouldn't let me follow you. It's never done that." His eyes met mine, and all I could see was the man from the Fae War, covered in blood, deep pain cutting into his eyes as he howled into the night air over the loss of his friend.

"You and Janos..."

"What?" Ash jerked back, his eyes wide. "Janos... How-how do you know that name?"

"Janos is Ms. Kitty, isn't she?"

Ash sucked in sharply. "What did the book show you?" I could see panic fluttering his chest, letting me know there were secrets he hoped I hadn't seen.

"The war twenty years ago. The night the wall fell. Warwick." I cringed, shaking the bad memories away.

His shoulders lowered, but his throat bobbed with emotion, focusing back on his duty. "That night still haunts me. Why would it take you there?"

"Not sure." I bit down as he finished cleaning the wound, grabbing the gauze. "Did you know I was born that night?"

"What?" His chin lifted from his work, meeting my gaze, his eyes wide.

I swallowed, my head bobbing. "The exact moment the barrier broke, my mother gave birth to me. She died right after. My father said her body couldn't handle the traumatic stress of my birth and the flood of magic."

"She was human?"

"Yes," I answered automatically, then slouched back with a poignant sigh. "I mean... that's what I assumed anyway. What Uncle Andris told me."

"But now you wonder?" He tied off the dressing.

I tried several times to swallow. "I know something is different about me. Even if I'm not fae, I'm... I'm something." The last part came out a whisper.

"You are." Ash's voice went low too, his hand touching my jaw, pulling my face up to look at him. "You are definitely something." His throat bobbed, and he tenderly stroked my cheek with his thumb. The same gesture he'd made with Janos. "I can't explain it. You are a light, but both life and death buzz around you. Drawing us all in like insects to honey."

"Honey." I chortled. "Never been compared to that before."

He smiled.

"Will you help me?" I felt scared and fragile, letting myself soak in his tenderness. He seemed like someone I could trust. A friend. "Find out what I am?"

His eyes searched mine, his hand still on my face. "Of course."

I felt the sudden hum, the change of air, but it wasn't from the guy next to me. The door burst open, turning our heads to the entrance with a jolt.

Warwick strode in, his gaze quickly taking in the scene between us. My skin still prickled where Ash touched me.

Ash dropped his hand, standing up, but it was too late. The rush of rage swirled around, digging deep. Warwick's presence coiled in on me.

"Move fast, don't you, princess." His voice growled in my ear, though he still stood in the doorway, silent as he closed the door from across the room. *"Your fan club is getting rather large, don't you think? You sure you have room for another?"*

"Fuck you," I snarled out loud, reaching out for Ash's hand to help me up. "Wasn't like that. Though I don't need to explain myself to you."

Ash's head snapped back and forth, as though missing what I was responding to.

"Don't you?" Warwick's ghost breathed against my neck. I felt teeth dragging across my shoulder, heating my body. I narrowed my lids on the real man, trying not to shiver at the sensation wrapping around my nerves, my adrenaline pumping. By now, I should have been used to him, but I wasn't. He entered, and he demolished everything else around me. Overpowering. Taking. Consuming.

"She pulled her stitches." Ash forced me to sit again, ignoring the glare Warwick shot him. "I was cleaning and rewrapping it."

"Is that what they're calling it?" Warwick muttered, making a sound in his throat, yanking his gaze from me, moving farther into the room, dropping a bag on the table.

"What's that?" I glanced at it.

"Thought you'd want clothes." He motioned to the bag, his irritation still curling around me. He had changed back into his own garments, fitting his frame like a glove.

"You got me clothes?" I opened the bag, seeing cargo pants and a T-shirt, knickers, and a sports bra. "Was this at Kitty's?"

"No." He strolled to a small table, picking up a bottle and pouring a glass of brown liquid.

Warwick was someone you had to learn to read because he gave so little away. One-word answers would drive most people insane if you weren't paying attention.

"Stole them?" Without moving or opening my mouth from the bench, I brushed the back of his arm. His back muscles tightened at my invisible contact.

"Does it matter?" he muttered over his shoulder at me, downing the drink.

Actually, it was the equivalent of getting me flowers, maybe even better, since the clothes were useful. He didn't ask Rosie or one of the girls to gather me some items; he got them himself.

I fought a smile as I tugged out the sports bra.

"Not sure I can wear this for a while." My ribs and wounds ached at the thought of anything binding them.

"All the better." He flipped around, leaning against the table, his aqua eyes burning into me as he guzzled another large mouthful.

I met his gaze, energy ping-ponging between us, my skin breaking out in bumps.

"A kurva eletbe." *Fucking hell.* Ash exhaled, running his hands through his hair. "And I'm supposedly the one with the overpowering sexual energy. Will you two fuck and get it over with?"

"Oh, is it happening now?" Opie darted out from the jars he was procuring, half-dressed in cotton balls and strips of gauze. "Bitzy would want me to wake her up for it. Do you need a vacuum?"

"A vacuum?" I turned to Opie.

"What?" He took in everyone staring at him, then started to chuckle forcefully. "Oh. Yeah. I was totally kidding. Why would you need one of those, right?" His cheeks flushed.

Chirp. Bitzy lifted her head, her fingers rubbing her ears.

228

"Oh, now you wake up and add your opinion."

Chirp.

"I have no idea what you're talking about." He huffed, glaring over his shoulder. "No one was asking you anyway."

Chirp.

Bitzy glared back. "It was a misunderstanding. How many times do I have to tell you that?"

"My head hurts." Ash rubbed his head.

Chirpchirpchirp! Bitzy pointed her middle finger at the tree fairy.

Opie's eyes widened at Ash. "Wow, she is pissed at you."

"Thank fuck, it's not me for once," I muttered. Bitzy flung out her two middle fingers at me, making me snort. "Ahhh, everything is right in the world again."

"Why is she mad at me?" Ash held out his arms. "And why do I give a shit?" He seemed bewildered.

"Welcome to my world." Warwick sniggered, downing the rest of the drink.

"She's not feeling so good right now," Opie replied.

"How is it my fault? She ate *my* mushrooms." Ash pointed back at her.

Chirpchirpchirpchirpchirp....

"Wow." I breathed as Bitzy went off on him. "You don't even want to know what she just called you."

"You understand it?"

"Gods, I hope not." I leaned my forehead onto the table. Again, I didn't understand her exact words, but I certainly felt her meaning, and I was pretty sure Ash should sleep with one eye open tonight.

"I think I prefer the imp high." Ash headed over to Warwick, pouring himself a drink. "Since when does my life consist of arguing with an imp and needing to hide my vacuum from a brownie?"

"When *she* entered your life." Warwick flicked his chin at me, taking the bottle from Ash, pouring a healthy amount of liquid.

"Hey now." I twisted my palm. "When did this become my fault?"

Both guys looked at me with their eyebrows raised. I looked over at Opie, who was back to fixing his cotton shorts, which looked like diapers, a gauze crop top, and his feet in fresh puffs.

"Yeah… okay…" I curled my hand for Warwick to bring me a drink. He pushed off the table, handing me his glass. It was silly, but I liked that he automatically shared with me instead of getting me my own.

The burn of extremely potent Pálinka watered my eyes. I watched his attention dart to the object on the table, brows furrowing.

"What the fuck is this?" he snapped at Ash.

"Right…" Ash cringed. "Look, man, I was going through it for *you* when she woke up… and…"

"And what?" Warwick sucked in, spine going rigid.

"I thought why not let her try to read it."

"Are you kidding me? You let her touch a fae book? Especially this one."

"She's fine."

"Fine?" Warwick barreled over to Ash. I squeaked, jumping up as he grabbed Ash's throat. A small cry of pain bent me forward, but I moved over to them.

"Warwick, stop. I'm all right."

He shoved into Ash, ignoring me. "You know what that book is capable of."

"I didn't let her do it alone. I held her hand, but Warwick, I've never seen the book respond this way. It took to her instantly, shoved me out instead."

Warwick's mouth pinched. "It blocked you?"

"Yeah." He nodded in shock. "I could feel it. It wanted her. As though it had been waiting for her or something."

Warwick let go of Ash, whirling to me, staring at me like I was some mystery.

"What?" I stepped back. "Was it not supposed to? I thought you said it couldn't hurt me."

"Not physically, but if you are weak or have nefarious plans for it, it has been known to make people go crazy or to hold them prisoner."

"Prisoner?"

"It has the power to trap your mind in it, not letting you out."

"And you let me touch that thing?" I yelled at Ash, motioning back to it.

"The book only protects itself. You have to have ill will toward it. You do not. It was a gut feeling. I just felt the need for you to touch it… like it was asking me to."

"What did it show you?" Warwick leaned into me.

I stared up into the very eyes I saw look upon me on the battlefield.

"You," I whispered.

His jaw rolled, but he didn't respond.

"It showed me Ash and Ms. Kitty, I mean Janos…"

Warwick inhaled when I said the name, stepping back, running his hand over his face as he started to pace.

"Yeah, I had the same response," Ash said.

"Why?" I looked between them.

"No one else knows that name but the three of us. Kitty said Janos died that night in the war. She has never allowed us to mention the name or acknowledge him again. To her, he did die. There's no way you'd know it unless..." Ash trailed off.

"I was really there," I filled in.

"What else?" Warwick demanded.

"I watched them find you..." My legs started wobbling from fatigue, and I lowered myself onto the bench. "Dead."

He didn't react, but his shoulders strained against his dark shirt.

"You-you were..." The images of him dead had me shaking my head, my throat tightening with nausea. "What they did to you."

"Yeah, I know what they did," he grumbled. "That was it?"

"Yeah," I lied, scared to admit he woke up and saw me. I could feel it in my bones, his gaze embedding into me. But it was ridiculous. There could be no way I was actually there at that moment. The book replayed what had already passed, so I couldn't interact with it.

Warwick's eyes went back and forth between mine, sensing there was more. I hiked up my walls, keeping my face emotionless and not letting him in.

We stared at each other; the pressure of him trying to push in thumped at my skin. He had always been able to just invade me, take what he wanted, see and feel my emotions.

"No!" My shoulders rose defensively, and I could feel myself pushing back, trying to not let him in.

He jerked his head, his chest rising in huffs of fury, but he eased back.

Holy shit, I had never done that before. I could block him out like he had me.

"Szent szar," Ash muttered, his head wagging in disbelief. "You two..."

Warwick snarled over at him. "There is no us."

"You can lie to yourself all you want." Ash poured more liquid into his glass, drinking it down in a gulp. "But I can practically feel colors sparking off your auras."

"I don't have one," both Warwick and I said in unison.

Ash's regard lingered on me. "How do you know you don't have one?"

"Tad..." I swallowed nervously. "He told me I didn't have one."

Both guys stared at me, a memory tickling at the back of my head from the night of the attack.

231

"She has no aura; I don't sense anything there. Like you."

"Don't."

"Don't what. I'm simply stating facts. Seems odd neither of you have auras…"

I nipped my lip. "Tad said it was most likely because I got good at blocking…" Though I was starting to doubt that.

"Tad? Who's Tad?" Ash asked.

"Tadhgan." Warwick rubbed at his scruff.

"The *Druid*, Tadhgan?" Ash's mouth parted.

"Yeah, why?"

"I thought he was dead. I mean, that guy is probably the same age as the book." Ash motioned to the ancient item on the table.

"He was in Halálház," Warwick added. "They kind of became friends."

Ash pinched the bridge of his nose, tilting his head to me. "You and the oldest Druid known to exist just happened to become prison buddies?"

"Yeah." I looked to Warwick and back to Ash. "Why?"

"Seems odd out of all people, the Druid gravitates toward you… And what the fuck was he doing in there anyway?" Ash set down his glass.

"I didn't ask." I shrugged.

"No, I mean, Druids' magic is different from fae. As powerful as Tadhgan is, he could have probably walked out any time he wanted."

I had learned Druids were different from fae. At one time, they were normal human witches who did favors for fae gods when fae had ruled Earth. The fae gods were so taken by them, they gave a few clans gifts of true magic, long lives, and extraordinary powers. They lived for many centuries and could heal similar to fae as well. Their magic had first been coveted by the fae leaders, working as healers, future tellers, and spirit guides, until they became more powerful than the fae. The jealous old Seelie queen in the Otherworld had almost obliterated them from existence, except those who went into hiding. It was why they were so rare now.

"Who gives a shit why he was there?" Warwick turned to me. "He said you had no aura? *Saw* nothing there?"

"Yes." I nodded, peering at Warwick through my lashes. "Like you."

In frustration, Warwick dragged a hand over his face.

"The coincidences finally making you wonder, old friend?" Ash smirked into his glass. "I could sense them, but a Druid can see them. Or the lack of them."

"Fuck off," Warwick grunted, pacing the room. The room grew silent, tension growing as Warwick moved around the space, finally growling,

"Fine, let's say there is a reason we both don't have one, and we have this strange connection. What does that mean, and how can we break it?"

"I need to learn why and how it happened before I could possibly start trying to figure out how to cut the link," Ash responded.

My mind went to the image of me leaning over Warwick's dead body, my palm touching his skin, a whoosh of magic slamming through me… the feel of death. Of life… The book had taken me there for a reason.

I already knew the answer to Warwick's question. It felt like it had been waiting for me to acknowledge it… I just didn't want to. But I also couldn't deny what I saw. What I felt. What I knew in my soul.

"Then do it!" Warwick's voice ordered his friend.

Perched on the edge of the bench, I stared at my toes. I could feel the buzz of the book from across the table, still rolling through my system, the moments replaying over and over. Fear clotted my throat, and I wrapped my arms around my body.

"I know why." I spoke too softly for them to hear me. So I cleared my throat, picked my head up, and said louder, "I know why."

Ash and Warwick stopped, all attention pointed at me.

"Know what?" Warwick rumbled.

"Why we are connected."

Both men stared at me, tension saturating the air.

"It was me."

"What was you?" Warwick's deep voice prickled against my skin with the anxiety of running too fast at a cliff's edge to stop.

My eyes looked straight into his, the same ones that opened on me the night on the field.

"I think I was the one who brought you back to life that night."

Chapter 24

Silence exploded and flourished in the room like smoke, expanding and sucking out all the air. Heat stomped down my spine, leaving beads of perspiration over my skin.

Warwick's burning eyes stayed on me, his nose flaring.

"What do you mean you brought him back to life?" Ash cut through the tension, his tone eerily detached.

My eyes didn't leave Warwick's. His jaw gritted together, but he didn't speak.

"You saw me there, didn't you?" Every syllable was choppy and terrified.

He went still.

"Didn't you?"

His head started moving back and forth, his throat darting up and down. "No," he muttered so low I barely heard it. "No." He turned away, his feet retreating from me. I automatically reached out for him in my head, projecting myself over to him, my hand pressing into his back.

Warwick jerked at my touch. He swung around, glaring at me. "Don't." I backed off, pulling back into myself, but my physical body took a step toward him.

"Look at me," I demanded.

Warwick's gaze darted all around, not landing on me.

"I said, look at me," I ordered. As if he couldn't ignore my request, his fury-filled eyes snapped onto me. "I was there that night, wasn't I?"

234

"No." He scoured his neck. "This can't be possible. I dreamed it... a hallucination."

"It wasn't." I had no idea where my assurance came from, but it sat in my gut, identical to truth.

"How is it possible? You weren't even born yet." Warwick tossed up an arm, his agitation rising.

Technically, I was, barely, but I got what he meant. I couldn't have been there. My mother was at our home giving birth to me. I was nowhere near the war. And was a newborn.

"Wait... wait." Ash held up his hands, strolling in the middle of us. "What the hell is going on?"

"I don't know, but when I was in the book, I wasn't simply viewing events passively. I could feel the magic, smell the grass and blood, see the barrier between the world falling... felt it... like I was there."

Ash jerked, his eyes opening wide.

"Is that not normal?"

"The book shows you what previously happened. You view it like a movie, history that has already passed. Yes, it can feel like you're right there, but you aren't. You can't touch or smell anything and certainly can't interact with it," Ash said firmly.

My muscles constricted around my throat and lungs, making it hard for me to breathe.

I recalled how it felt when the dirt rained down on me, the taps on my skin, the mud and guts squishing between my toes. The feel of Warwick's burnt skin against my fingers.

"When I asked you if you saw anything else, you lied." Warwick's rumble cut my attention to him like a magnet.

I nodded, my throat struggling to swallow.

"You saw me come back to life." A nerve in his jaw jumped.

"And you saw me."

He inhaled sharply, turning away.

I was right.

"*Szent fasz!*" Holy fuck! Ash whirled to Warwick. "This is *sötét démonom?*" *Your dark demon.*

"Dark demon?" I repeated it in English. The saying felt familiar, my brain rolling back trying to recall why it did.

A memory of the night we escaped from Halálház, hiding at Kitty's, came back to me. He started to tell me a little about his past. He had uttered those very words.

"It was the night of the Fae War. Right before the final barrier fell, I

was jumped by many enemies at once. A hunting party." He stared out of the window, taking another drink.

"How is it possible?"

"Sötét démonom."

My dark demon.

"How the fuck do you know about that?" Warwick's chest puffed with fury, his shoulders rolling toward Ash.

"A few times when you were here healing after the war, you muttered about a dark demon saving you, her eyes and hair black as night." Ash peered at me, stopping on those features, exactly the color of night. "I thought it was because you were fevered and imagining shit."

"I was," Warwick declared, but it fell flat, splatting on the floor, heavy with denial. He started to pace again. "I had just fuckin' come back to life. I wasn't exactly in a coherent state of mind."

"Gods, listen to yourself." Ash chuckled dryly. "You have no problem accepting you came back from the dead, like *dead* dead, but it's too much to think that she was there?"

"And you can believe she was?"

"I'm not saying this isn't all crazy as shit. *None* of it should be possible. The only people who can bring people back from the dead are the highest-tier Druids dabbling in black magic, and necromancers. And neither can bring someone truly back. They are basically the walking dead. A shell of themselves, tortured and trapped—begging to die."

"Do I fuckin' look or act like a zombie?" Warwick moved over by the fireplace, putting more distance between us.

"No, you act like a full living bastard," Ash shot at him.

"Exactly!"

"Warwick." I tucked hair behind my ear, my bare feet padding toward him. He shifted on his legs, his eyes darting all over again. I stopped in front of him, my neck craning back to look up at him.

"Warwick."

His regard finally came to me, his eyes tracking mine for a long time before he uttered, "Dark. So black, they felt bottomless. Like they could save me and destroy me."

"What was?"

"Her eyes." His hand reached up, his thumb skating under my lashes. "Your eyes."

The moment he touched me, energy crackled between us, and I once again saw that moment where I'd leaned over him, his figure jolting with life violently, our eyes connecting. I saw myself through his eyes: The girl leaning over him, pale, with cuts and bruises on her face. Her dark hair tangled and wild, only wearing a man's dark green T-shirt.

Exactly what I was wearing now.

"Fuck." Warwick lurched away as if he had been electrocuted, his chest heaving, and I knew he had seen the same thing. The dark demon who saved him twenty years ago was the *exact* girl in front of him now, down to the shirt I was wearing. Even though it was long ago, tonight, I had saved him.

We stared at each other for a long time. The sound of the clock ticking built up anxiety until it sounded like someone shouting.

"This can't be possible," Warwick blew out. But we both knew it was. "It was you." His heavy gaze dragged down my body, taking in my shirt. "You were wearing that. How?"

I shook my head, having no clue.

"Wait." Ash held up his hand, traveling to us. "What are you saying? What do you mean she was wearing that?" Ash pushed his palms into his head like it was going to explode. "Are you saying the vision you had twenty years ago was Brexley from tonight?"

Veins along Warwick's neck throbbed and strained.

"That isn't fucking possible!" Ash's arms flew out, his voice bouncing off the walls. "The book records history; it doesn't alter it."

"I know," Warwick snapped, his fingers skating back over the seam of the T-shirt, near my shoulder. "But even this little hole... She was wearing this shirt." Warwick's fingers pinched at the shirt, tugging at the hole, his other hand moving to my face, his thumb sliding over my cheek. "This bruise. The cut on her lip. I remember it all."

A hiss of swear words came from Ash as he bent over his legs, taking deep breaths. "How the hell is this possible?"

"You tell me, tree fairy," Warwick barked, backing away. "Fuck..."

I stood there. Numb.

"Fuck!" Warwick bellowed, whirling away from me. "This is... Fuck... I can't..." He growled, pacing for a moment before striding for the exit.

"W-where are you going?"

Warwick didn't respond as he stomped out, the door slamming shut behind him, leaving palpable silence in his wake.

I stared at where he exited, lost, scared, and overwhelmed.

It took several moments for Ash to stand up, centering himself.

"He needs a moment to calm down, gather his thoughts. He'll be back."

I nodded, slumping forward, feeling fatigued and heavy, plus extremely sweaty, dirty, and gross. My mind and emotions were a mess. This was all too much.

I could feel myself shutting down. I needed to do something so I wouldn't lose it.

"I'm gonna go take a shower," I said formally, no emotion in my voice. My head was overloaded, and my body was exhausted.

"Right now? Don't you want to figure this out? I need every detai—

"No." I held up my hand. "I need a moment." I headed for the bathroom, hearing Opie and Ash mutter to each other. I stepped into the room, falling back against the door. My emotions went so many ways. I didn't know if I was going to cry, scream, hyperventilate, or laugh.

Automatically, I reached out for Warwick, feeling a solid barrier there. I understood. This was a lot to take in. We hadn't even gotten into the hows and whys.

What was I? How was it possible?

I had no idea of anything, except I had been there. I had brought Warwick to life. Some way, somehow. I was there.

Sötét démonom.

I was his dark demon.

The shower water cascaded gently down from the spout, tapping the stone floor, begging me to step under the stream. I itched to be clean, to wash everything away. Forget the world for a moment.

"Brexley?" A knock tapped at the door. "I have the clothes for you to change into. Plus, I want to wrap your side so it doesn't get wet."

"Oh, of course," I replied. "Come in."

The door glided open, Ash's stunning face poking in like he still wasn't sure if he was allowed. He moved in cautiously, smiling warmly at me.

"You probably want to soak for hours, but you need to keep it dry." Ash set down the clothes Warwick brought me, strolling to me with a sheet of sticky film to cover my wounds. "I know this must be a lot right now."

I snorted as he lifted up my shirt, covering the dry, clean bandages with the film, his touch tingling my skin. His sexual nature was always there, pulsating under the surface.

"We'll figure it out." His green eyes met mine with determination. "I promise. And you know fae don't make promises unless they mean it."

A promise was a bond in the fae world. They didn't throw them around or break them as humans often did.

"Thank you," I croaked, biting on my lip, not able to think of all the things I wanted to say. He had only known me for a day and already treated me as a friend, once again blowing to shreds the notion that fae were evil and less than humans. "You have been beyond kind to me."

"It's what family does." His fingers pressed into my skin, making sure the film stuck around the edges of the gauze.

"Family?"

"You saved someone I consider a brother; that makes you family to me." Ash continued to work, not realizing the effect of his words. I tried to fight the tears sliding down my cheek, my emotions from the day, hell, the past few months, hitting me. "I can't explain it, but the moment Warwick brought you in, I felt as if I've known you forever, like you are part of us."

I wiped at another stray tear.

"And if tonight tells us anything, in a way you have been." He winked cheekily at me.

A dry chuckle twisted in my throat, several more drops escaping down my face.

"Hey." Ash straightened, noticing them, cupping my face. "You're not alone, okay? We'll figure this out."

My lids closed briefly, the warmth of his comforting words washing over me, driving up my emotion. His energy filled the room, coating my body, making me inhale.

"Sorry," he muttered, his mouth only inches away. "I'm trying to suppress it as much as I can, but it's difficult. Especially around you."

"I don't want you to not be yourself." My gaze went to his. He was so calm, caring, and sensual. I wanted to wrap myself up in him, let him take away the pain and feel wonderful for a moment. He would be easy to fall for... if I were another girl.

Or at least a smart one. But I seemed to be drawn to the dickheads.

"Don't let Warwick's mood bother you. He's always been a bullheaded, cranky asshole." Ash's description brought a slight smile to my lips.

"And egotistical," I added.

He laughed, nodding. "He is certainly that too." Ash's expression went serious. "For twenty years, he's held revenge and death in his heart. Vacant of life. But with you? I haven't seen him this way in a long time."

"What do you mean?"

"He was almost a machine before. Only killing made him feel alive.

But with you…?" Ash's eyes tracked mine. "You have a power, Brexley. Something I can't explain… it pushes all the death and ugliness away. It's like he can breathe again."

His proximity rattled my nerves, forcing my head to look down and step back. Ash's compassion, sexual nature, and honesty were difficult to fight.

"You need help getting undressed?" Ash grinned playfully. "Hair washed? Body scrubbed down?"

"*I've* got it." Deep, raspy, and vibrating with ire, Warwick's voice snapped over Ash's shoulder. He filled the entire doorway, leaning against the jamb, his glare set on the back of Ash's head. "You can get the fuck out."

A huge smile curved on Ash's face, stepping away. "Guess I will go see what I can gather up for dinner. Take a long walk to my vegetable garden a really long walk." He winked at me before heading out, patting Warwick's arm as he squeezed past him, shutting the door, leaving us alone.

"You're back." Captain Obvious reporting for duty here.

His gaze crawled over my skin, heavy and intense, his face void of emotion.

"What?" I tugged on the ends of my hair with aggravation. "I'm too exhausted to deal with this right now. Get to it or get out."

He pushed off the wall, taking a step toward me, his eyes never leaving me as he tugged his shirt over his head, his abs rippling as he moved, ink rolling over muscle.

Oxygen filled my lungs, my eyes locking on his sculpted torso. Marred and inked, it was even more beautiful because of its scars. The stories it told, the battles it won. Fuck… This man's physique. He needed to warn me before he did shit like that.

He kicked off his boots, his hands moving to his trousers, yanking them off, his boxer briefs following…

Holy mother of all that's massive. I was never prepared for this man clothed, but naked, he flipped my entire world off its axis, emptying my brain.

"What are you doing?" My voice came out small and flimsy, reminding me of the first time he stepped into the shower room at Halálház with me.

He strolled toward me, hard, feral, and confident, smashing the energy Ash held into smithereens. Everything about Warwick was unapologetic, raw, and severe.

My thighs clenched, my eyes darting away as fierce desire lit my nerves on fire. Naked, this man was a sin. One I wanted to commit over and over.

He gripped the bottom of my T-shirt, gently pulling it from my frame, my body responding to his, need coursing from my head to my toes. The cool air licked over my skin. "Warwick...?" My chest heaved, feeling his presence coating me, invisible hands sliding down my thighs, over my arms.

"No talking," he rumbled, turning me around to face the shower, tilting my head under the spray. His fingers paused at the top of my knickers, I could feel him searching for an answer, waiting for some kind of no, but he wouldn't get one.

His hands glided down my legs as he pulled off my underwear, my back arching as heat scored up my spine. He reached over, grabbing the homemade shampoo, and poured it into his hand. His fingers tangled through my hair as he massaged my head.

This reminded me so much of the first time we showered together, when I first felt the pull to him and the strange sense of him touching me without physically doing it.

Little did we understand then what was ahead.

I could no longer deny it or pretend it was all in my head. I leaned into the solid feeling of his spirit hands running across my stomach and over my legs, as his real hands washed my hair. There was no difference between either kind of touch. The connection between us seemed only to be getting stronger.

Water cascaded down me as he washed the soap from my hair, careful to keep my left side mostly out of the water stream. He pushed in closer to me, his hips pressing close enough for me to feel him hard and pulsing against my ass. I bit back a moan, invisible hands caressing and sliding over my figure, my nerves humming to life, and stilting my breath.

Pain was gone. Only lust and desire raked through me, my head floating away as I gave in to the sensations.

His hands coated the ends of my hair in conditioner before grabbing a bar of soap. I sucked in as he glided the soap between my breasts, then slid it slowly over one nipple. With a soft groan, I tilted my head back into his shoulder, his free hand wrapping firmer around my waist. Soaping up my breasts, nonexistent hands traced and pinched at my nipples, leaving my entire body on fire. Need throbbed my core, my ass curving back into him.

A noise vibrated from his chest, the soap slipping down my torso, stopping right at my pussy, making me ache with need. His cock throbbed against my back, and I spread my legs, needing him.

241

"Warwick," I whispered his name, pushing back into him.

He drew the bar of soap up, cleaning the dry blood around my wounds. His real hands stayed up higher, but I felt his phantom hands continue down, the sensation of fingers slipping through my folds making my breath hitch. He held me firmer against him as he fitted his enormous length between my ass cheeks, letting me feel every vein and pulse.

Logic evaporated into the steam, my body rolling back into him. The ghost fingers prodded my legs to open more as they found their way inside.

"*Baszd meg!*" Air rushed through my teeth, and I parted my lips. His head didn't move, but I could feel his mouth skating up my neck, drawling out a louder moan. I could feel the intensity as he pumped his fingers into me, then a tongue slid through me. "Oh, gods... don't stop."

His tongue flicked and nipped so powerfully I started to tremble. Pleasure hit so deep in my bones, I no longer felt I was tied to anything real, losing all track of when and where we were. A loud cry broke from my lips, and my teeth drove into my bottom lip. Warwick was everywhere; his mouth, teeth, and fingers touched, nipped, kissed, and licked my skin as a pressure rubbed over my core.

"Oh, gods... fuck... Warwick."

I lost all control of myself as he moved quicker, building the friction, my climax racing toward me. His ghost fingers curled as his thumb worked the sensitive part. I felt his warm mouth consume me, sucking on my clit. Then he nipped down.

A guttural cry sprang up my throat as everything shattered, my body violently thrashing as my climax consumed me, everything in me going limp.

Warwick clutched me to him, holding me up, his palm pressing into my chest like he wanted to feel me gasping for air, feel every ounce of life throbbing through me.

I wheezed and heaved for oxygen, slowly coming back to myself. "Fuck," I muttered, my limbs feeling like jelly.

"And think... I didn't even *actually* touch you." His voice was thick and rough in my ear.

Shit. I didn't know if I could handle the real thing.

Rinsing us off, he shuffled me out of the shower, wrapping a towel around me and gently drying the places near my wounds. Wordlessly he dressed me in a tank and fresh underwear before ushering me into the bedroom.

"Get some sleep," he muttered, helping me crawl into bed, my body boneless and my mind empty of thought or worry, as if he knew exactly what I needed to sleep.

Warwick grabbed some of his clothes out of the bag he brought, pulling on sweatpants, outlining everything he was trying to cover underneath. His erection tented his pants so sinfully, heat pulsed through me again.

Fuck. Me.

I curled onto my good side, away from temptation, wanting him to stay, but my mouth wouldn't open to ask.

The bed dipped with his weight as he crawled in, scooting behind me. "Just tonight." He answered the question I never asked.

A truce for the night, nothing but him and me before everything tangled and weaved into knots again. We could deal with all this in the morning.

His massive frame curled behind me, blanketing me in warmth and security. My insanely unbelievable orgasm only took the edge off the desire building back up as his body wrapped around mine, his cock still pressed into the back of me.

"Sleep, princess," he muttered in my ear. Sighing deeply, content and relaxed, I let go.

Darkness took me quickly, but right before I went under, I felt his lips brush my temple.

"Te valodi vagy... sötét démonom."

You are real... my dark demon.

Chapter 25

A tickling in my nose stirred me awake, my lids opening to Bitzy's fingers.

Chirp. The noise sounded like "good morning."

"Bitzy." I batted away her hand, noticing a lazy smile on her face. "Oh shit." I peered around. For once, it was just her; Opie was absent. My gaze drifted over the bed, finding myself alone, the bed and pillow still imprinted with Warwick's outline, suggesting I hadn't dreamed he slept next to me.

Exhaling, the feel of him still throbbed through me—the memories of what happened in the shower, the images of this huge violent man washing my hair... my body.

Chirp.

My attention returned to the imp, her hand holding something as she munched.

"Bitzy, what are you eating?"

She peered down at the item, then peered up at me innocently.

"Is that a mushroom?"

She rolled in her lips coyly, her eyes huge, her ears lowering to the side, and she giggled.

"Oh hell, Bitzy." I groaned, palming my face. "Are you high again?"

Her smile showed the few teeth in her mouth. How could she be so adorable and unsettling at the same time?

I fought the grin curling my own mouth, trying to sound angry. "Give it here." I held out my hand.

Chirp. She shook her head, tucking the piece of mushroom away.

"Bitzy. Now." My hand opened for her to put it there.

Her brow furrowed.

"Noooow."

She drew the piece out again, but instead of giving it to me, she shoved the whole thing in her mouth, her cheeks stuffed like a squirrel as she chomped on the huge piece.

"Oh, just you wait, young lady. When you come down from your high, you won't be looking so proud of yourself then," I chided.

"Phhhfffttt." She stuck her tongue out at me, bits of chewed mushroom flying out.

"Nice." I pushed back the covers, climbing out of bed, still stiff and sore, but I was starting to feel much better. I swore the orgasm was a miracle cure. Knowing Warwick, it probably was.

I still felt the aftermath of him, and now I craved more. Soon I'd become an addict like Bitzy, but it wouldn't be mushrooms I was stuffing into my mouth.

"Come on." I nodded to her, and she scaled my arm up to my shoulder, not flipping me off once. Her pleasant side felt all wrong, as if my day was already starting off upside down. "I need coffee."

After going to the bathroom, I headed for the common room, sensing the man my body ached for nearby.

"Fuck, Warwick. You can't leave. Not with everything going on." Ash's voice stopped me, stilling me in the doorway.

Bitzy made a small sound, and I put my finger up to my mouth to quiet her. She mimicked me, her long finger at her lips, her eyes wide.

"She needs you. This is some crazy, scary shit, and you want to walk out on her?"

My gut dropped, terror, hurt, and anger bubbling in my belly like a cauldron.

"I'm not walking out on her. I just need to deal with some things. I won't be long." His voice was like a drug, washing over my skin, leaving me high and hooked. "I need to move them, make sure they're safe. After what I did, Killian will have men searching for them."

Searching for who?

"Warwick…"

"Ash, I will do everything to protect them. He deserves to grow up happy. Safe. The opposite of what I had."

"I know, but what am I gonna tell her?"

"For fuck's sake, you act as if this is some horrendous burden." A wood bench squeaked as it slid over the wood floor. "I've seen you around her, so don't act like you wouldn't mind me staying away permanently."

"Screw you, man. You know I'm a flirt, and I won't deny there is something about her that draws me, but you made your position pretty clear last night. In my bed, may I add."

"Nothing happened."

A strangled laugh broke from Ash. "You're an idiot and a bad liar. I could feel you guys from over two miles away. I kept having to go out farther, trying to find a distance where I could no longer feel the intensity between you two. You know what that kind of energy does to a tree fairy? I was so tense, I had to go to Kara's to take the edge off."

"Kara? You two still fuck buddies?"

"It's convenient. River fairy-tree fairy sex exchange." Water fairies were another group who were constantly sexually charged, not that many fae weren't, but I guess the current of the water, the energy and life in it, riled them up. "But you're missing my point."

Bitzy started to sway in my hair, humming to herself.

"Shhh," I tried to shush her.

Chiiiirrrpppp. She batted at the air, falling over and hitting the ground with a thump.

A strange giggling chirp burst from her, her little legs and arms kicking as if she was swimming.

"Thanks, Bitz." I frowned as Warwick and Ash turned in my direction, forcing me to step out.

"Is she high again?" Ash's look went to a jar on the table, his mouth dropping. "That little shit! She stole my mushrooms again!"

"There are pieces on your pillow if you want some." I motioned over my shoulder, progressing farther into the room, my gaze running over Warwick. Dressed in dark cargo pants, T-shirt, and boots, his expression was detached, but his attention traced every inch of my skin, covering the tight tank and stopping on the tiny knickers I didn't bother covering up. Everybody here had already seen me naked.

The feel of his energy landed right between my legs, causing my pussy to pulse in response, like it knew where his focus stopped and was screaming out for more attention.

My jaw locked down, and I guarded myself against the surge of desire plunging through me.

Ash pulled his attention from Bitzy still wiggling around on the floor, taking me in. "How are you feeling?" He rose to his feet.

"Amazing!" I exclaimed, my arms tossing out.

"Really?" He tilted his head, his eyes wide in awe.

My face and voice went flat, my arms folding. "No. I feel like crap."

He grinned, shaking his head, something about his smile making me shift on my feet.

"What?"

"Nothing." But the same knowing smile stayed on his lips as he looked back at Warwick. "I'll get you some toast and tea."

"Coffee?" I could hear pleading in my voice.

"Uh, I'll check, but don't think so." Ash went to the kitchen, busying himself with my breakfast.

I folded my arms tighter, glancing at my toes. "So... you're leaving?"

Warwick pushed back, rising from the bench, gathering his jacket and bag on the chair.

"Seriously?" I shook my head, anger dancing at the edges of my tone. I should have known better, taken "just for tonight" literally.

Warwick moved in front of me, his body almost pressed against mine.

"I have to." The scents of rich woods and soap filled my nose, making me want to flatten myself into him. "For a week or so. Try to stay out of trouble." He stared down at me, but I felt an aloofness this morning. A line he was trying to redraw after last night. "It's not like you can't contact me anytime."

My response was to step away, giving him free access to the door.

He didn't move. "You'll be safe with Ash."

I nodded.

"Last night—"

"Nothing happened." I cut him off. "Right?" I lifted an eyebrow.

I had never been a jealous, bitchy girl. Even when Caden dated all those other girls, most of them I was friendly with. I had no idea where or to whom Warwick was going, but it caused my shoulders to bristle, resentment spiking out of my spine.

"Have a safe trip," I said flatly.

His mouth opened, then shut, his jaw rolling. He huffed as he stepped over Bitzy, stomping out the exit and slamming the door.

Just like that, he walked out. Left me.

Again.

I guess it was an upgrade he didn't sell me back to Killian, but his aloofness still cut deep, reminding me the only person I could really count on was me.

"Fuck you," I whispered at the door, but I knew he felt and heard it.

I turned around to the kitchen, picking up Bitzy and heading for the table, setting her down on some cotton balls. "Where's Opie?"

"Oh, he's found my trunk." Ash pointed to the far corner. The lid was open.

"What's in there?" I asked right when Opie popped out.

"Fishy!"

"Oh, gods." I rubbed my eyes.

Opie had designed a knee-length skirt out of bay leaves, which fanned out as he twirled around. His chest was bare but painted with dark crimson markings. On his back were large fairy wings made from dried calendula flowers and leaves; his eyelids were painted the same berry red. His beard was braided with leather ties and flowers, and on top of his head he wore a spray of lavender fanning out like a crown.

"Wow." I blinked.

"I know, right?" He scrambled onto the table. "This has to be one of my best." He spun again, the leaves dancing in the air.

"Like you are ready for a ball." *In Carnal Row*.

Chirp. Bitzy laid on her back, reaching at things in the air that weren't there.

"No, she wasn't speaking of that kind of ball." Opie huffed at her. "And that was a misunderstanding too."

Chirp.

"It was!" Opie stomped his foot. "You came in at the wrong moment. It wasn't what it looked like."

"Toast." Ash came around, setting a plate and cup in front of me.

"Oh, thank gods." I didn't want to know any more about this "ball" incident.

"Sorry, only tea." Ash slid down next to me, leaning his back against the table.

"Suddenly, Halálház isn't looking so bad." I smirked, taking a bite of my butter and jelly toast, trying not to moan as it melted on my tongue. "At least there they served coffee."

"I could see how it might make you want to go back," he teased back. "It's rough here."

Shoving more bread into my mouth, I snorted at his comment.

"Can I?" He motioned to my wound.

At my consent, Ash unwrapped the gauze around my waist, sucking in sharply.

"I thought so," he muttered, his fingers grazing my side.

"Thought what?" I looked down, toast getting stuck in my throat. The wound that had split open the night before was healed shut. As though the injury was weeks or even months old.

"That you would be completely healed this morning."

"What the fuck?" My hand prodded at the raised skin, a permanent scar on my side. I healed faster than ordinary people, but this was way beyond my normal.

"How?"

"I think whatever supposedly *didn't* happen last night with you and Warwick healed your wounds." Ash's eyebrows tipped up, mocking.

I blinked at him.

"Certain fae have the power to heal through sex."

"We didn't have sex. Nor am I fae."

"Well, whatever *connection* you guys share, it seems to diminish each other's pain and help you both heal. The power I felt coming from you two last night must have done the trick." He shook his head, ripping off the rest of my bandages and tossing them onto the bench, no longer needed. "Warwick told me he healed from the injuries he got escaping Killian's far quicker than normal. And you should have died the night you came here. I watched with my own eyes as Warwick bore some of your pain. I think he also helped keep you alive."

My head fell forward, my shoulders slouching. Another thing linking us together. It was starting to twist and coil so much, I couldn't see a way out.

"Don't think about it right now. You need to eat. You're still weak."

Ash was quiet, watching me pick at my breakfast before he spoke again.

"I thought we could work with the book again today; maybe it will show you more."

"Yeah." I nodded, sipping the milky tea. "Sure."

"He'll be back." Ash propped his elbow on the table, slanting more toward me. "Warwick's always been an island unto himself, even more after he 'died.'" Ash curled his fingers in quotes. "He's harsh, violent, rude, deadly, and arrogant. He kills and tortures without thought. But if he deems you part of his family, he will fight to the death for you. There is nothing Warwick won't do for those he cares about. It's why I've been friends with him so long. He's more like my brother, and I would die on any sword for him as well."

I set the cup down, lapping up every insight I could on Warwick. "Tell me more."

"Knowing him before and after his death, I saw the fierce part of his personality only intensify. He used to laugh a lot easier, smile, have fun, was passionate about things. When he came back from death, he seemed to lose the joy of life. I thought those qualities were gone for good." Ash tipped his head, his meaningful gaze hitting mine. "But around you, I see them coming out again. I feel the fire and drive he used to have."

I scoffed. "Most of the time he can't stand me, nor I him. We're always at each other's throats."

"Exactly," Ash smirked. "He never cared enough before to argue with anyone. He certainly wouldn't have given up his liberty from Killian's hold to save simply anyone."

"Where is he going?" I stared at my plate.

"To the reason he turned you over to Killian in the first place." Ash tucked his wavy hair behind his ear. "But that's his story to tell you."

I pushed away my plate, not sure how to respond.

"I'm just saying, you saved his life twenty years ago, but you are also bringing him to life now."

Dressed and fed later that morning, Ash and I sat at the table, the book lying before us. Nerves braided in my stomach and seemed to twist up my throat. This time I understood what I was getting into. What the book could do.

What if this time it took me and didn't let me go?

"I will be here next to you the whole time." Ash intertwined our fingers. "If you get scared or uncomfortable, focus on my touch. Remember, this is your reality, not whatever the book is showing you."

I nodded, my throat dry. I took in the imp passed out on my breakfast plate, her tongue out, crumbs of toast covering her mouth, a spot of jelly on her ear. Opie had disappeared in Ash's trunk again, probably designing his next outfit.

Thick fog and angry skies outside dimmed the light in the room. The weather was turning colder daily, but the crackling fire warmed the space. I lost count of days the moment I left HDF, though autumn had definitely arrived.

"You ready?" Ash squeezed my fingers.

"Sure," I breathed out, a hint of a crazed laugh following. Terrified didn't even cover it, but I needed to know more, to figure out what happened that night and how I was involved.

"Who knows… it might not even let you in today. It can be finicky like that." Ash tried to ease my fears, his small smile producing one from me.

"Okay." I swallowed, lifting our joined hands toward the open cover.

"Be open to whatever it wants to show you, but also remember it's not real. I am." His serious green eyes met mine.

I licked my lips, my fingers lowering slowly.

The book hummed with energy, and I had the sense it was conscious of me, clamoring for my touch.

My fingertips made contact with the page.

I gasped as I felt myself tumble, energy bursting through me as the book yanked me down, bile burning up my throat.

"Brexley Kovacs." The same raspy inhuman voice said my name like it had been waiting for me to come back. "The girl who challenges nature's laws."

Images and voices flipped so quickly in front of me, I curled over, covering my eyes with my hands.

The spinning stopped as loud screams, metal clanging, and booms of guns yanked up my head. My attention darted around, soaking in the same scene as the time before, the book returning me to the battle. Out in the dark field, death lay all around me, and the bitter smells of blood, urine, and fear soaked the earth. The vibrant colors of the Otherworld's magic ripped Earth's atmosphere almost to shreds. Pops and crackles hissed in the air, and the press of heavy magic on my bones was so dense I could taste it. The barrier was scarcely there, just webs holding it together, the final thread barely hanging on.

Turning toward where Ash and Janos had come, I waited for them to reenter, but the scene felt a little off. A different location. It also seemed to be later in the night than the last time I'd come.

"Scorpion!" A guy's voice boomed as he ran past me, jerking my attention to a man I knew. Maddox. Dressed in all black, wounds and blood covering him, his dark hair knotted on his head with only a single tattoo inked on his neck, not the multiple ones he had now. He called out his friend's name again, my gaze shooting to a figure in the distance fighting a creature that had to be part giant.

I ran, catching up with Maddox. We were yards away when the beast's ax swung down for Scorpion. He was too close to get out of the way.

"Scorp!" Maddox wailed, watching the blade slice into his friend. A scream wrenched from my throat as I watched the axe drive all the way through with a sickening sound of tissue, muscle, and matter being hacked before the blade came to a crunching halt when it hit Scorpion's spine. The monster roared, yanking his blade out, leaving a gaping hole in Scorpion's form. The monster didn't even wait for the body to drop before he stomped off, battling his next victim.

"No!" Maddox screamed, sprinting forward as Scorpion's body plunged for the ground.

A booming crack splintered through the night like lightning, more magic slamming into us. A bolt of light tore across the field, coming sideways instead of from above. Energy scraped at my skin with a strange familiarity.

As Scorpion's corpse dropped, the bolt of energy collided with him at the same moment. I could feel its power crackling through me, taste the magic in my mouth… And I recognized the thick bittersweet smell. Dirt on a spring morning, a bloom at midnight. The darkest chocolate with a sprinkle of salt.

It smelled like both life and death. *Like when everything is coming back to life after a long winter.*

My heart slammed in my chest, seeing the energy strike his body. Electricity ignited his frame, charging through and flapping him like a fish before he hit the dirt. One second slower or faster, and it would have missed him completely.

"Scorpion!" Maddox dove to his knees, his dirty and bloody hands fumbling to turn Scorpion onto his back. "Fuck! No, man, don't fuckin' die on me!"

But I could see by his demeanor he already knew his friend was dead.

There was no way *anyone* could survive that.

Maddox's gaze went over him. It was hard to see in the dark, but I knew from its location the ax had taken out Scorpion's entire side and his vital organs with it.

Gutted him.

Maddox sat back on his heels, peering up at the sky, taking in a shaky breath. The sorrow and grief of losing his friend was etched on his face, his chest shaking with sadness.

But then, with a sharp inhale, Scorpion's frame jerked, his eyes opening, his body jackknifing up. Maddox lurched back on his ass, a scream wrenching up his throat.

Scorpion sucked in long draws of air, his eyes wild, his head jerking around as if he didn't know where he was.

"Scorpion?" Maddox's voice shook with hope and terror. "What the…?" Maddox gaped, looking around as if something was going to give him a logical answer. "You-you're alive? How the hell… I watched you get sliced in half."

Scorpion's head lifted, his hands clawing where he had been axed, as if he recalled the same thing. He tugged at what was left of his shredded shirt. I could see a deep cut, tissue and blood oozing out, but most of his side was intact.

"What. The. Fuck." Maddox sucked in, fear lacing his tone. "How is that possible?"

Scorpion's wide eyes met Maddox, his head shaking.

I knew. Me.

I curved around, peering through the darkness and the moving figures. I couldn't see, but I knew, the same way the book knew that Warwick and I were not far away… The bolt that happened to hit Scorpion was from me.

It was why the book brought me here. To show me. My connection to Scorpion. Our link had been forged on this same night. Nowhere near as strong, but it was there just the same.

The commotion was quieting slightly as though the war was coming to an end. In the distance, a baby's wail rang in the air, piercing through me and snapping my spine straight.

A gasp burst from my lungs, the sound touching something deep inside me. Chills ran over my body, and my stomach dropped, a fluttering of understanding tapping the back of my mind.

I could feel the pull as the baby cried again, my feet moving…

Whoosh.

Darkness cloaked me, everything spinning and moving as I felt the book shoving me out.

With a scream, I went flying back onto the wood floor with a thud, my lungs scrambling for air as my eyes flew open.

Two figures stood over me.

"Barely any improvement from yesterday." Opie shook his head, his hands on his hips. "Sorry, I still only give you a two, maybe a two and a half. The head bounce was a nice touch."

"You all right?" Ash reached down and helped me sit up, ignoring Opie.

"Yeah." I rubbed the back of my head, my stomach swaying like an ocean. "Just nauseous."

"I'll get you some ginger tea." Ash pulled me the rest of the way up, plunking me down on the bench I'd fallen off. "How about next time we move to a chair with a back." He massaged my shoulder before heading for the kitchen.

"Have any more of those tea biscuits?" Opie bounded onto the table next to me, his skirt swishing, the sharp smell of the bay leaves flicking my nose.

"Gone," Ash grumbled.

"What? You had a jar full yesterday," Opie exclaimed.

"Yeah, someone got the munchies." Ash's lids narrowed on the passed-out imp on the table.

"Oh, is that why her farts smell like cookies?" Opie replied.

Ash shook his head, returning to making the tea. "So, what did it show you?"

I stared down at my fingers. Neither Warwick nor Ash knew about Scorpion, and for some reason, I felt protective of him. He was innocent in this. One more moment, and he would have missed the magic current. He would have died. Good or bad, he was still a victim of whatever the hell I had done that night.

"More of the same," I said evenly, my mind going back to the scene, something itching at the back of my neck. I felt restless and antsy, as if I was on the verge of something, but I couldn't see what yet.

"Here you go." Ash set down the steaming cup next to me, along with some crackers, and pulled up a chair beside me.

"Thanks." I grabbed the tea, giving half a cracker to Opie, my stomach not wanting anything in it.

"Is this sweet?" He sniffed at it.

"No, it's a cracker." Ash kneaded his temples. "Salty."

"Brownies prefer sweets. You sure you don't have any more cookies? Pie? Scones? Cake?"

Ash dropped his head onto his arms. "I'm getting a cat."

"Cat! Where?"

Their voices swirled around me, but I was no longer listening. My knee bounced, the aggravation in my limbs too much to contain. My insides crawled with the need to move. Irritated. Aggravated.

"I'm gonna go for a walk." I bounded up, desperate to move. "I haven't been outside in days."

"I'll go with you." Ash stood up.

"No." I moved to the coatrack, grabbing the jacket Warwick brought me. The fabric was heavy and thick. "The last few days, hell, few months… have been a lot. I just need a moment by myself."

Ash shifted on his feet. "Warwick wouldn't want you to go by yourself. We are in Killian's territory."

The mention of Killian spiked fear and guilt through me. Yet as much as the humans painted him as a monster, he had been kind to me. I had no idea how he'd act if our paths crossed again. Probably not favorably now. He probably regretted ever kissing me.

The night on the balcony fluttered back in my mind, his words prickling the back of my neck.

"I cannot see clearly when it comes to you. I cannot explain it, but you make me feel alive. I'm drawn to you."

Drawn to you.

What Zander had said to me.

What Ash had said…

"I will stay close. I need some air." I pulled on the coat, my lungs tightening.

Ash sighed. "Fine. But don't go far. There's a nice woodsy area right behind here. Stay within fifty feet of this house."

I nodded, already out the door, the need to run making my muscles twitch. Though I knew no matter where I ran, I could never run from this… or Warwick.

Chapter 26

Fog hugged the foliage. Sodden leaves hung with weight, curling the branches closer to the earth. The sky was swathed with gray clouds, but I could tell the sun was already drifting near the horizon, the shadows clinging in dark patches. It was chilly, autumn setting in, the crisp air snapping in my lungs. My shoulders lowered as I took in another deep breath, wrapping my arms around me, tucking deeper into my hood.

I let my mind shut down, my legs moving deeper down the overgrown trail, loving the feel of fresh air on my skin. My muscles and bones ached, and I was still nowhere near my best, but stretching my legs, moving around, helped ease the anxiety crippling my body.

My brain looped around and around with what I had learned just in the last day, not even taking in finding my uncle alive and him confessing what my father had suspected. All those trips he went on, leaving me, were to find any leads on what I was.

If I was fae, he could have found that quickly, but I wasn't.

But I wasn't human either.

Somewhere between.

Like life and death.

Love and hate.

Did my father find out anything? Andris said he got more secretive, saying it was for their safety. Did he find answers then?

Bringing back a cat from the dead seemed impossible, but what about the deep understanding that I went back to the night of the Fae War and brought Warwick and Scorpion back to life?

Neither of them was a shell of himself. They were full of vivacity, vibrating with danger, violence, and death.

"Danger and violence," Lynx's words came back to me. *"They follow you."*

She was right. They really did. And I didn't think it was a coincidence anymore. I needed to figure out who I really was… *what* I was.

Lost in my mind, my feet absently moving as my mind whirled with questions, I wasn't paying attention to anything but my turbulent thoughts.

I went through every detail of what the book showed me. What was happening when I was with Warwick, down to the shrill of the baby crying, breaking through the thick haze of magic like a sword.

Lost in my thoughts, it took me longer than it should have to feel the prickles down my spine, alarm skating across my chest, realizing I was much farther from Ash's than I had planned on being.

I stopped, wisps of my breath billowing in the deep shadows. My heart thumped in my chest, my skin bristling, recognizing something was off. Soldiers always trusted their intuition. I tilted my head, straining my ears, listening to every sound.

I knew wild animals had taken over park areas, moving back into the territories humans no longer used as recreation. Life here was not made for picnics or playing games.

What I sensed was more deadly than the kinds of animals that probably lived around here. There were no noises or movement, but the warning tapped loudly at my instincts. My heart thumped in my ears, adrenaline filling my veins.

Move, Brex!

Slowly, I circled around, facing the direction I'd come from, the tiny cabin nowhere in view. I had gone at least a mile or so out. Ash was going to kill me.

Icy fear scraped up my neck as I moved quickly down the path, steady and quiet.

A shrill squawk came from over the tops of the trees, making me jump.

A hawk circled overhead.

Terror dried out my mouth, my heart hammering against my ribs.

Nyx.

Brex, the world is full of wild animals and birds. There are wild hawks here too. It doesn't mean it's her.

But my feet picked up their pace, the chilly feeling of something behind me clawed at my back like fingernails scraping at bone.

Another squawk filled the sky, deep terror burning in my ears as I took off running. I could feel my muscles cramping, but I pushed them faster, ignoring the stiffness and pain.

At the sound of rustling leaves and snapping branches, I turned to look. Dark hooded figures burst through the foliage from all angles, moving for me.

Fuuucck!

My intuition had sensed what I could not see or hear.

Danger.

It followed me.

Killian had found me. Though something about this sneak attack didn't strike me as his style. He would have just burst through Ash's door and taken me. Why hide in the forest in hopes I would come out?

Not the time to contemplate. I darted down the path, hearing boots pounding in the dirt, getting closer.

I could see the smoke from Ash's chimney far in the distance.

I screamed his name, hoping I was close enough he could hear me.

"Shut up!" A hand grabbed the back of my jacket, hauling me back. A cry broke from my lips as I whirled around, my fist cracking into a person's face. The man grunted, blood bursting from his nose as he stumbled back. Another figure grabbed for me. I twisted and kicked, my boot landing in their groin, the hooded figure falling to the ground, hissing swear words in my direction. Punching and kicking, I knocked another coming at me, trying to ignore the multiple shrouded figures moving in on me, my strength already dipping, pain already tearing through my muscles.

Grunting, I punched the figure to my right as hands from behind grabbed my shoulders, yanking hard. I slammed onto the rocky ground, agony tearing up my spine. I tried to flip over and climb back to my feet, get out of the defenseless position, when a foot slammed into my gut, right where I had been shot. A scream tore up my throat as I fell back flat. A gun cocked and pointed at my face, and a boot pushed down on my chest. I could tell it was a girl, her dark blonde braids falling out of her hood, showing part of her unfamiliar face.

If she was Killian's, I had never seen her before.

"Don't move," she ordered. More than a dozen hooded figures moved in around me, my body motionless with terror, understanding I had no chance.

Was this how it ended? After all I had been through?

A large hooded figure pushed through the group, blood still dripping from his nose. His light brown eyes narrowed on me, his face and voice younger than I was expecting. "He warned us you might be feisty."

A squawk sounded overhead, circling the trees. Terror drowned my lungs at the idea that Nyx was near me. I had a feeling she would even go against Killian's rules and kill me before I even got to the palace.

My mouth filled with saliva. "Fuck you and fuck Killian."

The man chuckled softly, kneeling next to me, some kind of cloth in his hand, a slight sweet smell teasing my nose.

No. Fuck. No! Chloroform.

I tried to wiggle away, but the girl's heel dug into my ribs more. None of these people felt familiar to me from the palace. None wore the lord's insignia.

"Who are you?" My pulse jackhammered against my neck, my eyes darting around, taking in their worn cloaks and dirty faces, a realization hitting me.

These were not Killian's men.

"You'll find out soon enough." The man smirked, covering my mouth and nose with the rag.

Terror soared through me as I sucked in the sweet, odd taste of chemicals.

Fright shredded through all layers and walls.

Suddenly I stood in a small rundown small room with only an old sofa, table, and chair. A beautiful dark-haired woman peered up at Warwick like he was her world, her arms around him, as he held a young boy of maybe six in his arms, the boy hugging him like he never wanted to let go.

Like a son would a father…

I blinked, taking in the intimate scene, hurt slashing over my soul. He had a family… a wife? Or a lover and son. They were who he left me for? Why he didn't want this link between us… he was with someone else.

Fear pushed everything away as I felt myself slip toward unconsciousness, the effects of the chloroform wrapping around my legs, trying to drag me down into darkness. I only had seconds left.

"Warwick!" I screamed.

He whipped around, his eyes going wide, his shoulders expanding in alarm at the sight of me. "Kovacs?" He set down the boy, moving to me, searching the scene behind me. "What's happening?"

My mouth would no longer move, the darkness dragging me down. "Kovacs!"

I could no longer fight it. Slipping away, I clawed and scraped to stay with him, but it swallowed me, pulling me away from consciousness.

"Brexley!" His voice howled in my head as the chemical claimed me. The sound of my name on his lips wrapped around me like a blanket. Then nothing.

Nausea rolled through me, vomit purging up my throat before I even totally woke, my bones trembling with the aftereffects of the chemical. My head pounded as I tried to open my eyes, but only obscurity surrounded me. A cloth wrapped around my eyes, keeping me in the dark.

Grunting, I tried to move, my arms pinned behind my back.

"Go slow. Your body needs time to recover." A deep voice jolted me. My head automatically angled toward the sound, my senses groggy.

I felt so sick I wanted to vomit again. My instinct drove me to try and sit up, not be so defenseless. Hard to do when your hands were tethered.

"I apologize for the restraints, but seeing what you did to a few of my men, we couldn't be too careful." Something about his voice, the way he spoke, was oddly familiar to me.

"Who are you?" My throat croaked over the question.

"Well, that's a complicated question. I go by many different titles." Shoes clipped over stone, his voice growing closer, and I sensed there were other figures in the room. "Most here call me Kapitan."

The name touched something in the back of my mind, but I was too foggy to place it, my mind still trying to catch up with itself.

"You have stirred up a lot of trouble, haven't you? So many want to claim you."

"You adding yourself to the list?" I snipped.

"Not the way you suggest, my dear." The man scoffed, a laugh bubbling up his throat. The sound struck a chord deep in my gut. "That would be highly inappropriate."

"Cut the bullshit. What do you want? Why kidnap me?" My headache shoved all my patience out the window.

I heard a noise, then heavy footsteps moved toward me. Hands grabbed my arms, hauling me to my feet, undoing my arms, blood flooded back into my limbs, the pins and needles keeping them limp at my sides.

"Go ahead." The man ordered someone in the room. I could tell a smaller figure moved in front of me. Then fingers wrapped around my blindfold and ripped it off my head.

Light made me flinch back. I blinked desperately until I could finally see clearly the figure in front of me.

My breath hitched in my throat, my mouth parting, as I jerked back.

Oh. My. Gods.

The woman twirled her blue hair around her finger, a coy smile on her lips.

"Hey, little lamb."

"K-Kek?" I whispered, my muddled mind not able to understand. "How—why? Wha-what is going on?"

"Missed you too." She winked playfully at me, looking over her shoulder as a man stepped around her.

"Sorry for the extra precautions. Couldn't have you waking up and seeing the location of our hideout."

A guttural cry heaved from my soul, my body stumbling back into the figure behind me.

My heart lurched.

The man who stood there looked so similar to my father it was like seeing a ghost. Grief splintered across my chest, opening the hole in my heart.

He was tall and broad-shouldered with short black hair, a beard, and soft brown eyes. He was slightly thinner than my father and his face more oval, but so much of him looked the same.

"Right." The man dipped his head. "I should have foreseen your reaction. I apologize for not giving you more warning."

"H-h-how?" I squeaked, tears building in my eyes. Now I understood why his voice seemed so familiar. It sounded the same as my dad's.

"Brexley." The sound of my name felt like I had stepped back in time, hearing my father call my name. After all the times I wished I could hear his voice again, I wasn't prepared for how much it would hurt.

He took a step toward me, stopping when I tried to move away.

"I-I don't understand."

"Brexley, I'm your uncle. Your father Benet's younger brother, Mykel."

"What?" My uncle?

"But… He-he's a criminal hiding in Prague." I had never met him because he had run off to Prague, hiding from the law.

"True on both accounts." He rubbed his beard, nodding. He seemed aloof, lacking the kindness my father had, but the physical similarities were startling. There was no way to deny their relation.

"What some think of as criminal activity, others call a revolution." He motioned to the room full of people, all wearing dark clothes: young, old, male, female, fae, human. My gaze landed back on Kek, my eyes pleading for answers. What the hell was she doing here?

"Revolution?" I swallowed.

"Welcome to the Povstat Militia." Mykel held his arms out. The name felt like a punch to my gut. Povstat was the huge insurgence in Prague, bordering on fanatical, violent… Terrorists, as Istvan described them.

261

Kapitan, their known leader.

"Holy shit," I muttered. My blood uncle was the leader of Povstat, while my pseudo uncle was running Sarkis's Army.

"There is a revolution coming, Brexley." He clasped his hands, looking directly at me. "And you are going to help lead us straight into it."

I stared at him as my world tipped over once again.

Ó, hogy baszd meg egy talicska apró majom," I muttered under my breath, stealing Birdie's phrase.

Oh, may a wheelbarrow of small monkeys fuck it.

Dead Lands #3 Available Now!

Thank you to all my readers. Your opinion really matters to me and helps others decide if they want to purchase my book. If you enjoyed this book, please consider leaving a review on the site where you purchased it. It would mean a lot. Thank you.

About the Author

USA Today Best-Selling Author Stacey Marie Brown is a lover of hot fictional bad boys and sarcastic heroines who kick butt. She also enjoys books, travel, TV shows, hiking, writing, design, and archery. Stacey is lucky enough to have lived and traveled all over the world.

She grew up in Northern California, where she ran around on her family's farm, raising animals, riding horses, playing flashlight tag, and turning hay bales into cool forts.

When she's not writing, she's out hiking, spending time with friends, and traveling more. She also volunteers helping animals and is eco-friendly. She feels all animals, people, and the environment should be treated kindly.

To learn more about Stacey or her books, visit her at:

Author website & Newsletter: www.staceymariebrown.com

Facebook group: www.facebook.com/groups/1648368945376239/

TikTok: @authorstaceymariebrown

Instagram: www.instagram.com/staceymariebrown/

Facebook Author page: www.facebook.com/SMBauthorpage

Sex, Lies, & Blank Pages Podcast: https://linktr.ee/sexliesandblankpages

Goodreads:
www.goodreads.com/author/show/6938728.StaceyMarie_Brown

Pinterest: www.pinterest.com/s.mariebrown

Acknowledgements

I hope you guys have fallen in love with this world as much as I have. It's always hard starting a new series, even though its set in the same world. I thank you for giving *Savage Lands* a chance and loving it so much you have been hounding me for *Wild Lands* release! Best thing an author can hear! The others I'd like to thank for getting this book out:

Kiki & Colleen at Next Step P.R. - Thank you for all your hard work! I love you ladies so much.

Jordan Rosenfeld at Write Livelihood - Every book is better because of you. I have your voice constantly in my head as I write.

Mo at Siren's Call Author Services – You have been my savior! Thank you!

Hollie "the editor"- Always wonderful, supportive, and a dream to work with.

Jay Aheer- So much beauty. I am in love with your work!

Judi Fennell at www.formatting4U.com- Always fast and always spot on!

To all the readers who have supported me: My gratitude is for all you do and how much you help indie authors out of the pure love of reading.

To all the indie/hybrid authors out there who inspire, challenge, support, and push me to be better: I love you!

And to anyone who has picked up an indie book and given an unknown author a chance.

THANK YOU!

Printed in the USA
CPSIA information can be obtained
at www.ICGtesting.com
LVHW011530100923
757777LV00006B/105